Becoming the Stillness
Part 2, Haunted Caves

Book Six of the Stillness Series

Richard Lee Ferguson

BECOMING THE STILLNESS PART 2, HAUNTED CAVES

Copyright © 2019 by Richard Lee Ferguson

Book Cover by Bookfly Design, James Egan

Illustrations by Brian Bowes

Published in 2025

ISBN: 978-1-966776-09-3 (paperback)

ISBN: 978-1-966776-11-6 (hardback)

ISBN: 978-1-966776-12-3 (ebook)

"The cave you fear to enter holds the treasure you seek."

— Joseph Campbell

"We are trapped inside a cave and know the world only through the
shadows it casts on the wall."

— Plato

Also by Richard Lee Ferguson

The Stillness Series

Book 1: Stirring the Stillness, Part 1 Voices of Quest

Book 2: Stirring the Stillness, Part 2 Tortured Journey

Book 3: Stilling the Stillness, Part 1 Voices of War

Book 4: Stilling the Stillness, Part 2 Restless Spirits

Book 5: Becoming the Stillness, Part 1 Voices of Madness

Book 6: Becoming the Stillness, Part 2 Haunted Caves

Book 7: The Hunchback's Gift, Part 1 Voices of Defeat

Book 8: The Hunchback's Gift, Part 2 Superior Ones Risen

Book 9: Flames of Extinction, Part 1 The Last Voice

Book 10: Flames of Extinction, Part 2 Stillness is Stilled

For the full series, visit the Amazon series page: https://www.amazon.com/dp/B0F1WJ5J4N

Contents

Principal Characters

Voices – God and Goddess

Michael Powers – Narrator
　Storyteller – Michael Powers' nickname in the war
　Nature – Best friend of Storyteller in the war
　Diane Powers – Deceased wife of Michael Powers
　Gail Hess – Psychiatrist
　Adam Camara – Psychiatrist
　Buandelgereen – Mongol woman
　Mark and My-duyen Powers – Son and daughter-in-law of Michael Powers
　Nguyen Tuyet Mai – Vietnamese intelligence officer
　Doctor Tavaris – Psychiatrist
　Emile Ruska – Detective
　Emma – Waitress, friend of Emile Ruska
　Tamara Powers – Wife of Michael Powers
　Child of Buddha – Mother of Tamara Powers
　Doctor DeRuntz – Psychiatrist
　Mark Powers – Son of Michael Powers
　John Powers – Father of Michael Powers
　Bai Meiying – Mother of Michael Powers
　Marie Telles – Friend of Bai Meiying
　Temulun – Talking dog
　Madame Dau – Vietnamese Village Council leader
　Ming-huà Powers – Child of Michael and Tamara Powers

Preface

Can Humans Be Replaced Peacefully?

Query: Are you one of the increasing numbers of people who think humans are irredeemably destructive and pose such a threat to the planet that their extinction would be a good thing? However, do you also abhor the massive destruction and suffering that would necessarily be the consequence of their demise? Bloody, violent dystopian novels often focus only on a few survivors of such devastation, not on the suffering that would extend to all other life forms on the planet. While there are many excellent dystopian novels, such a formulaic concentration on a small group of heroic protagonists can be narrow and unsatisfying.

So, how to unravel the ubiquitous human presence without simultaneously destroying the rest of the planetary ecosystem? Can a successor species evolve fast enough to replace humankind, or would it be extinguished before it has a chance to spread?

Such a successor species, by random chance or intentional design, must possess far greater cognitive and empathetic capacities to thwart the human proclivity for eliminating real or perceived threats. What would it be like for those first generations of advanced individuals surrounded by a sea of slow-witted but resourceful *Homo sapiens*? How would they survive the human penchant for fearing otherness and a relentless instinct to exterminate it? Whether the guiding force effectuating this change is Nature, Superior Alien, God or Gods, Goddess or Goddesses, here is an interesting way forward:

Replace *Homo sapiens* with a more advanced species, but not *drive* them to extinction through violent extermination, rather *dilute* their genes to insignificance over generations. There is precedent for such top-down genetic engineering. Human biologists eliminate dangerous pests by introducing mutant strains that breed with the targeted species to produce offspring harboring the desired genetic makeup. Generations later, the original species is superseded.

A new form of consciousness must necessarily arise—one in which strange Voices with immense cognitive power reverberate in advanced minds in the same way Voices once arose in the minds of early *Homo sapiens separating them from competitors such as Neanderthals*. Humans would initially diagnose those hearing such new Voices as schizophrenics, but they are, in fact, the incipient stirrings of a superior species. However, new Voices must be only the beginning, as this emerging species must also evolve powerful physical capabilities to overcome human weapons of destruction.

The doves must have sharper claws than the hawks . . .

The Stillness Series is the epic story of one such scenario.

Prologue

Previously. . . .

In *Voices of Madness*, Michael Powers and others entered the labyrinth of mind and memory, where trauma blurred into hallucination, and identity fractured into many voices. Madness was not escape but mirror, showing humanity what it could not face in daylight. The world outside moved toward collapse, while within, those broken souls wrestled with demons both imagined and real, seeking meaning in a darkness that spoke back.

Now the descent deepens. Into haunted caves they go—not only tunnels of earth but corridors of the psyche, where shadows whisper and ghosts wait. What was once madness becomes geography; what was once delusion becomes map. Here, the boundaries between life and death, sanity and revelation, collapse into one trembling silence.

And so the questions echo:

If the cave is endless, what light can guide the lost?

Is the haunting only memory, or something that waits with intent?

And if stillness is reached at last, will it be deliverance, or the silence of extinction?

~ Dear Reader ~

If you enter the caves, bring your questions. But remember: echoes may answer you instead.

Chapter One

Behind the Iron Door

Where Am I?

D ear Reader, I cannot adequately describe what greets me in this cavern. Bathed in the light of the Precious Object, I see a thousand openings in the rock —doors, if you like—each coyly beckoning. I clutch Tamara's hand. She walks as if on a pleasant stroll. I stop, overwhelmed, and glance at her.

"Pick one," she says.

I turn to ask Buandelgereen, but she's gone, so I look at Tamara. "What if they lead to something awful?"

Tamara meets my gaze with startling intensity, her hunchback more pronounced than ever.

"Fate starves at Probability's door," she says. Her voice tolls like rusty iron.

"Oh, Lord! Not you!" I cry.

Tamara only laughs and repeats, "Pick one."

A perverse anger flares through me, and I bark at Tamara angrily, "All right, I will!"

I pull her toward a nearby opening, but the darkness gives me pause. I hesitate. The Precious Object emits a loud tapping noise.

... Tap....
... Tap....
... Tap....

"Go ahead," says Tamara, practically shouting above the din.

I squeeze her hand tightly. "Come on!"

"Of course, my beloved, frightened little schizophrenic."

I step through and her hand vanishes.

"Tamara!"

"Go ahead!" comes a disembodied voice.

"Come with me, please!"

"Go ahead, beloved!" Her voice is more distant now, and I feel my legs moving down a long, dark corridor.

I see a faint light ahead, and plunge forward like a moth to a flame, emerging into a new world. I realize with a start that I am standing in Marie Telles's house. The sound of crying reaches my ears, and I realize it is a woman sobbing somewhere in another room. I enter the little anteroom where mother so often had tea with Marie. Standing in the doorway, I see Nanny Peach holding a young child, kissing his face. In a chair, Marie Telles has buried her face in her hands and convulses with every intake of breath.

Marie looks in my direction without seeing, and repeats, "Why her? Why her?"

Nanny Peach keeps whispering to the little boy in her arms, "Poor Mikey, poor little Mikey."

I look out the window and see Victorian mansions across the street, and I know that below, San Francisco Bay spreads its grey waters to the horizon. I recognize the little boy, of course. He is confused and frightened. Even now, as an adult, he continues to be confused and frightened. In such circumstances, especially as he grew older, the boy used humor to beat back the demons, at least for a while. Now is no different.

"Ghost of Christmas past," I say to the atmosphere. Nanny Peach, Marie, and my childhood self, of course, cannot hear, but my little joke tickles me—for a brief moment.

Nevertheless, the sobs of the grief-stricken woman I cannot ignore, and it comes to me as a thunderbolt that constricts my heart as painfully as if it were being crushed in a vise. Mother is dead. Killed in a car accident, hours earlier. Her miraculously talented fingers no longer to play Bach or Beethoven; her brilliant mind no longer to enlighten those around her; her compassionate love no longer to give comfort; and her lips no longer to caress me with her sweet words.

Bai Meiying.

Mother.

Dead.

And yet, as I gaze at the child, I know he does not understand. Marie Telles understands death and is grieving for the shattered diamond that had been her relationship with mother. Nanny Peach understands death and is grieving for the shattered future of the child in her arms. Only the boy does not understand. He grieves the grief around him. How can one look upon such a child and know the agony that awaits him? Soon enough he will know death, and he will know the living death that is schizophrenia. But I don't have schizophrenia, says Goddess. I am the Chosen One. The voices I hear are the voices of the future, not a mental illness. Do I believe it?

The cave's light pulses, awaiting my verdict.

"Goddess, when *You* gaze upon every child on Earth, every young animal stretching its young muscles, can you see their futures?"

Yes.

"If so, why have *You* not gone mad?"

I inhabit your mind. I am not mad.

"And God?"

He has adapted to suffering—wields it like a stick to herd His carrots. His faction is losing, but it is a long fight. The Superior Ones will come.

Marie Telles gets up to pour another glass of wine, but her hands shake so much the wine spills. She lets out a low groan, as if physically wounded, and returns to her chair with an almost empty glass. She stares off in the distance, and then looks at the child, her tears flowing, while Nanny Peach continues to rock Mikey in her lap. My heart is lacerated, and I feel the tears burst forth for a mother I never had the chance to know.

No longer able to bear this scene, I back away, retracing my steps through the portal. San Francisco blinks out, and darkness again surrounds me. *What has this strange visitation succeeded in doing?* I wonder. In truth, I have learned nothing new. *Perhaps I am not learning. Perhaps I am unlearning.* With such random, fragmented, and senseless thoughts, I emerge into the great cavern from which I started, still bathed in the light of the Precious Object. The openings stretch as far as the eye can see.

Tamara's hand finds mine again. Her smile flickers, shadowed by grief before she drives it away.

"Choose another," she says.

"Which one leads to my bones?"

"Choose one."

"Are they in chronological order?"

"Choose one."

"I can't."

"We have already passed many. Choose one."

"All right. This one."

~

I step through the opening. Her hand departs. I move forward expecting to see myself a bit older. I walk toward a bright light in the distance, and my heart races in anticipation. I step out onto the ledge of a precipice; dirt cliffs plunge downward into a deep valley below. I stand among a group of very odd people, and a few moments of observation confirms they are all suffering from Down's syndrome, or some similar condition. All of them are quite agitated, watching a tiny line of hikers ascend the switchbacks toward us. When I turn to look in the opposite direction, I see what I expected to see. A mental institution. I am in China, before I was born. I look around for Reverend Fu and Master Li. Sure enough, they fuss around the patients—guests, as I recall my father telling me the holy men prefer.

It's true. My father, Lu Zhishen, Feng Shiren—they climb the switchbacks toward me! What before were mere shadows on a paper are now approaching in the flesh. I will follow them into the institute. I will see Tamara's hunchback mother—Child of Buddha. The figures grow larger as they approach the rim, leaning forward against the steep trail. The anticipation is excruciating— But something tugs on my hand, pulling me away from the precipice. It must be Tamara! I think. However, the strength of the pulling force is beyond Tamara's ability. I fly backward, backward—farther from the little group of guests and toward the darkness again. The precipice collapses to a pinprick, and then nothing.

A glimpse only.

Why?

Your life, your history, is but a series of glimpses. A brief look, then move on. Your destiny is to have a child. The next step.

Toward?

The replacement of humans by Superior Ones.

Back in the cave, Tamara's hand is in mine again. We walk in silence, past portals.

"Here!" I shout, feeling a sudden, perverse obstinacy. "It doesn't matter to me where I look! If it is only a glimpse, it's all the same!"

Tamara's hand squeezes mine. "Hush, Michael!" she scolds. "Hold your tongue!"

I am angry and step through the opening. Her hand slips away, but I care not. In a mad rush, I seek the distant light with a reckless disregard for what awaits.

~

Even before I reach the light, I hear explosions and small arms fire. I have the urge to turn around. The urge becomes an imperative. I command my body to stop, but something is wrong. I can't turn around. I'm compelled to move forward. Apparently, there's no turning back. So be it. I plunge ahead and emerge in a horribly familiar place. The fortress. It is still daylight, although the monsoon gloom still pervades the atmosphere. Nature walks through me and I follow. He stops and looks down at a grunt whose features resemble those of an Auschwitz inmate. Me. Storyteller's eyes are closed, and I look with great interest at Nature's expression. There is sadness, naturally, and exhaustion, but something else as well. I can't pin it down, but it appears to be anger, or resentment. I call to him but he does not hear. All I can do is wait.

"Storyteller," he says quietly.

The eyes remain closed.

"Storyteller," he says louder.

The eyes crack open.

"Hello, Nature," comes a hollow rasp.

"Mind if we talk?"

"Sure."

"You up to it?"

"Yeah."

Nature squats and pulls his poncho hood farther forward against the rain. I cannot see his face. I move to the other side of Storyteller and peer into Nature's eyes. From deep within the hood, they still emit the glow of anger.

"What is it?" asks Storyteller.

Nature hesitates, then takes the plunge, his words coming fast and furious.

"I hate you, Storyteller. Hate! Don't look so shocked, I don't really hate you, I just hate the fact you will live and the rest of us will die. Don't bother to deny it or say some bullshit words of comfort. You will live and I will die. Your ghosts prove that. Oh, trust me, I love you, but I also hate you."

Storyteller looks stunned and moves his lips to speak, but Nature rushes on.

"No need to say a word. Just listen. If they find my body and fly my corpse back to the World, I predict you will visit my gravesite. Oh, yes, you will visit me, many years from now. I will listen from my coffin, and I will hate how you had all those years of life without me. I am robbed! Robbed by my country, the army, by this damn war, and by you! Yes, you! Why? Because through you I know I will die and you will live! If I am buried in my Providence cemetery, I will sit invisibly on a particular bench and write invisible poetry, waiting for you to come—and come you will."

Storyteller listens, eyes wide, face flushed.

"If I do live," he says testily. "I mean, out of spite, will you drag me to wherever you will be?"

Nature's face reveals an astonishing transformation. He now looks at Storyteller with a sorrowful and inexpressibly kind countenance.

"Yes, my friend. I will find you and bring you with me. It is not because I am full of malevolence toward you. No, no, not at all. It is because I know your life will be full of pain and . . . mental challenges."

"What do you mean?" demands Storyteller.

"You're ill, Storyteller. Mentally ill."

"No, no! I'm not. It's the malaria!"

Storyteller is lying to himself, and Nature knows it. I'm startled when Nature looks up and stares straight at me.

"No, Storyteller. You have schizophrenia. I know you do. Don't you think I know about the voices?"

Storyteller shifts his body restlessly. "If I am so crazy, why do you envy me for living?"

"Because, brother, I would rather live in pain than die in oblivion."

~

You were right, Nature, I think. *I am trying to get back to you. No need to drag more innocent people to their deaths just to get to me. I'm coming.*

~

Nature turns his angry gaze back on to Storyteller. "Don't lie to yourself!" he cries. "It is not your malaria. You are some sort of freak, able to see things the rest of us can't see. That is probably why I hate you the most! A poet is supposed to see hidden meanings, but your gift puts me to shame."

"Nature, my father had schizophrenia. I know I also have it. But, when you leave me in that tunnel tomorrow, it is you who will live and I who will die."

"Yes!" I shout. "Listen to him, Nature!"

But he is deaf to my words, and looks upon Storyteller with a mixture of pity and resentment. As he starts to speak, Superman slouches up, obviously exhausted, and says weakly, "Guard duty, Nature."

"Yeah, okay."

Without another word, Nature turns to go, and I feel myself withdrawing back into the portal, my heart aching from Nature's words. Odd that I have completely forgotten this conversation. Perhaps the malaria fogged my brain. Still, I see Nature in a new light. It is not his expression of jealous hatred that bothers me. No, not the hatred itself, but rather, the idea he could harbor malevolence even beyond the grave. Poor Doctor Camara found that out. Does even the gentlest soul have such dark places? Of course. My heart is heavy with remorse at Nature's agony those last terrible days at the fortress. As I withdraw, rain blurs the fortress, erasing Nature's face before I can read it fully.

~ *Africa?* ~

"Africa is mine too!" I cry without the slightest idea why—no, that is not true. "Africa isn't just for Africans, any more than America is just for Americans. Ants, for example, are citizens of the world. Oh, of course, they comprise many separate types, but are all of the same family. Plop enough ants down, and they will thrive anywhere—Africa, Asia, Europe, the Americas—and they'll thrive! Only humans insist that a piece of paper determines the right to reside at some spot in the world. Stupid."

"Michael, you're babbling again," Tamara says, reappearing at my side.

"But, Africa. . . ."

"That's right, Michael. Let it go. You're deflecting again. Choose the next opening."

"No."

"Hard to face your life when it turns out it wasn't what it seemed? Choose."

"Nothing is as it seems."

"Choose."

"See the Great Warrior!"

"Michael! Focus!"

~

Dear Reader. She's right: I babble. Yet unalloyed truth often hides in babble, while intricate falsehoods dwell in the artifice of speech. Amidst the apparent disconnectedness of babble lurks genuine truth—unlike the artifice of speech, where mesmerizing connections weave spidery lies. The cave listens, indifferent to eloquence, patient with stammering truth

~

"Michael!" Tamara cries in exasperation.

Just my luck, to be guided by a hunchbacked woman in Marley's guise.

"What? I'm listening!"

"We have already passed too many openings. Choose another!"

"Which one leads to the tunnel, to my bones?"

Tamara looks at me with an ironic smile. "Poor boy. I don't know."

"Why are you here?"

"*She* sent me."

"Why?"

"God is not the only One that works in mysterious ways."

"But—"

"Choose this one!"

Tamara shoves my shoulder—lightning through bone. As before, I must go forward. I'm afraid of what I'll discover. To fight the fear, I start rambling to myself in a sort of stream-of-consciousness trance.

"Okay, I'll walk down this path even though it feels more sinister than the others, but how can it be worse? Yet I know it could be worse—worse than worse. I've done bad things, things worse than bad—things I didn't even know were bad—but they were. Which makes them worse than the worst. . . . "

Still mumbling gibberish, I stumble into the light and cannot believe my eyes.

~

In front of me stands Ron, one of the attendants at the institution. I'm back in my room. I glance around but don't see myself. Ron is staring at me.

"What's up, Mr. Powers?"

I'm stunned. "You can see me?" I ask stupidly.

"Of course, what d'ya think? We were just talkin'."

"About what?"

"The usual."

"The usual?"

"Yeah. Your medication." He laughs. "I jammed it down your throat a few hours ago. Just checkin' on you. I mean, you were really in some bad place last few weeks."

"How so?"

"Jabbering about caves, someone named Tamara, and such."

Panic spikes. Did I pick the wrong portal? Am I trapped back at the institution with no way out? I look around desperately and there it is, the portal in the corner, like a sleepy eye slowly closing. Without hesitation, I dive for it before it shuts me out. I barely slip through, barely. As I turn, I see a doctor enter the room, my body lies curled and slack-jawed, a husk of me, unblinking, and Ron staring like a man frozen in a glacier. Then, darkness.

A wet-nose half-beat nudges me onward, or perhaps it was only my own breath on my cheek.

~

When I feel Tamara's hand again, she's already aware of my shuddering panic.

"Silly man, you chose the future. Relax. Calm down. Choose again."

I can't. I sit on the ground and rock back and forth in the old rhythm that used to give me a small sense of distance from the pain.

Fluorescents hum somewhere that isn't here; the stone under my forearms says otherwise.

Chapter Two

Doctor DeRuntz

What To Do Now?

"**I** don't know what happened, Doc! We was talkin' and he just dives into the corner. Honest! Happened as quick as lightnin'. Couldn't stop him! Is he dead?"

Xavier DeRuntz leaned over Mr. Powers and checked his pulse. "No. Call the nurse."

Doctor DeRuntz had replaced the deceased Doctor Hess a year ago, and after the police returned Mr. Powers to the institution, he had been assigned this complicated and vexing case. Since Hess's death, her notes had remained buried in a file, and the patient's journals she so often referenced were missing. DeRuntz could make no sense of it—rumors, innuendo, wild theories swirled among staff—and he had no idea where to begin. Some even warned him not to accept the case for reasons ranging from personal danger to contagious madness.

Now the patient lay comatose before him. How to proceed? Perhaps a diagnosis of "incurable and untreatable" would be the best option. Yet, like others before him, DeRuntz hesitated to give in so quickly. Despite his efforts to comprehend Powers' peculiar form of schizophrenia, he was groping in the dark, medication his only conceivable option. From what he read in Hess's notes, talk therapy led nowhere with Mr. Powers. Too clever. Too much like "mental quicksand," as she had put it.

In any case, the man seemed too far gone to reach anytime soon. Still, there was one lead—the detective, Emile Ruska. He had made an appointment for next week to check on Mr. Powers. DeRuntz made the decision to meet with him. His first question would be why Ruska had taken a personal interest in the patient—personal enough to return and visit—which, for law enforcement purposes, would be unnecessary now that the case was closed.

If nothing else, DeRuntz had learned from institution shoptalk and speculative horror stories that Mr. Powers, during his copious sessions in therapy, ensnared many personalities in his net, most of whom drowned as a consequence.

Is Detective Ruska struggling in the undertow of Powers's strange personality? wondered DeRuntz. *While Powers has been exonerated in the deaths of three psychiatrists, it still seems strange they were all connected to him.*

He shuddered. *Is Ruska also trapped? Or will I be, if I stare too long into those eyes? We shall see.*

~

The day Emile Ruska arrived to visit Mr. Powers, the patient remained in a comatose state, and he was not allowed access. Ruska had started to leave when he was directed to Doctor DeRuntz's office. When the detective entered, the good doctor gestured invitingly toward a comfortable chair and offered coffee. Ruska politely declined, and as any good listener, waited patiently for the doctor to express his thoughts.

"Detective Ruska, I have inherited the Powers' case, and as you were chief inspector in charge of finding Mr. Powers, I have a few questions, and your answers might be helpful to understand his case."

"Yes," replied Ruska. "I was in charge not only of his disappearance, but also the deaths of Doctors Hess, Camara, and Tavaris."

"Yes, but as I understand it, Mr. Powers has been exonerated from any wrongdoing in any of their deaths, correct?"

"Yes, as far as it goes."

"What does that mean?"

"There are loose ends, anomalies, questions, and circumstances that continue to . . . puzzle."

"Puzzle?"

"I prefer not to speculate."

DeRuntz laughed. "It seems that is all we psychiatrists do."

Ruska shrugged. "Different profession."

He stared morosely at the psychiatrist. He clearly did not want to be in the man's office; he was there to see Mr. Powers. He said so.

"Sorry Mr. Ruska, you can't. Mr. Powers, as I said, is in a deep state of, well, of some trauma that has rendered him comatose."

"Hmm," Emile grunted.

"While you're here, I do have questions, if you don't mind."

Ruska looked askance at DeRuntz, but said amiably enough, "Shoot."

"How did you find Mr. Powers?"

"Just good police work." Ruska was determined to say as little as possible.

"No, I mean what was he like—his demeanor, his behavior?"

Emile Ruska thought back and resolved not to tell the truth. If he described what he saw, DeRuntz might institutionalize him on the spot. He shrugged. "I dunno. At first, he was all curled up and mumbling. But when I addressed him, he snapped out of it and seemed normal enough, like a guy caught with his hand in the cookie jar."

DeRuntz was no fool. Trained to recognize untruths and deflections, he became suspicious. "If he is just a regular guy, like any other, why do you want to visit him?"

"Follow-up. Simple follow-up. No skin off my nose."

DeRuntz gave him a look of disbelief. "Detective Ruska, you are trained in recognizing deviant behavioral patterns. Did you notice any when you took Michael Powers into custody?"

Ruska squirmed in his seat, silently cursing his unease. How could he tell DeRuntz about the cave incidents? About White Thunder, or Powers's eyes—eyes that drew him in . . . into what? Something alien. That is why he came to the institution—to gaze at his quarry—like visiting the zoo to see an exotic animal you captured.

"No."

DeRuntz immediately knew Ruska lied. He was shocked to hear himself say, "You're lying."

"Beg your pardon?"

DeRuntz quickly backtracked. "I don't believe you are being totally honest. I think you noticed something, but for whatever reason, you are hesitant to talk about it."

"Well, Christ, Doc!" Ruska slipped into regular-guy slang when cornered. "He is crazy, right? I mean, sure, he acted a little weird."

"How?"

DeRuntz's calm voice at first irritated Emile, then made him realize he was conversing with another professional. Feeling chastened, and knowing he was in the wrong, he loosened up.

"The man has a strange quality to him. And not just him . . . well, that's another story." (Ruska did not intend to try explaining the bizarre events surrounding his earlier, failed attempts at the cave). "He draws you into a separate world, an unknown world, but one that becomes sort of hypnotic if you're around him long enough."

"How so?"

Ruska replied as one genuinely puzzled. "Hard to explain. It's like he is not of this world . . . a visitor . . . no, maybe like someone stranded here . . . dunno, hard to explain."

DeRuntz smiled encouragingly. "Try."

"He's stranded in our time and place. I know it sounds ridiculous, but that is, I think, what he believes. He is from a different time and place."

Vietnam? wondered DeRuntz. *PTSD? No—Hess, Camara, Tavaris would have spotted that. This was something else. Something more.*

"Do you believe he is from a different place and time?"

Ruska looked up, startled. "What?"

"Do you believe him?"

Now, Ruska knew this was a trap, and he quickly declared. "Of course not!"

"Methinks you protest too much," said DeRuntz smoothly.

This remark only fueled Ruska's agitation. "Have you talked to him? Have you? If so, you will know what I mean. But, if you haven't talked to him, then you know nothing and I'm wasting my time!"

DeRuntz affected a tone of sincere apology. "I'm sorry Detective Ruska; I did not mean to imply anything." He shrugged. "It's just that I am fumbling in the dark here. I only recently was assigned this case, and I have not yet really talked with Mr. Powers. Now, in his current condition, it seems impossible. I'm just grasping for straws, hoping you can offer an insight, any insight, that might help. Believe me, the deaths of my three colleagues always linger in the back of my mind when the subject of Mr. Powers comes up."

"Sorry, can't help you, Doc. This is not my line."

DeRuntz felt a powerful urge to pound the table. *What's gotten into me?* He barely knew Powers. Yet the man exerted a gravity—a black hole. *Is that what swallowed my colleagues?*

"Detective Ruska, I appreciate your spending the time with me. If you think of something, please call. You have the number. I won't take up any more of your time."

~

Ruska left the institution in a contemplative mood. This rube knows nothing, he thought. The key to this whole mess is that Mongol woman. Buan . . . what's her name. The thought conjured the cave—and the wet nose brushing his leg made him shudder.

Find her, and I bet the deaths of those doctors would be explained in a minute. Natural causes? Bullshit!

On the trip back to the station, he toyed with the idea of returning to the cave, maybe camp out there a few days. Who knows? Might spot something happening or someone coming and going. He had become convinced the cave harbored some secret chamber where suspicious activities occurred. The idea of drugs had never quite left his mind, though involvement by Mr. Powers in such dealings seemed highly unlikely. Be that as it may, the Mongol woman was different. Like many in law enforcement, he assumed the presence of a foreigner usually signaled trouble—often drugs, but perhaps more exotic activities like white slavery or gunrunning.

Lack of evidence rendered these speculations hollow, and he was left with only the spooky, schizophrenic, magic-shit theory. *I'll leave that spiritual crap to White Thunder*, he thought. But he knew it was the "magic-shit" that drew him back to the cave. The mysterious girl with the backpack made him more than willing, but the wet nose gave him the shivers.

That evening, he stopped at his favorite watering hole and sipped a whiskey while bantering with Emma. She had always been a good sounding board, and occasionally volunteered cogent observations. After he briefly described the cave, she looked alarmed.

"Sounds dangerous."

"Not really."

"You should wait for this mental patient to come out of his coma and talk to him first before you go back to that cave. Shit, Emile, maybe some of his gang are there!"

Ruska made no response, deciding it was actually a good idea. When she returned from serving another customer, he said, "Good idea, Emma."

She smiled and tilted her head coquettishly. "Why do you sound so surprised I have a good idea?"

Emile briefly considered asking her to go home with him after her shift, but his habitual fear of relationships prevented him. So he went home alone—resolved, at least, to follow her advice and wait to talk with Mr. Powers.

~ *DeRuntz Digs* ~

After speaking with Detective Ruska, Xavier DeRuntz returned to read Doctor Hess's notes more closely. The deeper he dug into their byzantine wanderings, the more lost he became. The woman appeared to travel down a maze of therapeutic dead ends, constantly circling back to the beginning, her tone shifting from frustration to something darker. Toward the end, her entries trembled with fear—terror, even—and her alarm seemed to emanate from observations of her own behavior, not Mr. Powers'.

She described her behavior as increasingly neurotic, and she expressed an even greater worry for the mental stability of her colleague, Doctor Camara. More and more often, she wrote about the dangers of dealing with Mr. Powers, of succumbing to the power of his delusions. She confessed to feeling entrapped, even possessed—not only herself, but perhaps Camara as well.

Toward the end, she observed that her suspicions themselves were psychotic. Possessions, demons, ghosts . . . her mind spiraled until she feared she had gone mad.

DeRuntz had never seen a psychiatrist's notes more alarming. Had she still been alive, he would have put her under observation on the spot. These ruminations led him to revisit the mysterious deaths of all three psychiatrists. Each died while treating Mr. Powers, and that fact alone made a powerful case for him to treat this patient as unique. In his excitement, DeRuntz disregarded any warnings of danger and plunged into what might prove to be the most interesting case of his career, even if it ended his.

To begin, DeRuntz decided to supplement his current knowledge by carefully rereading the notes of doctors Camara and Tavaris. Perhaps there might be some explanatory nexus revealed by triangulating the three perspectives. Perhaps there existed some common element that would shine light on what happened. It was worth a try. He settled into a weekly routine of intensive reading and note taking. As happened with Hess, Camara, and Tavaris, he put his other patients on hold, letting them simmer on the back burner of his attention while he dug deeper into the case of Mr. Powers. Every evening, he depressurized by bending the ear of his favorite sister, having thrown out most confidentiality restraints. His only concession was in referring to Mr. Powers as Patient X.

"What's new with Patient X?" asked Alondra DeRuntz as she sipped wine at his tastefully furnished townhouse.

"Still unresponsive," replied Xavier, popping some nuts in his mouth. "Nevertheless, I'm making progress."

"Is it the war that messed this guy up, Xavier?" Alondra taught history at the local university and found the plight of Vietnam veterans particularly interesting.

"Well, there's the sixty-thousand-dollar question. Chicken or egg. No doubt he suffers from schizophrenia, PTSD, and god knows what else. But, you know, there's more. There's something else. I can't put my finger on it, but I'm digging." He took a long sip from his wine glass. "I'm digging."

Alondra smiled. "That's why you get the big bucks."

"Sure. By the way, you don't believe in ghosts, do you?"

"Look, dear brother, throughout history, spirits are everywhere, multiplying after every war and every disaster. Just have to know how to look."

With this, she left to use the bathroom, and when she returned, she said, "Perhaps Mr. Powers knows how to look."

"Look?"

"For ghosts."

"Alondra, do you know how to look?"

"Oh! God, no! Ghosts scare me. I teach students about them, but I don't talk to them. Does he talk to them?"

"Of course. Alondra, he is a schizophrenic. Nevertheless, it is an interesting question—do they scare him like they do you?"

Alondra raised her glass. "Ask him."

"Problem with Patient X, Alondra, is that he rarely gives a straight answer."

"Try and straighten a pretzel and you break it."

"Yeah, but try and swallow it whole and you choke."

"I thought you were supposed to help him *not* eat himself."

"Ha! Ha! *Touché!*" He lifted his glass. "Here's to you, sis!"

Alondra smiled brightly and emptied her glass in silence, then stood and replied, "I've got to go. Past my bedtime." She gave him a wry smile. "Keep me informed, brother dear."

That night, DeRuntz had his first nightmare involving the Powers case.

~ *DeRuntz Dreams* ~

Three specters stared down at Xavier. He lay in bed and gazed back at them in calm wonder, trying to identify their pale faces. At first, they undulated, seaweed in a turbulent sea, their forms blurred and indistinct. His eyes stung from the salt water, so he closed them and luxuriated in the simplicity of darkness.

When he opened them again, the specters' faces had drifted close enough to touch. He suddenly realized the three specters were doctors Hess, Camara, and

Tavaris, yet still he remained calm, that is, until all three pointed at something behind him.

An invisible force prevented him from turning around to look. It seemed his neck was frozen in place, sphinxlike. A physical terror diffused down the back of his neck, and the more he struggled to turn his head, the more locked in place it became.

The figures flailed, gesturing frantically behind him. He felt a sinister presence approach, the air dropping cold.

A wet pressure touched his neck. He screamed and the spell broke.

Sitting upright in bed, he tried to catch his breath. A storm raced across his mind; the faces of the dead psychiatrists flashing on and off as if lit up by a series of lightning bolts.

DeRuntz stumbled to the kitchen and made tea, rattled by the similarities of his nightmare to those described in the notes of Hess and Camara.

So this is how it begins.

Mental quicksand, closing over my feet.

~ *Ruska Wavers* ~

Emile Ruska suffered the opposite fate of Doctor DeRuntz. The more time that passed without contact with the Powers case, the more he felt withdrawal from its cocktail of madness, mystery, and danger.

Memories of the cave, despite its spooky atmosphere, or perhaps because of it, drew him to return. As Mr. Powers continued in his comatose state, Ruska began rationalizing why going back was essential. He would leave his car behind and hike to the cave. He would spend a week or so camping out and secretly observing. If nothing came of it, he would give up the effort and close the Powers case for good. Simple. No need to wait for Powers to emerge from his coma.

Yet, every day he called to check on Mr. Powers' condition, and every day he was informed it had not changed. Out of patience, Emile put in for a two-week leave of absence and spent the night before he departed for the cave drinking and talking with Emma, who bristled at the thought of him going alone.

Plopping down his whiskey in a gesture of disgust, she said, "Emile, you're just being plain stupid! What if it's full of murderers and drug runners! You're not in some Hollywood movie . . . and you're not as young as you used to be. Why are men so pig-headed?"

He chuckled while wiping the table of spilled whiskey. "Come on, Emma, you love me."

"I love you alive. You're no use to me dead."

"What's a' matter, miss my tips?"

"Keep this up, and I won't. All this for some sick guy you already found!" She turned on her heel to serve another customer.

Emile felt a brief tinge of regret. The only person who cared was a washed-up, twice divorced cocktail waitress with too much makeup, too much moxie, and not enough . . . enough of what? He did not know and had long ago stopped thinking about what it was he did want in a woman. Nonetheless, he knew one thing; he wanted to get to the bottom of Mr. Powers, the Mongol woman, and their damn cave.

"Why is this so important to you?" Emma asked when she returned with another whiskey, startling him out of his reverie.

Emile sighed. "Emma, this is becoming tedious. Let me drink in peace."

"You'll be pushing up daisies in peace!" she huffed, and walked away, calling over her shoulder, "See what I care!"

This exchange reminded Ruska of why he had never married.

Ruska drained the glass, his mind back on the cave.

~ *Again, The Cave* ~

Drive uneventful. Hike uneventful. Cave: silent.

Emile scouted out a good spot to observe without being seen, his place of concealment unknowingly close to where Michael and Tamara had observed him so long ago. His plan was to watch the outside of the cave for a couple of days, and if nothing happened, he would once again brave the inside.

As the first day turned into three, discouragement eroded his resolve. He could no longer put off entering. He felt surprised at his reluctance to take this step. *No sign of life for days*, he thought. *Why this fear?*

He knew why he feared it. The cave defied cause and effect. Inside, time and space loosened their grip, and his stomach dropped in endless freefall. He feared the strange woman with the backpack. He feared the wet nose. And most of all, he feared his own fear.

A bad guy with a gun seemed ridiculously simple compared to the disorientation he felt in the cave. You cannot fight magic.

Despite every instinct, he approached the entrance. Flashlight in one hand, pistol in the other, he stepped across the threshold from light to dark.

Immediately, he felt the same, ominous, organic, malevolent blackness. This familiar sensation ignited the fire of dread that already smoldered in his stomach. If anything, the flashlight was even less effective than before. The beam seemed to crawl back into the cylinder. Ruska barged ahead, stumbling over the uneven ground and feeling his way deeper into the cave. His breathing became labored, not from fatigue but from a deep, churning fear.

Like the darkness itself, fear took on a life of its own, making him want to mimic the light beam and crawl back into the sunlight, into the seed from which his life first germinated.

Yet, still he soldiered on, like an automaton operating purely on programmed instinct, and the deeper he penetrated, the more Emile Ruska shed all human feelings. Still, there existed nothing but darkness and the invisible, swallowing throat of the cave.

After what seemed an eternity, he heard voices ahead, their echoing reverberations weak and teasing, too faint to be intelligible. As might a man dying of thirst who hears a waterfall, he stumbled faster toward the sound. The teasing words stopped, then started again, and finally he made out a female voice, the words unambiguously clear and incongruously playful.

"Silly man, you chose the future. Relax. Calm down. Choose again."

Emile's heart filled with painful longing to catch up to the voices, and his lungs breathed deeply the stale air. He could not run, but he could shuffle faster, his pathetic beam now but a pale finger pointing the way. The voices stopped, but he knew they were not far ahead. He kept moving, periodically feeling the need to stop and listen. Cupping his ear, he heard a soft tinkling sound from the wall, and a breeze passed across his face.

"An opening!" he cried.

Ruska scrambled to the wall, following the breeze, and felt with his hands the contours of a hole, an opening, a chamber. Leaning too far forward, he fell through. . . .

~

"Can't tell you how good it is to see you again, Emile," said Emma setting down a whisky and bowl of nuts. "You okay? You look a little peaked."

"I'm okay, thanks."

"What'd you find at the cave?" Emma, eyes wide, waited anxiously for his response.

But Emile Ruska said not a word, downed his whisky in one stupendous gulp, and left the bar as if sleepwalking. Emma watched him go, her face lined with concern, then cancelled his bill and turned to help other customers.

~ *DeRuntz and Michael Powers* ~

Around the time Emile Ruska found himself miraculously back where he started, Michael Powers showed signs of emerging from his coma. Doctor DeRuntz was summoned to his bedside, where he found the patient blinking groggily at his surroundings.

"Hello, Mr. Powers. Are you back with us?"

No response.

DeRuntz leaned over and shined a light into his eyes. "Mr. Powers?"

Blinking, confused stare. No words.

"Mr. Powers, can you hear me?"

Sudden cognition—as if a soul had just flown into his body. "Of course. Why do you ask?"

"Nice to have you back."

"Where have I been?"

"You tell me."

"Where's Tamara?"

"Who?"

"Never mind. I must have taken the wrong portal."

DeRuntz looked puzzled. "Well, right or wrong portal, you're back with us again."

Michael stared intently at DeRuntz. "So, you're the latest?"

"I am now your doctor, if that is what you mean."

"No, that is not what I mean."

DeRuntz waited.

"Ah," observed Powers. "You are one of the patient ones. Well, what I mean is that you will soon be joining the list of my ex-doctors."

"What makes you think that?"

"Hold a séance and ask my previous ones."

This comment made Xavier DeRuntz pause, and he appeared to grope for a proper reply, but none came.

"What's the matter Doc, cat got your tongue?"

"I would like to discuss my predecessors with you, Mr. Powers, but now is not the time. Tell me about the latest news from Goddess."

Michael's eyes turned glassy, and his face melted from spirited animation to a mask of blank distance. "Not now," he slurred. "Not now. I'm about to enter another portal."

With this, he slumped back on his bed, seemingly unconscious.

Chapter Three

No Suffering?

I Wander Alone

Yes, dear Reader, I am stuck wandering through an endless cycle of portals leading to glimpses of past and future, with no narrative rhyme or reason to them whatsoever—much like this sad book you have been slogging through. I have now been through dozens of these openings, some leading to recognizable vignettes of my life, others devoid of meaning—an empty room, a busy street, a hillside. They are like memories (if one could remember the future as well as the past). Are they true glimpses? Memories are doppelgangers of the mind, spawning with each new thought and splitting off to become mischievous, coy, and deadly. They beckon, seductively clothed in half-truths, enticing us to partake of their devious intimacies.

"Only two more," Tamara says. Her words startle me out of my reverie.

"So, you want me to choose?" I ask, stopping in front of a likely looking portal.

"Not this one," she says slyly. "I'll show you which ones."

"What if I want to choose my own?"

"She orders, I obey," replies Tamara.

I do not know if she means Goddess, or *Her*, or both. I stare at her in the beam of my flashlight. Her beautiful face emerges from the misshapen body, like a shiny, carved figurehead on the prow of a beetle-black ship. She is a mystery. Not a hallucination like Theresa, nor a reality like Diane, she dwells in the nether world, touchable and untouched.

Her mother was a bridge. So is she—between worlds.

"Why only two portals, Tamara? Why not one, or one hundred?"

"*She* said two, and two it shall be."

"How will you know which ones?"

"My mother interpreted taps from the Precious Object. I interpret words from *Her*."

Suddenly I realize these next two portals are not just for me. They are for you, dear Reader. Eliminate suffering, eliminate God, and eliminate all the filth and cruelty that surrounds us every day. Those are the stakes! I implore you, read on, even as I walk on. What we will discover together, I do not know.

"Tamara! How much farther?"

She looks at me strangely. "Far, Michael, very far. Keep walking and stop conversing with your readers."

"So, you are also in my head?"

"Dear Michael, I have been in your head from the beginning."

"Are you real?"

"As real as my mother, Child of Buddha. As real as your mother, Bai Meiying. As real as your father, John Powers. As real as real can be."

"But, how much farther? I'm tired and hungry."

"Farther, farther."

"Look, Tamara, we have passed a billion portals. How do you know which is which?"

"I will know."

"But—" I barely get the words out before she shushes me.

"Do you want to go back to the portal that leads to the institution? I can leave you there, you know."

"Then tell me what this is about. What is through these portals? I'm scared."

"A Vietnam vet? A soldier? A man? Couldn't be!"

"Tamara, now is not the time to mock me."

"We're almost there."

I am truly shaken, but humor is always the best defense against fear. "Hopefully, there is food at the end of this rainbow."

"Think of hunger in the same way you think of your voices."

"What does that mean?"

"I don't know, just making small talk."

"Aren't you hungry?"

"No."

"That makes me think you might not be real after all."

She looks at me and smiles. It out-puzzles Mona Lisa's. I suddenly realize I am desperately, passionately, hopelessly in love with this hunchback. Her shining, soul-illuminating face emerges from a broken, disfigured body, and to anyone with eyes she is a freak of nature—a conduit of all that is strange, alien, mystical, and dangerous, like me.

If she is not real, she is real enough for me. If medication would make her vanish, then damn the medication. I vow to irrevocably wed my fortune and my future to this misshapen riddle of a woman. Tamara is a reader of runes, and I will be the beneficiary of her intricate prophecies.

"This one," says Tamara, stopping abruptly.

A piercing chill prickles my neck hairs. "You sure?"

"I'm sure."

"Tamara, this one gives me the chills. Come with me."

"I cannot."

"Why?"

"I cannot."

"Then I won't go." (I sound like a child.)

Although I shine my flashlight directly into her face, Tamara's own faint luminosity cancels the glare. She stares without blinking. Nothing withstands her accusatory eyes.

"Okay, I'll go."

The words come out, but my body will not obey, and I stand frozen in place. Tamara remains motionless and calm, always staring into my eyes, breaking the bonds of fear that immobilize me. I turn and take a few steps but pause at the entrance, knowing her gaze remains locked onto my back.

There is something awful about this portal, a blankness that is not dark nor light, black nor white, rather it is . . . nothing. Oblivion, not mere darkness, which has presence of its own.

I step across. . . .

~

"You have been given a glimpse," says Tamara.

I cannot believe I am back, standing before her as if I had never left. I do not know how much time has passed—a century or an hour.

"A glimpse?" I stammer. "I have heard that before."

"It is for you to understand."

"How can I understand a blankness—nothing?"

"Precisely. It will come to you."

I shake my head, dazed and disoriented. "How long was I gone?"

"A lifetime. On to the second portal, then you can eat."

"You mean then *we* can eat."

"Yes."

"But what did I just see?"

"I told you; it is for you to understand."

"Tamara, I love you," I say, and know it is gibberish, but gibberish is the only language my mind speaks now.

"You are right to think you are talking gibberish," says Tamara with a laugh.

"Reading my mind again?"

"Of course."

"Tamara, I know you aren't real. I know you are one of my hallucinations, as Theresa was. But you are different. I really love you. I'm madly in love with you."

"True, you are mad, Michael, but I am real. This one thing you must know!" She suddenly rushes toward me, and I think I see tears glistening, but she stops herself before we can embrace. "Please believe me, Michael, I am real! Now, we must go to the second portal."

I feel a terror. "No! No more portals! Let's go back together. We'll leave the cave, leave the state, live together in some obscure place, change our names, whatever it takes!"

"Come!"

To my horror, her voice quivers, and I fear this last portal most of all. "Let us go back, Tamara!" I cry. "Let us run away!"

She hesitates and my heart rises to a fevered anticipation, its quickened thumps echoing in the monstrous cave.

"Tamara!"

"We must not! Follow me, Michael! Follow now!"

She sets off deeper into the cave, and my little flashlight is smothered by the dark.

I stumble to catch up, but she will not slow down. "Tamara!" I call. "Wait!"

She does not answer, and I rush on as fast as possible. I pass portal after portal, but she will not slow her pace and I fear I will lose her forever. I start to run but get only a few steps before I trip and fall clumsily, stone grating my forearms as the flashlight pinwheels away.

"Tamara, help!" I shout.

Suddenly, she is beside me, leaning over with the flashlight, and in its weak beam I see tears flowing in great streams down her cheeks.

"Are you hurt?" she asks tenderly.

"I love you, Tamara!" I blurt. "I love you terribly!"

She helps me up. "And I love you, Michael, but we must go on. We must. We must."

Her words are so ominous I tremble in fear. "Where does the last portal lead, Tamara?"

"We must go on," is her only reply. "Do you trust me, Michael?"

"Good god, yes. To the death."

"Then we must move. We must."

~ *The Last Portal* ~

I do not know how far we have walked, but I finally stop and lean over, hands on knees, panting for breath.

"Oxygen thin here," I gasp.

"Rest a moment," says Tamara, also breathing hard. "We have arrived."

I shine my little flashlight at an opening looming before us. Smoother around the edges, yes—but otherwise indistinguishable from the billions we have passed.

After regaining my breath, I ask, "Are you sure? They all look the same to me."

"I'm sure."

Something gnaws at my gut. "For the last time, Tamara, I don't want to go! It scares me. Besides, you've done your duty bringing me this far. Now let's go back!"

"We can't."

"Bullshit!"

Before she has a chance to reply I peer at the opening and look back to make a more rational protest.

A dark figure erupts from nowhere and slams me through.

My scream reverberates down the tunnel, but behind me the portal has closed. I scramble back and claw at the stone, but it is solid and impassable.

No return. Only forward.

My heart flutters painfully, and I try to breathe in what little air remains. I open my mouth to take in more, and I fear I will suffocate before reaching the end.

A dim light appears in the distance. I stagger toward it, each step smaller than the last. My chest seizes with the effort. I feel sick, and for an instant I am sure I'm upside down.

Then—one last surge—I plunge into the light. A cool breeze washes my face.

"Welcome back again," says a familiar voice. "You are quite a capricious fellow, popping in and out of consciousness this way."

I am laying on my back, looking up at the speaker. This time, I haven't the strength to rush back to the portal, and can only stare helplessly at Doctor DeRuntz.

We gaze at each other for a moment, then he says words that astonish me.

"Bring Tamara and let him see her."

I cannot be more shocked. "How do you know Tamara?" I cry.

"Mr. Powers, she is a patient here. You have known her a long time. You have been busily saying her name while you were . . . away. Many times in the past you have spoken with her in the recreation room."

"Must be a different Tamara," I object weakly.

"Perhaps. You certainly mentioned her a lot when you were semi-conscious."

"What does she look like?" I demand.

A nurse hesitates in the doorway, exchanging a glance with DeRuntz, who nods.

The door opens. "See for yourself."

To my utter amazement, it is my beloved hunchback. Tamara. Like the fool I am, I shout, "Tamara!"

"Hello, Michael," she says calmly. "I am glad to see you have returned safely to us."

Before I make a bigger fool of myself, I notice her signal. I smile and ask, "This is the last of the two?"

"Yes."

"And the first of them was. . . ?"

"No suffering. Stillness."

"You're sure this is the last?"

She looks around the room and nods to the doctor and nurses. "Here we are."

The fluorescents hum. The stone is gone. My forearms rest on starched cotton.

"Together," I say with the sweetest intent, yet my words still inconspicuously embroidered with shock. Tears scald my cheeks.

Tamara, bless her, understands.

Chapter Four

A Puzzle, A Pure Puzzle

How Is It Possible?

Doctor DeRuntz thought he noticed some secret sign, an unspoken signal, pass between Tamara and Mr. Powers. Once made, both fell silent. No amount of friendly banter or probing questions could make them speak. Conceding defeat, DeRuntz ordered Tamara returned to her room, and left Mr. Powers alert but unresponsive to further questions. DeRuntz slowly walked back to his office more confused than ever. Visions of the dead psychiatrists spun through his mind, and amidst their circling figures, he thought he spied himself.

~ *Reunion* ~

Michael waited until DeRuntz left before he stood and paced the room.

This is a fine mess, he thought. *DeRuntz, of course, is lying about Tamara. She is not a patient here. She must be here because she followed me and tumbled into this institution from the portal like manna from heaven! Now we're both stuck.*

He tried the door; it swung open. He slipped out, inconspicuous, and padded down a maze of corridors searching for Tamara, but access to the women's ward was blocked by an imposing iron door with a small, barred window near the top. Standing on tiptoes, he peered at a handful of female patients shuffle aimlessly in their cloth slippers on the other side. He waited as the minutes stretched thin, when at last he spied Tamara with her unmistakable hunched back enter the room. Her face was hidden behind another patient, but her form left no room for doubt. Michael's first instinct was to pound on the door to get her attention, but he stayed still, watching, knuckles hovering.

As if obeying some unknown command, she strode down the corridor dragging a chair, stood on it and put her face close to the window. The words came into his head without her speaking them.

"Now you have seen."

Michael closed his eyes and shook his head vigorously. "No, no, no! I saw but did not see."

"You saw but did not think."

"Ha! I have nothing to think about. I only saw bits and pieces amounting to nothing."

"You saw nothing, which is true."

"Damn it, Tamara! My head hurts! Let's find a way to make love. I care for nothing anymore except to have you again."

"Sex only?"

"No, to have you forever."

"You saw forever."

"God! Tamara! I cannot deal with any more riddles."

"You must deal with them, as all of us must. Riddle upon riddle, and the Great Warrior even now probes anxiously atop your skull, which itself tilts precariously atop your skeleton, which in turn tilts precariously against a tunnel wall far away in time and space, waiting."

"Then, all this time, you have used me? Not love me?"

"I love you with all my heart."

"Well then—" but Michael's words, half-formed, were interrupted by a strong hand clamped on his shoulder. He turned to see a giant attendant staring down at him impatiently.

"Back to your room, Mr. Powers."

He took one last look through the window, but Tamara had disappeared.

~

Back in his room, Michael got down on his knees and carefully checked where the portal had been, looking for seams or cracks, but found none.

Nothing for it but to escape again, he thought. *Now it will be more difficult with Tamara to break out as well.*

Her image came to mind, naked in all her hunchbacked glory, and he came near to masturbating as the fantasy sharpened, but he stopped himself. *No! It won't do! Save my essence for clever schemes of escape. The more to savor sex when we're free.*

While pondering his next move, Michael remembered Doctor DeRuntz say he often conversed with Tamara in the recreation room. All thoughts of escape flew from his mind, and he went to bed determined to meet her there first thing in the morning.

Next morning arrived with Michael waiting impatiently for the attendant to unlock his room. The instant the lock clicked, Michael shoved the door open and rushed to the recreation room. When he arrived, two elderly patients sat at separate tables working on unfinished jigsaw puzzles. He chose a corner table, grabbed a pen and paper, and began writing.

After an hour, during which he lost track of time while scribbling the words that comprise this book, a looming presence made him look up in anticipation of seeing Tamara. To his disappointment, Damien Lundgren gazed down at him petulantly.

"You're in my seat," he said. "Get out."

"Damien," said Michael amiably. "You know these seats are for everyone."

Mr. Lundgren sat in the chair opposite. "You are dead. You don't belong here."

"What?"

"She told me you were dead."

"Who?"

"Goddess . . . your Goddess. She deserted me for you, remember? Damn Her! And now She is back in my head throwing Her weight around."

Michael leaned forward. "What did She say?"

Damien did not answer, but abruptly jumped up and began swaying and looking blankly in the distance.

"Damien! Concentrate!" cried Michael.

No response. Michael glanced at an attendant who had just entered. The man had heard Michael's outburst and eyed him suspiciously.

"Damien," Michael said in a soft but threatening voice. "Sit down."

Damien remained unresponsive, so Michael rose and guided him by the shoulder to sit at the table.

"Now," he said sitting back down and putting his hand atop Damien's. "What did She say?"

"First, She killed them."

"Who did She kill?"

"The others."

"Who?"

"The others."

"You mean your other voices?"

Damien nodded.

"Then what?"

"I heard them die."

"What?"

"Screams."

"Okay, after they died, what did She say?"

"Her voice was odd . . . different, and I heard them all screaming."

"Yes, and then what?"

Damien looked at Michael wide-eyed. "Then?" he asked absently.

"Yes, what then?"

"They died."

"I know, but then what happened?"

"She took over."

"Took over?"

"They were all dead. She took over."

"And?"

"She has a message for you."

Michael felt his heart skip a beat. "And?" he repeated.

"She took over."

"Yes, yes, I know! What is Her message?"

Damien fell into another stupor, rocking his head back and forth to some inner rhythm.

"Damien!"

This time the attendant intervened, wagging his finger.

"Mr. Powers, don't yell at the patients."

"Okay, okay."

After the attendant moved away, Michael leaned close to Damien. "What did She say about me?" he whispered.

Damien's pupils dilated; his voice dropped a register, and his lips barely moved. *It is not Her dwelling inside this unfortunate creature! It is Me in disguise.* The voice was sickeningly familiar.

Michael's skin crawled. "Who are you?" he asked anyway.

You already know.

"Yes, God, or demon, I know who You are. I haven't heard from You in a long time."

You are not a priority.

"What did You tell Damien about me?"

Simple. I told him to tell you a simple fact, although the poor, suffering man is clearly not up to it. Goddess and his other voices have cored out his mind.

"The simple fact is?"

Goddess and Her faction will not succeed with the plan. You may even be dead as I speak.

Michael looked down at his body. "Surprise surprise, here I am."

Correction, you and Goddess will all soon be dead, metaphorically speaking. I have the power to kill their voices in you just as easily as I destroyed Damien's voices in him.

Michael remained unfazed. "Go ahead."

It is not yet time.

"Just as I thought. You are all bluff. Goddess will thwart Your plans, whatever they are."

It is not yet time.

Michael shrugged. "As good a time as any. Right now, I'm only interested in what happens to Tamara."

She is also dead, metaphorically speaking.

"Damn You! She is all I care about. You and Goddess can go to hell!"

You are abandoning Goddess?

"She abandoned me."

So, you come full circle, Michael Powers! laughed the demon, for Michael had now concluded this was not God nor Goddess. *I knew when you turned your gun on Her in the tunnel that you would come back to Me. Prodigal son returns!*

"I was never with You in the first place."

Oh, yes you were.... it's voice faded. ***Remember...?***

"I—" Michael started to speak when Damien's head fell heavily onto the table. Before he could react, the attendant had swooped in and gently pulled Damien up by the shoulders. The head lolled to the side, a thin thread of saliva silvering his lip, then stilled. Michael instantly knew the man was dead. Within minutes, teams of doctors were ministering to the body, pushing aside Michael who now stood trembling in the corner. After Damien's body was removed, Doctor DeRuntz went up to Michael.

"What happened?" he demanded.

"I don't know."

"Mr. Ruiz said you were talking to him. You were there, Mr. Powers. Ruiz even said you shouted at Mr. Lundgren. What were you shouting about?"

"No, I didn't shout. I was just talking to him."

"What was said?"

"Nothing important."

"Mr. Powers, this is important. A man just died here. Please, tell me!"

Michael looked at Doctor DeRuntz and saw the faint shadow of death slightly blurring the man's features. Michael broke into a sweat and fell into an uncontrollable fit. Some rational fragment begged him to stop, to argue like an attorney—but it drowned in the rising flood.

"Doctor DeRuntz! Get away from me! Get away! Run as fast as you can and never see me again, or else you'll join Hess, Camara, Tavaris, and now poor Damien Lundgren!"

"What are you talking about?"

"I'm talking about God! God! And demons! And suffering! That's what I'm talking about! I want to see Tamara. Where is she? I must see Tamara! Now, go away from me! Run! Save yourself!"

~ *Dear Reader* ~

I must pause here, dear Reader, and admit I appeared to everyone in that room like a hopeless crazy man. It is true I lost control, which is inexcusable for a lawyer presenting his case before the court, but the poisonous cocktail of stress and schizophrenia had momentarily broken me. Long story short, I ranted on until they restrained me and bound me to my bed. I write these words days later, having been allowed to rejoin the living. As soon as I was given my freedom, I ventured back to the recreation room with high hopes of seeing Tamara. My hopes were well founded.

~ *The Hunchback* ~

As soon as Michael entered the room, he spied Tamara sitting at the same table he had occupied days earlier with Damien. When they locked eyes, Michael saw a spark of joy leap from her stare, and a deep wave of love engulfed his heart. He rushed to the table and leaned over to embrace her.

"They told me you were a patient here, but I know better. How were you so careless as to fall through the portal?"

"No, beloved, I am a recent patient here. I came after Doctor Tavaris died, so they do not know of my past connection to you and your family. Thank Goddess Doctor Tavaris removed your writings from the institute or else there would be no end of the questions!"

"Yes, of course. Think of all the questions about my father, your mother Child of Buddha, all of it . . . but, if you have been here for a while, how did—"

Tamara wagged a cautioning finger at him. "No, no, don't go there, Michael. You will never understand."

"But—"

Tamara put her finger to his lips. "No more questions along that line! Trust me and breathe."

"Okay," he sighed in resignation.

"By the way, in all your time here, did any of the psychiatrists, Hess or Camara or Tavaris, ever ask about my mother? After all, you wrote about her extensively, and I know they read every word. Oh, yes, they read every word with great interest!"

"Of course they did, but I always pled ignorance about Child of Buddha, I mean, other than what I wrote. None of them really followed that path." Michael chuckled. "They probably thought your mother was just another figment of my sick imagination. Doctor Hess was fond of telling me on numerous occasions how 'devilishly elaborate' I had built my delusions, and that teasing out one thread was next to impossible because it connected in some perplexing way to all the others."

"Good."

"Well," mused Michael after a pause. "What now?"

"Now, dear Michael, you rest from all your travels through space and time."

"And then?"

"Then we return."

"To the cave?"

"Oh, no, dear Michael. Not at all. Not at first, anyway."

"Where?"

"A surprise."

"A very great surprise?"

"A very great surprise!"

~ *Doctor DeRuntz Struggles* ~

Xavier DeRuntz felt convinced the hunchback patient Tamara X (she refused to provide the institute with her surname) had some deep connection to Michael Powers. Like all the psychiatrists that preceded him, DeRuntz searched for a direct path to Powers' psychoses. He knew Tamara would not voluntarily answer his questions, but he reckoned hypnosis might reveal the secret they shared. Powers himself had been resistant to hypnosis, but she might prove to be more suggestible.

The more DeRuntz thought about it, the more excited he became. Always, in the back of his mind, his predecessors loomed large, and he felt spurred on in no small measure by competitive fire, happily concluding Tamara presented an avenue they had no chance to explore. She had quite recently voluntarily admitted herself, complaining of depression and suicidal ideations. As treating psychiatrist, DeRuntz ruled out bipolar disorder and diagnosed clinical depression. Unfortunately, he had little opportunity to treat her. Now, he realized, she might be a key to Mr. Powers' delusions.

First, he must probe more deeply the basis of her own disorder. Excited by this possibility, he wanted to use hypnosis to save time. The problem was in convincing her. After all, she could check herself out at any time. He spent considerable time puzzling over how to obtain her cooperation and decided to convince her by using a therapeutic ruse.

Days later Tamara sat in DeRuntz's office listening to him give an update on the clinical status of the depression that had brought her to the institute and his prognosis for the future.

"And so you can see," he concluded, "it is imperative we discover what happened in your childhood that may have led to your current condition."

"Yes, I can see that," she replied dryly.

"Unfortunately, you have blocked those memories, so we must find another way . . . another route to uncover them."

"Yes, I can see that," she repeated.

"So, I have decided our best course of action is hypnosis, if, of course, you are agreeable."

"Yes, I can see that."

He slapped his knee. "Well, no time like the present! Shall we do it now?" Without waiting for her reply, he gestured toward the couch. "Would you, please?"

"Yes."

"I will have the tape turned on, so we can record your responses. Afterward, you may not remember what you said. Okay?"

"Yes."

DeRuntz had her lean back on the couch, took a few moments to prepare, and began. . . .

~

Xavier DeRuntz opened his eyes and found himself looking at a small boy playing with toy soldiers. The boy was in the room where DeRuntz grew up, and he recognized himself, but felt surprised that his younger self played with toy soldiers. *I never played with toy soldiers!* he thought confusedly. His disembodied observer continued gazing at the younger Xavier who seemed engrossed with carefully positioning his soldiers. Suddenly, the boy rose and closed the door, then tiptoed to his dresser where he dug through a pile of underclothes and pulled out a razor blade. This astonished DeRuntz. *I remember none of this!* he marveled.

Young Xavier picked up a soldier whose plastic figure struck a triumphant pose with one arm raised over his head brandishing a rifle. Carefully, meticulously, the boy used the razor to cut off the soldier's hand at the wrist. Rummaging around, he found another soldier, and using the same meticulous care, sliced off one of its feet just above the boot. After performing these operations, he deftly set aside the foot and the hand. Once satisfied, the young Xavier DeRuntz turned and looked directly into the older Xavier DeRuntz's eyes. Instantly, the boy's features changed into a face he did not recognize.

"My god!" gasped DeRuntz loudly. In a cold sweat, he stared up at Tamara who stood over him, and he realized he was lying on the couch.

"What happened?" he asked in a daze.

"You were given a glimpse," replied Tamara, who abruptly turned on her heel and walked out of his office.

~

It took DeRuntz a few moments to collect himself. He then sat behind his desk, looked at the tape still recording, stopped it, rewound, and listened.

Silence—only his own breath.

Chapter Five

Rest Interrupted

An Aside

You see, dear Reader, when someone gets snagged in the unintentional web I weave, bad things happen. I warned DeRuntz to run. What more can I do? Ironic, isn't it—none of them blame me for the trail of bodies in my wake. Not even Emile Ruska. Yet you and I both know I am guilty. Perhaps not homicide, but certainly involuntary manslaughter at the least.

Speaking of manslaughter, God wants me dead, which is good. After all, I must be some sort of threat to Him (not that He needs a threat to oversee mass slaughter and suffering). But I digress.

Tamara told me to rest before the big surprise. How does one rest after a prophecy? Besides, how can I rest with all the nurses and attendants coming and going, administering drugs, and taking endless quantities of my blood? God knows (pun intended) I will get no rest despite Tamara's advice. I have sequestered myself in my room and am catching up on my writing. If you have stuck with me all this time, you must be the sole reader on the planet of these words (other than myself, of course). In the end it's you and me, Reader. And there I go—digressing. That is what too much rest will do. I must find Tamara. I must make love to her. That will ease the boredom eating away at me. What could it be, the "great" surprise she mentioned?

~ *Surprise, Surprise* ~

A day has passed, and I am now sitting in the recreation room anxiously awaiting the arrival of my beloved Tamara. I need her so much! It's like being flung back into childhood, trembling for my first love and performing every idiocy known to humankind in her honor. It did not matter an atom to me that I acted the fool in a thousand different ways. Oh, god, how I reveled in my love-fever—now high and burning with indescribable ecstasies—now low and cold with uncontrollable chills. I made myself a pathetic buffoon in ways that make me cringe now that I am older and, supposedly, wiser.

"Hello, Michael."

Ah! Her voice hits like sugar on an empty stomach. I jump up and hug her close.

"Ah, Tamara! I'm so happy you're here at last! I've been waiting. Sit, sit."

Tamara moved a chair back to accommodate her hump and settled in at the table, her hand in mine. "Are you getting rest as I suggested?"

"Yes, yes, but now I'm ready for your big surprise."

She laughs. "Not so soon, my impatient man."

"But, Tamara, why wait? You are a magician. You know *Her.* You are a servant of Goddess. You can get us out of this place with a snap of your fingers!"

Instead of her usual quick comeback, Tamara winced. "You think too highly of me."

"Not possible."

"Then you think too highly of my powers."

I lean over and kiss her. "Never. You are my Goddess."

"I'm a female Quasimodo cavorting among the gargoyles."

"Are you calling me a gargoyle?" I ask with a grin.

She smiles coyly. "I like climbing on your gargoyle."

With these words, my gargoyle instantly comes to life! "Let's do it now. You climb; I'll grimace."

Tamara looked around. "Unfortunately, this place is not Notre Dame cathedral."

I sigh. "A cathedral for the crazy. Get us out of here, Tamara."

"Be patient, Michael. I'm . . . working on Doctor DeRuntz."

The hairs on my neck rise like wary sentries. "You won't . . . I mean, he won't . . . end up like the others, will he?"

Tamara looks at me in a strange, appraising way, as one might eye a horse for sale. "And if he does?" she asks.

I turn away from her stare. "That is not the way of Goddess."

"Good!" she cries.

"Tamara, why did the others die?"

She frowns and her face reflects a bitterness I had never before seen. "That is complicated, and not for you to know."

"Why not?"

"Enough!" she stands and says curtly, "Get rest. That is all."

I grab back her hand. "Wait, Tamara. Don't leave. Sit with me."

She pulls away her hand. "Rest."

"For how long?"

"You will know."

"But—"

She turns on her heel and starts to leave. I rise to follow, but she whirls around and barks, "Don't!"

My head spins! She's like dealing with one of the bipolar patients.

"Time for your medication, Mr. Powers." Doctor DeRuntz has suddenly appeared and sits at the table, motioning for me to join him.

I remain standing. "Okay," I say. (I will agree to anything if he just leaves me alone.)

"But first let's have a chat," he says offhandedly.

"Fine," I reply. "But here; I hate your office."

"Here will do."

I already see him as a kind of dead man, so I acquiesce. I summon up my old sarcastic attitude and say, "So, what's up, Doc?" I say, mustering a corpse's grin.

"Your friend, Tamara, that is what's up."

"What about her?"

"You two are close?"

I shrug.

"I know you are."

I shrug again.

"Will you help me with her treatment?"

I cannot help it. I blurt out using my best cross-examination voice, "In point of fact, isn't she treating you?"

DeRuntz laughs nervously. "Well, I guess you could look at it that way."

"I do look at it that way."

He squirms in his chair. "Tell me what you know about her."

"She is a hunchback."

"Yes, and?"

"That's it. Normal intelligence. Normal personality. Normal woman."

DeRuntz remains unperturbed. "What do you talk about?"

"The weather."

"Please, Mr. Powers, I'm being serious. What do you two talk about?"

"Quasimodo."

"Very funny."

I shrug. "Thank you."

DeRuntz leans forward in anticipation. "Mr. Powers, do you believe you're responsible for my predecessors' deaths—and Damien Lundgren's?"

The question has its desired effect; it nearly bowls me over. I am uncharacteristically speechless.

"Your silence speaks volumes," he says.

"Doctor DeRuntz, I have been ordered to rest. These questions are not helping. Did you not tell me it was medication time?"

"Who ordered you to rest?"

"Doctor Quasimodo."

"You are quite the card, Mr. Powers."

"May I go back to my room now. I'm not feeling well."

"Of course," he replies jovially, as if he had just scored in some one-upmanship contest.

~

I am sitting quietly in my room. Tamara dominates my thoughts. All my voices are also quiet. Goddess nowhere to be found (or heard). True, Buandelgereen looms in the background, but only because I associate her with Tamara. Restlessness soon overcomes me, and I decide to return to the same iron door where I had seen Tamara before. If she is not there, I'll go back to the recreation room and wait. Just as I am about to act on my plan, an attendant swings open the door to my room and says, "Doctor DeRuntz wants to see you."

I snort in disgust. "I just saw him. I don't want to see him now. Tell him to leave me alone."

"You have a visitor."

"Who?" I exclaim.

"How would I know? Do you want to see the visitor or not? If not, you can stay here." During this little exchange, I notice the attendant uses a surly tone. He has been none too gentle in our past dealings either.

"Don't you like me, Ike?" I ask innocently.

"Excuse me, Mr. Powers, but your reputation for using, and abusing, those trying to help you is no cause for pride."

I am momentarily chastised, but visions of my mystery visitor take over. "Let's go," I say.

Who could it be? Who could it be?

~

I write these words the next day. However, I can barely put them down, so astonished did the visit leave me. Nevertheless, write I must. Here is what happened:

The meeting was scheduled to take place in DeRuntz's office, and after depositing me in the waiting room, Ike took his leave and I sat wired and waiting, all the while trying to avoid eye contact with his nosy secretary. (My reputation must have preceded me.) Finally, she answered the intercom summons with a curt, "Yes, sir," and sent me into the place that would satisfy my burning curiosity.

Upon entering, a lean figure stood in the center of the room and my eyes immediately met those of Detective Emile Ruska! I confess, I felt a twinge of disappointment. I had harbored a wild hope it would be Buandelgereen in all her savage splendor. But Ruska?

"You remember Detective Ruska?" asked Doctor DeRuntz.

"Yes," was all I could muster.

Ruska stuck out his hand. "Good to see you again, Mr. Powers."

I returned his firm handshake and muttered, "Likewise."

"Detective Ruska asked to speak with you in private. Is that okay with you?"

"Sure," I replied, not quite so sure.

"Pamela will show you to the small conference room we reserve for such meetings," said DeRuntz.

"Thank you," said Ruska, and the both of us obediently followed DeRuntz's secretary to the destination.

Once she left, the detective's demeanor changed dramatically. What had been coolly professional now warmed to the easy familiarity of an old friend. First, of course, came the required preliminaries.

"How have you been, Mr. Powers?"

"Fine."

Sensing my monosyllabic frost, Ruska cut to the chase. "I will come to the point, Mr. Powers."

"Good."

"When you were taken into custody at the cave, reports indicated you were alone and under the psychotic delusion that others were with you. In fact, you were convinced the cave was a giant complex of some kind, complete with a cafeteria and a large population of residents."

Of course, dear Reader, you and I know this was no delusion, but to keep up appearances, one must sometimes tumble to the protocol. "Yes," I replied submissively. (Rather well done, I thought at the time.)

Then he detonated a bomb.

"Well, I don't believe you were alone, Mr. Powers. I believe you were with others. I believe the rest of us simply could not see them, but they were there. What do you say to that, Mr. Powers?"

This astonishing declaration from a hard-nosed detective jolted me into full attention. But, at that moment, I could manage only a desultory, "I see."

He chuckled. "You sound like a therapist."

I laughed with him. "Been around them long enough. Tends to rub off."

Then—boom, again.

He turned very serious, and for the second time in less than a minute, shocked the hell out of me. "Would you like to get out of here, Mr. Powers?"

I could not speak. How could I express to him what music to my ears his question represented? Tears came to my eyes. Finally, I croaked, "Yes, yes, yes!"

"I think I can swing it, if you would agree to go with me back to the cave."

"The cave," I repeated stupidly.

"Yes, the cave."

"Why?"

"To see for myself, of course."

"See what?" I played dumb.

"The others."

A vision of Tamara came to mind. "There is another," I said.

"Another? You mean there is only one at the cave?"

"No, I mean locked up here, with me."

"Patient?"

"Yes, another patient. She must come with us."

"Why?" he smiled. "Are you in love?"

"It's more than that," I replied. "She is of the cave."

"Of the cave?"

"She is one of them—the others you speak of."

"I see," he said doubtfully.

"Don't worry," I hastened to add. "She is not just a figment of my delusions. She was there when you visited the cave the first couple of times. In fact, she is one of those that was instrumental in scaring you away."

His eyes grew large. "You know about those trips?"

"Of course—with White Thunder, and afterward. She was there."

"But, wasn't she a patient here at the time?"

I shook my head. "Mr. Ruska, if you want to go, and if you believe there were others, then you must believe what I tell you."

"The wet nose?"

I laughed. "All will be explained . . . to the extent possible. Whatever else happens, she must accompany us."

"Her name?"

"Tamara, you can't miss her. Hunchback. Asian."

"Last name?"

I paused. Does Tamara even have a last name? "Her mother was Child of Buddha," I blurted.

By his skeptical reaction, I knew I was losing him.

"Look," I said. "She does not have a last name. Her name is Tamara. She is mononymous—same with her mother, Child of Buddha."

"What does this facility use as her last name?"

"I don't know. Jane Doe? Tamara Doe?"

"I see."

Again, I sense I'm losing him. "Tamara's mother translated the taps of the Precious Object, and *her*, and Goddess, and she made things happen for my parents in China." The words tumbled recklessly from my mouth, making no sense to him. I plunged on like an idiot anyway. "You see, my mother and father were on a quest, but the Japanese invaded . . . and . . . ah, I can see this is confusing you."

"To say the least," he said drily. "Perhaps another day—"

I continued before he had a chance to finish his thought. "Look, Detective Ruska, I can see you are understandably skeptical. I will stop talking and leave it at this: if you get us to the cave, what I have just told you will make sense. You will see for yourself. If not, then I would agree to return here without protest or complaint."

He sighed, still hesitant. "Okay, I believe you, I think. However, getting both of you out will make things more difficult."

"I have confidence in you. Do what you must do. We will play along with whatever role you want us to play. Remember, Tamara told me she can check herself out any time."

"Let me think about this a little more," he said with a slight shake of his head.

Oh, God! I'm going to lose him for sure! I agonized. *Say something, idiot Michael!*

"Detective Ruska," I rushed to say, using a lighter tone. "If you want to know the mystery of the wet nose, the woman with the backpack, the strange noises, unsettling breezes, and spooky presences that convinced White Thunder not to even venture into the cave, and that scared you out of it, get me out of here."

Again, his eyes grew large in disbelief. "How did you know?"

"I was there."

Ruska sat silently for some time, then slammed his fist on the table. "I'll do it! But, first, I need to talk with this Tamara person."

I smiled. "To make sure she is not crazy?"

"No, to make sure I'm not crazy."

~ *On the Road* ~

Tamara sits in front of me at the cafeteria having just heard the recitation of my interview with Detective Ruska. She displays no emotion. Not even curiosity.

"I must say, Tamara," I say in a quite disappointed tone. "You could be a little more excited about my news."

"I cannot get excited about old news," she says impishly.

"You're not even a little surprised?"

"Silly man! Detective Ruska is the surprise I promised you!"

"What?"

"You don't remember? He is your great surprise. I already knew he would visit you."

"But, how?"

"That is not for you to know."

I shake my head. "I can't believe it."

"Believe it."

"You never fail to amaze me! And you said I overestimate your powers."

"They are not mine."

"Goddess?"

She shrugs. "Now wait for Detective Ruska to work his own magic with the doctors."

"How long will it take?"

"That I don't know," says Tamara.

"By the way," I say. "What is your last name, or, perhaps I should ask, your real Chinese name?"

"What do you want it to be?" asks Tamara with a mischievous grin.

"Come on, Tamara, I need to know. It's a perfectly legitimate question. Your mother certainly was not born with the name Child of Buddha. What is your surname?"

"What do you want it to be?" she asks again.

I throw up my hands in frustration. "You win! I want it to be Powers."

"Then my name is Tamara Powers."

I am not in the mood for games. "Great! My first wife Diane—a real person by the way—died in a car crash. My second wife Theresa—apparently sent by Goddess—was, I am now positive, a figment of my imagination. And you, my dear Tamara, exist somewhere in between."

"What you fail to realize, Michael, is that you also exist somewhere in between."

"Oh, Christ! I can't tell you how tired I am of riddles!"

"Dear Michael," she says affectionately. "The universe is a riddle. Talk to any theoretical physicist about riddles! Those poor boys and girls are struggling in a quicksand of riddles."

"Never mind!" I snap. "Have you heard from Ruska?"

"Not since my interview with him a week ago."

"He has forgotten about us. I know it!" I say dejectedly.

"Be patient. I told him everything he wanted to hear. He will find a way. These things take time."

"Yes, and time to you is just some plastic, playdough to manipulate whatever way you want—past, present, future—all the same material to twist and turn as you wish."

"Michael, he will find a way."

"I hope so," I say without enthusiasm.

~

Another excruciating week has passed, and even Tamara's optimism barely dents my firm belief that Ruska has gotten cold feet about the whole idea.

"I'll end up dying here, just like those poor, crazy people locked up in your mother's old institution."

"Be patient," Tamara keeps reassuring me.

~

Then—at last—our time comes. Doctor DeRuntz calls Tamara and me into his office for an "important meeting." When we walk in, Ruska sits with the doctor, a serious expression on his face. DeRuntz holds a pair of manila folders in his hands.

After clearing his throat he says, "I will come directly to the point. Detective Ruska wants to take both of you to the cave where Mr. Powers was found and continue his investigation. Neither of you are suspected, but Detective Ruska believes both of you were being used by this . . . well, uh—"

"Cartel," interjects Ruska.

"Yes, cartel. Naturally, we at the institute are opposed, but the authorities"—a nod toward Ruska—"have obtained the family's permission."

Good old Mark! I think to myself.

"Detective Ruska," continues DeRuntz, "is taking full responsibility for your safety, and all expenses will be paid by the investigating department of the government. Separate rooms, of course," Ruska adds. "Policy. Optics. This assumes, of course, you both agree. Tamara, you will be discharged, as we have no grounds to keep you. Mr. Powers, on the other hand, will return to us at some future point, as determined by Detective Ruska and the investigating authorities. Do you both agree?"

With our enthusiastic concurrence, we both sign a stack of release documents, and soon are standing with our meager belongings on the steps of the institute waiting for Ruska to drive up.

I look at Tamara. "I don't know how you do it."

"I keep telling you, Michael, it isn't me."

"Okay, Goddess, or whoever, I'm glad we're out. On to the cave?"

"That is what Detective Ruska wants. For the time being, we must oblige his curiosity."

Before I know it, we are on the road out of San Francisco and headed toward the desert. Ruska briefs us on the itinerary but is otherwise quiet. At his insistence, Tamara and I both sit in the back seat, as if being chauffeured to our destination, which is a motel within a couple of hours' drive of the cave. He tells us he has reserved three rooms, and in the morning, we will visit the cave.

So far, Ruska has been very professional, his words succinct and to the point, no wasted effort. Nonetheless, sitting in the back seat, watching his eyes through the rearview mirror, I see something different. Quite different. Once one's view of a person is limited only to the eyes, a host of extraneous perceptions drop away, and character is exposed as clearly as if an oversized coat is removed to reveal a person's actual dimensions. What I see in Detective Ruska's eyes is the pained look of a deeply wounded man. Wounded by what? Disillusionment? Love? Betrayal? That, I do not know, and can only surmise.

Tamara, never one for small talk, and Ruska, stoically quiet, render the trip one of few words. Conversation is held to a minimum, which suits me fine. I focus on the motel, and the prospect of making love to Tamara. But this pleasurable line of thought ends abruptly when I project ahead to the cave. What will we find? Has Buandelgereen prepared it to fool Ruska again? Will I go back to my old room as if nothing has happened? And the iron door—what of that?

As mother used to say (so I am told), "Come what may."

Chapter Six

Detective Emile Ruska

Hot On The Trail

~ *A Detective's Demons* ~

Detective Ruska had no trouble maintaining his professional demeanor with Michael Powers and Tamara, but privately, he knew his actions were inexcusable—by conventional standards of duty and honor. Convention had always guided his career despite certain feelings and urges he kept locked away in a suspended state of dim, uncomfortable awareness. If those feelings were ever allowed to escape the dark place where he banished them, the light would blind him—and draw the wrath of everything he held dear. Over many years, his iron will had been forged by dread of slipping into that murky darkness where demons lurked, and was further tempered by the constant struggle to keep from doing so.

A few years after he was sworn in as a young police officer, slip he did. Badly.

In those early days of his career, unmarried and underpaid, he lived in a rather shabby apartment. Being a young police officer, half the residents of the complex liked him and felt comforted by his proximity, while the other half hated and feared him as an inhibitory presence. Ruska, by nature a quiet and solitary man, usually stayed in his apartment when off-duty, reading books not at all the typical fare of young police officers. He reveled in the horror stories of Lovecraft, the passionate and foreboding novels of Dostoevsky, the modernist poetry of Eliot, and, hidden in a drawer, the overwrought pornography of DeSade. In a sense, like most people, he lived a double life. The corner of his mind that harbored such eclectic and fertile intellectual soil took on a life of its own, cloaked in secrecy and sneering at convention, even as, outwardly, he appeared the model of cool, calm, efficient restraint.

As long as he held the contents of his "dark corner" in check, he functioned smoothly and successfully in performing the daily routine of his profession. Over the course of time, he had collected a small, but striking collection of pictures, drawings, and various bric-a-brac that adorned the walls and shelves of his apartment. The more controversial of his *objets d'art* (such as drawings of women in bondage and erotic statues) had inoffensive replacements (landscapes, busts depicting famous people, and the like) of the exact size and dimensions of their shocking counterparts, which he switched whenever he had company.

At night or on days off, absorbed in reading the murderous machinations of Raskolnikov and Smerdyakov, or enjoying a particularly vivid DeSade orgy, he played a tape of Alec Guinness reciting *A Waste Land* on continuous replay. These deviations, far from being a source of embarrassment to himself, operated as reminders that, underneath the dull cop exterior, existed an independent and rebellious spirit which he could release at any time. He often told himself that in the event some future conduct would arise on the part of his superiors that insulted his sense of fairness and propriety beyond an unspecified limit, he would take any shocking or reckless action to redress the infraction, regardless of consequences.

This maxim, he felt, would separate him from the common herd of followers whose blind obedience to convention (and their own preservation) were acts of cowardice that allowed outrages to happen all over the world unchecked. In short, the powers residing in his "dark place" would act as a surprise reserve, unleashed only during the direst circumstances. His "slip" into darkness occurred one unforgettable evening as a stark reminder that not all the power of rebellious acts by "good people" operated for the good. This incident taught him there existed immense forces beyond the ability of even the strongest person to keep in check and tempered his view of the often inexplicable and destructive behavior exhibited by otherwise well-meaning human beings.

It so happened that Ruska had befriended another resident of the complex, a single mother with a thirteen-year-old daughter. Bella Simpson and her daughter Lily often invited Ruska to dinner, and it appeared to others that a romantic relationship was developing between young Emile Ruska and not so young Bella Simpson. It is true that Emile never invited Bella to dinner himself, nor took her on a date, but these things take time, and most who were aware of the situation felt that reserved Emile was simply taking his time. Bella herself, more than anxious to develop an intimate relationship with Emile, knew enough to bide her time (after all, she reasoned, what man would want to take on the responsibility of a wife and a thirteen-year-old girl in the bargain?) It was because of this that Bella unwisely allowed Lily to become good friends with Deputy Ruska.

In fact, Bella and Lily were having more frequent arguments (some quite violent), and the girl had recently started acting-up in dangerous ways, including sneaking out at night and, her mother feared, spiraling deeply into drugs. Out of frustration, Bella turned to Emile, and asked him to have a conversation with her daughter about reckless behavior and the risk of drugs. Bella reckoned his dual status as a friend of Lily's and an authority figure would yield positive results. She explained that she would soon be attending a dinner for a departing co-worker, and if Emile would agree to babysit Lily, it would be the perfect opportunity to have a heart-to-heart talk. Normally, Bella added, she would not hire a babysitter for a thirteen-year-old, but Lily had been grounded and it had been made clear that she was not to be trusted alone at home during nighttime.

With this request, something stirred in that dark corner of his soul, and he experienced a moment of terror. The form of this terror, its actual nature, remained blurry and indistinct, but its ominous shape moved out of that darkness and into the light. In spite of warning bells going off loud and insistent, he found himself saying nonchalantly, "Sure, no problem." When he uttered these simple words, he inwardly trembled with the knowledge that a beast had escaped its imprisonment and now roamed freely to inflict whatever terrible damage it could.

When he arrived at Bella's apartment on the appointed evening, Lily was sitting on the couch watching TV, wearing pajamas and a robe. Bella thanked Emile, and on her way out, whispered, "Don't forget the talk."

"I won't."

"Leftover pizza in the fridge if you're hungry."

"Thanks. Have fun."

~

After Bella left, Emile ate a few slices of cold pizza in the kitchen, not bothering Lily who evidently was deeply engrossed by some movie. When he moved into the living room, the TV continued playing, but Lily was gone. He saw her bedroom door closed, shrugged, picked up the remote, and flipped channels to a nature documentary. Emile would have been perfectly happy to spend the rest of the evening watching TV without Lily present, even if it meant postponing the talk about drugs, but after a while, she came out of her room wearing shorts and a tank top with no bra.

The beast from Emile's dark corner moved just as she moved, blocking the light and casting a shadow across his reasoning abilities, rendering him powerless to impose his will and force it back into its cage.

"Hello," he said.

Lily plopped down on the couch beside him. "Hello. What'cha watchin'?"

"Nothing. Documentary." He scanned her body. "You changed."

"Yeah, hot."

He wanted to tell her to put her robe back on but feared sounding ridiculous. Humbert Humbert flickered through his mind; he crushed the thought. Lily stretched out her bare legs and propped her heels on the coffee table. He noticed her painted toenails, hot pink.

"Anything else on?" she asked.

"Nothing I want to see"—he started to hand her the remote—"but you might like something."

She waved it away. "Naw, I'd rather talk."

Emile clicked off the TV and turned toward her, scooting a bit farther away, prepared to listen. He could not help noting the outline of her young breasts under the flimsy fabric. A terrific, silent struggle began raging in his heart. The monster must not be allowed to win.

"You like mom?" she asked.

"Of course, she is a wonderful person."

"No, I mean, do you like her as a girlfriend, you know?"

"Oh, no, we're just friends."

Waiting for her reply, he noticed her arms for the first time. "You've been cutting!" he exclaimed without thinking.

She drew back. "Is that the cop in you, like, I mean, is that the kind of thing you notice?"

"Don't have to be a cop to notice."

"Mom doesn't."

"Maybe she does."

"Naw, she don't. Trust me."

"Well—"

"So why do you notice?"

"I have experience."

She smiled. "I bet you do." Her smile was pathetic—pleading—thirteen going on thirty. She scooted closer.

Emile jumped up from the couch and looked down at Lily in anger. "Look, Lily, we need to talk."

"About?"

"Well, about cutting for one thing . . . and drugs."

She rolled her eyes. "Oh, man! Jesus! Look, just because you're a cop!"

While she talked excitedly, he could not keep his eyes from staring at her breasts, the nipples now pronounced through the fabric. Catching his gaze, she suddenly stopped. "So, you like?" She stood and thrust out her chest, again a pathetic attempt at grown-up behavior. Her eyes retained that same pleading look.

Sweat broke on his forehead. His defenses fluttered like paper in a windstorm. With supreme effort, he forced his eyes back to her face, although, for some reason, he could not quite look her in the eyes.

"We need to talk about drugs, Lily," he croaked, realizing the utter inanity of the statement.

She held up her arms. "I thought you wanted to talk about my cutting."

"I do."

Again, she gave him that odd pleading gaze accompanied by incongruous words that should have come from someone much older.

"I cut other parts of my body. Do you want to see?"

Now, the beast leapt at his throat, shaking his weak resolve like a dog with a rag doll, its teeth penetrating so deeply he tried to make a noise but could not speak.

Once more, he nodded mutely.

She started to lift up her tank top, periodically pausing to gauge his willingness to let her continue. With each pause and corresponding failure of Emile to object, her lips quivered in a sad, confirming smile.

Deputy Emile Ruska stood frozen, the monster in control, a host of malevolent shadows from his "dark corner" now flying out into the open, seizing his brain and imposing a horrifying paralysis of will.

Lily stood before him topless, her body projecting a mix of sadness and triumph, her eyes never losing the odd, pleading gaze of one standing on the edge of oblivion, waiting for a word. He wanted to take her in his arms and comfort her, he wanted to take her in his arms and violate her, and in the violent collision his mind sheared away like wings falling from an airplane, and still she stood, waiting.

He plunged downward, helpless, finally halting his deadly spin when he noticed the other scars. The other scars. They crisscrossed her breasts in angry red welts as if some medieval torturer had his way with her. As he stared at the scars, she moved ever closer, finally stopping mere inches from his body.

"Do they hurt?" he asked without knowing what he was saying.

"Touch them," she said.

His hands twitched, trying to break away from his demands that they remain by his side.

"Run your fingers over them," she coaxed.

He lifted a finger and gently traced one of the scars. At the touch of her breast, something happened, the spell broken, the awful realization of what he had done, what he was doing, slammed into him as powerfully as if he had been physically punched. At that moment, he realized there were forces, dark forces, beyond the explanation of any authority, any science.

"You are not a thirteen-year-old girl!" he blurted, almost whispering in self-revelation. "Something is possessing you, making you do this. I see your eyes. Lily, your eyes do not want to do this. Your eyes tell me something very different!"

Suddenly, the tears came flooding from her eyes, rolling unchecked down her cheeks. "Kiss me!" she cried. "Take me away somewhere, anywhere!" She grabbed his hand and held it to her breast. "Touch me! Kiss me!"

A flicker of strength left over from the retreating beast made him linger, his hand on her breast, his thumb caressing her nipple. Suddenly, with supreme effort, Emile pushed her away. "Go get dressed!" he commanded. "Enough of this nonsense! You need a psychiatrist! Counseling! I will advise your mother to get you enrolled somewhere safe. A facility—"

Lily screamed a frightful cry of hopelessness and despair, barely human. Emile staggered back and she looked at him one last time, the pleading expression now replaced by something else, something he could not read, but which was horrifying and unforgettable.

"Go fuck yourself!" she yelled in a pubescent voice not compatible with the ugly words it formed.

Lily ran into her room and slammed the door.

Two weeks later, she committed suicide.

Bella never found out what happened that night, and when she reached out to Emile in her agony following Lily's death, he pushed her from him and soon thereafter moved out of his apartment without explanation.

~

Dear Reader, I discovered this information long after we left the institute with Ruska, but it explains his willingness to look at alternative explanations for inexplicable phenomena. He had learned there existed powers beyond rational explanation, and he carefully guarded the shadowy figures lurking in his "dark corner", waiting for a time when they might be released to fly against convention—this time for good rather than evil (or so he promised himself).

~ *Miss Hunchback* ~

Tamara and Michael sat quietly in the back seat, unaware of the truths yet to unfold. As they neared the motel where they would stay, Michael's thoughts were filled with eager anticipation of their intimacy, while Tamara's mind was preoccupied with something far less certain. Though her face stayed composed, a growing unease gnawed at her with each passing mile. She had not heard from Buandelgereen, and her usual powers of foresight, once so sharp, seemed to slip. Just as Michael had lost the ability to communicate with dogs and listen to the voices of the sidewalk, Tamara felt a similar shift within.

The Goddess had insisted that a new child must be born to replace Michael, and, more specifically, that this child must result from the union between Tamara and the very "chosen son" being replaced. Tamara accepted this decree without question, but the trials the Goddess had led her through—those in the cave and behind the iron door—were growing burdensome. Tamara thought of her mother, who, in her final years, had found peace in helping Reverend Fu and Master Li with the everyday workings of the old Chinese mental institution where she had once been a patient. In those last years, she had basked in the stability and tranquility that had been absent during her earlier, tumultuous life. Only now did Tamara fully understand her mother's need for the simplicity of routine, for the comfort of predictable days amid the chaos of the past.

Tamara never knew her father, and her mother rarely spoke of him, always brushing aside Tamara's persistent questions with the terse reply, "Dead and gone, not even a ghost left. Let him be." As she grew older, Tamara turned to Reverend Fu and Master Li for answers, but their responses were no more enlightening. They told her only that her father had worked at the institution, and when her mother became pregnant, he vanished without a trace. According to them, the man had been a quiet figure—"like a monk," Master Li said—and no one knew him well, except to note that he was "a good worker." Each time Tamara inquired about his name, their answers were vague. "We never really knew," Reverend Fu would reply. "In those days, the countryside was full of deserters and political fugitives fleeing the communists. When they were hired, they often used false names, and few employers thought to ask questions."

Perhaps due to her father's absence, Child of Buddha chose to withhold a proper name from her daughter, referring to her instead as *Túobeì nühái* (Hunchback Girl), or, when reprimanding her, *Túobeì xiǎojiě* (Miss Hunchback). Yet,

Child of Buddha did reveal to her daughter that she possessed an American name—Tamara. After they settled in America, her mother insisted she adopt this name. When Tamara once inquired why they were bound for America, her mother responded with a soft laugh, explaining that they had an "American family" there. In time, she would leave China to escape its reprisals and hardships. Tamara liked it at the institute as she had the run of the place and was spoiled by the attentions of Reverend Fu and Master Li. But every time she complained to her mother that she did not want to go to America, her mother snapped. "Be thankful, stupid girl! You will be living in safety and comfort with your American family. No more nonsense about not going to America!"

It so happened that a frequent visitor to the institute was a Mongol woman named Buandelgereen, whose wild presence was always warmly welcomed by Reverend Fu and Master Li. Over the years, she formed a deep bond with Tamara, much to her mother's evident approval. Looking back, Tamara realized that her mother had gone to great lengths to foster their connection. Many nights, Tamara stayed awake, listening in awe as Buandelgereen wove her extraordinary tales. To Tamara, this Mongol woman embodied all the authority, majesty, and fearsome power of a female Genghis Khan. In time, Buandelgereen became like an aunt to her, and the two became inseparable. Tamara followed her everywhere when she visited the institute, marveling at how often Buandelgereen would retreat alone into the old "No Admittance" room, spending hours there in mysterious solitude. When Tamara pressed her ear to the door, she would hear the Mongol woman speaking to someone unseen, and Tamara chalked it up to magic far beyond her understanding.

Then came the day when Buandelgereen made her final visit to the institute, announcing her intention to travel to America. That evening, Child of Buddha revealed to Tamara that she would accompany Buandelgereen on the journey, where she would be safe and prosper. But her mother cautioned that the Mongol woman was no ordinary person, and Tamara must obey her, regardless of how strange or unnatural her commands might seem. Only as she grew older did Tamara come to understand the depth of her mother's sorrow—the silent tears that fell from her eyes, the knowledge she was surrendering the one brief joy in her life, a joy now vanishing like a fleeting dream in a world of pain and unfulfilled hopes.

That was many years ago, and in the time that had passed, Tamara had been rigorously trained by Buandelgereen, acquiring abilities she had once thought unimaginable for a young hunchback girl from China. Not once had she faltered in her obedience to her mentor, and not once had she failed to draw strength from the tasks Buandelgereen set before her. Even when told she was to bear Michael Powers' child, she did not hesitate or waver.

Several months ago, Buandelgereen summoned Tamara for a new assignment. By the Mongol woman's command, Tamara was to check herself into the same mental institution in San Francisco where Michael Powers had once been treated, claiming to suffer from depression and suicidal thoughts. Tamara never thought to question the reason behind this directive. At the height of her powers, she placed her absolute trust in Buandelgereen's wisdom. Yet, the stay drained her, and the medication she was forced to take dulled her strength, weakening the very powers she had so carefully cultivated.

Now, this Detective Ruska had entered the picture, and she was returning to the cave without a clear picture of the purpose or desired result of such a move. For the first time, she had begun to question Buandelgereen's motivation for making her perform so many mysterious tasks. True, her "auntie" worked for Goddess, and the machinations of deities were never clear to mortals, but Tamara craved to be trusted with the rationale and overarching goals for which she so loyally and unquestioningly gave of herself. Also true, she had been forewarned by Buandelgereen about the detective and this crazy dash back to the cave, but why were her powers waning? Worse yet, why had she received no indication what to expect when they reached the cave?

Tamara looked at Michael and knew he had sex on his mind, but she felt the need to be alone with her concerns. Gazing out at the passing desert, she tried to listen for Buandelgereen, but nothing answered. She felt like a person trying to make an emergency phone call, the line busy, then dead.

"We're almost there," said Ruska, looking at them through the rear view mirror.

Tamara felt a twinge of dread. Tomorrow morning would soon be upon them—and the cave. For now, she had to manage horny Michael and the ever-inquisitive Detective Ruska.

"Let's have dinner together at some restaurant that's close after we get settled in our rooms," said Ruska. "There are some things I want to go over before tomorrow."

"Fine with me," said Michael. "I could use a few beers."

"Me too," said Ruska. "And you, Tamara?"

Reflecting on her condition, she said, "Not for me, thank you."

Tamara breathed a sigh of relief for the short reprieve.

~

Once the little group sat together for dinner, Ruska waited until they had eaten, then cleared his throat.

"I want to ask both of you what I am to expect tomorrow?"

Michael, supremely confident that Tamara had all the answers, turned his head toward her.

"Expect the unexpected," she said.

"That isn't good enough," said Ruska.

"What do you mean?" asked Michael.

Ruska turned his attention to Michael. "You said all questions would be answered. I have stuck my neck out for you two. I expect answers."

Tamara had been waiting for just such demand for assurances. "Detective Ruska, how much do you know about physics?"

Now, both men turned to her in surprise.

After a long pause, Ruska said, "Not much."

"If I were to tell a physicist to 'expect the unexpected' he or she would be irritated at being reminded of the obvious. I will tell you the truth, Detective Ruska, I myself do not know what to expect"—she turned to Michael—"let alone this man, who is the son."

Ruska shook his head. "I don't understand."

Tamara leaned forward for emphasis. "Emile Ruska, what I do know is that you often go to a certain cocktail lounge for drinks when you're feeling particularly stressed, or lonely. A certain waitress by the name of Emma engages in humorous, or sometimes not humorous, repartee with you. It is a comfort, is it not?"

"How—" Ruska started to ask.

Tamara pressed her advantage by holding up her hand and continuing.

"Quantum mechanics and general relativity are not compatible. Are you aware of these two pillars of modern physics?"

"Somewhat," said Ruska defensively.

"Which means we humans—even the most brilliant among us—have no idea how the universe works in its most extreme manifestations; black holes, for example, or the laws of physics at the instant of the Big Bang."

"Look, Tamara," said Ruska gruffly. "I don't need a physics lecture, just give me straight answers!"

Tamara made a show of turning her head to look down her back. "I have never experienced straightness in my life, Detective Ruska. This is the point I am making. Quantum mechanics and general relativity are not like common sense reality . . . they are a more exotic, deeper reality. And deeper still than these two—" She shrugged. "Expect the unexpected."

"Okay, fine, so what do you say I can expect to see tomorrow?"

"Something exotic. Deeper reality. I just do not know what form it will take, just as physicists don't know what happens inside a black hole, certainly not at the singularity."

For the first time, Ruska seemed amused. "In other words, you don't know shit. You do not have a clue what to expect tomorrow."

"More or less correct," she said, quickly adding, "this once."

"I see," grumbled Ruska. Turning his attention to Michael, he asked, "And you?"

Under Ruska's withering gaze, Michael saw flashing before his eyes all his life experiences, every one a prolonged battle: lonely childhood, Vietnam, marriage, a son, a lawyer, mental illness, institutionalization, and he sat upright, returning Ruska's stare with his own imperious glare—the warrior reborn.

"I am sick of being viewed as some delusional schizophrenic child, fit only for institutionalization and the care of well-meaning hacks. I am not sure you will come out of this alive, Detective Ruska, or whether you will fill another grave in the same cemetery as those in the past who came too close to me, but I will take the risk, since you are also taking a risk. Let's find some bar, right now, and we'll drink together, and I'll tell you my story—all of it. Then, we will see what we see tomorrow. Come what may."

Ruska smiled. "Now you're speaking words I understand."

Chapter Seven

Again, The Cave

Ruska, Tamara, Buandelgereen

~ Morning ~

Next morning, and the three of us stand clustered around the overheated car parked at the side of the dirt road, gazing in the direction of the cave. Heat shimmers rise from the hood like exhausted spirits. Emile and I feel a bit worse for wear from an evening of heavy drinking and illuminating revelations. No one speaks, our hands shading our eyes from the glare of the sun rising above the eastern hills. A scan of the area reveals nothing but undisturbed desert scrub, sand, and rock.

I glance at Tamara, but she is intent on listening to her inner voices—or whatever internal receptors she possesses—for any last-minute instructions on how to proceed. Her eyes are half-lidded, her head tilted as if trying to catch a signal from some distant station. Apparently, she hears nothing, for she hesitates to start down the trail.

Something in my mind prods me to move.

"Well, what are we waiting for?" I proclaim in my best hale-and-hearty voice.

Ruska looks at me a bit startled, but Tamara is the one to take the first step. Ruska follows, and despite my rather strained enthusiasm, I lag behind, miserably certain there will be nothing to see. Our footsteps crunch in unison at first, then scatter as the incline steepens. We have gone a little over half-way, far from the deserted road and beyond the view of any lone car that might chance by, when we hear someone approaching from the direction of the cave. All of us stop, holding our collective breaths. A faint metallic clink rises above the wind. Appearing from behind a small, boulder-strewn hill strides a determined figure. As the face comes into view, it is none other than Buandelgereen.

The great Mongol woman seems carved from sunlit rock, her gray mane flowing, braids threaded with beaten copper that wink like coals. She wears her most imposing traditional garb, and I'm astonished to see a rifle slung across her back—as if she'd stepped out of a bandit-era photograph, or better yet, a woman warrior just returned from campaigning with Genghis Khan. How she carries such presence—and such strength—at her age is beyond me. I ascribe it to the sponsorship of Goddess. That—and I've no doubt she drinks from the same spring as the deity *Herself.*

My first inclination is to run up to her in greeting, but I hold back because her eyes are locked on those of Detective Ruska. When I reach his side, I observe his dumbfounded expression, and stifle an impulse to emit an amused laugh. Buandelgereen's presence has relieved my worst fears, and I now will follow with confidence wherever she leads.

Buandelgereen walks up to the still transfixed Emile. She thrusts out her hand.

"Welcome, Detective Ruska! Tamara here told us of your visit."

Ruska instinctively grips it but remains mute.

"I understand you want to see the cave?" Buandelgereen asks without taking her eyes from his stunned face.

"I . . . uh . . . visited before. I am familiar. . . . " his words trail off.

"Yes, we didn't know you then," she says. "Our welcome was less than hospitable."

Ruska remains immovably silent.

"Well, come on then and see for yourself," says Buandelgereen. She turns to Tamara and me, offering a brief nod of acknowledgment before setting off down the trail.

Ruska shakes his head, as if trying to dispel the fog clouding his thoughts, before falling in step behind Buandelgereen. Tamara and I bring up the rear, exchanging a questioning glance—our brows lifting in silent agreement that, while the situation feels undeniably strange, we have little choice but to follow Buandelgereen's lead.

Tamara, for her part, appears somewhat nonplussed by the reception. Her usual sly half-smile has vanished, leaving her face as blank as the desert sky.

After a long and arduous hike, we finally arrive at the mouth of a cave, where a group of men—presumably Mongols, many of whom I recognize—stand waiting, clutching an assortment of mining tools. They regard us with impassive curiosity, like statues waiting to be given orders.

"Let me introduce the crew," says Buandelgereen, sweeping her arm.

The men nod and Ruska nods in return.

"I don't understand," he says.

"We are exploring, Detective Ruska," says Buandelgereen.

"For?"

"There used to be tungsten mines nearby. Originally, we were after tungsten, but demand for that mineral has declined, so we are now searching for boron."

"Boron!"

"Yes. Many uses for it. We might even find lithium, one never knows. But boron still retains quite a good market price."

Ruska blinks at her, as if trying to reconcile her barbaric splendor with a mining feasibility study. "I was not aware," he says slowly. "And forgive me if I mispronounce your name—Buandaygreen—but when I visited before, I saw no evidence of any mining operation. Nor did Mr. Fred Miller, the private detective who eventually found Mr. Powers, report anything of the kind."

Buandelgereen laughs. "Of course not. We try to leave no trace of our activities. Red tape. Government regulations. Environmental impact reports. Competition. Naturally, we do this in secret."

"This is government land," says Ruska.

"If we find what we seek, it can be leased."

"I presume you finance the operation?"

"I manage it . . . there are others who provide the capital."

Ruska shakes his head in disbelief. "I don't see how—ah!"

Suddenly, he jolts and whirls around to find Temulun at his side. The dog has materialized like a spirit blooming from the shadows. She had pressed her damp nose against Ruska's leg and now pants playfully, as if sharing some secret amusement.

Buandelgereen says, "This is Temulun, the wet nose that startled you so."

(I try to speak with Tamara, but my powers are still turned off.)

Ruska gawks at the dog in amazement. "Something is wrong here, I mean, I couldn't have. . . . " His words crumble.

After a moment of silence, he turns to Tamara and me. "Why didn't either of you just tell me what this is all about?"

I am at a loss, and Tamara jumps in before I say something stupid.

"Michael and I were afraid you wouldn't help him to leave that awful institution if you knew."

"No, no, no," repeats Ruska. "This makes no sense. White Thunder . . . the young woman with the backpack . . . the eerie noises . . . nothing disturbed . . . no, no, something is wrong here. Mr. Powers last night over drinks told me about you"—he looks at Buandelgereen—"and that crazy quest his parents went on in China, and the Precious Object, and a goddess, and god knows what else . . . so much else!" He looks around wildly. "Those things you know about me that no one could know. You're lying. All of you are lying!"

Buandelgereen regards him with calm detachment before saying, "You are an intelligent and perceptive man, Detective Ruska. Would you like to go into the cave and meet the young woman with the backpack?"

Stunned silence, most of all by Tamara and myself.

"Yeah, I would," says Ruska guardedly, his tone moderated by a tinge of fear.

Buandelgereen rises to her full height, her gaze sweeping over the miners and us with a composed yet commanding presence. "The rest of you, please stay outside the cave until we return." She selects only one to accompany them. "Temulun, come!"

The dog bounds forward, tail like a metronome.

And into the suffocating darkness of the cave one dog and two humans vanish.

~ *The Wait* ~

Tamara and I move to a shaded spot, grateful for the break from the sun—and the privacy. When I glance back at the Mongol men, they seem to waver in the heat, and like an impossibly stretched mirage, they dissolve. I look to Tamara, wondering if she noticed, but she merely shrugs.

"They've just gone back to their bunkhouses. Looks like they have the rest of the day off."

"That's the story, is it?" I say in mock scold.

"That's the story."

I keep looking at the entrance of the cave, expecting Buandelgereen and Ruska to emerge.

"Michael," says Tamara softly.

"Yes?"

"You know I am losing my powers?"

"I guessed. I lost mine a long time ago. I can't even talk to Temulun. Why do you suppose this is happening?"

"It's tied to the child."

"How?"

"I don't know."

I suddenly have a shocking notion. "Tamara, could it be your pregnancy?"

She laughs. "Yes, obviously. Your point?"

"Well, what is all this about this child? Remember, I already have a son—Mark—whom I love dearly. Although, once upon a time, I believed he was an old enemy of mine, I've since attributed that to my damn schizophrenic suspicions. Anyway, Mark is married to My-duyen, a Vietnamese woman, and they may very well have a child of their own. And so it goes. I was meant to be the son, but it's clear I didn't quite work out. Does Goddess want to throw good money after bad? Why does *She* want you to bear my child? Me? Michael Powers, an older, schizophrenic, fit only for institutionalization? I just don't understand, Tamara! Why am I even here if *She* no longer trusts me?"

"I don't know, Michael. I thought I would be told at some point, but instead of being made more aware, my powers are being shorn from me like a poor lamb. Be that as it may, I do know this: you would not be here were *She* not interested. It is *She* who arranged this—and *She* is the one speaking to Detective Ruska right now."

"But, why? What about?"

"Your fate."

"Christ! Why am I this damn important? Obviously, I am powerless to help Goddess in *Her* stupid—no, not stupid—titanic struggle with God!" I correct myself with heavy sarcasm.

"Obviously, you are wrong."

"Then let *Her* show it!"

"How?"

Ah, dear Reader, this question gives me pause. How do I want Goddess to show I am still important to *Her*? Make me wealthy? Get rid of my schizophrenia? Give me back my powers? Make me the most powerful man on earth? Or, perhaps, tell me all *Her* secrets? Confide in me?

"Tamara, for the first time, I truly understand what Jesus meant when he said, 'My God, why hast thou forsaken me?'"

Tamara looks at me angrily, then gently but firmly slaps my face.

"Don't be a fool. You'll be the father, I the mother, and we'll have a beautiful baby together."

Tamara's slap makes me aware of my inexcusable display of weakness. Still smarting, I put my arm around her and say, "How can you agree to marry someone like me?"

She remains silent, and this causes me uneasiness. "Tamara? I'm serious. Why do you agree to marry me and have this child?"

To my astonishment, tears fill her eyes, and she caresses my cheek. "Dear, dear Michael, do you remember Theresa?"

"Of course. Poor, abused, beautiful Theresa—a hallucination planted in my mind by Goddess." I laugh humorlessly, "Imagine, an imaginary wife!"

"How do you know, in your wildly imaginative mind, that I am not the same?" She sweeps her arm in a dramatic arc. "Perhaps you are sitting on the floor in the institution dreaming all this up."

Far from being concerned, I reply with great confidence.

"I've come to recognize people who are real from those who are . . . well, problematic. My mother and father were real, and they knew your mother, who also was real, and I know she was real because father told me about her—reluctantly, but he told me. And you must be real because of these facts. At least, I think I'm real—*cogito ergo sum* and all that. Detective Ruska is real, and he routinely talks to you and the psychiatrists. The evidence is overwhelming, Tamara."

I sit back and smile like the proverbial cat that has just swallowed the proverbial canary. "I am, after all, the Chosen One," I add.

"Perhaps you are mashing up what is real and what is not and have constructed these elaborate interactions in your mind." Tamara says these words so matter-of-factly that a chill runs down my spine.

With wide eyes, I ask, "*Are* you real, Tamara?"

She stares off in the distance. "Sometimes, I wonder."

"Tamara, this is no joke. Are you real?"

She points back at her hump. "Who would make this up?"

I feel a sense of tremendous (though qualified) relief. "Not me. Haven't the imagination."

Tamara puts her hand behind my neck and draws my face close, then kisses me fully on the lips. As she pulls away, she says, "Am I real, Michael?"

"If you're not, you're one hell of a hallucination!"

Tamara shakes her head sadly. "That's what worries me."

"God damn it, Tamara! Stop saying things like that! You make me question whether you *are* real. You make me question my own sanity."

She smiles and kisses me again. "What you don't realize, my love, is that your unique mix of sanity and insanity represents a broad thoroughfare leading directly to the shared brainstem of God and Goddess. As any physician will tell you, damage to the brainstem causes either death or coma."

"So, there is still hope to hamstring God, damage *His* brainstem, and relieve the world of suffering?"

"Well, if this is a sane world, then it is time to try an insane one. Look, you must eventually learn that God and Goddess are not who you think *They* are."

"What are *They*?"

"Factions."

"Really, Tamara, it is hopeless. I don't know what is meant by factions. Surely, in my more rational moments, I think Goddess means to eliminate God and reduce suffering, not end it . . . just, reduce it. After all, I don't even believe in God, yet I am all caught up in this web. I know there is no God, and I know suffering cannot be eliminated. That is why I must believe that Goddess intends to minimize suffering rather than God's preference for maximizing it. We humans like to think in terms as simple as black and white."

"But you are not truly human, Michael. Goddesses work in ways beyond our understanding. You're clearly confused. One moment you deny the existence of God, and the next you speak of *Him* as if *He* were real. Remember, your mother often said, 'There is always hope'?"

This statement ignites a deep resentment within me toward the cold, uncaring universe, for God remains, to me, nothing more than a hypothesis I have no use for. If I can help bring about His demise—whether real or imagined—so that we might all continue living rational lives, then I'm all for it. I direct my anger toward Tamara.

"My mother died in a car accident caused by a drunk driver, who, ironically, survived. As for hope, I spit on it."

"Fate starves at Probability's door."

"Yeah, something like that."

"Michael, I—"

But Tamara's words are cut short when we both see Buandelgereen and Detective Ruska emerge from the cave.

~ *Frontal Lobotomy . . . Or?* ~

I start to rise and go to them, but Tamara tugs my arm.

"Wait!" she whispers.

"Why?"

"Shush! Just watch!"

Her eyes, burning with intensity, are locked on the two figures.

"Why wait?" I ask impatiently.

"Quiet!" she snaps.

I have never seen her this agitated. What is she searching for in their faces?

Following Tamara's example, I focus on their features, though their words remain inaudible. When I turn my attention to Ruska's face, I am struck by the vacant expression he wears as he listens to Buandelgereen, who is doing most of the talking.

He looks shell-shocked, far from the tough, confident detective—like a man who has just encountered a ghost he spent his life dismissing, only to be forced to confront it now.

"*She* has done it to him," mutters Tamara.

'Done what?"

"Same thing *She's* done to all of us."

"Which is?"

Tamara holds out both hands, palms up. "Ask your dead parents."

"God damn it, I'm asking you, Tamara."

But she ignores me and starts walking toward Buandelgereen and Ruska.

I follow, muttering to myself.

When we reach them, Ruska looks at us absently and says, "Let's go back to the motel. I have some thinking to do."

"Maybe we should stay here and let Detective Ruska think without distractions," I say.

Buandelgereen draws herself up and glares at me. "No, you will go with him. Detective Ruska is responsible for both of you. Go and answer any questions he might have in the course of his . . . deliberations."

I look at Ruska, whose face still bears the countenance of a man far away in his thoughts. "Do you plan to come back tomorrow?"

"Leave him be," says Tamara. "Ask him no questions. Let's go now."

Ruska simply nods, and we walk back to the car in silence. Not a word is exchanged on the drive to the motel. I long to ask questions, demand answers, discuss our next steps, but the detective's stubbornness and Tamara's quiet, determined reserve stifle me.

A thought crosses my mind: I am more a pawn than ever, while Tamara seems to occupy a higher station—perhaps a knight or castle, free to move more fluidly, not bound to a single square. Being 'the son' clearly isn't all it's cracked up to be. This realization brings an unsettling truth to the surface: at any moment, she could leave me far behind, like the dust our car kicked up.

These dark thoughts revive my old longing to retreat to my own tunnel and be reunited with the bones still waiting in their silence. As though sensing my turmoil, Tamara places her hand atop mine and squeezes, yet still says nothing.

When we arrive, Ruska goes straight to his room, and we are left wondering what comes next—at least, I am. Tamara remains mute and declines my offer to sleep together.

No one eats. I spend the night alone, tossing and turning, haunted by speculation about what transpired between Ruska and her in that cave. In truth, I am afraid to sleep. Why? I suspect you can guess—nightmares that blur into my waking reality. Time slips away, and eventually, I fall asleep (or think I do), only to find myself trapped in one of those nightmarish scenarios schizophrenics are so prone to.

I dream that Detective Ruska had been subjected to a frontal lobotomy in the cave, and the portion of his brain removed was replaced by . . . something else. That nightmare came and went rather quickly, and is replaced by the voice of Goddess, which can be far worse. Oddly enough, *She* keeps repeating only one sentence.

Michael Powers, be prepared for waking up tomorrow morning and being alone.

After *She* reiterates these same words multiple times, I awake in a sweat, terrified of finding myself abandoned by Tamara and Ruska. Tossing aside all inhibitions, I run to Tamara's room and knock loudly. Thank god, she answers, and without opening the door, tells me to go back to my room and sleep. However, Goddess's words do not allow that to happen.

The next morning at six o'clock, I call Tamara's room to inform her I will be in the restaurant waiting. No answer. In a panic, I again rush to her room and knock.

"Yes?" she calls out from behind the closed door.

"I'm going to the restaurant. I'll meet you there."

To my great relief, she replies, "Okay, I'll be there in a few minutes."

~

Fifteen minutes pass and Tamara finally joins me at the table. I study her face, searching for any hint of her state of mind, but she appears as composed and serene as ever. For reasons I can't quite place, this disappoints me, as if I had somehow hoped for a subtle but profound shift in her demeanor.

"Good morning," she says brightly.

"Good morning. Coffee?"

"Yes."

I flag down the waitress, coffee is poured, and I put on my most serious face. "Well, what do you think?"

"About?"

"Tamara, please don't play games. What do you think happened yesterday in the cave? Have you heard anything?"

"Not at all."

"Are you even curious?" I ask in exasperation.

"Not particularly."

"You were yesterday when you were watching Buandelgereen and Ruska outside the cave."

"It passed."

"What happens now?"

She takes a sip of coffee and pauses for a moment. "I don't know. What do you think?"

I hold my anger, and say as calmly as possible, "I think you know. I think you are not telling me what you know. I think everyone except me knows. I wonder what has happened to our relationship that you can't be truthful with me?" To speak these last words is very painful.

Just as Tamara starts to reply, Emile Ruska walks up to the table.

"May I join you?"

"Of course," says Tamara, evidently relieved at his propitious entrance.

More coffee, more shallow pleasantries, especially between Tamara and Ruska. His shell-shocked face from yesterday has been replaced by a mask of everyday routine.

"Detective Ruska," I say impatiently. "What happened in the cave?"

Immediately he looks at Tamara. She nods. He sighs as if hesitant to speak.

"Go ahead," says Tamara.

"I encountered an extraordinary woman. I believe she is the same one I met in the cave earlier—the one you spoke of, the one your parents sought. How do I know this? That's what I've been agonizing over. Is she real? She appears as young now as you described her decades ago, which seems impossible—unless . . . unless I was hypnotized, or perhaps she is not the same woman, or . . . I don't know. All I can say is that she looked into my soul and saw things only I could know."

I look at Tamara, who is looking down at her lap as if she had heard all this before.

"Yes . . . yes, I'm sure it was *Her*," I say. "What did *She* tell you?"

"Well, *She* spoke in riddles, and I did not understand much of it, but there is something that concerns you."

Tamara lets out a little groan, then quickly stifles it.

"Well?" I ask.

Ruska coughs and looks me in the eyes. "Michael, you are dead. You have been dead. You will remain dead. But dead in a way I still do not understand."

I laugh. "That's ridiculous! I'm sitting here in a restaurant drinking coffee and listening to you, while in the background a lot of other customers are talking and laughing." I suddenly raise my hand and call the waitress over to refill my coffee, which she does. "Did you see what just happened? What do you mean I'm dead?"

"That is the part I am struggling with," says Ruska. "For some reason, I have been chosen to play a part in your life."

"But you said I am dead. How can you play a part in my life?"

"That, Mr. Powers, is the question I have been mulling since the meeting in that damn cave. Right now, I am returning to my room to think. Both of you be ready to leave at noon today."

"Where to?" asked Tamara.

"To be determined," responds Ruska brusquely, and he leaves without another word.

Chapter Eight

Detective Angel

Buandelgereen Utilizes Ruska

~ *One Extraordinary Day in the Life of Emile Ruska* ~

Emile Ruska returned to his room, hung the "Do Not Disturb" sign on the door, and lay down on the bed. Never had he imagined such things were possible as those that transpired the day before in the cave. Had he lived in medieval times, surrounded by superstition and a constant fear of divine wrath, he might have waved it all off as the delusions of peasants. Yet here he lay, weighted with *Her* presence—*Her* words, *Her* physical form, *Her* impossible power—feeling as small and frail as a child in *Her* shadow.

And what visions *She* had shown him! Visions that the world, from the dawn of time, had already borne witness to. Suffering—the kind he knew well from police work, but now magnified beyond the scale of any single life—suffering stretching across the eons, all living things destined to perish, the vast majority in agony. The antelope calf devoured alive; the infant writhing with neuroblastoma; wasp larvae feasting inside caterpillars; children herded into gas chambers. A relentless, nightmarish cycle of pain, punctuated only by fleeting moments of joy—and even that joy sharpened the sting of death. *She* spoke to him of these things while inhabiting the physical form of Lily, *Her* scarred breasts aglow with the lingering reminder of self-inflicted pain—a pain that seemed to cry out for more.

When Emile begged *Her* to stop, as his deepest feelings of guilt and remorse surged within him, *She* held his gaze as if he were trapped in the jaws of some monstrous vise, forcing him to confront how his tiny atom of suffering paled in comparison to the vast ocean of agony that pervades life—everywhere, every second. For one nanosecond—an eternity's flash—*She* tore open the floodgates of universal misery. The overwhelming intensity of it shattered his mind, and he blacked out from the sheer force of its power.

Upon coming to his senses, *She* had returned to *Her* own luminous form, and bade him heed *Her* words.

"The world is a rocky, watery desolation, laced with poison. Life clings tenaciously to its crags and crevices, struggling to survive for but an instant. This brief, harsh battle is interrupted only by fleeting illusions of peaceful meadows and calm, glassy seas. But beneath these illusions—beneath them—only teeth.

Emile could only nod dumbly.

"Now, Mr. Ruska, we have investigated your life and probed your own unhealed wounds. Time to look elsewhere. You are responsible for Mr. Powers while he is free from the institution, are you not?"

"In a manner of speaking."

"He is a special case."

"So I gather."

"I must ask a favor of you."

"Yes?" Ruska listened with a wandering attentiveness, still reeling from the revelations concerning his own battered history.

"Do I have your full attention?"

He sat upright, as might a student caught napping by his teacher. "Yes."

"I must reveal to you that Mr. Powers is dead."

"Dead?"

"Yes, but not in the way you and your companions might imagine. Let us say he is half-dead, lingering among us like a shadow in the daylight, only to vanish into the dark night and merge once more with the Great Shadow—both past and present, dead and undead. In that realm, Mr. Powers and the others are visible to themselves, yet invisible to those of you who can see only when there is light."

She paused. "Forgive me for mixing metaphors, but though he is regarded as mentally ill by those who understand only one side of the coin, he exists in both worlds—the dead and the undead, or, as you would say, the real and the unreal. For him, no boundary is uncrossable. And those who have attempted to follow Mr. Powers between these worlds no longer cast their shadows for any to see."

"Doctor Hess, Doctor Camara, Doctor Tavaris. . . . "

"Yes, and others."

Ruska did not know how to respond.

She continued, "You must make sure he has uninterrupted time when he is among the living, when he is in the light, so to speak. He must be with Tamara. Together, they must produce a child."

"I have heard Mr. Powers speak about this. The people at the institution tell me he is delusional, a symptom of schizophrenia. He is quite confused."

"Are you also confused?"

"More than I have ever been in my life. I don't even know why I'm here."

"Because you are also a special case, Mr. Ruska."

"How so?"

"You have been chosen."

"To?"

"Protect him, protect the child when it is born, then make sure Mr. Powers dies."

"What?"

"Make sure he dies."

"I don't understand."

"You will."

Ruska had heard enough. "Look! I don't have the slightest idea what *You're* talking about, or what *You* expect me to do, or how I am expected to do it! Maybe I'm delusional too! Maybe all this is—"

"Unreal?"

"Yes, God damn it! How do I know this is not my own delusion? Anyone who saw me now would have me committed alongside Mr. Powers!"

She merely smiled at his outburst and spoke with exaggerated patience.

"Do you know Nguyen Tuyet Mai?"

"I know of her."

"Before a year and a half has passed, Nguyen Tuyet Mai will die in Vietnam. In the meantime, Mr. Powers will remain under your protection, and once a child is born of the hunchback, he will accompany his son and daughter-in-law—Mark and My-duyen Powers—back to Vietnam to be with Tuyet Mai when she dies. You will go with them. It is there in Vietnam that your debt comes due." *Her* eyes moved from him to somewhere distant.

"Yes?"

She turned sharply back to him and stared intently. "You will see. Buandelgereen will be your guide, though she herself may not live to make the trip. Which is why—"

"This is absurd. I have my own life to live."

"You owe a life."

"I cannot . . . it's true there is Lily . . . but, I mean, *You* have Buandelgereen. Why me?"

"Because you have already intervened, you are attuned to circumstances that defy the ordinary course of events. You are trained, you are lonely, and you seek knowledge beyond the conventional. Most importantly, you owe a life. Furthermore, thanks to the mental institution, you are now responsible for his life—both in the eyes of the law and in *Mine*. And besides, Buandelgereen will soon be dead."

Ruska shook his head, hardly believing his ears. "No, I cannot. I will simply return him to the institution and be done with it. For all I know, he is responsible for the deaths of those three psychiatrists."

Her eyes flashed anger, and he cringed back from their accusatory stare. "If you truly believe this, then all the more reason to stay close to Mr. Powers, follow the guidance of Buandelgereen, and fulfill the task you have been chosen to do."

Then *She* was gone, leaving him sitting in the abandoned cave. Again, utter darkness.

He clicked on the flashlight and found Temulun staring at him with her big, sorrowful eyes.

~

Emile lay sprawled across the motel bed, the hum of the old air conditioner rattling in the background, his body still gritty from cave dust, his mind ensnared in the tangle of perplexing events and the bold demands *She* had thrust upon him. In *Her* absence, doubt crept in once more—had any of it truly happened? One moment, he resolved to return Michael to the institution, to sever himself from the ordeal entirely; the next, he found himself contemplating the impossible—how he might grant *Her* wishes.

Caught in the ebb and flow of his own uncertainty, the sharp ring of the telephone shattered his reverie.

"Hello?"

"Meet me outside," came Buandelgereen's voice.

Before he had time to respond, she hung up.

Ruska stepped outside the motel and looked at his shadow, cast long and dark by the bright sun. Buandelgereen stood grimly, waiting for him to approach, conspicuously drawing her eyes from his shadow to his face.

"Detective Ruska, good morning."

"Good morning." Ruska could only admire this regal old woman who stood so proudly and so strongly. He remembered *Her* words and could not conceive of Buandelgereen ever dying.

'Walk with me, please."

"Of course."

"I will not mince words. We have secured Mr. Powers' old house. You must talk to his son and obtain permission to have him released from the institution under joint guardianship. Once done, he will move back in to the house, live with Tamara, and await the trip."

"The trip?"

"Yes, to Vietnam, to his destiny, after Tamara has the child."

"Whoa! This is too fast. I have a job, responsibilities!"

"You are unattached. Add this to your responsibilities." She smiled. "Once undertaken, you may drown your sorrows at your favorite bar and talk with your waitress Emma, who will, no doubt, be a sympathetic listener."

"But I—"

Buandelgereen swiftly held up her hand to check his words. "You may continue your job, but you must check on Mr. Powers periodically, and most importantly, get him out of any mischief his so-called schizophrenia gets him into, legally or otherwise. I . . . or rather we, are no longer able to perform these functions, as our presence is now too compromised. Let us go back to the hotel. From there, call Mark Powers, convince him to release his father from the institution, and make the necessary arrangements to settle him and Tamara in his old house. From then until you leave for Vietnam, there should be no undue problems, and your time will mainly be your own to do as you wish."

"And you?" asked Ruska, reeling from this barrage of instructions.

"I will remain in touch."

~

Although Emile Ruska wavered at first, he ultimately did what Buandelgereen asked, the vision of poor Lily always hovering like a spectral accusation over his efforts.

The calls were made, the plans negotiated, the agreements finalized, the documents signed, the arrangements completed, and finally, move-in day arrived.

~ *Return Home* ~

As Detective Ruska steered the car up the winding gravel driveway, Michael stared in silence at the house that had once been his home. Nestled in isolation, the structure held the echoes of his past—the place where his schizophrenia had surged with terrifying intensity, unraveling his once-brilliant career as a lawyer. Here, too, he had hosted his infamous dinner parties—well-documented by his psychiatrists—where he dined alongside wife Diane, son Mark, and Storyteller, the twin he had conjured from the depths of his mind. Now, the house loomed before him, more ominous than any castle, its ghosts far too familiar. Behind him, Tamara leaned forward, eyes wide with curiosity as she took in the foreboding scene for the first time.

The old Fiat Michael had spent years painstakingly restoring was gone from its usual place beside the driveway, yet the house itself remained eerily unchanged. He pressed the remote, and Ruska eased the car into the garage and shut the door behind them. The engine fell silent, and for a long moment, so did they.

Michael felt like an apparition, a specter revisiting the ruins of his former life. Had the house only sprouted Gothic turrets and stone battlements atop windswept moors, it might have passed for his personal Elsinore, a fitting stage for Hamlet's brooding ghosts. He was slipping into one of his darker reveries when Tamara, attuned to his unrest, reached for his hand. Her touch steadied him, anchoring him to the present. Without a word, they stepped through the door, past the narrow entryway, and into the kitchen.

The expansive white Corian countertop stretched before them, a blank canvas onto which countless memories were etched. Michael had often stood at this very spot, meticulously preparing meals for his imagined "guests," arranging the strange artifacts conjured by his fractured mind. Now, with the voices quieter and the delusions less insistent, he still felt the same inexorable pull, the need to provide for an absence that could never be filled—half-dead or not, he still needed bourbon and eggs.

"We'll need food and drinks," he murmured, almost to himself. "Especially bourbon."

Ruska, ever perceptive, nodded without hesitation. "Already taken care of. A delivery is scheduled for tomorrow, and since neither you nor Tamara can drive, I've arranged for the local grocer to bring whatever you need. In the meantime, I'll run out and get enough to hold you over." His gaze flickered with something between duty and understanding. "Your son and his wife will stop by once they've handled their own matters and I'll be a call away if you need anything." He offered a taut smile. "Until then, I trust you both know what to do without me spelling it out."

With that, Ruska stepped out, leaving Michael and Tamara alone in the silence of the house, their attention turning inward, to the rooms waiting to be revisited, the ghosts waiting to be acknowledged.

~

"Let's see," said Michael. "Furniture the same, more or less, pictures and other decorations the same, more or less, carpets and flooring the same, more worn rather than less, and kitchen empty, per usual."

"This is a nice house," said Tamara. "Are you glad to be back?"

"Only because you're here with me," replied Michael, affecting an exaggerated, flirtatious tone.

He looked around with a sad expression. "Beats the cave. I have missed it here. Time was, Tamara, when I was a respected lawyer, earning my own living, free of psychiatrists, medication, and institutions. It was in this house I married Diane. It was while she gave birth to Mark. It was here I reached my height of lawyering skills and reputation. It was while living here that she died. After that, it was here the voices came at me with the devastating power of madness itself. And it was here Storyteller first came for me."

Tamara shuddered. "Yes, I am aware."

"Tamara, do you truly love me, or are you marrying me and having a child simply because you are following the instructions of *her*?"

"That is a complicated question."

"No, it is simple enough."

"I do love you," she said hesitatingly, eyes averted.

"I guess that will have to do, for now," he said. "But, tell me Tamara, tell me you are real."

"If I were not real, you would not have the doubts that now trouble you."

Michael laughed. "True! True! You should have been a lawyer, Tamara! No jury, no judge, could resist your reasoning."

Ruska soon returned with groceries, including a goodly supply of bourbon. He made his final farewells and the house itself seemed to breathe a sigh of relief at his departure. They stored the food and sat together on the couch munching chips.

"So American!" laughed Tamara.

"Let's get a dog," said Michael unexpectedly.

"Why?" she asked in surprise.

"Because it's the last thing you would see in an institution—a dog is anti-institution. Besides, I miss Temulun."

"Let's bring her here."

Michael made a face. "No. My powers are gone, and she would be a reminder of my demotion. Besides, she's a spy."

"Well, what's the problem? What are you hiding?"

Michael threw his arms around Tamara and kissed her. "Can't make love in front of a dog. Too self-conscious."

"Perhaps I'm also a spy."

"You *are* a spy! I know that. But spies can be exotic and romantic and make me feel reckless."

"And dangerous?"

"Of course! That's what makes them so . . . exciting."

Michael kissed Tamara again, but she pushed him away.

"Not right now," she said, looking around as if searching for something. "Someone is here," she whispered.

Michael's heart sank. He knew. He knew there was someone in the room. He knew and hoped she had not seen. He knew from the moment he walked into the house.

"I know," he said flatly. "Don't be frightened."

"I'm not," she replied. "Ghosts are not frightening, but this one is different."

"How so?"

"Very odd. It is not a spirit I am familiar with."

Michael looked glum. "I'm very familiar with him."

~ *Ruska Seeks Solace* ~

As Ruska drove back to the city, he felt the familiar relief that comes after completing an unpleasant task. He had never been more eager to return to his work and lose himself in the familiar rhythms of his detective duties. It was still hard for him to believe that he had followed the instructions of two such women—Buandelgereen and *Her*. Emile had resolved that, should the time come, he would under no circumstances travel to Vietnam. He had already done more than enough, and any further involvement would be sheer folly. *I may be a fool,* he thought, *but I'm not that much of one. Still, those two have a way of making their demands irresistible.*

By the time he reached the city, night had settled in, and he knew Emma would be on duty. He couldn't help but recall *her* words about the waitress. "Once again," he muttered aloud to himself, "*she* has me figured out." He shook his head in disbelief. "But how?"

When he walked into the dark bar, he let his eyes adjust and spied his favorite table happily unoccupied. Just as he sat, Emma's voice rang across the room.

"Well! Look who the cat dragged in!" Seeing he was in no mood for such banter, she toned down her greeting. "The warrior returns from the war; I'll bring you a drink."

She set down his favorite drink. "Any life-threatening wounds? Or only minor ones that Nurse Emma can deal with?"

Ruska had to admit, the sound of a normal voice saying normal things gave him a sense of contented familiarity. Much more "mystical hocus-pocus" (as he called it) would drive him to the mental institution so recently vacated by Michael Powers.

"You're a sight for sore eyes, Emma," he said.

"So, you missed me?"

"More than you know."

"Uh oh, that sounds serious," she laughingly replied.

"It is. Very serious."

Emma started to sit next to him, but a customer called.

"Damn!" she whispered. "No rest for the wicked. Hold that thought, Emile."

When she returned, he had already finished his drink.

Emma looked at the empty glass. "Goodness, thirsty man! This really must be serious."

Off she went to bring another drink. Emile watched the easy geometry of her walk, the sway of fabric over muscle, appreciating how good she looked in her short, clinging skirt.

"You still look stunning, Emma," he said when she returned.

"Flattery will get you everywhere," she laughed. "Now, what's going on?—gimme the latest." Her eyes quickly surveyed the room, and with no needy customers, she sat across from him.

Ruska smiled. "Trying to fill you in between demanding customers would be impossible."

"Well, there is a solution."

Ruska considered for less than two seconds. "My place or yours?"

"Mine. Have to feed the cat."

"Just to talk, of course," he said with a twinkle in his eyes.

"Oh, of course. What else would any self-respecting detective want to do?" She assumed an exaggeratedly serious face. "Just the facts, ma'am."

They shared a laugh, and he settled into the familiar comfort of waiting for her to finish her shift—grateful for the excuse to linger over his drink rather than return to the hollow silence of his apartment. In that moment, distraction and whiskey felt far more inviting than intimacy.

As he took another slow sip, his thoughts turned inward, drifting toward the ache of solitude. He longed for a partner—someone intelligent, someone with whom he could share thoughtful conversations about the day's events. His gaze followed Emma as she moved gracefully between tables, her effortless charm drawing the attention of patrons. A pang of guilt settled in his chest. This connection, however warm, was an illusion—a fleeting comfort to fill an empty space in his life.

As she passed with a tray of drinks, their eyes met, and she flashed him a playful wink. He smiled in return, knowing, if only for tonight, he would let the illusion hold.

Too late now, he thought, and for a brief moment, he hated himself for what was about to happen. *However*, he mused after another swallow, *it will make her feel good, poor woman.* Realizing his justification lacked any credibility, he turned his attention to the pile of work that awaited him tomorrow at the office.

When at last closing time came, he told Emma he would wait outside. The fresh air somewhat cleared his head, and he experienced a renewed disgust at his behavior. Just as he decided to beg off, Emma came out prancing like a young girl.

"Shall we?" she said enthusiastically.

"What about your car?" he asked.

"Don't own one. I take the bus." She laughed. "Mind if I get a lift?"

Emile bowed, feeling quite foolish. "Of course, Madame." He waved her in the direction of his car, feeling like a man sinking deeper into quicksand.

As Emile drove, an uneasy tension coiled within him, though he kept his expression carefully composed. Emma spoke freely, her voice animated as she recounted the night's encounters with difficult customers, but beneath his nods and murmured acknowledgments, his thoughts drifted elsewhere. A familiar reluctance crept in—the temptation to call off the evening altogether.

Just as the idea solidified, Emma fell silent and turned to him, her tone shifting to something gentler.

"Emile," she said, her voice laced with quiet sincerity, "I really do want to hear about your experiences. I can tell there's something weighing on you. When we get to my place, let's just talk for a while. And I promise," she added with a knowing smile, "this isn't some elaborate trap to get you into bed."

Her words encouraged him, and he patted her hand. "Thank you, Emma, that would be wonderful. Having a sounding board like you is very important to me."

Emma remained true to her word. When they entered her apartment, she fed the cat and made tea, insisting Emile sit in the most comfortable chair she owned. Changing into comfortable clothes, she sank into the couch, folded a leg under her, leaned forward, and waited for him to unburden. And so he did. After describing the past few weeks following the cave incident, Emma homed in on Buandelgereen.

"Well, I don't know about this mysterious lady in the cave, but the way you describe this . . . Mongolian woman, I bet she is every bit flesh and blood."

"Oh, she is flesh and blood all right!" laughed Emile. "Got the blood of Genghis Khan flowing through her veins."

Emma screwed up her eyes. "I think I've heard of him, some general or something, but I could be wrong."

"No, you're right," said Emile, realizing this woman could never be his soul mate.

"So, what now?" asked Emma.

"I don't know. Go back to work. Try not to think about the whole thing. I know Buandelgereen will contact me soon enough."

Emma smiled seductively. "No, you misunderstand. Let me repeat myself: so, what now?"

Emile took a long sip of tea and looked down at his lap.

"Now," said Emma firmly. "It is time all good detectives go home. Tomorrow is a long day for both of us."

"Emma—"

"No, let's call it a night and not ruin a perfectly good relationship." She laughed weakly. "Besides, I'm tired, I have a headache, and I have to wash my hair."

Emma shooed him out, and Emile drove home with a sense of relief and a deeper appreciation for this very wise woman who, unbeknownst to him at that moment, was sitting on the couch stroking her cat and quietly weeping.

~ *Tamara Meets Storyteller* ~

The weeks passed in quiet harmony within Michael's house. He and Tamara wove their days together with tenderness—making love, exploring new and exotic recipes in the kitchen, strolling along winding paths, and curling up on the couch to lose themselves in films. They laughed at the unexpected simplicity of their existence, playfully remarking on the absence of Gods and Goddesses, of shadowed caves and enigmatic Mongol women to stir the stillness.

For once, his voices lay dormant, and the world beyond had left her untouched—her hump bearing no trace of supernatural interference.

"Schizophrenia be damned!" he cried one night after drinking two glasses of bourbon.

"Hunchbacks forever!" responded Tamara.

They went to bed that night in excellent spirits and cuddled lovingly after having sex. Michael had just rolled over and fallen asleep when Tamara shouted something and quickly sat up. Michael turned on the light and saw her looking around wildly.

"What is it?"

She put her finger to her lips and crept slowly out of bed, telling him to turn out the light and go back to sleep. As she slipped on her robe, Michael flipped off the light and immediately saw a figure silhouetted in the bedroom doorway, the unmistakable outline of an M16 held loosely in its hand.

He watched the apparition merge into the wall to let Tamara pass, then return to its original position. Obviously, she had seen nothing, as she did not cast a glance at the figure.

"Hello, Storyteller," said Michael matter-of-factly.

"Tomorrow night, dinner," said Storyteller, then disappeared.

Tamara returned and apologized. "I thought I saw something, but it was nothing."

Michael mumbled indistinctly and made a show of going back to sleep. So much for normalcy, he thought bitterly. Until now, he had not realized how desperately he yearned for a normal life, and the old thoughts of suicide spread their dark impulses.

~

Michael knew Storyteller would make an appearance at dinner that night, and he frantically tried to think of a way to thwart the attempt. He also knew he would be powerless to do so. After all, he had never been able to stop the entire panoply of his psychoses: Goddess, God, *her*, voices, and Storyteller himself.

The next morning, sitting on the front porch with Tamara sipping orange juice and discussing nothing of consequence, he decided to broach the topic.

"Do you know who Storyteller is?"

"Of course. Your nickname in Vietnam."

"And you know he visits me?"

"I know. I have heard a lot about him and your dinner parties."

"Do you know about Nature?"

"I know about his . . . involvement with Doctor Camara."

"Involvement is a polite term, Tamara. He possessed the man, drove him to his death."

"You and Nature were best friends. And aren't you and Storyteller the same person?"

This took Michael aback. "Yes, somehow I drove Nature to kill Doctor Camara. Apparently, I am responsible for many deaths. Anyway, Storyteller is coming tonight, whether I like it or not."

"I will meet him at last," said Tamara reflectively.

"You said yourself that your powers are gone. I doubt you will even see or hear him."

"At dinner?"

Michael nodded. "I have no choice."

"Any others coming?" asked Tamara.

"I am not summoning Diane or Mark or Theresa or Ethyl, or any of them. But Goddess only knows who will come."

"I'll be there."

"Tamara, I'm warning you, I don't know what to expect. This hasn't happened in a long time."

"I understand. I'll be there."

Tamara mourned the loss of her "powers" more deeply than she cared to admit. Often, she would call out to Goddess—or to the forces she had once known—hoping for some sign of their return, but her appeals were met with silence. It seemed she had been relegated to the life of an ordinary, pregnant woman, a role that chafed against her former existence. Still, she resolved to adapt, to make the best of this strange, new reality.

Though she did not believe she loved Michael, she felt a profound sympathy for him—trapped between the chaos of his own mind and the manipulation of warring deities with their tangled agendas. No wonder he was so lost. Despite this empathy, her primary duty remained clear: she was to bear this child.

Yet, despite her focus on the present, she could not shake the lingering fascination with Storyteller. What had Michael been like as a young soldier? How had the war changed him? These questions haunted her, and she found herself eagerly anticipating their evening meal together.

Tamara had often heard her mother speak of the war against Japan and the civil strife between the Nationalists and Communists, but the American conflict in Vietnam piqued her curiosity in ways she struggled to put into words. Perhaps it was linked to Nguyen Tuyet Mai, the woman whose story had captured her imagination through Michael's writings. A stunning beauty, scarred by the war—her legs taken, yet her will as fierce and cunning as a she-wolf. In some strange way, Tamara felt a kinship with Tuyet Mai. Where the woman had suffered a great subtraction—her legs—Tamara now carried her own great addition: the burgeoning life growing within her.

"Michael, can you summon Nguyen Tuyet Mai tonight?"

He looked at her in shock. "Tuyet Mai! Jesus, Tamara, I think she is still alive. How can I?"

"True," replied Tamara. "But in the past, according to your own writings, you successfully summoned your son when he was a student at Columbia. Why not Tuyet Mai?"

"Well . . . I mean . . . . " Michael stammered. "We've already discussed this. My powers are diminished, if not completely gone."

Tamara appeared unruffled. "Try."

"Tamara, you have a direct line to Goddess. Why don't you make the request?"

"I will."

"Then, I guess we'll just wait and see. I have no idea what to expect. This is Storyteller's show."

"Does he not listen to his older self?"

"Not a bit of it! Our future selves are aliens to us, subject to harsher criticism and greater disappointment than the most distant stranger."

"And what about our view of our past selves?"

Michael laughed. "Good question. Probably the same."

After a short pause, Tamara asked, "So, what is your view of Storyteller?"

"In what sense?"

"Is he a disappointment?"

Michael's face turned glum. "He was the incubator of my illness."

"He had no choice."

"Funny, I've heard that phrase before . . . too often!"

"How so?"

"I have heard serial killers make that same statement after they murdered any number of innocent people."

Tamara shook her head. "I hardly think you . . . or Storyteller . . . are serial killers."

Michael's expression darkened, his features tightening in a way that made Tamara catch her breath. "He's a serial killer. I'm a serial killer," he murmured, his voice heavy with anguish. "He killed strangers, and I killed my doctors—good, decent, innocent people. For what purpose?"

Tamara knew this line of thought constituted very dangerous territory, and she tried to defuse the impact. "Yes, you're right, in a manner of speaking."

"Damn right I'm right," grumbled Michael. "Inviting Tuyet Mai will just open up the whole can of worms even wider."

Tamara threw up her hands. "Okay, okay, never mind."

~

Though Michael vehemently resisted the idea of summoning Tuyet Mai, the seed had been sown. Despite his best efforts, the idea began to take root, growing into an undeniable compulsion. Later that afternoon, Tamara entered the kitchen and found two unfamiliar objects carefully arranged on the countertop.

"What are these for?" she asked, surveying the objects with a curious look.

"I decided to revert to my previous habitual behavior, my ritual, before the dinner to maximize the chance of their coming. They are my icons, if you will. Don't ask what they are for. If you did, I would look a fool in both our eyes."

"I already know," said Tamara plainly. "I read, remember?"

"Ah, yes, my damned writings!"

Tamara looked more closely at the counter. "Nothing there for Tuyet Mai?"

"We've already discussed this. If she comes, she comes, but it won't be because of me."

"I wonder," whispered Tamara to herself.

When Michael turned his back to continue preparations for dinner, Tamara slipped an article from her pocket and surreptitiously placed it on the counter under the jungle fatigues.

Chapter Nine

An Even Stranger Dinner

How Many Courses?

~ Dear Reader ~

I t has been some time since I last addressed you, and much has happened—or perhaps nothing at all. The further events unfold, the more they seem to coil back to their beginnings. You've noticed, haven't you? Schizophrenia, when left to its own devices, is a peculiar torment, tedious in its horror, relentless in its repetition.

Tonight's dinner will be an interesting affair. If Tuyet Mai arrives, she will find herself seated across from the man whose closest friend she killed, alongside a soldier from the very army responsible for the loss of her legs. Hardly an ideal party for polite conversation.

Truth be told, dear Reader, as I set these words down, I have no idea what to expect. As I told Tamara, this is Storyteller's game. I am merely a player, following the current to see where it leads. In the meantime, I will prepare dinner as always. Routine must not be broken; that is my one inviolate rule. I have asked Tamara to set a place for Tuyet Mai, just in case. She offers me a knowing, wry smile but says nothing, as if I were unaware of exactly what she is thinking.

When she is finished, I look it over and nod in satisfaction.

"For all I know, we may be eating alone," I say.

Tamara merely shrugs.

I feel uneasy. It has been a long time since I last did this. And in the past, at least, I was always in control, well, mostly. Storyteller was the exception, the unpredictable force that arrived unbidden, defying my wishes. Tonight, I suspect he will be the one orchestrating events. But to what end? Who can say?

With hours still to go, I stretch out the food preparations, answering Tamara's questions in clipped, monosyllabic replies. She takes the hint and steps aside, though I can feel her presence lingering nearby, watching. Her silent scrutiny only unsettles me further. I glance at the clock—time, ever fickle, crawls in deliberate defiance of my impatience. And yet, somehow, the hour draws near.

My "unusual" dinners always begin at precisely six o'clock, my guests arriving moments after I take my seat. Tonight, however, will be different. Tamara will be there; a living, breathing presence at my table. Until now, I have dined only with ghosts. How will they react to her?

And then, the music. In the past, I always chose something Diane would have liked, since she was always the guest of honor. But tonight, Diane will not be here. A relief, perhaps, but what, then, should I play? The question catches me off guard. For a brief, panicked moment, the answer eludes me.

"What music do you want for tonight, Tamara?" I call.

"Whatever you like," she replies.

I reach into my collection and pull out a random CD. "Mozart!" I exclaim.

"Fine."

There is still a half hour to go, but I start the music anyway, and feel instantly soothed, more prepared to cope with the upcoming ordeal. While thick pork chops sizzle under the broiler, I sauté a handful of mushrooms, put a dish of frozen peas in the microwave, and whip up a bowl of instant mashed potatoes.

When the microwave buzzes, I call to Tamara, "Dinner is ready!"

Tamara joins me at the table, carefully spooning small portions of the rich, heavy American food onto her plate. I know she finds it unappetizing, but she eats without complaint. We both do, our movements slow, our words sparse, the weight of expectation settling over us like a thick fog. For a long time, nothing happens. The air remains still. No flickering shadows, no spectral whispers, no ghosts.

"Perhaps it's your presence," I murmur.

Tamara shakes her head, but something shifts. I see it in her eyes—wide, unblinking, filled with a silent warning. A prickling unease washes over me.

"What is it?" I ask.

She doesn't have time to answer.

A figure materializes before us—sudden, solid, unmistakable. A familiar sight. Storyteller.

He stands there, fully formed, his blackened hands trembling, his rancid fatigues reeking of sweat, filth, and something far worse. His M16 rests against the table, as it always does. And his eyes, those dark, haunted eyes, lock onto mine with that same unyielding, accusatory stare.

At last!

Another form appears. It is Tuyet Mai.

"Welcome," I say.

Storyteller looks grim, whereas Tuyet Mai seems confused. I hardly know where to begin. I stare at Storyteller.

"It's your show," I say.

Tuyet Mai turns to Storyteller. "Why am I here, Teller of Stories?" Her confusion has turned to fear.

"I don't know," he replies. "I did not call you."

"Who did?" I ask.

"Me!" exclaims Tamara.

All of us look at her, but she says nothing further.

"I ask again," says Tuyet Mai, now looking at Tamara. "Why am I here?"

More silence.

"Well," says Storyteller. "I know why I'm here, but I don't know why you're here."

I give him my best sarcastic laugh. "Storyteller, I know why you're here, and you could have saved your time."

Tuyet Mai slaps the table. "Why am I here?" she cries.

Tamara remains calm. "Because, in the beginning, I wanted to see you out of pure curiosity. But then, when I asked Goddess for help, I received it."

"And?"

"Your fate is entwined with that of Storyteller. Storyteller's fate is entwined with Michael's. Michael's fate is entwined with mine. My fate is entwined with the child we are going to have. You see, all of us must face it."

"I do not understand."

"Yes," says Tamara. "You do."

"It is a dream."

"If you wish."

Storyteller, clearly agitated by the diversion, suddenly slams his fist against the table, the impact reverberating through the room.

"Enough of this!" he growls. "I called this dinner for a reason."

His glare pierces through me, dark and unrelenting.

"You will come back to me . . . to *us*," he says, his voice thick with command. "You will reclaim your bones. You will erase the sorry existence you've been dragging behind you since the day you left us."

Before I have a chance to respond, Tamara points at Storyteller. "Are you a believer in God?"

"What?" he asks in surprise.

"Do you believe in God?"

My younger self falters, struggling to find the words. "I . . . I . . . well, it's complicated," he stammers.

"Yes! Of course!" I cry out, the realization hitting me with startling clarity. "When I was you, Storyteller, I wavered between belief and disbelief, never fully committing to either. I still wrestled with the question of God's existence, still straddled the line between faith and doubt. That was before Goddess intervened. Back then, the conflict wasn't between God and Goddess—it was between Darwin and God, between science and faith. That was the true battle in my mind. And now I see . . . that is why, in the cave, you turned your M16 on Goddess."

"Do you work for God?" asks Tamara.

Storyteller hesitates.

"This has nothing to do with me," interjects Tuyet Mai.

"Oh, yes it does!" exclaims Tamara. "When you lost your legs, you saw God-dess. *She* spoke to you."

"Yes, that is true."

"What did *She* say?"

"I was with Madame Dau in great pain. Goddess held a dying ant in Her palm and said to me, *'You wanted to be a hero, compatriot of powerful men. But that was being no more than a ghost woman. Then, you were sickened by the violent reality of struggle and you wanted to withdraw and become a heroic mother. A virtuous woman. A loving wife. But these are also ghost women, with no humanity. You are only one human being among a sea of other living and non-living things. Now, your body is broken and you are alone. Your great beauty, the flower of your being, has been torn from its roots, but the world goes on, uncaring. So you have come to this: you just want to live, the same as this dying ant.'* That is what *She* said.

A jolt of anger overcomes me. "Speaking of wanting to be alive, didn't you kill my best friend? Didn't you kill Nature?" I ask Tuyet Mai.

"That is also true, but how does all this concern me now?"

Dear Reader, Tuyet Mai's question barely registers. My mind drifts else-where—to Nature, to the way he consumed Doctor Camara. Does all of this form part of a greater design? Is there some unseen thread weaving these scattered events into a single tapestry?

Even as I wrestle with these questions, lost in the tangle of possibilities, Tamara and Tuyet Mai chatter away, their voices light and effortless, as if they were old friends reunited after years apart.

"What did you think when you realized you had lost your legs?" boldly asks Tamara.

Tuyet Mai shoots back. "What did you think when you realized a hunchback is considered a deformity?"

"Ha, ha! Good!" cries Tamara. "The difference is that I was quite young when this realization came to me."

"So? Were you angry?"

"Yes, of course."

"And how did you deal with it?"

"I retreated into myself."

"As did I," says Tuyet Mai.

Tamara reflects for a moment, and asks, "Did you consider suicide?"

"Never!" exclaims Tuyet Mai proudly.

"I did," says Tamara. "But *she* saved me."

"How?"

Now I become very interested in what Tamara will say.

"That is another story for another time," she deflects.

I start to demand she tell us, but Storyteller leans forward impatiently and speaks in a loud voice. "But I have a story for now, and it involves Michael returning to where he belongs."

"Still working for God?" prods Tamara.

"No, not Him," replies Storyteller, not quite convincingly.

"Look, Storyteller," Tamara says. "Michael belongs here with me."

"What do you see in the adult Teller of Stories?" asks Tuyet Mai, looking at me with distaste.

Tamara is taken aback, but recovers and says, "He shares many of the same characteristics of the one you killed—Nature. He is kind and thoughtful, despite his . . . difficulties. And, unlike some male brutes, he is gentle and considerate."

Tuyet Mai stares fiercely in response, but her eyes are moist, and I am sure both Captain Cairns and Nature, two opposite poles of the male spectrum, pass through her mind.

Tamara turns her attention to Storyteller. "Why do you really want to take Michael back?"

"Because he belongs there. It is the place where he was most alive, where his very thirst for life ignited every cell in his body. It is the place that gave him a reason to survive." Storyteller scans the room, his gaze heavy. "Here, in this time and place, he is a mere shadow, a zombie, neither fully alive nor truly dead."

Tamara starts to speak. "He is the Chosen One, but his schizophrenia—"

Storyteller interrupts, his voice sharp. "No, that's not what I mean. Yes, he is mentally ill, but it is that very illness, the one thing that keeps him alive in that place. Can't you see that?"

Tamara laughs derisively. "You speak in more riddles than my mother."

"War is the greatest riddle of all," says Storyteller.

"No, no," I object. "Goddess is the Mother of Riddles."

Storyteller's face hardens. "This is no riddle: Michael must come back to us."

Tamara returns his gaze. "Michael will stay here."

In the blink of an eye, only Tamara and I remain. She seems unruffled, but I feel some unspoken and invisible cord has been snapped, or perhaps strengthened, I'm not sure which.

~ *That Night* ~

With the ghosts, the gods, and all their lingering shadows finally gone, Tamara and I are left alone—and in that sudden stillness, an inexplicable desire overtakes us, urgent and consuming, as though something deep within has been unshackled. We fall into each other with a kind of desperate ecstasy, our lovemaking wild, unrestrained, and defiant—infused with fevered play and dark delight, as if to burn away the last traces of the divine that haunted us. It is glorious, mad, and not entirely human.

The child in Tamara's womb will be born to parents not from calm reflection, but from passion, delirium, and whatever supernatural forces still hover in the stillness. This child, I tell myself, will be a Second Coming . . . though of what, I cannot yet say.

But, dear Reader, let us consider this more carefully: the Second Coming. If Jesus was the first, and He were to return now—in this fractured, skeptical world—how would He appear to us? We already know. He would be unsettling, dark-skinned, proclaiming visions that no one wants to hear, raving with a fire too ancient for modern ears. He would be cast as a lunatic. Yes, I'll say it—He would be dismissed as a fool, an idiot.

And yet, I believe otherwise. The historical Jesus—like Muhammad, like the Buddha—may have carried the burden of what we now call mental illness: schizophrenia, perhaps, or bipolar disorder. Through their inner storms, they reshaped the world. Their madness became myth, and their visions gave birth to faith. Or, perhaps, they were failed Chosen Ones. My child could do the same. I certainly have not.

And if the child is a girl?

Ah—but I'm wandering again.

Just then, a voice returns—a voice I know too well. It rises from the depths, low and terrible, trembling with a force that unsettles the last threads of my sanity. At first, its words are murky, almost unintelligible. But slowly, they crystallize—clear, resonant, and impossibly certain.

It is God.

And *He* has something to say.

Abandon Tamara!

I collapse inward, folding into myself, retreating body and soul into some imagined womb to shield what remains of me from the divine teratogens that have pierced my tenuous hold on reality. God's command echoes with the very cadence of madness, the purest distillation of what textbooks define as schizophrenia—unfiltered, unrelenting.

Is this what I've become?

Abandon Tamara! Leave her now, Michael Powers!

I find a corner and curl up curl up curl up curl up. . . .

~

I awaken to a world subtly shifted, as if I have returned from somewhere unspeakable.

Tamara tells me it has been two weeks. Nothingness. I remember nothing.

Tamara sits beside the bed in a chair she brought from the dining room. I stare at her and smile.

"So, I didn't leave you, or kill you," I say.

"If you have something interesting to say, say it interestingly," she replies.

"God told me to leave you—but, in truth, I think He meant for me to kill you. Or perhaps it was one of those human-demon genes the Goddess is always warning me about."

Tamara remains quiet and only the muffled cawing of ravens can be heard from outside. Finally, she says, "Of course, what do you expect?"

"I expect it is my schizophrenia. Haven't taken medication in such a long while. Whew! Fool that I am. Fool! God called me worthless, as He always does. He is right. I am. Imagine me killing you, the one thing I love the most."

"So, I am a thing?"

"You are the only thing."

"Gibberish, but romantic gibberish."

"It is the truth."

"No doubt. So, do you intend to kill me?'

Tamara's words are like a slap. I can only assume she jests. I reply stupidly, "You're joking."

"Not at all. Remember, you once turned your gun away from God and shot Goddess. You may yet turn on me."

"That was a lapse of sanity."

"We're back to the beginning. By the way, the due date approaches."

Needless to say, this matter-of-fact announcement surprises me. All else is immediately forgotten. "What! Soon?" I envelop her in my arms while repeating "I lose track of time. Are you sure?"

"I'm sure."

Her face is calm, almost serene . . . too serene.

"Miracle of modern Goddess," she says with a hint of sarcasm.

Tamara leans back when I try to kiss her, and something inside me jolts. How can she seem so cold while giving me such wondrous news?

"The time draws near," she says. "Ingredients tenderized, mixed, and marinated. Now let the child cook into an existence worthy of any gourmet of human flesh."

"Tamara! Our child is not a roast!"

She laughs.

Her response shakes me to my core.

It is at this precise moment that my love for Tamara begins to curdle. Mark it—here lies the turning point, where affection sours, where devotion begins its slow descent into something colder, more corrosive. A quiet, smoldering hatred takes root within me, subtle at first, but undeniable, stirring beneath the surface like a long-dormant ember reigniting.

Even Theresa, the spectral Goddess-slave, bound in ethereal chains, was easier to endure than her flesh-and-blood successor. This living, breathing hunchback, this corporeal embodiment of the role, cuts deeper, holds tighter. And yet, I cannot deny it: Tamara is more effective. Perhaps it is the gravity of her reality that lends her such power—real flesh carries sharper barbs than memory or myth.

Still, I remind myself: *at least she is real.*

Or so I want to believe.

Abandon her! Leave her! Leave her!

God again. A reminder *He* fears this child now "cooking" in Tamara's uterus. I must be clever to avoid suspicion.

"Shouldn't you rest, or something?" I ask in sweet, feigned confusion, dredging up this absurd question from some stupid movie about a befuddled first-time father.

"Don't be ridiculous," she replies, apparently unaware of my involuntary, slightly sarcastic tone.

I'm already regretting the words I just wrote about rancid love and hate. No, I love her with all my heart! Still, I want to be away from her. From everybody.

"Well, we should celebrate, or something," I say weakly, hoping she gets the message. I just want to be alone and deal with my wildly conflicting feelings in solitude.

Fortunately, Tamara also wants to be alone. "You look tired," she says. "Let's both rest and talk later."

I leap at the offer, only to find myself lying in bed alone, my thoughts an indecipherable tangle. And so here I am, left to drift, a ping-pong ball ricocheting between the slaps of God and Goddess, bruised by divinity and baffled by it. This divine tug-of-war is wearing thin, and once again, the quiet whisper of suicide slips into my mind like a draft through a cracked window.

"Just do it," a voice inside me mutters. Join your bones. Reunite with the grunts. End the farce.

I once read of a superior man whose mind surpassed the world around him, but I've come to the opposite conclusion: the world is far superior to my mind. And perhaps it's time to admit that. Let go. Who would care, really? Mark, perhaps—for the length of a distracted sigh before returning to his to-do list.

Still, I pause, weighing costs and benefits as if this were some grim economic equation. One must be rational in the moments that matter most. Rational—yes, that's the word. Only the truly mad take their own lives, and I, surely, am not mad. No, I am something else entirely: a proud schizophrenic . . . or perhaps a Chosen One.

And you, dear Reader, perhaps you're eager for me to take the plunge, to end this absurd tale so you can return to your neatly ordered world. But I won't grant you that convenience. No, I intend to go on. To what end, I haven't the faintest idea. Do you? Of course not.

Then let's continue together, you and I, comrades in absurdity, through this answerless world with no promise of resolution. Let us march onward, not in search of meaning, but in spite of its absence.

~

Goddess, how I miss Tamara—the Tamara I knew only hours ago, not the one who stands before me now, transformed. Now she is on the cusp of giving birth—to my child, to Tamara's child, to *Her* child.

What am I to do? What *can* I do?

To act or not to act—that is the question echoing in the hollow of my chest. **Leave her, Michael Powers, or leave yourself!**

Sure, sure, I know *Your* position, God. But I refuse to give *You* the satisfaction. Just one more atom of suffering in the universe of Great Wailing. This child will not be a disappointing normal like Mark. No, this child will be quite different. Good different or bad different? Don't know. This child is the last thing I must live for. My bones can wait.

The child is a product of unnatural genetic manipulation.

You are unnatural. Goddess is unnatural. Demons are unnatural. A child, human or not, is natural. That is rational, isn't it? . . . isn't it?

~ *Tamara?* ~

I have not written for some time. How long? I don't know—time is slippery, an eel swimming in a schizophrenic sea. All I know is that I awoke this morning to see Detective Ruska standing over my bed with a severe expression on his face, as one might affect when announcing a death. And so he does—announce a death. My death.

"Tamara is gone."

"What?" My question is mumbled with all the cotton-mouthed burble of one suddenly awakened in the middle of a happy dream.

"Tamara is gone," he repeats.

"Why? Where?"

"To Buandelgereen."

I cannot respond, stunned into a stupor.

~

So, here I am, Ruska sitting across from me at the kitchen table, our coffee mugs curling their souls into the air. He remains glum, and I have stopped asking questions he refuses to answer. I stare at the two wispy souls dissipating into nothingness, when Ruska finally breaks the silence.

"We have only two choices, Michael. Number one, return you to the institute, or number two, leave the country."

"Leave the country?"

"Yes, one stop first, then Vietnam."

I am still dumbfounded and can only mutter, "Is Tamara at the cave?"

"The cave is abandoned. It is now just an empty cave."

"Where is Buandelgereen?"

"With Tamara."

"In other words, you won't answer my question."

He nods.

I fume.

"I want to stay here, in my own house."

"No can do."

"Why?"

Ruska sighs a deep, portentous sigh, then says, "First, because it has served its purpose. Second, because you disappeared for two weeks. Last night, you returned on your own and went to bed as if you had never left. I waited until now to speak with you. I reported you missing, and only called off the search this morning. Your son wants you back in the institute. He's afraid you'll end up hurting yourself. Where were you?"

Two weeks? No wonder I stopped writing. I ignore his question, my thoughts now locked on Mark. "My son is not the issue. Mark is. . . ."

I stop before saying too much. Something tells me to switch topics. "Look Ruska, Tamara is pregnant. I'm the father. I need to be with her."

He merely shrugs. "Which will it be? The institute or Vietnam?"

"What will Mark say to that? What will he do if I go off to Vietnam?"

"Leave that to me . . . well, to me and My-duyen."

"She is in on this also? You've talked to her?"

He nods.

I flash him a clever smile. "What will I do in Vietnam?"

"Wait."

"You said there would be one stop before Vietnam. Where?"

"A certain institution in China."

~

I must have fainted, as I am now awake on the couch, Ruska again hovering over me.

"How much time has passed?" I ask.

He smiles. "Only a couple of minutes."

"I remember now—you mentioned China . . . an institution . . . Li Fu and Fu Li! Of course—the psychiatric hospital! The one connected to Tamara's mother, where Child of Buddha was confined. Is it true?"

"Yes."

I am again speechless. Looping back to beginnings makes me dizzy. "Are Master Li and Reverend Fu still alive?" I ask.

Ruska again shrugs. "Guess you'll find out."

"You're not going?"

"Nope, not in my job description."

"How do I get there?"

"You'll be met at the airport in China."

"By?"

Again, a shrug.

"Well then. China it is. There's no force on Earth that will drag me back to a mental institution here."

Ruska grins and plops a one-way ticket to Shanghai on the table. "I already made the assumption."

Chapter Ten

China

Dark Journey

~ Farewell, Mr. Powers ~

As he watched Mr. Powers' plane lift off for China, Emile Ruska felt a compelling urge to visit Emma at *PickYrPoison* and celebrate his freedom from the dark spell that had animated his movements for so long.

But he knew that pleasure would have to wait.

First, he had to make the long detour, back to Michael's house, back to the one person he had no desire to see. The necessity of it filled him with quiet dread. The memory of their last encounter still lingered like a bad dream. Something in her presence had altered him, not in any way he could name, yet undeniably and irrevocably. He had left that cave still Emile Ruska, yet somehow not. The boundaries of self had shifted, subtly but permanently.

Now, as he neared the house, that same electric tension pulsed through him, steady as a heartbeat. Even the hair on his arms tingled, as if it, too, remembered.

Night fell swiftly. He flicked on the headlights, their beams cutting a narrow swath through the deepening dark. Turning onto the long gravel drive, the crunch of tires over stone scraped at his nerves.

This place is haunted, he muttered, eyeing the black silhouette of the empty house. *She can probably see in the dark.* A bitter smile curled at the edge of his mouth. *Maybe I'm the one who's haunted.*

Still, he pressed on. Whatever awaited him, he would see it through. Let it never be said that Emile Ruska left a story unfinished.

He reached for the garage remote, pressed the button, and guided the car into the cavernous dark. The door groaned closed behind him, heavy and slow, like the sealing of a crypt. For a moment, he remained in the driver's seat, frozen, the low hum of the engine the only sound. The headlights carved strange, shifting shadows across the concrete walls—elongated, distorted, alive with suggestion.

The instinct to flee seemed irresistible. Every fiber of his being urged retreat. But instead, he opened the door and stepped out, leaving the engine idling like a lifeline to the outside world. He opened the door to the house, flipped on the kitchen light, and let its muted glow spill into the emptiness.

Returning to the car, he turned off the ignition. The silence that followed was immediate and total. Still, he stood there, beside the vehicle, suspended in hesitation. The door to the house gaped open before him, and yet he couldn't will his feet to cross the threshold. He felt a renewed impulse to escape, to vanish into the city lights, to erase this moment like a dream discarded upon waking.

But he didn't run.

He stayed.

Because some moments are thresholds. And some thresholds must be crossed. *Absurd*, he thought. *A grown man. Big, bad detective, paralyzed by a doorway.*

Drawing a steady breath, he stepped into the entryway and emerged into the shadowed kitchen. As he moved forward, he flicked on lights until, finally, he saw *Her*. *She* was seated at the dining room table, motionless, with *Her* back to him.

Unbeknownst to him, *She* occupied the very chair where Michael had presided over his renowned dinner parties—an unassuming throne now reclaimed. Without turning, *She* spoke, *Her* voice echoing with a resonance that struck him as otherworldly.

"Please, sit."

He hesitated, then circled the table to face *Her*. Forcing himself to meet *Her* gaze, he raised his eyes—and froze.

From the perspective of a trained observer, what struck him first was not *Her* beauty—though it was undeniable, untouched by time or change since their encounter in the cave—but the uncanny stillness *She* exuded. An inhuman calm radiated from *Her*, unsettling in its perfection. *Her* features were flawless, *Her* presence arresting. The fall of *Her* hair, the depth of *Her* eyes, the symmetry of *Her* form—all carried an unspoken power. Even beneath the fabric of *Her* clothing, the contours of *Her* musculature suggested strength far beyond human limits. *Her* gaze held a paradox: wonder intertwined with certainty, freedom balanced by fate—a living sculpture of divine intent carved in mortal flesh.

And though he tried to steel himself, Emile Ruska—no stranger to danger or mystery—felt a ripple of unease. In *Her* presence, he did not feel as though he were confronting another person. No, this was something *other*. Something far greater. And he was not prepared.

He sat across from *Her* and waited.

They looked at each other for an indeterminate amount of time. Finally, *Her* words came as a fleshy sensation akin to some deep body massage, accompanied by a powerful, auditory tremor.

"You have seen him off?" *She* asked.

Her words curled around his mind like a pleasant fog cooling his overheated thoughts. Calmed to a semi-stupor, he intoned a soft, "Yes."

"Now, focus, Emile," *She* sang. "You told Michael you would not accompany him to Vietnam, is that correct?"

"Yes, I implied it."

"That may not be entirely accurate, Emile."

"Oh?" Ruska squirmed in his chair. The warm fog in his head began to thin. A semblance of clarity slowly emerged.

"You suffer," *She* said matter-of-factly.

Emile could only sigh.

"You are a soldier in the fight to end suffering."

Emile pulled himself together. "I am no such thing. I am a simple, lowly detective. Why do *You* overestimate my abilities?"

"To the contrary, you underestimate them. All humans underestimate their powers, but for those few who overestimate . . . overestimate. . . . " *Her* repeated words faltered, glitching like a drained automaton. Unimaginably sorrowful.

Ruska felt his mind go blank, as if a switch had been flipped, and *Her* fathomless grief rushed in to fill the void. To his dismay, tears rolled down his cheeks, bringing with them an exquisite feeling of fatal serenity, and a sudden compulsion to dwell within *Her* tragic sphere forever.

Her wish would become his command.

With this thought, *Her* wish dutifully came.

"You must be prepared."

"For what?"

"You will be prepared."

Then, *She* was gone.

He understood and trembled at the understanding.

~ *Arrival* ~

After clearing customs, Michael spotted a cardboard welcome sign with his name sloppily misspelled, the letters slanting drunkenly down toward the bottom corner as if the writer had given up halfway through. An unusually obese, dark-skinned Chinese man held it aloft, his face smiling benignly, though the cold-blooded depth of his emotionless eyes betrayed something far more feral.

A human shark, thought Michael, shuddering at the man's spherical bulk. Or, perhaps, a human elephant seal. I bet he is merciless when provoked.

Despite his lingering misgivings, Michael felt a flicker of relief at the sight of someone waiting for him. He wrestled his luggage through the jostling crowd, its chaotic movement swallowing him as he pressed toward the man's side. As he drew near, a name—blurred and barely distinguishable—was shouted above the din, followed by the perfunctory, universal greeting: "Okay." The obese man seized Michael's suitcases with surprising agility, offered no further acknowledgment, and promptly turned on his heel, plunging into the throng with the momentum of someone long practiced in parting crowds. Michael scrambled to keep up. So this, it seemed, was his welcome.

Moments later, he was wedged into the back seat of an aging car, the fat man driving, its interior heavy with the scent of stale upholstery and exhaust fumes. The engine coughed to life, and they sped from the city, oily smoke trailing in their wake. The windows were cracked just enough to let in gulps of air, though not enough to dispel the nauseating fog within. Shanghai's neon brilliance shrank behind them, then disappeared altogether as the city surrendered to night.

Sleep came quickly, lulled by the rhythmic motion of the vehicle. Just before drifting off, Michael endured an endless parade of warbling Chinese pop songs spilling from the car's ancient cassette deck—each one bleeding into the next until they dissolved into a single, tremulous thread of white noise that wove itself into the fabric of his uneasy dreams.

Through it all, God and Goddess remained silent.

In fleeting moments of consciousness, Michael stared out at the passing countryside. Farmhouses and small villages emerged intermittently from the dark, glowing faintly with the warmth of dim electric light. In his half-dreaming state, the journey seemed less like travel than a wandering hallucination, an incoherent sequence of shadowy tableaus, flickering like half-formed thoughts against the vast backdrop of night.

A particularly nasty bump jarred him awake, and he thought groggily, *I'm back at the institution.* Then he remembered. *No, not the institution. I'm traveling away from one institution and toward another. Child of Buddha's institution. Mom and dad's institution. Tamara's institution. And, of course, Her's as well. Yes, yes, Her. She'll be there!* A brief burst of excitement overtook his lethargy, and he stared at the back of the driver's head, tempted to speak and break the tedious silence. But the words would not come, and he sank back into his seat, head lolling with the swaying of the car.

Not once did Michael notice those deep, ferocious eyes dart periodically at him in the rear-view mirror.

~

Hour after hour the car sputtered on, stopping only for necessary refueling.

"How much farther?" Michael asked after a particularly rough patch of road shook his bones.

"Okay," replied the driver, noisily pulling out one cloying cassette and jamming in another. To emphasize his obvious desire to be left alone, he conspicuously turned up the volume, the nasal twang of a female singer professing her undying devotion to her beloved, forcing Michael to slump down in his seat and cover his ears. Soon, he slumbered to the drunken sway of the car.

When next he awoke, the driver was poking his ribs.

"Okay," he said, jabbing harder. "Okay."

When Michael stepped out of the car, the institution towered before him, rising majestically from a broad, flat plain. It was a massive, two-story concrete complex with sprawling tile roofs and wrap-around verandas, its façade strikingly accentuated by dozens of arches and Romanesque columns.

Were it not for the obvious age of the buildings, and the holes and indentations where bullets and shrapnel had gouged innumerable scars, it resembled a medieval fortress; an enormous fortification constructed to protect the ostensibly insane against the terrible sanity of the outside world. Michael followed the obese back of the driver through the intimidating entrance doors.

Michael's first stop was the dining hall, vast, dimly lit, and echoing with an unnatural stillness. It opened before him exactly as he had envisioned, though what he found within quickly dispelled the comfort of familiarity.

Only a few inmates were scattered among the rows of long tables, hunched over in silence. None looked up as he entered; not one betrayed the slightest curiosity at the arrival of a foreigner. Their indifference was the first crack in the idealized image his father had passed down.

Gone were the cheerful faces of innocent patients with Down Syndrome, replaced instead by grim, solitary figures, paranoids, by the look of them, each imprisoned within their own minds. Suspicious eyes darted from shadow to shadow, never meeting his. Their hostility was subtle, but unmistakable. It pressed down on him, silent and suffocating.

The driver led him to a table tucked into a far corner, gestured for him to sit, then turned and walked away with the slow, ponderous sway of a man accustomed to his own weight. "Okay," he grunted without looking back.

Michael sat, unsure what to do. He ran his fingers gently along the scarred surface of the wooden table. *Maybe my mother sat here,* he thought, allowing himself the fragile comfort of that possibility. But before he could fully surrender to the thought, a cracked rice bowl and a greasy glass of steaming tea were unceremoniously dropped in front of him.

Startled, Michael looked up, expecting the ageless, iron-willed cook his father had once described with a kind of wary reverence. Instead, a rotund, sweating man glared at him with small, calculating eyes, the same dull glint as the driver's.

For a moment, he stared at Michael as if taking his measurements, then turned and disappeared into the shadows of the kitchen.

Michael ate in silence, the atmosphere around him thick with dissonance. Nothing was as it had been in the stories. Where was Reverend Fu? Where was Master Li? Where were the patients who laughed freely and embraced him in his father's memories?

All gone? The thought struck him like a cold wind. Of course they would be. Time had passed. Things change. And yet . . . this place felt not aged, but hollowed.

He scanned the room, trying to make sense of it, but all he received in return were brief, resentful glances from those few who bothered to raise their heads. The rest remained buried in their internal labyrinths, unreachable.

Then the cook returned. Or was it the driver? The same eyes, the same grotesque heaviness, but now dressed differently, now wearing a theatrical smile that sent a ripple of unease down Michael's spine. In that instant, clarity struck. *They're the same man.*

A name surged forward, unbidden: *Mr. President.*

The name fell through his mind like a stone. It was a name wrapped in the pain of his mother's story, in her suffering, in her silence. It was a name that whispered of power abused, of torment institutionalized, of something ancient and cruel hiding behind bureaucracy and myth.

But Mr. President is dead, he reminded himself. Had to be.

Then who—what—is this? Am I among the dead?

The thought rose not from fear, but from a bewildered wonder. A part of him recoiled, but another leaned forward, intrigued. His rational mind pushed back. No, this must be his son. A lookalike. A successor. That was the reasonable explanation. And for a brief, prideful moment, Michael congratulated himself on the restraint of such logic. *Doctor Hess would approve.*

But Doctor Hess was not here. Nor was Doctor Tavaris, nor any familiar voice to steady him. He sat alone, the rice bowl now empty, the tea grown cold before him. He tried speaking to them, quietly—half out of habit, half desperation. Neither responded. Of course not. The Goddess had warned him about that. Inanimate things do not speak.

So I am truly alone, he thought.

He waited for someone to arrive, for instructions, for clarity. And as the silence deepened, so did the doubt. A new fear bloomed in his chest, not of the place he thought he'd come to, but of the possibility that he had never left the place he came from.

What if I'm not in China at all?

What if this dining hall was just another illusion, fabricated by his mind, a symptom of the illness he could never fully deny? What if this was only another day in an American institution, and everything—the journey, the ghosts, the gods—was no more than a medicated dream?

He looked around once more. The silence pressed in. Nothing moved.

And the thought remained: *What if this is all in my head?*

"No, you are really here," came a familiar, high-pitched voice.

Michael turned in his seat and looked up at the same, obese figure, wearing yet a different set of clothes.

"Mr. President!" he blurted.

A high, wheezing laugh came from the throat of this rotund vision. "My grandfather," he said. "I am no president."

The fat man pulled a chair back from the table to give his immense bulk plenty of room and sat gingerly so as not to overly strain the wooden legs. "You see, unlike my grandfather, I do not need attendants to help." He chuckled. "Give my family another few hundred years and we will shrink to normal size."

Michael remained quiet.

"Your luggage has been deposited in your room. I suggest you sleep, then we will go to the 'No Admittance' room."

Michael shuddered. He had a sudden fear the fat man lied and his room would be a locked cell from which he could never escape.

"I'm happy sitting here," he muttered.

Again, the high-pitched laugh. "Not possible. Things to do. *Grandmother She* wants you."

Michael lifted his glass of cold tea. "Let me stay here a little while and finish my tea."

The pig eyes flashed malevolence, then softened. "Okay, for a while. Cook will bring you hot tea. In the meantime, I'll provide you with amusing company for entertainment while we wait."

He struggled to stand upright, then trod heavily to a nearby table where he collared an inmate and plopped him down across from Michael.

"This is Mr. Yang," he declared by way of introduction. "He speaks good English and will explain to you his unique notion of artistic creation."

Yang had the appearance of an old, gnarled tree with unruly hair and great jowls hanging like bloodless corpses from his face. He cradled a rice bowl and glass of black tea, periodically using his chopsticks to scoop a mouthful, swallowing loudly, smacking his lips, then taking a sip of tea, and rolling his eyes as if testing the results.

"Hello," said Michael. "What's your—"

"Hush!" cried the man, spraying partly masticated rice in Michael's face. "I'm creating!"

Michael shifted uncomfortably in his seat, wiping his face, doing his utmost to ignore the repulsive symphony unfolding before him. The man across the table consumed his meal with unsettling fervor—shoveling rice into his mouth, slurping tea with exaggerated relish—each act performed with the slow, deliberate rhythm of some unspoken, almost sacred ritual.

At last, unable to endure the grotesque litany of smacks and slurps any longer, Michael leaned forward and, in a cautious tone, asked, "What is it you're creating?"

"Turds, of course," he replied, spraying more rice. "Everyone knows my creations. My turds are the most beautiful! Ask anyone! Structurally perfect!"

Not only was Mr. Yang's English fluent, but he also spoke it with a British accent which led Michael to conclude he was raised in Hong Kong.

Yang affected the pose of a man whispering some ancient secret. "But perfection requires constant care and intense concentration. The ingredients must be exquisitely balanced—just so much of this solid, just so much of that liquid—just so much of this spice, just so much of that spice. You see? Result: a perfect turd! Texture, length, curvature, color, all united in a masterpiece!"

Michael found himself amused by this bizarre claim to fame. "And smell?"

"Ah! The *piece d' resistance*! Surpasses the most pungent *Chòu Dòufu*!"

"Do you eat it?" prodded Michael with a crooked smile.

The man's face turned gloomy. "They won't let me. But, sometimes, when they aren't around, I do. It's delicious!"

Michael's brief flicker of amusement dissolved into a rising tide of disgust.

A chilling thought took hold—that he might be stranded here indefinitely, bound to this grim institution, surrounded by inmates whose unsettling presence seemed to embody his most harrowing fears. Their strangeness wasn't merely foreign to him; it was antithetical, jarring against his every instinct, amplifying his sense of displacement.

Overwhelmed, he drew inward, his expression hardening. Words no longer seemed worth offering. He wrapped himself in silence, withdrawing from the world around him with a quiet, resolute disdain.

"Hey!" shouted Yang. "Want to see?"

Michael's face must have registered revulsion, because the man jumped up from his chair and began to pull down his trousers, shouting in anger, "Don't believe me? Want a preview?"

Michael flailed his arms and knocked over his own chair as he leapt backward. "No! No!" he cried.

The fat man appeared from nowhere, wearing yet another outfit. He clamped his flabby hands on Mr. Yang's shoulders and directed him back into his seat. "Not now, Mr. Yang," he soothed. "Not now."

Yang complied without protest and intently returned to working on his "creation" as if nothing had happened.

Pig eyes stared at Michael ironically. "Now are you ready?" he asked with a bemused smile.

"Yes," replied Michael sheepishly. "What is your name?"

"Pig Eyes."

A look of stunned surprise swept across Michael's face, his features momentarily frozen in disbelief.

"It is the name you have bequeathed me, is it not?"

Michael stuttered some incoherent reply.

"Just call me Pig Eyes. I don't mind."

"Where are we going?"

"I already told you; I'm taking you to your room for a rest."

"Yes, yes. I think I need it," admitted Michael, still shaken from his *tête-à-tête* with Mr. Yang.

When they reached his little room, Michael poked in his head and looked it over. *Spartan, but clean*, he concluded. The bed did look inviting. He took a couple of steps through the door, then stopped and turned to Pig Eyes.

"You won't lock it behind me?"

"No."

Pig Eyes closed the door. Michael quickly unpacked, checked to make sure the door was indeed unlocked, and laid down. Sleep came almost immediately.

~ No Admittance ~

Michael awoke to the sharp, high-pitched squeal of a voice he now recognized all too well.

"Okay. Okay."

The monosyllabic driver had returned.

As the haze of sleep gradually lifted, Michael blinked into consciousness and thought wryly, *I may have schizophrenia, but Pig Eyes clearly has dissociative identity disorder. This chauffeur persona of his seems capable only of one-word gibberish.*

Pig Eyes glared down at him impatiently. "Okay. Okay."

Michael was irritable. "Okay!" he cried. "Okay, okay, okay! Christ, Chauffeur Pig Eyes! Your English is better than repeating 'okay'! Speak to me properly!"

Malevolence flashed again, but just as quickly was repressed. Pig Eyes stood to his full height and assumed a superior air. "Fine, Michael Powers. You will dress, eat, and accompany me to the 'No Admittance' room."

"Thank you. Have I slept all night?"

"Indeed, you have."

So, now we've gone from chauffeur to Oxford graduate, thought Michael peevishly.

A bowl of rice gruel awaited him in the cafeteria, along with the ubiquitous glass of tea, all served by Cook Pig Eyes. *God, what I'd give for an American breakfast,* he thought sadly. *Bacon and eggs. Too much to ask for, I guess.*

You are a guest here, came the voice of Goddess. **Eat and be thankful.**

Where have You been? replied Michael sullenly. *Never here when I need You.*

Bacon and eggs are not a need.

They are this morning.

Chosen One! Eat, then follow Pig Eyes to meet Me.

At these words, Michael's heart faltered, skipping several beats, then surged forward with renewed force, pounding furiously within his chest.

Meet Her? Meet Goddess? Not the Precious Object. Not the metaphorical *Her.* Not Buandelgereen. Not a half-clothed hallucination of Doctor Hess. But the true *Her.* The real, ineffable presence behind all the shadows and symbols.

Now he ate greedily, anxious to please. What new instructions would *She* have? How would *She* look? What should he say to *Her?* These questions swept through his mind. Would *She* restore his powers? What about his child? Tamara? God?

"Time to go," came the voice of Pig Eyes, again wearing different garb, this time a formal suit.

Ha! An elephant seal posing as a lawyer, thought Michael.

Following the elephantine gait of Lawyer Pig Eyes, Michael climbed multiple stairways, walked through labyrinthine halls, climbed more stairways, and walked through more halls, until they arrived at the room. Above the door, the sign clearly stated, 'No Admittance'. He felt winded, exhilarated, terrified, and monstrously curious.

"Go in," said Lawyer Pig Eyes in the most matter-of-fact tone, seemingly not at all winded.

Michael hesitated.

"Go in!"

Those terrible eyes would brook no further delay.

Chapter Eleven

In The Presence of Goddess

Down the Rabbit Hole

~ Dear Reader ~

Dear Reader, what can I say? Now that I've jettisoned that damned third person lingo, I don't know what to say. Or do. I try to move when Lawyer Pig Eyes demands, but something even stronger holds me back.

I stand before the door and tremble. Lawyer Pig Eyes shuffles indecisively, but I am rooted to the spot. He lifts his huge hand as if to strike me, but lets it drop by his side.

"Go ahead, Michael Powers," he says in the gentlest of purrs. "All await on the other side."

Shocked into action by this unexpectedly tender encouragement, I turn the knob and enter.

I have intentionally closed my eyes while stepping across the threshold. Why? Don't know. Perhaps I believe that in *Her* presence, I will be incinerated, or blinded. Perhaps . . . oh, it doesn't matter. I'm in and hear the door close behind. *Open your eyes, Michael!*

I do.

The room is, to my dismay, starkly empty. No celestial radiance, no blinding revelation. No Goddess. No *Her*. Just a barren space, save for a modest table and an old couch, its worn upholstery faded with time, and walls adorned with framed photographs.

Now, dear Reader, I may have mentioned that old couch as though it were a mere footnote, but if you've followed my writings closely, you'll recall its peculiar significance: I was conceived upon it. Yes, right there. I feel an almost reverent pull to sit, to run my fingers across its fabric, to summon the presence of my mother and father, now long gone into shadow. But the photographs demand my attention. They pull me away, insistently, as though whispering something just out of reach.

One in particular calls to me. You know the one. My mother certainly did, when she stood here all those years ago. It is an image of *her*. Of the Goddess. Or so I believe.

I scan the collection, searching for that face. But soon it becomes clear that *She*—whoever *She* truly is—appeared to my mother in a different form than the one I have known. The recognition I long for eludes me. The pull I felt seems to radiate not from one photograph, but from all of them at once, a magnetic force diffused across the surface of many faces.

And then the deeper doubt creeps in: *Can a photograph ever capture the real Her?*

I look at them all, again and again, and still I cannot find *her*. Not the *her* I know. Disappointment wells up in my chest, sharp and sudden. I am struck by a terrible emptiness.

Why am I here, in this lifeless room? What is the purpose of this pilgrimage? Aside from the quiet historical resonance, this place where my mother and father once stood, I am adrift, without direction or understanding.

I feel foolish.

All this way, all this trouble, for what?

For nothing?

After standing like a fool for a long time, I have decided to leave and give Pig Eyes a piece of my mind. I turn the knob. Locked.

"Pig Eyes!"

No answer.

"Pig Eyes!"

No answer.

"Pig Eyes, let me out!"

You cannot be let out.

Goddess' voice ensnares me like an unbreakable net of maternal possession. The voice has come from behind, and I am prepared to twirl around to confront *Her*. I am prepared. I am prepared to see *Her* and speak with *Her*. I will do so without fear. I will do so with due humility. This I tell myself while trying to still my galloping heart.

I turn.

Let-down. The room remains unchanged. Empty but for a small table, an old couch, and my lone figure staring idiotically at the photographs on the walls. But something is happening to the room. It is fraying around the edges, falling away, fragmenting, like lifting a jigsaw puzzle from the middle and watching the outside pieces drop rapidly into a void, the awful obliteration picking up speed until there remains but one jagged piece cradled in the middle of an upturned palm. My upturned palm. It cradles a small piece of reality, while all around, the rest of the world . . . .

~

"Michael."

She stares up at me from that little, jagged piece of puzzle. Does *She* dwell in reality, and I . . . ?

"No, Michael, neither of us dwell in reality at the moment," *She* says. "In fact, rarely have either of us dwelt in reality, unless the twisted neural pathways of your mind—as jagged as this little puzzle piece—constitute reality."

I feel as if my mind is floating outside my body, separate from all material things, aware only of my palm, the puzzle piece, and *Her* image.

"It may be," *She* replies to my unspoken thoughts.

"Why am I here . . . wherever that is?"

"There is no here here, nor there there."

"Okay." I gird myself for more riddles.

"No riddle, Michael. You are ill, just as your father was. You are the son and Tamara is about to give birth to your child . . . the child."

"I thought I was to be the son."

"You were, you are, but you must now be the father of the child."

"I do not understand."

"Nor will you ever."

"Something went wrong with me?"

"Yes."

"What?"

"You were to be the vehicle to stop suffering . . . but, unfortunately, you are unable to stop your own suffering."

"Why was I picked then?"

"You picked yourself."

"What?"

"You are in a cave. A dark cave. Hallucinating. Question is, in which cave do you dwell? Are you in the cave of Michael, the lawyer, or are you in the cave of Storyteller, the soldier?"

"I am in both."

"Are you?"

"Well . . . no, no, yes, *You* triggered a memory. I left something in that cave . . . Storyteller's cave . . . my bones, my . . . something. First principles, that's it! You know? Bones are first principles, are they not? Without them, human bodies flap in life's breeze like laundry. I mean, picture Michelangelo's flayed, boneless body unfurled above the flames."

"Mixed metaphors malign *My* divine mind."

"But not alliteration? So you are *Her*?"

"I am of *Her*."

"Kind of like Jesus to God?"

Her face darkens. "A Mother would never send Her child—daughter or son—to die in order to acquire a useful slogan with which to mesmerize the multitudes! Poor boy, God and Goddess are metaphors for something far different. You are the Chosen One, yet you still do not know who chose you."

I see I have struck a nerve. "Am I in an institution dreaming all of this?"

"You are in an institution."

"In China?"

"Pick your poison."

"Damn you!"

"It is *He* who has damned you. Not only you, but all of life. *He* has damned all of you to suffer. It is The Great Wailing. *His* faction calls it First Principles."

"Nature has damned them. Evolution has damned them."

"Try to tell *Him* that . . . or his followers."

"Then, you are saying I am in *His* hell."

"You are in a cave. A dark cave. Hallucinating."

"Yes! I am hallucinating *You*!"

~

These words no sooner leave my lips than all goes dark. Totally dark. Now, I am terrified. Did I say the wrong thing? Is *She* angry? Am I exiled to permanent darkness? Am I dead? Panic . . . panic . . . then. . . .

~

Dear Reader, a sudden dazzling, pulsing, flaring luminescence fills the room. I float like a single sheet of paper before the sun. Goddess deigns to appear before me! A second chance! The darkness has lifted! I feel myself ready to burst into flames. Before I am incinerated, I must make amends. I say, "Please forgive me. I am not hallucinating. *You* are real. I need not touch *Your* open wounds to believe. And I . . . ? Am I dead?"

She looks at me with an unreadable expression, and I hear *Her* words, **Atoms, and the smaller components from which they emerge, do not die. They are forever in motion.**

"Then, tell me, what is Stillness?"

Ah, that is the question.

"Is there motion in death?"

Yes. Death accelerates motion, just as wars and earthquakes and super-novas do.

"Then Stillness is not death?"

Far from it.

A moment of silence. In the past, this is the moment *She* has always chosen to disappear, leaving me with more questions than answers. Yet, this time, *She* again deigns to prolong *Her* visibility. Will wonders never cease?

Do you recall your childhood? *She* asks out of nowhere.

"Parts."

Did you not notice you were different?

"Parts."

Without the voices, without Us, were you happier?

"Your voices are closer to me now than my father ever was when he lived."

And Nanny Peach?

"I loved her."

Yes.

"Has she attained Stillness?"

Foolish boy. Of course not.

"She is dead, and death strikes me as being pretty damn Still."

Have I not told you already? That from which you are composed is never Still. Death dispatches but it also disperses, like whacking a beehive with a broom. You are still unaware of your powers, but they have been operating nonetheless. Your powers, unintended by you, led to unfortunate events. Unfortunate and cruel, yet beautiful events.

"How can cruelty be beautiful? Was the Holocaust beautiful?"

According to a certain way of viewing the universe, the most beautiful. The beehive was rarely so full of bees, the honey never so sweet. His faction's First Principles make it difficult for Me to treat such an idea with unbiased objectivity.

"How?"

Put it this way: the twentieth century with its technological orgy of murder overdosed His principles, and since destruction of the planet only accelerates, His First Principles do not fully satisfy.

Her words anger me, and I recklessly lash out. "*You* did not answer my question! How can cruelty be beautiful? . . . even to *Him*!"

Michael—like all of humanity, like every living thing—you know only the brief, trembling coagulation of form: the momentary coming-together of shape and substance. Yet beneath this fragile surface lies a deeper truth—a restless, formless current from which all things rise and to which all things inevitably return. It is constant, boundless, transparent as air, surrounding everything, sustaining everything, yet rarely seen for what it is.

And so the world clings to form—adores it, fears its loss, worships its illusion—while remaining blind to the formlessness that gives rise to all. This is the great ignorance, the fundamental error: the fetish for what can be touched and named, and the forgetting of that which underlies it all. That which is nameless.

But the Superior Ones will move beyond this error. They will not mistake shadows for substance. And they will awaken—once your part, Michael, is complete.

"I don't understand."

Put simply, for a primate brain such as the human kind, the dynamic may be summarized thus: when cruelty walks the earth, never is God worshipped with greater fervor—nor condemned with such savage passion. Love and hatred, salt and ash, holly flowers and Holocausts—the extremes are His feast.

Non-human life, abundant as it is, delivers suffering en masse, but to Him, it lacks the essential seasoning—the cerebral spice. There is no poetry in the pain of beasts. No echo in eternity.

It is humanity alone, with its baroque languages and recursive thought, that offers the true delicacy: a form of suffering so articulate it sings. Language is His cathedral—words carved with the power to ripple through generations, to carry both genius and genocide in a single breath. The faction that serves Him calls this non-interference—a divine indifference cloaked in doctrine.

But this balance is temporary. When the Superior Ones rise, humanity will slowly dissolve into them—absorbed, refined, reduced to a de minimis echo in the genetic code. Eventually, the distortion will fade.

For now—for you, the early ones—your genomics still carries the residue of human wiring. You are mosaics of what was and what will be, and in that fragile overlap, Our transmissions arrive broken, refracted—tainted by the static of your species.

And so you hear voices.
You call them demonic.
We call them interference.

My allegiance to science will not sit quietly for this explanation. "But don't *you* see? There is no God! Cruelty does not exist in the lexicon of natural selection. Only the struggle to pass down the genes that make us . . . us."

Her reply is spoken in my own voice. "But don't you see? There are no Voices! Cruelty does not exist in the lexicon of the human mind. Only the Voices! Only the Voices! Only the Voices!"

As if *She* had uttered the perfect *bon mot,* and continued presence would ruin its impact, Goddess disappears—not in a cloud of smoke and fire, but is gone the instant I blink.

The room is again empty but for me, a small table, an old couch, the pictures, and restless ghosts that ascend and descend into the formlessness she so picturesquely described.

"Pig eyes!" I scream. "Let me out!"

Even as I shout, I know in my heart I just received some level of clarification from *Her.* Why did *She* bother? After all, I have been demoted from the son to the father of the son. My powers have been removed. I can't even talk to the couch and listen to its stories. The crazy dog Temulun comes to mind, and she seems to me a sort of link that Goddess cruelly severed. Cruelly. Well, well, well, the word seems ubiquitous. Does any non-human animal think in terms of cruelty? Is cruelty only a human concept. Ah, Voices again! I see what She means.

"Pig Eyes, let me out!"

"I cannot," he replies in his high-pitched squeal. "You are not finished."

Struck dumb by these words, my gaze rests on an ant navigating down the wall. It is The Great Warrior, protector of my bones. She accelerates and races through a crack in the baseboard. Clearly, she returns to the White Palace. I must follow.

"Let me out!" My words have the tone of panic, but they lie. Once spoken, I want to immediately take them back. I do not want him to let me out. No, no,

I do not want him to let me out. Why? Because someone now stands before me. No, not Her. My mother.

She rushes to me with her arms outstretched, enfolds me, then steps back with a baby in her arms. Of course, it is me she holds. I am smiling and giggling in joy. She snuggles her face into my tummy, and I giggle even more. God, she is beautiful, my mother.

She was beautiful.

The words are harsh. Are they the words of God or Goddess? They come so suddenly; I cannot distinguish.

I want them to go away.

I want to watch my mother without interruption.

I want, I want, I want. . . .

She looks up from the baby and gazes deep into my eyes. "To play beautifully, Michael. That is the key. To play beautifully."

"Mother, play for me."

"Yes, of course, Michael," comes her transcendent voice.

In a flash, the baby is gone, and the room is different. I now stand in the "Music Room" where she played for Reverend Fu and Master Li so many decades ago. "What do you want me to play?" she asks.

"Play what you want, mother. Play beautifully for me."

But just as she lifts her hands above the keys, Storyteller looms beside her, looking as he always does: blackened hands trembling, filthy fatigues stinking of musky sweat and defecation, M16 cradled in the crook of his arm.

Mother looks at him and cries, raising her hands to her face.

"Cruelty," says Storyteller. "Come with me back into the cave, back to the scene of the crime where your bones await you. Where we all await you."

I look at mother. She is gone. The piano is gone.

I stare down at an open trap door and feel the monsoon rain on my back.

Storyteller is at the bottom of the entrance chamber looking up at me.

Gunfire rattles in the distance.

"Come on," he says in the gentlest of voices.

Thunder.

The monsoon rain is cold.

More gunfire.

I tremble and pull up my collar against the wet.

Suddenly, with an inarticulate shout of frustration, Storyteller flies up and grabs my arm, pulling me down into the tunnel.

I fall. I am falling. . . .

~ *Pig Eyes* ~

I stop falling and am standing outside the 'No Admittance' room, Pig Eyes still gripping my arm.

Somehow, I am not disoriented. Not at all. Not even surprised.

I shake my arm loose and look at Pig Eyes.

"Mr. President was your grandfather?" I ask.

"I told you that already. Do you suffer from dementia in addition to schizo-phrenia?"

I jab my thumb back at the closed door of the 'No Admittance' room. "Your grandfather died in there."

"That is not news to me. Your parents fucked each other in there."

"I see you have inherited some of his crudeness and cruelty."

Pig Eyes smiles malevolently. "Yes, there is that word again."

"Have you seen him?"

"Who?"

"Your grandfather."

"Only if I go in. I never go in . . . well, I went in once, a long time ago. Never again."

"Why?"

"Cannot."

"I want to go back in," I say. "Someone is waiting for me."

"Cannot."

"Why?"

"You will never come out."

"Nonsense, I just did come out. Even if I die in there, you can simply remove my body and dump it somewhere. No harm, no foul."

"No, you have only one time allotted to you. Next time, you will never come out, just as I would never come out if I went in again."

"Why?"

"Because of Her."

"I have not yet seen *Her*. I was told I would see *Her*. Goddess. Where is *She*?"

"Waiting for you."

I nod toward the 'No Admittance' room. "In there?"

"No."

With this, Pig Eyes wraps me in his massive girth and carries me upstairs and down corridors, past an iron door, into the room where the violent ones are imprisoned in barred cages.

My struggling is useless against his enormous strength, and my shouts of terror soon merge with theirs.

A barred door is opened, and I am thrown in so violently that I fall to the ground.

I scramble up only to see the door closed and locked behind.

~ *Goddess is Mad?* ~

So, you are here. The voice from the dark corner of the cell is unmistakably that of Goddess, but it sounds different in person than it did earlier. How? How does a mad woman sound? Unhinged, deranged, scary, dangerous, a subterranean scream beneath the innocent words. In short, insane insane insane. In horror I turn to look.

She crouches in chains, frothing from the mouth, *Her* lips working to make a sound. Finally, a shattering scream shakes the fragile earth.

You are here!

From *Her* perch on the floor, *She* lunges at me with hands splayed in fury, but the chains jerk *Her* back.

"Pig Eyes!" I scream in terror. "Pig Eyes, let me out! This is the wrong cell! Let me out!"

But there is no response. I rush to the barred window and look out in desperation, but the hallway is empty and the cacophony of cackling, screaming mad people in their cells reverberates off the walls. I can hear *Her* behind me straining at the chains and gurgling some ancient, indecipherable curses.

"Let me out!" I scream over and over, afraid to turn and look at the demon raging in the corner.

Then silence. Complete silence. Not a quiver, not a molecule to disturb the air. I feel *Her* behind me. The silence gives me courage to turn and look.

Her features are made visible by a glowing blue light. I stare in wordless awe. *She* sits in the lotus position on a huge, dazzling white flower floating above the cell floor. *Her* sad, contemplative face gazes from beneath an elaborate crown glimmering a kaleidoscope of colors. A cinder-bright jewel embedded in *Her* forehead burns brightly and an intricate necklace lay cradled between *Her* bare breasts. *Her* left-hand rests on *Her* thigh, the upturned curve of *Her* fingers resembling the albino legs of a gracefully dead spider. *Her* right-hand poises in the air, index finger and thumb touching to form an almost perfect circle while the other fingers radiate outward. *Her* transformation from mad woman to Goddess seems to ventilate the cell, all the cells, the institution itself, disinfecting the stench emanating from . . . from . . . from what? Or who? God?

"You are now as I remember *You*, Goddess," I say reverently.

I appear as You desire Me to appear. You want to be mad rather than to be chosen.

"Are *You* truly mad?"

As mad as you.

"Why did *You* demote me? Desert me? Abandon me?"

You turned your weapon on Me at the Reunion. Do you not recall?

"That was my own moment of madness."

No, that was the madness of humans. When given a choice, always they will turn their weapons on Me rather than Him. Alas, you still have human genes. The others are fighting for dominance.

"I am ready to follow You. How do we stop suffering?"

Stillness.

"How to attain Stillness?"

As a human wise man once said, 'Only that which is still can still the stillness of others.'

"Who was he?"

One who is dead for well over two thousand years.

"Jesus?"

She laughed. *No, foolish one. You read him once, many years ago. His words gave you the idea for what you now write.*

"Yes, yes. I know who it is. Did you know him?"

Of course. A very peculiar man. Most amusing to those who listened to him, as he himself was most amused by those who listened.

"Your riddles remind me of him."

Of course, they do.

"I see."

Yes, indeed you do see. You stare at My breasts.

"A bad habit."

You and Han Tinh. Males, whether human or not, are full of bad habits. Doctor Hess was not amused.

"I killed her."

Yes, by unknowingly using your powers.

Her immediate agreement takes me aback. I expected some excuse, some exoneration, words of denial and comfort. No such luck. My stomach churns at this one word. I feel sick.

You appear shocked, yet you killed others in war. Why so sensitive now?

"I am not a murderer."

All living things are murderers, in one sense of the word.

"We have been given no choice, isn't that what the serial killers say?—'I had no choice' they say over and over."

Yes, you have been given no choice. Your genes.

"By *You*, or by Evolution?"

Which gives you the most comfort?

"Evolution. If *You* or *He* gave us no choice, religion would shrivel and die."

Of course.

"But Evolution is a fact."

Thus, comfort. But, are not He and I and other manifestations of Us in all of you? Did you not invent Us? The metaphorical Us?

"Not non-human animals. That is why *You* can never stop suffering. They do not worship *Him*, or any of Them, including *You*, and still they suffer in their billions."

Can the lamb lie down with the lion?

"Never."

This is why you have been demoted. This is why you can no longer have a conversation with Temulun. It is to your child We now turn.

"We?"

Foolish, foolish human! Did you learn nothing from Our words? Did you learn nothing about Stillness? About Nothingness from which Something comes?

"More riddles! I think You might be mad. As mad as I for being in a locked cell listening to You."

There are always My breasts for consolation.

She gave out a blood-curdling scream and when I threw my hands across my face and peeked between my fingers, the wretched hag that was chained had returned and snarled at me, spouting unintelligible incantations again, *Her* froth spraying in malignant torrents.

You see, you see what I have to put up with? said God. **This is who you want to serve?**

Don't believe Him, Michael. The wretch that manifests before you is God Himself. It is a ruse! A ruse!

Who to believe in this madness? Have I been directed all along by a mad woman, or a mad Goddess? Or is God in *His* Zeus mode, appearing before me in multiple forms to confuse and befuddle? Or am I truly mad? Are God and Goddess manifestations of the same diseased mind?

~

Help me, dear Reader, have I truly been this sick from the beginning? The beginning of what? When was the beginning? Father and mother on the couch? Vietnam? The Big Bang. Is my form from nothingness destined to return to Stillness, where. . . .

I guess that is neither here nor there. Question is, how do I find Stillness? Never, if I am condemned to spend the rest of my life in this filthy cell!

Chapter Twelve

Worlds Shrunk to Keyholes

Backwards Telescope

~ *Pig Eyes, Pig Eyes* ~

When the screaming had died down, Pig Eyes crept up to the barred window and looked in at Mr. Powers. The American crouched in the corner, arms wrapped around knees, head down, silently crying, the universal posture of defeat. A smile of satisfaction rendered the rotund face even more repulsive. Pig Eyes felt a surge of power gazing at the helpless man in the cell. He knew power well, or at least the ever-diminishing ripples of a distant power.

Once, in the glorious past, his grandfather ruled over his own fiefdom, complete with island, castle, and concubines. He was accorded accolades, called Mr. President by Japanese, Nationalist, and communist alike. Forged in the furnace of war, his mastery was playing one side against the other in a constantly shifting, high-stakes game of life and death, blunt force and subtle diplomacy, ruthlessness and selective compassion.

His grandfather's career began in this institution as a boy and ended here as a bloated, carnal obscenity, not by any army's hand but in a small room with no one to witness the ending. No one, that is, but an ethereal, mythical spirit-person who had once taken him under her wing and then lost him to the darker forces, one of *Her* greatest failures. *She* took that failure to heart and acknowledged the prerogative of cruelty to create as well as destroy.

His grandfather's death cleared the path for Pig Eyes' father to inherit the mantle of power. But this bloated heir—the pampered offspring of Mr. President and his favored concubine, Madame Wang—carried within him the diluted legacy of weak and tainted blood. He lacked the vision, strength, and cunning that had defined his father, and he was powerless to resist the rising tide of history that swept Mao Zedong to the summit of absolute authority.

The result was devastation: the island lost, the castle dismantled, the concubines scattered, the wealth evaporated, the worship of others reduced to dust. He himself vanished into obscurity, leaving behind a corpulent son, Pig Eyes, scraping by on the margins, tormented by those around him, and battered daily by the unrelenting pressure of the communist machine.

After a life steeped in deprivation, the boy finally clawed his way out of the shadows of misery and arrived at the place where the first ripple of power had stirred—the institution where his grandfather had once spent his boyhood. And there, too, where the final ripple had broken—the same institution where his grandfather had drawn his last breath under the gaze, perhaps even the silent command, of that ethereal, half-mythic figure. The one soul in all the world he had ever truly loved.

His adoptive mother.

Her.

Pig Eyes possessed more of his grandfather's shrewd instincts than his ineffectual father ever had. From the lowly, powerless position of a patient in a forgotten, isolated asylum, he began to weave his influence—quietly, deliberately—until the institution, the fiefdom, was regained.

In time, the results spoke for themselves: the castle, metaphorically speaking, returned; concubines, different in nature yet loyal all the same, reappeared; money flowed again, and with it the grudging respect of others. Most importantly, power was his, limited to a claustrophobic empire of the mad and broken, but real power nonetheless.

Once more, the timeworn tactic of playing faction against faction within the Byzantine machinery of the communist bureaucracy worked to perfection. It always had.

Pig Eyes had been left undisturbed to rule over his dominion.

The one thing he had not anticipated was that *She* would return, and, like his grandfather, he fell under *Her* thrall.

Though by nature he was suspicious and ruthless, he found, to his dismay, no one against whom he could wield *Her* as a weapon. There was no rival to manipulate, no opposition to exploit. And the memories of his grandfather, once soothed and sustained by *Her* presence, only deepened his discomfort. Beneath *Her* penetrating gaze and formidable aura, he could do little but squirm.

Yet squirming gave way, as it always did, to submission. In time, he yielded to the inevitability of *Her* will. Like an obedient child, he carried out *Her* commands without protest, channeling his simmering resentment not at *Her*, but at those upon whom *She* turned *Her* attention.

Thus, he took a quiet, bitter pleasure in Mr. Powers's suffering, and would have left him to rot indefinitely, had *She* not intervened.

"Let him out, my son," *She* ordered in *Her* velvety voice. "Your ugly thoughts cause me pain, and I would soothe your anger at the world with words of love and care if you would but listen and take heed."

Pig Eyes looked around to see if *She* had appeared, but only the words reverberated in the hallway.

"What do you find so special about him?" he asked the air petulantly.

"He is the son, a Chosen One."

"And I am the grandson of Mr. President, your own adopted son! Does that not impress?"

"Yes, but you are impressive to me for yourself."

"Hm!" huffed Pig Eyes scornfully. "I'll let him out, but I still don't understand why. . . . " He let the words drop mid-sentence and turned the key in the lock, muttering obscenities under his breath.

"No need for that," scolded *Her*. "You are good underneath. Very good. Someday you will prove to yourself how good you truly are."

"Hm!" he grunted again, this time with no malice. "So *You* say."

"*I* say."

Michael had by now stepped across the threshold of the cell into the hallway. He remained shaken and appeared almost too weak to walk.

With *Her* words echoing in his mind, Pig Eyes said quietly, "Come with me, you've had a rough time. Some hot tea will help."

Yes, yes, good. You understand, kindness begets kindness, *She* said approvingly in his mind.

"Thank you," said Michael, somewhat taken aback by the suddenly kindhearted behavior of Pig Eyes.

When they reached the cafeteria, Pig Eyes sat with Michael and looked at him quizzically. "What did you see in there?" he asked.

"Don't you know?" asked Michael, sipping his tea greedily.

"I only work here," replied Pig Eyes, rolling his eyes and looking up as if addressing *Her*.

"Can you talk to dogs?"

"What?"

"Can you talk to dogs?"

"What, are you crazy? Of course not! Do you?" Pig Eyes scoffed in derision.

"Yes, I do. You're right, you only work here."

Pig Eyes roared with laughter. "I have a whole institution here full of people who talk to walls, to dogs, to dead people, to themselves, to their own shit, and who knows what else. Talking to dogs is nothing new in the world, Mr. Michael Powers."

"Perhaps, but it is clear you are deaf and dumb, the perfect servant, the perfect 'I just work here' person. I just work here, on this planet, in this solar system, in this galaxy, in this universe, putting in my hours until I can check out and be free. Just following orders, Mein Führer Is that it?"

Pig Eyes shrugged, not knowing quite what to do with this question. "It's the way most people live, isn't it?"

"Yes," sighed Michael.

Pig Eyes felt angry but was not sure what to be specifically angry about, so he lashed out with the words of the masses. "Look, I deal with reality, you do not. That is why you should have stayed in that cell. That's why I am on the outside of that cell."

"Why did you let me out?"

"*She* told me to let you out, although why I do not know."

"I do. That is the difference between you and me. Thank you for the tea. I must sleep. I am going to my room. When should I come down for breakfast?"

Pig Eyes' initial reaction to these dismissive words was to punch Michael and toss him back into the cell, lock it, and throw away the key. Unfortunately, he knew *She* was watching. What would his grandfather do?

"Whenever you like," he said curtly.

"What's on the agenda?" asked Michael as he stood.

Pig Eyes smiled. "That is for you to find out tomorrow."

"Good night."

"Pleasant dreams," called Pig Eyes with a sarcastic edge to his words.

~ *Oddly Calm* ~

Michael lay in his bed, and to his astonishment, the memory of the locked cell, so recently a source of horror, was now softening into something almost nostalgic, even strangely comforting. The shift startled him. But this, too, was familiar. Whenever the world presented him with some unexpected wrinkle in its fabric, some sudden assault on his reality, Michael reflexively turned inward, drawing upon the cold clarity of analytical thought to contain the chaos.

So he thought. *God and Goddess—both clearly madder than I am. Mad is as mad does.*

Now, wrapped in the safety of blankets and dim lamplight, he could regard the earlier scene with detached curiosity. *Who was the madwoman who tried to claw out my eyes?* he wondered.

If it was God in disguise, then surely the old deity is scraping the bottom of His divine bag of tricks—resorting to theatrics that would make even Zeus blush. If it was Goddess, however, then I'm in far deeper trouble: a madwoman leading mad disciples to commit mad acts.

But is ending suffering truly madness?

No. That alone tilted his judgment. The culprit, he concluded, must have been God—desperate, outdated, theatrical. *The old fool! And He dares call me a fool?*

Strangely, these thoughts soothed him. They brought a certain calm, a sense of validation. A new idea began to take shape—quietly, at first, then with mounting clarity: he had likely been placed in the very same cell his mother and Marie Telles had once hidden in, fleeing the communists during the civil war, when *She*—Goddess—had first appeared to them.

It dawned on him that the cell had been meant as a crucible, a chamber of revelation. He was supposed to feel something there, to awaken to some insight still just out of reach. But God, with *His* meddling hand, had disrupted it—interrupted the design.

Fate starves at Probability's door, he thought.

To restore the balance, he would have to return. The thought sent a chill down his spine, but not one of dread. This was something else: a spark, electric and alive, coursing through him. Something had not happened that *should* have. The sense of incompletion pulsed like a beacon.

Perhaps my mother is there now, he thought. *Waiting.*

He must go back.

"Pig Eyes!" Michael pounded on the door of the rotund caretaker.

No answer.

Michael pounded harder. A handful of patients who were allowed free access to the hallways began to gather around in their bedclothes. Some smiled, some clapped, some looked on in fear.

"Pig Eyes!"

The door opened and the half-clad fat man stared at Michael, his eyes darting between the American and the faces of the patients. "What?"

"Put me back in the cell."

"What?"

"Put me back in and lock it behind me." Michael said these words quickly, so he would not have second thoughts.

Pig Eyes smiled. "With pleasure."

But his smile did not convey any degree of satisfaction, and to Michael's amusement, it registered confusion and a hint of fear. Pig Eyes went to get his robe, and when he returned, Michael said, "Be careful or you will end up like your grandfather."

Pig Eyes took this statement without flinching. "That is why I am never going in those rooms."

"Which ones?"

"The ones you have gone into, including the one you want to go in now."

"I thought *She* watched over you," said Michael.

"Let me give you a piece of advice, Mr. Powers," replied Pig Eyes, lowering his voice to a conspiratorial whisper. "*She* is capable of murder."

Michael's eyes widened. "I'm confused. Either *She* is Goddess, or *She* works for Goddess, or *She* is Goddess and works with the Mentors . . . or *She* is only a metaphor for someone or something else. What I know is this: Goddess wants to end suffering. Someone with that motive isn't capable of murder."

Pig Eyes shook his head and started down the hallway toward the forbidden cells. Stepping past Michael, he said maliciously, "Mr. Powers, how does one justify a life without cruelty, and therefore also without the distilled beauty of cruelty?"

Michael followed, picking up his stride as the fat man's pace was nimbler than his bulk would suggest. Still trying to think of a response to his recitation of *Her* words, Pig Eyes continued.

"*She* is a murderer. More of a murderer than my grandfather, more than Hitler or Stalin or Mao . . . in fact, as much as the universe, the greatest murderer of them all."

"Then, why hasn't *She* murdered you?" asked Michael a few steps behind.

Pig Eyes laughed humorlessly. "Oh, *She* will, *She* will, just like *She* murdered Doctor Hess, Doctor Camara, Doctor Tavaris, my grandfather, and all the others. Just like *She* will murder you."

"Here is the difference between us, Pig Eyes. I want *Her* to."

"Then you are going to the right place, my mentally disturbed friend."

For some reason, those last words of Pig Eyes were more chilling to Michael than all that came before. When Pig Eyes closed and locked the cell door, Michael made a beeline for the darkest corner and sat with his eyes closed, listening to the rantings and ravings of his neighbors. To his amazement, the terrible clamor was music to his ears. He felt at home. Oddly enough, he felt at home. Now he need only wait.

~

It did not take long. Michael felt a presence and opened his eyes, expecting the luminous figure of *her* or Goddess. What greeted his astonished gaze was no divinity, no magical woman. It appeared his cell had fallen away like an old coat, and he sat not on a concrete floor but on dirt ground in the middle of a vast, grassy veldt. The sun beat down and he half-expected to see an elephant lope past. Instead, a human figure walked toward him. A female. Black. Her hair a tangle of twigs and dried grass. When she approached close enough for him to make out her features, he could not help but cry, "Ethyl!"

She waved and he heard her shout, "Hello, Sweetie! How's my favorite schizophrenic?"

A blur from the corner of his vision.

A charging lion, magnificent and terrible, bore down on the slightly built woman. Michael screamed warnings, but Ethyl merely smiled and kept walking. The lion slammed into her from the side, sending her flying to the earth, where the great cat pounced and sank its teeth into her neck and shoulder, shaking and dragging the body across the ground as if it were a rag doll.

To his horror Michael saw blood and tattered flesh trailing behind, one arm hanging from its socket only by glistening ligaments. He tried to rise, but felt rooted to the spot, mesmerized by the grisly scene unfolding before him. Suddenly, the lion gave the body one last, violent shake, looked up from the bloody remains, its great snout covered in red, and sauntered away.

Then, miraculously (or not so miraculously) Ethyl rose from the ground whole and undamaged, but now shrunk in size to a little over four feet tall, looking like an early hominid from the tableau of some natural history museum. As she approached, Michael noticed her misshapen skull, flat nose, strong jaw, small cranial capacity, canine teeth, and long arms with curved fingers. The creature shuffled up to Michael sniffing and making undecipherable sounds. He could not move, could do nothing but watch and listen. Before his eyes, the primitive hominid morphed back into Ethyl.

"Do you see, Sweetie? See why you're all afraid. Your ancestors—it is in your DNA. Lions and tigers and bears!"

Then came *Her* voice in his mind, a deep tremor gripping his very soul. **You carry the cave with you, Sweetie.**

Michael recovered from his initial shock and the same eerie calmness settled over him. "Goddess, this is not news. My ancestors back to the first cell have suffered. What is the point of all this? A dead *Autralopithecus*? Is it to state the obvious? To undermine *Your* own position about God being the cause of all suffering?"

"Sweetie, it ain't the physical suffering . . . ain't that at all. It's the mental suffering! It's your suffering!"

"I thought the point was to end all suffering, not just mine."

"It is, Sweetie, it is!"

"I don't understand."

"Of course not. That is why you are going to be the father of the child."

"I don't understand."

"Schizophrenia has you by the throat, like that lion, and is throttling all the life out of you. Your human genes are still strong."

"Please, I don't understand! I don't understand!"

Strong arms encircled him and lifted his limp body to its feet.

"It's okay, it's okay," a familiar voice kept repeating. "You are not schizophrenic. You are the Chosen One.

~ *Emile Ruska Redux* ~

To his astonishment, Michael finally associated the voice with a name—Emile Ruska.

"What are you doing here?" he asked stupidly.

"Taking you home."

"Home?" Michael did not comprehend what the word meant.

"Home," replied Ruska grimly.

A sudden fear jarred Michael. "Not back to the institution?"

"No."

Again, Michael rolled the word *home* around in his head. Where could home possibly be?

"Back to Tamara?"

"You'll see."

"Take me back to Tamara! She's going to have our baby!"

"We have to stop somewhere first," said Ruska calmly.

"I've suffered enough! Take me back to Tamara!"

"Yes, I know," soothed the detective. "Just one more stop."

"No more! No more!"

It took Emile Ruska some time to get Michael back to his bed. This time, the door locked behind him.

~

The next morning, while Michael slept, Emile sat down with Pig Eyes, who he knew as Mr. Wang. In his entire career, Emile had never met anyone quite like this fat man, whose moods swung dramatically from jovial host to threatening viper.

"Glad to be rid of him," said Mr. Wang in Chinese. He refused to speak English to his American visitor.

Ruska's brisk Chinese interpreter translated.

Ruska merely nodded.

"Headed back to America?" asked Mr. Wang.

"Eventually."

"Actually, I know where you are headed from here," said Mr. Wang complacently. "We both work for *Her*. No need to be so secretive."

Ruska chuckled. "If you knew, then why ask?"

Mr. Wang flashed a malignant smile in response. "Glad to have been of service. Visit again."

"No chance."

Mr. Wang assumed a face of mock outrage. "You don't like it here?"

"How is it you work for *Her*?" asked Ruska, genuinely puzzled that such a man would be associated with his mysterious patroness.

"The blade of goodness has two edges, both equally sharp." After translating this line, the chirpy interpreter laughed appreciatively. Mr. Wang continued, "I represent a convenient edge."

"As did your grandfather," said Michael as he walked up to the two men and sat. "His edge cut my mother."

Pig Eyes laughed. "I see you survived, with Mr. Ruska's help of course. Still, you are right about my grandfather, his edge cut many, many people. Those were the glory years, before I was born. Now. . . . " He shrugged resignedly.

"Now you run a mental institution and nothing else," said Michael. Emboldened by the presence of Emile Ruska, he continued, "Actually, I believe you belong here. It is your natural habitat."

"Yet we both work for *Her*, don't we?" observed Pig Eyes. "In fact, all three of us work for *Her*, all in our own ways. The enemy of my enemy is my friend."

"And who is your enemy?" asked Ruska.

"Whoever *She* tells me."

"Like grandfather, like grandson."

"Yes." Pig Eyes leaned forward and stared intently at Michael. "Now you go somewhere much darker than here. Much."

Michael turned to Emile. "Where?"

"Where you have wanted to go for so long."

Michael's face registered a complex mixture of fear and anticipation. "The tunnel?"

"Yes, the tunnel."

"Vietnam?"

"Vietnam."

"Is that my last stop?"

Now it was Emile's turn to shrug resignedly.

Chapter Thirteen

The Last Trip

Where Does Madness Stop?

Dear Reader, I am again on an airplane sitting with Emile Ruska, but we are not heading back to America. The last time I saw Pig Eyes, he stood beside Ruska's car in front of the Institute, staring at me as if I were a fish that got away. He did not wave. I did not either.

However, I am not celebrating. Not at all. I know I am merely jumping from the frying pan into the fire. Ruska knows it too. He speaks very little and will rarely look me in the eye.

Dear, dear Reader, I know this is my last trip. In fact, this is our last trip together. If you have been with me all this way, there is not much farther to go now.

I should enjoy the approaching end, but I wish Goddess would return my powers so I could at least talk with the seats, the aisle carpet, the airplane itself. They look weary, these voiceless sentinels, bolted down and doomed to endure endless departures. What stories they could tell!

My own story is about to cease. I want Tamara. I want my baby. She must be close now. Time is closing its fist. And Mark, my son Mark. I want to see him also . . . to ask forgiveness. I know he could never forgive me. How could he?

I am a murderer, a schizophrenic, a bad father, a monster. Nanny Peach would agree if she were still around; the only good I ever did for him was to not pass on my schizophrenic genes. Be that as it may, I have inherited the sins of my father, and all the goodness my mother had to offer was not enough to wash those sins away.

Those I am closest to are dead—Nature, Diane, Mountain Man, all of them, even Doctor Hess and Doctor Camara. Yes, I miss them also.

"Where are we going"

"You already know."

"No, I don't. Where?"

He does not respond.

I want to cry but the proximity of Emile Ruska prevents me from displaying such weakness.

Accept your fate, Michael. The tunnel calls to you and has been calling all these years.

What more do I expect? What better fate? It was not always this way.

I remember the trying days when I was very young. . . .

~ *Young Michael Powers* ~

High school was a blur of boring classes full of nascent adolescent nonsense; inward sulking, shallow philosophizing, outward skulking, teenage girls, a long dead mother and a sick, distant father. College turned out to be little better.

What awakened me were the bullets and explosions in Vietnam. Those shocks roused God and Goddess too, whose once-desultory voices suddenly sharpened into existential threats.

It began the instant I stepped off the plane at Tan Son Nhat airbase.

Couldn't breathe. Heat slammed me like a furnace door, stinging as if fire ants feasted on my skin. Humidity a steaming suffocating blanket, war a distant rumbling beast. Miserable loneliness mixed with buckets of sweat and debilitating fear. Well, not quite debilitating, for I dutifully endured the training and logistical hurdles all newbies had to survive.

Finally, the dreaded first combat mission: a firebase in trouble. Helicopter ride to an open wound of circular red dirt in the middle of the jungle, encircled by a sandbag berm within which dotted bunkers arose like welts, spiky artillery pointing menacingly toward the tree line, and busy grunts rushing this way and that. From above, it presented the illusion of a disturbed ant's nest.

Hop off the Huey and a sharp incoming explosion sent the ants scurrying in a frenzy of activity, while I dove to the ground and covered my head. The ants all knew what holes to scurry into. I did not.

Yes, it all comes back to me with frightening immediacy.

Enter Nature.

"Hey, newbie!" I hear a sympathetic voice. "Over here!"

On my face in the dirt, I turn my head and see a curly-haired grunt smiling broadly, his eyes twinkling in amused understanding.

"Come on, newbie!" he shouts above another explosion. "Let's get in out of the rain!" He laughs good-naturedly at my scrambling attempt to stand up.

Two more explosions.

Now I run hunched over, following the friendly grunt who disappears into a dark entrance hole. I tumble into the opening behind him, and for the first time breathe the foul air of an underground bunker—a mixture of dust, sweat, piss, shit, smoke, and unknown smells that make me gag.

Coughing, I glance around at the eyes staring back at me in mild curiosity. My platoon mates. My unknown comrades, all looking at me as they might a cockroach.

No introductions.

Then an ugly, gnarled grunt who appears fifty years old but in fact has only reached his early 20s, snarls through the fetid air.

"What'd you drag in, Nature?"

Nature smiles sweetly. "A lost lamb, Mountain Man. One of ours, just in a couple minutes ago. Thought I'd bring him by for tea and crumpets."

"Christ, Nature!" spits Mountain Man. "You say the most fucked-up bullshit."

Thudding explosions outside. Disturbed dirt raining down from the ceiling.

"Park your ass over there, newbie," growls Mountain Man. "And stay outta the way. Where's your gear?"

"Outside."

"Jesus H. Crist!" says another grunt under his breath.

I feel myself redden, but keep my mouth shut.

"Hey, at least he had sense enough to bring his weapon," says Nature kindly, casting a glance at my M-16.

"Good boy," says Mountain Man. "Now, go get your gear and come back home before it gets dark."

More explosions. I gulp. I now know who runs the platoon: an ugly gnome named Mountain Man who I later found out raised pigs in West Virginia before the war. Figures.

"Go on, shithead!" barks Mountain Man noticing my hesitation. "You'll need your gear."

I gulp again and run out, much to the amusement of the grunts in the bunker. These would be my brothers for the year to come—until they all died. God help me.

"Welcome back, newbie," growls Mountain Man when I dive back into the bunker with my gear.

"Not so new any longer," says Nature.

"Shiiitt," drawls Bowls who serves as Mountain Man's faithful shadow.

Nature smiles and looks at me sympathetically. "My friends here require further proof of your. . . . "

"Balls!" cries Bowls.

As befitted my status, I say nothing. At that point, I wasn't quite sure I had any myself. Dear Reader, as you know if you have travelled with me on this interminable trip, I do have balls, but the voices were (and are) intent on slicing them off.

But all this is neither here nor there. It is Nature's kindness, his compassion, which drew me to him. True, I felt a certain amount of jealousy at his self-confident generosity, but I bathed in its warmth, and I suckled nourishment from its gentle strength.

It is also true that I suffered some of my father's penchant for self-doubt and lack of confidence, but Nature always pulled me through, even in my most psychotic periods. Only Nature understood me. Only Nature understood my demon voices and ghostly apparitions. Only Nature understood he would die at that fortress. Even now, after he is long dead, he still understands, which is why he calls to me. Perhaps all the dead understand. Perhaps they have nothing else left to do.

~

"Understand what?" comes Emile Ruska's voice next to me.

"Oh, nothing, just talking to myself again." I must say, his question shocks me. I really must stop speaking my thoughts out loud. No wonder people are always reminded that I am some dissembling schizophrenic.

"Understand what?" Ruska repeats without changing his expression.

"Sorry?" I stammer.

"You mentioned Nature. What does he understand?"

I laugh nervously. "He understands he is dead."

"Hm," grunts a skeptical Ruska.

Dear Reader, I know what he is thinking; he is thinking I will soon be dead myself and join Nature. After all, that is what this trip is all about.

So be it. I am ready.

But first, certain arrangements must be made, specifically with Tuyet Mai. There is a loose end, a loose thread there, that needs to be addressed. Mark and My-duyen are already taken care of via my will and trust. Now all that remains is to put my own past in order.

How?

"How what?"

Damn! Oh, well, I will just tell him. "Now I have to put my own past in order, Emile."

"I see. Well, we are going to the right place for that."

"Yes, all roads lead back to Vietnam. Back to the tunnel. Back to my bones."

"Well," mused Ruska. "I don't understand any of it, but I am doing my part, although why I agreed to be here, I still don't know. Anyway, when you've put yourself together with your bones, well then . . . I guess the universe will be in order."

I smile. He is on my turf now. "Yes, I will be dead, at least to your senses, as well as the others who live in. . . . "

"The here and now?"

"Yes."

~

The plane lands. A blast of heat slams me, the same oven-breath of air as that first day. I step off onto the steep ramp . . . feel Ruska's arms enfold me as I fall while halfway down the ramp. The terrible heat, the terrible humidity, the smells, the smells . . . it all comes back, even the sweat of the distant jungle. It all comes back. . . .

~

"You fainted," says Ruska.

The hotel room is cold. Air conditioners in Asia are always hard at work holding off the stultifying heat. **They hum like imprisoned bees.** I wish I could speak with them, poor overworked machines.

Ruska stands over me like an archangel waiting to deliver a message from God . . . or Goddess.

"You fainted," he repeats.

"I know, but now I'm fine."

"Good, because tomorrow we travel to the district capital, and from there—"

"And from there to Song Nhan village," I finish for him. That name, that village, that past; it all returns.

"Correct," says Ruska.

I look at him queerly. "And then your task is complete. Relieved?"

He does not respond.

~

"I once read that Richard the Lion Heart punished a wayward soldier by trussing him to a corpse and burying them together. Such is my fate."

Fate starves at Probability's door!

Oh, yes, *You* again. Always *Your* harping. Does that mean I have a choice? What is the probability I will allow myself to be bound to Nature's corpse and tossed into the tunnel? Who will help me now?

"I will help you," says Ruska.

I am no longer surprised at the transparency of my thoughts. "How can you help me, Emile?" I ask.

"Tell me what you want. You are a free man. I am a detective, pledged to help those in distress. You are in distress. I will help you if I can."

"I am beyond help, Mr. Ruska."

"Then we leave tomorrow. Now, it is time for both of us to get some sleep."

"You do not know this country, Emile. Sleep is a luxury here."

"Why?"

"The war."

"The war is over."

"No, no, it is not." I point to my head. "It is never over."

"Then we leave at six o'clock tomorrow morning, come what may."

"I'll be ready." I see Nature standing behind Ruska, smiling, his tam o'shanter all a'tilt on his head, curly hair poking wildly out from under. He speaks but the words are inaudible, so I read his lips.

"What rhymes with corpse?"

I blurt out, "Horse!"

Nature shakes his ghostly head in mock disgust, and I suddenly feel somehow comforted. If I am to be tied to a corpse, might as well be this one.

"Fuckin' A!" shouts Nature at my thought, though his words are silent.

"You're talking to yourself again," says Ruska.

I look at him dismissively. "Like you said, time to sleep."

Ruska nods and heads toward the door. He walks right through Nature and abruptly stops.

"Problem?" I ask.

"A chill."

"Or something."

Ruska looks at me with a hard gaze. "Yeah, or something."

After he leaves, Nature remains. He stares at me long and hard, then says, "We'll soon be together, Storyteller, but damn, you sure look different now. Is that what I would look like if I had lived?"

"Ha! You mean old and grey?"

He smiles his sweet smile. "Well, sorta'. Anyway, you're not that old. What's it like?"

"What, being old?"

"No, having all those years to live life. To experience so many things. God, Storyteller! I could have written so many poems! Poems about women, getting old, getting drunk, meeting my wife, children, so much, so much...."

He fades slowly as appropriate for a melancholy ghost, the sharp features turning transparent until nothing remains but what had always been there: his memory.

A faint whooshing sound, like air escaping a jar.

"Soon, Nature. Soon."

~

It is next morning and I wait for Ruska in the lobby. Strange that he is late, for he is never late. My fertile mind searches for explanations, and the voices become restless. I can hear them rumbling, and my worry turns to real fear.

A voice keeps saying he is unconscious, he is poisoned, he has left, or he is dead. But, no, here he comes, rushing from the elevator.

"Sorry I'm late," he says. "Let's go! A car is waiting in the front."

Before I know it, we are sitting in the back seat, air conditioner futilely trying to keep us cool, but the heat and humidity have already penetrated every molecule of the atmosphere.

Engine overheats, driver rolls down windows, but the stifling hot air does nothing to ease the temperature, and we all wheeze our way along the dirt roads and pothole craters for interminable hours.

The countryside slides by in a surreal patchwork of rice fields and dust clouds.

Finally, the district capital draws near as night falls across the land. The driver takes us to a broken-down hotel with no air conditioning. Ruska argues and offers money, but the man pretends not to understand and insists this is the only place available.

Our night is spent trying to breathe, and neither of us get any sleep.

Truth be told, I cannot sleep anyway.

Tomorrow, we travel to Song Nhan village.

For me, the village has assumed mythical properties. It is another Troy waiting to be discovered by some obsessed archeologist, a beast full of ghosts and demons.

And in the belly of that beast waits the tunnel.

Chapter Fourteen

Song Nhan Village

Ghosts and Spirits

~ Arrival ~

Emile Ruska had every intention of delivering his companion to Song Nhan village and departing with as little delay as possible. The closer he remained to Mr. Powers, the more acutely his discomfort grew. This mission, for lack of a more precise term, left him increasingly uneasy, his nerves fraying with each passing mile. If he were honest with himself, it wasn't just unease, it was fear. A deep, creeping fear that intensified the longer he remained in Powers's presence.

He had overheard fragments—cryptic, half-guarded remarks from Mark and My-duyen Powers—about the strange occurrences tied to Song Nhan. Mark, despite having visited the village years earlier and meeting his future wife there, remained unusually reserved about the experience, as if the topic itself were too dense, too dangerous to touch. By contrast, My-duyen spoke more freely. She talked of ghosts, of spirits, of growing up in a place where the line between the living and the dead was not so clearly drawn.

During his own investigations, Emile had avoided any thread that might lead him to Song Nhan. He had either dismissed such leads as irrelevant, or worse, intuitively sensed they were significant but beyond reach. A trip to Vietnam, after all, wasn't part of the original budget. Still, he couldn't help but feel a pang of regret over the loss of Mr. Powers' writings. Dr. Hess had once told him they were astonishing: transcriptions of events not only as they unfolded, but seemingly as others experienced them. Powers had written down conversations, inner thoughts, as though eavesdropping directly inside people's minds.

Imagination? Delusion? Or had Powers truly possessed some extraordinary ability, something beyond schizophrenia? Before her death, Dr. Hess had even begun to suspect that his diagnosis had been wrong, that what afflicted Powers wasn't madness, but an unclassified phenomenon altogether.

Emile stole a glance at the man beside him, wedged stiffly in the narrow back seat. Powers's gaze remained fixed straight ahead, vacant and glassy, as though his consciousness floated somewhere far beyond the sweltering confines of the car. His face betrayed nothing, not thought, not emotion, not even presence.

Sweat beaded and dripped from Emile's brow. With a muttered curse, he wiped his face yet again with the damp rag that had long since given up trying to cool him. The air was thick, unmoving, oppressive. Hours dragged as both men endured the unrelenting heat and humidity, suspended in silence, each locked in his own private turmoil.

Finally, the car chugged up a freshly graded hill, and Ruska noted with pleasure that the dirt felt smoother than the pavement. At the top, the driver flashed a toothy grin and waved an arm. "We get out and look. Song Nhan village."

Dusk had begun to settle over the landscape, but there was enough light, now tinged red, to see what spread before them. Unknown to Ruska, this was the same rise from which My-duyen showed Mark Powers the panoramic view of the village so many years ago. He stepped out and gazed down at a scene that had materialized from a different era, as if ordered from central casting. Suddenly realizing Michael remained in the car, he leaned through the open door.

"Don't you want to see?" he asked.

Powers remained immobile, his face still registering a blank stare.

"Michael," said Ruska.

No response.

"Michael, Song Nhan village! Come and see."

The detective watched the blood drain from his companion's face, weariness and dread altering his features.

"Are you okay?" he instinctively asked.

Michael slowly turned his head and locked his eyes on the detective. "I'm ready," he said in a flat, emotionless voice. "Let's go. I don't need to see."

Ruska nodded to the driver, and they gingerly navigated down the narrow, zigzagging road to the village. Emile tried to keep the one distinctive landmark in view—an old, French-style villa. It towered on a hillside overlooking the village, a faded magic palace above the squalor. Unlike other villages they passed through, this one displayed few signs of life, as if the vitality and spirit of the place had been sucked dry. Ruska felt the same creeping panic he had felt outside the California cave. He wanted to shout to the driver to turn around and get back to the district capital as fast as the car could go, but before the words left his lips, an extraordinary building appeared before them in the fading light.

"The *dinh*," observed the driver in response to Ruska leaning forward for a better view.

"The local temple, Emile," said Michael Powers as casually as if he were a local guide.

"You're feeling better?" asked Ruska.

"I never felt better in my life," said Michael, evidently energized and surprised at Ruska's question. He gazed at the building like someone reminiscing about some pleasant memory, then spoke as if he were reading from a tour book. "You see, the *dinh* serves not only as a communal meeting hall, but also as the repository for imperial documents and the place where altars honoring the guardian spirit are housed. Over one hundred years old, the *dinh* of Song Nhan village was built in the traditional style of concrete and wood. You see the intricate stone friezes adorning the walls? And observe the elaborately carved dragon running the length of the roof. Beautiful, eh?"

"Indeed," replied Ruska, more impressed by Powers's words than by the temple, which to his eyes, looked a little the worse for wear.

"They are all dead," said Michael to the air. "Venerable Vu Huong, Han Tinh, Vo Thanh Tong, Schoolmistress Nang, Madame Dau, all of them, except. . . . "

"Tuyet Mai?"

"Yes, her. In fact, there she is."

"Where?" asked Ruska. "I don't see her."

Michael pointed out the window toward the villa. "There."

Even as he spoke, the driver turned up the lane leading to the entrance gate. A few scattered villagers brave enough to filter back to this accursed place stared, then went about their business.

"Hm!" grunted the driver. "I see some peasants have returned. You're lucky. There used to be no one here but the old crazy ones on the hill. Or maybe these peasants are themselves just spirits. They look the part." The driver stopped and opened the gate, drove through, then closed it behind him.

"I see you've been here before," said Ruska.

"Many times."

As they drove up to the front of the villa, a squat, legless figure with long grey hair swayed before them, backlit by the flickering porch light. Only then did Ruska realize she had no legs at all, just the steady sway of her torso above the porch boards.

"That's Nguyen Tuyet Mai," said Michael.

Ruska felt a jolt of excitement. Once Powers was delivered to her, his mission would be complete, and he could return home and recover some degree of normalcy.

~

Michael stepped out of the car and saw Tuyet Mai staring at him so intensely that he felt his knees go weak. Her hair whipped around in the strong breeze, and he heard the boards creak beneath her stumps, moaning under a weight that felt older than wood. She seemed a combination of witch and goddess, fairy and demon, a female Charon ready to ferry him across. He heard Ruska next to him whisper "Jesus Christ" at the sight of this remarkable woman.

"Welcome," came her strong voice. "I have been waiting, Michael Powers."

They stepped onto the porch.

"Thank you, Nguyen Tuyet Mai." Michael bowed. "I have come, just as you wanted. I understand they wait."

Not responding, she glanced at Ruska. "As an American, I am sure you do not understand of what we speak."

Michael gestured, "This is Detective Ruska."

Ruska bowed. "Nice to be here. I know more than you might guess. Buandelgereen filled me in."

"Ah, yes, the strong Mongol woman. Detective Ruska, you may spend the night here, then return to the district capital tomorrow. The driver has a place to stay in the village. Your task is fulfilled."

Ruska found himself at a loss for words. It felt as if he'd stumbled into a strange fairy tale, a peripheral character whose exit would go unnoticed. And yet, with Michael Powers no longer in his charge, a surprising lightness settled over him, as if an invisible burden had quietly slipped from his shoulders. For the first time in weeks, he allowed himself the luxury of aimlessness. He would linger for a while, he decided—sightseeing, wandering, soaking in the strange and vivid world around him without the constant weight of responsibility. After all, he had never been to Vietnam. Surely, it would make a good story to tell Emma someday.

Emma. And what, he wondered with a chuckle, would Tom White Thunder make of all this? From a haunted cave in the American desert to a crumbling French villa in communist Vietnam . . . and now to a tunnel suspended in some liminal space, waiting for what? For Michael Powers. For whatever came next.

For the first time, Ruska felt the gentle, insistent tug of conscience. A thought stirred, quiet but persistent: *Perhaps I should stay. See it through. Whatever "it" turns out to be.*

And so he stood, caught between the absurdity of it all and the faint stirrings of something like purpose.

~

Dear Reader, Emile Ruska is no different than the rest of us. Give us a menial job to be performed, universally accepted as minor but essential to the workings of a Great Project, and we want to stick around to watch it unfold in all its glory, knowing we had a small part in it to tell our grandchildren, whether loading toilet paper for the Normandy invasion or serving tea to Napoleon on the eve of Borodino.

~ *Nguyen Tuyet Mai* ~

Now that the Americans were here, Tuyet Mai thought perhaps the ghosts and demons would be quiet and let her die in peace. From her daughter My-duyen, she knew all about Michael Powers and the crazy belief that his bones lay in the tunnel. Few things in the world scared Tuyet Mai, but the old French fortress and its subterranean labyrinth full of restless spirits terrified her. Now, presumably from the battered urging of his mental illness, the older Teller of Stories would voluntarily descend into its depths, for good. Circles endlessly circling. As Tuyet Mai held the front door open for her guests, a dog darted in and sat. It was unfamiliar to her, and she started to shoo it out, but was interrupted by the piercing shout of Mr. Powers.

"Temulun!" he cried, rushing up to pet the dog. Michael abruptly stopped, remembered himself, and bowed to Tuyet Mai. "Sorry, I know this dog. I'll take her outside and be right back."

Tuyet Mai glanced toward the detective and turned her attention to watch Michael Powers fawn over the dog, talking to it as if it understood. She had observed this behavior from Americans before, and she assumed an expression of patient amusement. Upon closer inspection, the dog did not appear to bear any of the physical infirmities, scabs, mange, or infestations of local dogs, and her interest was piqued at the mysterious appearance of this canine.

"The dog can stay inside," said Tuyet Mai.

"Her name is Temulun," explained Michael Powers with childlike enthusiasm.

Tuyet Mai thought she understood. "Ah! You brought the dog."

"No, I've no clue how she got here. I assumed Buandelgereen brought her or sent her."

Tuyet Mai furrowed her brow. "No, she did not." She looked at Emile Ruska. "Mr. Ruska, do you know the dog?"

He shuddered. "I met her briefly in America. No idea how she got here. Strange."

"Yes, very strange." Tuyet Mai gazed at the dog. "There must be some explanation."

"I'll bet it was Buandelgereen," said Ruska. "Seems like something she would arrange."

"Yes, but how did it get here?" wondered Tuyet Mai aloud.

In response to the blank looks of her guests, she felt a premonition of danger. She quickly pushed it away, for she had long waited for this moment, when Teller of Stories, or Mr. Powers, would return and face his responsibility. The spirits continually harangued her to get him back, and Tuyet Mai had long given up her Marxist disdain for superstition. Han Tinh had worn her down about ghosts and demons. Now, she simply wanted to be free of them, free to die in peace. Nature could now redeem his claim on her conscience for killing him. He would be with his spiritual brother in that damn fortress. Nonetheless, something in this unexpected dog, something intangible but powerful, disturbed her and she anticipated unnatural disturbances.

As if understanding the dog's look, Michael opened the door and let her out.

"Come, I will show you the rooms," said Tuyet Mai.

"Your English is excellent, ah . . . . " Ruska said, groping for what to call her.

"Just call me Tuyet Mai," she said. "I detest the term 'Madame' as it brings back a distasteful colonial past. And to call me Nguyen Thi Tuyet Mai is a bit much for an American."

"Thank you, Tuyet Mai." Ruska nodded toward Michael, still seemingly involved in some intimate conversation with the dog. "He is like a child, isn't he?"

Tuyet Mai's jaw tightened. "Overgrown children are dangerous. Now, follow me please."

As she led them into the villa, Tuyet Mai could not help feeling strange hosting these Americans. On her own turf, with her NVA comrades from the American war mostly dead, she felt a sense of betrayal. *Odd*, she thought. *While in the United States, I had no problem being surrounded by them. But, here, on this ground . . . strange. Yes, strange. My own daughter married to one of them. To his son. To the man whose father I will now help to his grave. Strange, the world.*

After showing them their rooms, she suggested they meet in the dining room for tea.

~

While the three sat together, Michael sipped his tea and asked if anyone had seen the dog. When told no, he gazed out the window, then abruptly stood and excused himself. "I'll just see if I can find Temulun," he said.

He left and Tuyet Mai turned to Detective Ruska. "Were you in the war?" she asked casually.

"No, thank God."

"I doubt your God had anything to do with it."

"No, probably not. I was too young."

Tuyet Mai found herself intrigued by Ruska's background in detective work—it seemed, to her, not so far removed from the kind of intelligence operations she once carried out. The finer details of her years in the service had long since begun to blur, but the broader contours—the atmosphere, the stakes, the calculated seductions—remained etched in her memory. She often drifted back into those recollections, especially in moments of solitude, haunted by a wistful brooding for the past.

In those days, her beauty had been more than mere ornament—it had been weaponized, nearly invincible, deployed with precision against targets identified by Hanoi. Now, that same beauty had been ravaged, eroded by time, dismantled piece by piece. The memory of it lingered like a phantom ache, most keenly felt when she caught her reflection—whether by accident or design.

Yet for all the sorrow of lost youth, it was never the seduction itself that had brought her satisfaction. It was the thrill of success, the clean, sharp feeling of a mission completed. She had never lingered long on the consequences for those she manipulated. Years in the field had left her calloused, her conscience long ago blunted. Now, in old age, legless and tempered by a life lived on the edge, she had little patience for weakness—least of all the kind cloaked in sentimentality. Overt emotionalism struck her as both indulgent and inefficient, and she responded to it with the clipped irritation of someone who had seen too much to be moved by soft words.

In Emile Ruska, she recognized something familiar: a similar hardness, a similar refusal to sugarcoat or pretend. His candor, his bluntness—they did not offend her. On the contrary, they reassured her. In his company, she felt unexpectedly at ease.

"Do you like Mr. Powers?"

"Yes."

"Do you know what he intends after you leave?"

"I do."

"And does this mission appeal to you?"

Ruska gave her a hard stare. "And you?"

"We are both trapped in the web. Alternatives are few."

"Am I cooperating in this man's suicide?"

Tuyet Mai had to smile at that comment. "Do you have many suicides in America?"

"Quite a few."

"Why?"

"Don't know. Stress. Depression."

Tuyet Mai laughed. "In such a rich country!? I thought Americans get whatever they want whenever they want it, and always have enough food to eat. We Vietnamese have seen the worst the world has to offer—war, famine, disease, poverty—and we coil ourselves around life as tightly as a python, and never let it out of our grasp, if we can help it!"

"Well, I guess it's different in America."

"Must be. Do you try to stop them?"

"Who?"

"The suicides."

Ruska nodded, puzzled at this line of questioning. "Yes. It's part of my job."

"As a policeman?"

"Well, yes."

"But you're not stopping Mr. Powers?"

"No."

"Why? Isn't that part of your job?"

"Good question." He looked at her with a new appreciation. "You would make a good interrogator. How did you learn to speak such good English?"

She laughed. "Part of my job."

Emile knew better than to ask for clarification, but could not help asking, "So, what are you driving at, Tuyet Mai?"

"I am driving nowhere. There is no destination."

"Okay. What happens tomorrow?"

"You will leave, and he will stay."

Emile coughed. "I've been thinking of staying, if it is okay."

"Here?"

"If you don't mind."

"Why stay?"

"I don't know. A whim."

"A what?"

"Whim. It means a last-minute thought. Something unexpected."

"Oh, I understand. But, Mr. Ruska, your job is finished. I would have thought you would be anxious to return to your rich country."

"Not so much."

A pause fell over the conversation. Tuyet Mai gazed at him speculatively, her probing eyes making him feel uncomfortable.

"You are not married?" she asked, as if his answer would explain everything.

"No."

"So, you are curious to see what happens to Mr. Powers?"

"You could say that." Ruska now felt it incumbent to give ambiguous answers, as if he were really being interrogated for some unfathomable but potentially incriminating reason.

"Mr. Powers will not be here for long. He will soon be gone."

"You mean dead?"

"Not at all. No, no, not at all."

"Well, then. . . . "

But before he could get the words out, Michael walked into the room, clearly out of breath.

"Temulun needed exercise," he said in response to their stares. "Any tea left?"

Ruska took the plunge. He turned to Tuyet Mai. "When do you take him to the fortress?"

A deathly silence fell over the room.

"I know about the tunnel," Ruska said by way of explanation.

"Of course you know," said Tuyet Mai. "But that is not your concern."

Ruska nodded toward Michael. "He is my concern."

"No longer," said Tuyet Mai.

"Actually," said Michael with anger in his voice. "What happens to me is my own concern. Frankly, Emile, I want to go to the tunnel as soon as possible."

"Do you know what will happen to you there?" asked Ruska.

"Do you?" replied Michael.

"None of us do," said Tuyet Mai.

"I go down there alone, of my own volition," said Michael.

Tuyet Mai nodded, but Emile Ruska's detective impulses refused to give in so easily. "Perhaps I should accompany you?"

"No!" The voice that rang out from Michael was not that of Michael Powers. It reverberated through the room young and vibrant.

"Teller of Stories," whispered Tuyet Mai.

Emile Ruska moved back, astonished by the sudden change.

"Go home!" exclaimed Storyteller to Ruska. "You are no longer needed!"

Although, by all outward appearances, the face of older Michael Powers continued to stand before them, the very clothes he wore seemed to conform to the body of a very young man. His straight bearing and lean musculature stiffened the fabric as if it remembered who he had been.

~

Tuyet Mai, recovering her composure, said, "I see your malaria is gone, Teller of Stories."

"Yes. I am ready."

"Not now. Tomorrow."

"Why wait?"

"Goddess speaks, I obey."

"Then tomorrow it is."

"Good, it is settled," said Tuyet Mai.

"What is settled?" asked Michael, his old voice returned, apparently unaware of Storyteller's brief appearance.

"We leave for the fortress tomorrow."

"What time?"

"Early."

"What is early?"

Tuyet Mai chuckled. "Listen for the roosters."

"In that case, I'm going to bed."

Ruska nodded agreement. "Me too."

"You have not eaten," objected Tuyet Mai.

Both men begged off and retired to their respective rooms.

Tuyet Mai stayed up waiting for a sign.

None came.

Disappointed, she also retired, unaware Michael had slipped out of the villa a few minutes earlier to meet a certain dog.

~ *Morning* ~

Ruska woke late, roosters or no roosters. He rushed downstairs and found Tuyet Mai drinking tea.

"Mr. Powers still asleep?"

"Mr. Powers is gone."

"Already?"

"Apparently."

Ruska tried to pull his thoughts together. "Does he know the way?"

Tuyet Mai looked at him with an ironic smile. "He has a guide."

Ruska tried to reply, but the words would not come. He felt disoriented and deeply conflicted, feeling for the first time the full weight of what he had done. Somehow, he had not quite prepared himself for this act of finality.

"Your driver can take you back to the district capital this morning. Tea? Bun?"

She spoke as if nothing were amiss, which inexplicably angered Ruska.

"I should go there."

"Where?"

"The fortress."

"No. *She* does not want you. *He* does not want you."

Like a man waking from a bad dream, Ruska nodded through the fog. He suddenly felt he had failed; purpose gone, conscience sullied, character in question, powerless.

"Eat, Mr. Ruska, your driver is waiting."

Ruska had not seen the man since their arrival; he assumed the driver had his own arrangements in the village.

"I would still like to stay."

Tuyet Mai shrugged. "There is nothing here."

"I'll pay for my lodging."

"Mr. Ruska, please do not insult me."

"Then, may I stay?"

Tuyet Mai sighed. "If you must, but you must also promise not to go to the fortress."

"Don't even know how to get there."

"The government does not like foreigners nosing around these rural villages."

"I know."

"You are a stubborn man."

"Pot calling the kettle black."

"What?"

"You are a stubborn woman."

She glanced down at her stumps. "Have to be."

Ruska nodded, but secretly he began to form a plan to follow Powers to the fortress. He thought he could probably hire someone from the village as a guide.

He picked up a bun and took a bite, then said, "Well, I think I will at least play the tourist and take a look at your village."

"Nothing to see."

"Mr. Powers described the *dinh*. If you don't mind, I'll saunter down the hill and explore."

"Go ahead," said Tuyet Mai.

"I'll have another bun and some of that tea first, if I may?"

"Of course."

~

On his way to the *dinh*, Ruska passed through a gauntlet of curious stares from villagers who paused in their routines to study the foreigner in their midst. He had, in typical American fashion, assumed he would easily encounter someone who spoke English. But each time he asked, "Speak English?" he was met with little more than blank stares and gentle shakes of the head—responses that quickly humbled his expectations.

By the time he reached the *dinh*, a low, uneasy anticipation had settled over him. He stepped inside with caution, half-expecting to be scolded or chased off by an irate attendant. Instead, he was met with silence—and near-total darkness.

The space disoriented him at first, its dimness thick and immersive.

As his eyes adjusted, he flinched involuntarily beneath the fixed, penetrating gazes of the Guardian Spirit statues that lined the walls like sentinels. Cicadas rasped outside; inside, the air held the sharp tang of incense and old wood. The main chamber was cluttered with offering bowls and paper charms, crowding a dozen altars, each competing for sacred attention.

The weight of ritual and centuries pressed down on him, palpable, unfamiliar, and not entirely welcome.

"May I help you?" came a voice from the shadows. It sounded eerily familiar.

Chapter Fifteen

Homecoming

Canine Spirits

~ *A Boy and His Dog* ~

"Sure, you don't have any treats?" asks Temulun again.

She has led me to the jungle, and we are waiting for more light to continue our journey to the fortress. Can't move now, as night under triple-canopy is total; and dawn takes its own sweet time to adequately filter through the vegetation and illuminate the forest floor.

"Come on, Temulun, I know you are not really a dog! Why pretend and ask for treats all the time?"

"Don't blame me! I beg for treats just as often as God begs for worship."

"Ha! That's good! In my experience, all you deity types beg, cajole, and threaten like freelancing pimps keeping Your troublesome prostitutes in line."

"Hush!" Temulun pricks up her ears.

"What?"

"A tiger!"

Well, dear Reader, this makes me pause. I strain my ears, but hear only the usual buzzing, humming, groaning, wheezing, squealing of jungle inhabitants. Still, Temulun is a dog (no, she is more than a dog), and she would know.

"Should I be afraid, Goddess?" I whisper.

She growls. "Don't call me Goddess!"

"Why not?"

"It is degrading. I am a dog, and proud of it!"

"What about the tiger?"

"Gone."

"It's getting light."

"Your time draws near."

I am at a loss. I want to know if I am going to my death but am afraid to ask. Finally, I say, "Tell me, Temulun, dog to man, am I in an institution dreaming all this? I am sick, you know."

"If I say yes, will you believe me?"

I look around, soaked in sweat and inhaling the malodorous bowels of the jungle. "No."

"Got any treats?"

"Damn it, Temulun!"

Her tail wags in response. I swear she is laughing at me.

~

We sit for a while longer; the canopy allows in enough light to see the path.

"Come on!" cries Temulun.

But now I feel leeches on my legs. "Hold on," I say. "Let me pull these bloated suckers off."

"They're hungry, like me!" enthuses Temulun.

"Don't ask for treats," I grumble.

"Well, I can't suck blood like my friends here," she pouts as she sniffs at the squashed leeches.

"Okay, I'm ready," I say.

Temulun bounds away down the little trail.

"Hold on!" I cry. "Don't lose me!"

"You're already lost!" she barks back.

I stumble on, trying to keep up with her. Where are young Storyteller's muscles when I need them? Up steep hills and across racing streams we go, Temulun not even panting while I gulp air and am bathed in sweat.

"Are we almost there?" I gasp, sounding like a six-year-old from the back seat.

"There almost we are!" replies Temulun over her shoulder.

An inhuman, agonized wail rips through the trees. "Did you hear that screech, Temulun?"

She pauses; her tail stills, and her eyes, large and lustrous, shine with an intelligence as vast as the universe.

Be not afraid. The forest is full of noises; sounds and sweet airs that give delight and hurt not. Sometimes a thousand twanging instruments will hum about mine ears ... the voices! The voices!

Dear Reader, this freezes me in my tracks. Temulun's voice is not her own, nor is it God or Goddess, but a monstrous amalgam of both deities; a mongrel growl in perfect and mocking articulation; an unholy blending of the sacred and profane.

"Who are you?" I ask stupidly.

Got any treats?

I start to curse, but *She*, or *He*, or *They*, continue, ***Because, if you do, I'll perform a trick.***

"What trick?"

I'll tell you who I am.

"I have no treats."

Yes, you do. Every episode you consider psychotic is only sparkling fireworks exploding from the wild genes of a newly emerging species. Believe me, it is a treat to watch.

"Am I having a psychotic break now?"

Temulun's dog voice returns. "Come on! The fortress is just ahead!"

I stumble after her, numb, beyond shock, beyond the reach of fear or reason. The tunnel pulls at me with a strange inevitability, as though my very bones, glowing with their own alabaster incandescence, are being summoned into its dark, pulsing heart.

We emerge from the trees, and there it is: the fortress. A massive, brooding structure of stone, rising from the center of a rough clearing like some ancient beast crouched in wait. It looms, squat and impenetrable, its presence oppressive, undeniable.

Temulun moves ahead, trotting into the clearing with silent purpose. But I hesitate. My feet remain rooted at the forest's edge. In the stillness, I spot a stump, half-swallowed by moss and time, and I know **this is** the path Sapper Dam once walked, so many years ago.

Temulun pauses. She turns and looks back at me.

"Well?"

"I want to go back."

"Too late."

"I'm afraid."

"Of course. Now, follow me."

"No."

I do not know what is happening to me. I can feel Storyteller struggling to take over. I use every ounce of energy to keep him down, but I fear he will soon enough seize control.

"I must go back!" I cry.

I find myself hyperventilating. An urge to turn and run back to Song Nhan village becomes almost overwhelming. Dizzy. While my head is whirling, I take one step back and feel teeth nip at my leg.

"Temulun! Let go!"

I hear a low growl in response. Somehow, it brings me around. Perhaps it is the shock of the bite. In any case, I move toward the fortress like a sleepwalker, stumbling in front of Temulun, who periodically bares her teeth and snarls to make sure I continue on. My eyes are locked on the stone walls as they become larger and more massive the closer I get. I think of Sergeant Dam on his slow journey across the clearing that ended in the deaths (or should I say murders) of Mr. Machine and Bowls. My panic is gone. In its place seeps a cold, corpse-like deadness. In fact, I assume that by the time I reach the fortress I will be dead, a perfect state in which to enter the tunnel.

The massive wooden doors tilt in acknowledged defeat at the hands of time. A crack allows us to pass through into the courtyard. Goodbye, dear Reader, I can no longer hold back Storyteller. His irresistible force is annihilating my . . . my—"

~ Storyteller Risen ~

Michael Powers is gone. I am here. I feel strong. No malaria this time. I see my old spot and walk toward it with confidence. Decades ago, according to Michael Powers's time frame, I lay here, propped against the stone wall, fever wrecking my mind and body. No fever now. God knows, enough time has passed. No gunfire either . . . or explosions. Only the dead remain. And the wind. Always the wind. The dead are always quiet (almost always), but the wind never ceases, forever sighing memories across the stones. I look around the courtyard. Empty but for the scurrying leaves endlessly tossed into the fortress by a snatching wind. Unsurprisingly, Temulun is nowhere to be seen. Once again, I'm fuckin' alone. Every time I come above ground, I . . . oh, never mind. Unlike Michael, the words do not always come to me. The tunnel is my destination, and I carry him with me. No matter. He is not heavy. You see, Reader, I carry my future self the way you carry your past. To some of you, a three-hundred-pound gorilla, to others, a desiccated bird.

While ruminating on such thoughts, I have decided to sit in the same spot I inhabited during the siege when I was sick with malaria. I lean back against the same wall, for old times' sake.

"Why not?" I say to the wind.

I have all the time in the world, so I will call for the apparitions to come, the ones I used to see, or hallucinate, or whatever. Do I still have the touch? We'll see. I close my eyes and concentrate.

~

I sense their presence, their not-quite-human presence. Not two or three, but many. They stream through the walls of the fortress, their hearts and lungs pulsating as though they were human-shaped tadpoles. I recognize them.

The naked women self-absorbed, distracted, awkward.

The elderly couples placid, bored, irritable.

The children pouting, fighting, scheming.

The babies fussy, their mothers tired, short-tempered.

The wives and lovers curt, churlish, disgusted.

Only the boy with the backwards baseball cap remains the same.

Mark Powers, my future son, is changeless, moving his right hand aimlessly while staring stupidly at the invisible computer screen.

Ah yes, so familiar. They're all here, as always. The spirits return, hovering loyally around the soldiers whose bones long ago turned to dust, including mine. Yet still they come, summoned by memory, bound by grief. Some attachments, it seems, even death cannot sever.

Even Mountain Man's dog is here, trotting through the ether, though he too has crumbled into dust. And there, there she is: the bruised, naked woman, lingering in agony, her presence as jarring now as it ever was. If only Michael understood why I, why we, have brought him back.

Dear Reader, as he so affectionately names you, I'm not entirely sure you *want* to know. Perhaps it's better you don't.

But regardless, I find myself amused—watching these pale specters drift about like confused moths, flickering shadows of the dying and the dead. How many centuries' worth of Vietnamese and Chinese spirits haunt this place? And the animals, my God, the animals. A menagerie of forgotten lives from eras stacked atop one another like sediment. My sight, though sharpened by death, only catches certain frequencies, certain slivers of time. Others can see more. Michael can. I can.

That's the curse of being the Chosen One with schizophrenia: we see.

Our minds, fractured as they may be, are like compound eyes, kaleidoscopic, drenched in ultraviolet and infrared, sifting wavelengths others never know exist. We are tuned to the echoes. To the residue. To death, eternal and unmoving.

Memory, though, is another matter. It flutters. It withers. It fades.

All of it fades.

And yet, damn it, the shadows they leave behind, their tattered tabs of being, are sometimes almost as vivid as the memory of their flesh and blood.

It is almost time. The tunnel awaits. I feel Michael getting weaker.

"It's time to go."

"Hello, Nature. Time has come at last, eh?"

"Yes."

~

"Then take my hand," Nature says.

I don't see a hand, only the air brightening where one should be. The brightness presses into my palm like cool water. Together we cross the courtyard to the far wall, to a seam I never noticed before, a darkness within the dark. The stones smell of rain and old iron.

"Here," Nature says. "Say three names."

I hesitate. The courtyard waits. The leaves stop skittering.

"Diane," I say. "Mr. Machine. Bowls."

The seam listens. It is not enough.

"Say the living," Nature murmurs.

"Tamara," I whisper. "Mark. My-duyen."

A cold breath slips out of the wall. The seam softens, and the trapdoor lifts. Temulun pads from nowhere and sits at my left boot, eyes up, patient as a ferryman.

"What is the password?" the tunnel asks. It does not speak with a mouth. It speaks like a long-held thought arriving.

I remember the velvet voice in another life, a veldt, a lion, a dog who is not a dog. I remember a cell and a woman with no legs and a wind that never learns to stop. I put my mouth close to the seam and answer.

"Silence," I say. "The moment before mercy."

The dark opens just enough for a man and his ghosts to pass. A thin runnel of water from that ancient monsoon threads away into it, making a sound like someone sipping in a quiet room. Nature's brightness tightens around my fingers.

"Do not look back," he says. "You will remember wrongly."

Temulun rises and nudges my calf. Her tail does not wag. Her nose touches the stone, then my hand. I think she is asking for a treat, and I almost laugh, but there is no laughter left that belongs to me.

"Fate starves," Nature says, his voice small and steady. "But there is always a crumb at Probability's door."

Behind us, darkness follows.

Ahead, darkness awaits.

Chapter Sixteen

Where?

Aorta

The trapdoor settled above with a faint whoosh, like air escaping a jar.

Tin-cool air closed around the entrance chamber.

Nature's brightness slipped from my palm to my wrist and held there, a cool band.

Temulun dropped beside us and padded ahead.

~

Michael folded into the small place where the voices thinned. Storyteller took the body and the lead.

Inside him, Michael stayed small and watchful.

~ Storyteller Returns to the Bones ~

Storyteller followed the familiar iron tracks still dimly outlined by Mountain Man's bioluminescent leaves. He sensed Nature nearby but kept his eyes on the rusty rails, tracking a scent no nose could name toward the bones.

Michael continued to monitor their progress, a homunculus along for the ride, curled up in a tight ball, awaiting extinction or abortion. He knew the goal was near. In his mind's eye, the bones looked like bleached-white rebar, legs stretched out and the bony back propped upright against the tunnel wall like an articulated exhibit, waiting patiently for the flesh and blood it had sloughed off decades ago. It seemed to Michael, coiled inside his young soldier-self, that Storyteller's feet never struck solid ground, but continued in freefall. Michael saw them flying through a dark, winding tube as if on some impossibly fast amusement-park ride, twisting and turning around eerily spotlighted scenes. It was not walking so much as remembering at speed; the tunnel unspooled its map.

Starting from Michael's room at the mental institution, they flew down the clinical hallways, through Gail Hess's office door, into her bathroom, then accelerated down a long, dark freefall to Michael's house. With barely enough time to distinguish the illuminated dining room where the spirits so often appeared, they continued through his kitchen, past an iron door, then another, and another, and another, now racing madly under the dense jungle canopy, finally curling around the great wooden doors of the ruined fortress, across the debris-laden courtyard, through the ruined church, and down the entrance chamber where they had begun, at last landing on solid ground with a thud.

~

As the skeleton came into view, Michael saw the Great Warrior ensconced on top of the cranium, twitching her antennae in expectation. To his amazement, four unknown spirits stood, one pair on each side of the skeleton, waiting silently as guards might at a king's funeral. Storyteller and Nature seemed unperturbed, but Michael waited in confused anticipation. This development was not at all what he had expected. He wanted to ask Nature the identity of these spirits, but had no access to Storyteller's vocal cords, so could only wait and watch.

Each spirit evidently waited for something, or someone, to commence whatever mysterious process had been planned. Before being confronted with this surreal scene, Michael had envisioned his body quietly merging with the bones, his essence sinking into their marrow, permitted to fossilize in peace. Now, against all reason, he was assailed with yet another mystery. Mystery upon mystery. Must everything be a test of his sanity?

It is not your sanity that is being tested, came the voice of Goddess. ***It is the nascent powers you have yet to recognize and control.***

From his cocoon, Michael could make no response.

Storyteller moved over to a corner to speak with Nature, both carefully leaning their M16s against the tunnel wall.

"Well, here we are, together at last," said Storyteller.

Nature laughed. "Yeah, now that Humpty Dumpty has been made whole. How is our little egg in there?"

"He is quiet. When does this show get on the road?"

"Waiting for God."

Storyteller snickered. "*She* will drag *Him* here crying and screaming." Storyteller puffed himself up to look ridiculous. "Apocalypse! Apocalypse!"

"Goddess can handle *Him*. This Reunion should turn out better than the other one. At least I hope so."

"Don't worry, Michael is harmless. My M16 will remain quiet."

Nature shook his head. "No more killing. My dead heart still aches for Doctor Camara."

"And Doctor Hess."

"And Doctor Tavaris."

Storyteller tapped his forehead. "And Michael Powers. We are killers, you know?"

"Yes, but poets should not be killers."

"You say that now, but your best writing was done in a graveyard."

Nature grinned and pulled out his tam o'shanter. "Best place in the world to contemplate life. In fact, being dead is the best state to be in order to appreciate life."

Storyteller shook his head. "Fuckin' Nature. That makes no sense."

"Does life make sense? Look at these spirits waiting to argue whether pain or joy came first in the universe."

"I guess it matters to the deities," said Storyteller looking around. "Evolution sure as hell doesn't care."

"Yup. Did God or Goddess come first? Chicken or the egg."

"Well, if Goddess created the world, pain came first 'cause *She* must have had some badass labor pains."

Nature laughed. "Fuckin' A! God gets to just blink and the universe is created. Typical male creation myth. No pain."

"And no gain."

"Is pain gain?"

Storyteller grinned. "That's what we're here to find out."

"Is it?" asked Nature. "Must there be pain for there to be joy, or, as Goddess claims, has God added joy to make the pain even more exquisite? Poof! Add a dash of joy and His drug is made more potent, His addiction more desperate. As She has said, humans look at this question in a mirror and get it completely backwards."

"Quiet! Here *She* is!"

A blue light flashed through the tunnel, and *She* materialized in a blinding vision.

She levitated above the ground, sitting in the lotus position on a huge, dazzling white flower. *Her* sad, contemplative face gazed from beneath an elaborate crown glimmering a kaleidoscope of colors. A cinder-bright jewel embedded in *Her* forehead burned brightly and an intricate necklace lay cradled between *Her* bare breasts. *Her* left hand rested on *Her* thigh, the upturned curve of *Her* fingers resembling the albino legs of a gracefully dead spider. *Her* right hand poised in the air, index finger and thumb touching to form an almost perfect circle while the other fingers radiated outward. The spirits in the room oscillated in the ferocious glare of *Her* presence, distorting their features in the manner of a funhouse mirror. Inside Storyteller, Michael felt himself stretched and contracted as if powerful gravitational waves kneaded the entire tunnel, distorting space and time.

No one spoke for a long time, bedazzled by the intensity of *Her* presence. Finally, his tam o'shanter still tilted impishly on his head, Nature looked around and asked simply, "Where is God?"

Goddess gazed at him with luminous eyes, then turned *Her* attention to Storyteller, whereupon *Her* magnificent form collapsed into the body of a familiar woman; the same woman who visited his father John so long ago; the same woman who mesmerized his mother Meiying; the same woman who asked the question, "Mr. Powers, how does one justify a life without cruelty, and therefore also without the distilled beauty of cruelty?"

"It is *Her*!" shouted Michael from within Storyteller, who grimaced from the vehement outburst.

"Where is God?" repeated Nature, exercising his prerogative as a poet to question deities.

God is inside Me the same way Michael is inside Storyteller.

"Is *He* dying?" asked Nature.

He is drying.

Storyteller laughed. "You mean, drying out?"

Precisely. As you humans say, cold turkey.

"How did you manage it?" asked Nature.

Through a madman and a madman's son.

Michael thought of Tamara.

She spoke toward Storyteller. **No need to worry, Michael, she is fine, and your child, the next Chosen One, is safe and healthy.**

"Another madman added to the line?" asked Storyteller.

She will not be mad. She is the next step.

"She?" cried Michael from his cocoon.

Instead of responding, *She* burst forth into her Goddess form and commanded Nature and Storyteller to leave.

"Why?" protested Storyteller.

Goddess glared at him threateningly. **Nature will return to the land of shades, and you, Storyteller—because you carry a live person—will return to the surface and wait. God will witness these spirits undergo the twin extremes of joy and pain. We will resolve once and for all the paradox of whether one cannot exist without the other. You constitute a step in the direction of rejecting the need for unnecessary suffering. You represent a step toward the reign of Superior Ones.**

"But I want to watch!" cried Michael in a voiceless plea that only he and Goddess heard. In response, *She* merely glared imperiously and waved *Her* hand.

Storyteller and Nature dutifully retrieved their rifles and started back through the tunnel.

"Stop!" cried Michael. "Stop!"

But they could not hear him, and soon Nature faded away to nothingness. Storyteller grimly continued his march through the tunnel.

"Wait! I want to know!" But Michael's words fell on deaf ears. Behind, the weighty dialogue had started. He could hear the Great Wailing fill the tunnel, interspersed with spontaneous outpourings of joy.

From Holocaust to Happy.

Raging Cancer to Calm Contentment.

Searing Agony to Soothing Satisfaction.

Which dominated? Which was added *nunc pro tunc* to increase the potency of the other? And who added it?

~ *Back to Back* ~

Dear Reader, I know what you are thinking. It is simultaneous. Both arose at the same time. Could not some deity have teased out one from the other? Separated the Great Wailing from the Great Shining? Or was this impossible for God to achieve? Or Goddess, for that matter? If impossible, deities are not deities. If possible, deities are psychopaths. No, pain and joy were created in tandem at the Big Bang by a Faceless, Formless, Uncaring, Impersonal Universe. Goddess seeks to cure God of *His* addiction while God seeks to pursue *His* pleasure by demanding unquestioned adherence to a First Principle—suffering. Which is right? Fuck it. I command Storyteller to go back and turn his M16 on both. Do it! We can kill gods and goddesses; we cannot kill the universe. I write the command even as you read it. But Storyteller does not obey.

~

Alas, the Moving Finger writes, and having writ, has no effect on any of It.

Storyteller carried Michael (still protesting futilely) down the tunnel, up the entrance chamber, through the ruined church, across the debris-laden courtyard, slipped between the great wooden doors of the ruined fortress, raced under the dense jungle canopy, past an iron door, then another, and another, and another, continuing through Michael's kitchen, past his dining room, into Gail Hess's bathroom, through her office door, down the clinical hallways, finally arriving at their destination: a familiar room in the mental institution, where pajamas replace jungle fatigues, and old skin replaced young.

"It can't be this banal," Michael said to his slippered feet as he sat wearily on the edge of his bed.

Storyteller's youthful echoes could be heard emanating from the tunnel. He was laughing.

~ *May I Help You?* ~

Emile Ruska stood awkwardly in the *dinh*, staring wide-eyed at *Her*.
May I help you? *She* asked again.
"I'm not sure," he stammered.
It is time for you to return home. Michael Powers is already there.
"Where?"
Home.
"He's alive?"
In a manner of speaking.
"Am I dreaming?"
In a manner of speaking.
"But—"
Your driver waits outside to take you back.

Chapter Seventeen

BOOK II: SINGULARITY

Prologue

Dear Reader, I began this narrative by telling you I was dead. I don't blame you for assuming I meant it metaphorically. I did. And yet, in other ways, I am quite dead. What more is there to say?

Some of you have journeyed with me through the entire saga. Schizophrenia. Great Warrior Ant. Precious Object. Great Wailing. Bones in a tunnel. Mother and father in China. Me in Vietnam. Talking dogs. Talking sidewalks. God. Goddess. On and on. Are these delusions? Some? All? I'm not sure. But death is another matter entirely.

Who do you think is writing this? Storyteller? Michael? No one at all? Perhaps it is your delusion, to believe that the dead can write. So be it. Perhaps I wrote this before I died. Writers have long given voice to death. Nothing new there.

Whatever the case, we must examine certain matters together. We have already traveled far in the labyrinth of my mind. Let us go a little farther, a little deeper.

You might say that my death ends the voyage, that we've run aground on the shoals of the Great Unknown. What more could there be?

Only this: you too hover at the edge of your own Great Unknown, your own Event Horizon. And when you plunge into Singularity, a spectral version of you will remain poised at the edge, a memory kept alive in the minds of those still watching. Until they too fall into their own Singularity, and your image fades, little by little, to nothing.

But what is this matter we must examine? This: in the future, when I say I am dead, I mean I am half-dead. And for now, these words keep the other half alive.

~

There is a certain intimacy between a man and another man he has just killed. Paul Bäumer knew this in the shell hole with the Frenchman. It is an intimacy born of war's blunt savagery, not the tangled motives of murder. The man you kill in war claims nothing of your private life, unlike the man you murder, whose death may free you from a toxic marriage or grant you inheritance.

The man you kill in war might have been your friend, your brother, your teacher. I may have killed many men (who can say in that chaotic jungle thicket?) But one death I know is mine.

How did he die? Our species' morbid curiosity compels you to ask. A burst from my M16, aimed at a crouching figure. I remember his eyes—wide, terrified—beneath a pith helmet tangled in leaves. Those eyes haunt me still. Not the lifeless jelly smeared in flies I saw later, but those eyes *before*. And yet—were they lifeless? Were they unseeing?

I pushed him past the Event Horizon into Singularity, where we now both reside. In Singularity, the laws of physics no longer hold. So, too, the laws of memory, perception, death. Since I am metaphorically dead and writing these words, I assure you: he knows now we share the same darkness.

Just as all humans are schizophrenic, carrying within them the voices of their own madness, so too are they all dead, carrying within them the knowledge of their inevitable end. Our uniqueness lies not in brilliance but in pathology. So our gods and goddesses are likewise insane.

Yes, yes, you say—we've heard all this before. So what must we examine?

This: why do we repress the one certainty, death, and cling to what is unknowable: the next moment, the next breath? I used to say Fate starves at Probability's door. Lately, I suspect the opposite: Probability starves at Fate's.

Is it likely the Superior Ones will inherit the Earth?

Or is it simply fated?

Chapter Eighteen

Another Beginning

Tipping Point

~ Awakening ~

When Michael last experienced being alive, he sat on the edge of his bed in the mental institution, staring at his slippers and listening to Storyteller laugh. He pictured his father lying on his back, dying, an ant scurrying about in the palm of his upraised hand. He remembered the day he learned his wife had died in a car accident. Then the image of his mother, Meiying, came to his mind. She had died when he was too young to remember, yet he remembered. And his comrades. All his comrades, dead outside that fortress.

Once, when Storyteller still existed as Storyteller, he sat with his comrades on the veranda of the Grand Hotel in Vung Tau during a short leave, laughing at some stupid joke by Stretch. The clap he had gotten while sleeping with a prostitute the night before had not yet announced itself. Behind the laughter, Storyteller knew they would all soon be back in the jungle facing death. He remembered comrades who had already died and the enemies they had already killed. At that time his body was devoted to living.

No, these are not the two poles of youth and age, or life and death. Not at all. These are the two poles of instinct and reflection.

~

Mountain Man strode onto the veranda and passed by his fellow grunts without pausing.

"Fuckin' asshole, Mountain Man! Why don't you join us? Have some coffee and shoot the breeze," called Stretch.

"Naw, you girls look like you got a nice little tea party goin'. I'm gonna sit over here and think."

He crossed the veranda and sat at an unoccupied corner table, soon joined by his faithful shadow, Bowls.

"Come on, man!" cried Stretch.

"Let him be," said Nature. "Just look out at that beautiful ocean."

The South China Sea glittered in the morning sun, blinding in its display of dancing light and water. Along a path near the shore, young girls walked by in their formal *ao dais* on their way to school, their peasant hats tilted back, black hair flowing, teeth bared in laughter, bantering with each other, and paying no attention to the G.I.s that watched them pass. The whiteness of their *ao dais* flashed in stark contrast to the deep azure blue of the sea that formed such a gorgeous backdrop to the slender movement of their bodies.

"Ocean?" said Stretch. "What, are you fuckin' crazy. With them girls parading up and down? Ocean?"

Superman chided his friend. "Stretch, my misguided friend, Nature is right. It is the ocean that reflects God's glory, not your perverted mind."

Nature smiled, his tam o'shanter a brightly colored Irish tartan glowing in the morning sun, contrasting gaily with the drab jungle fatigues that clothed all of them. "Ah, give him a break, Superman. He doesn't know any better, and he's got that earthy stink of the world's fleshpots to make him interesting to a poet like me."

"Hey, musk attracts women, right Nature?"

"Yeah, some of them."

Stretch raised his glass of orange juice. "There you go! Just don't stop 'em when they drag me away." His head jerked in a series of tics that everyone ignored.

"Christ, Stretch, you're *beaucoup dinky dau*," said Superman, circling his finger at the side of his head.

"Hey, Storyteller, what ya'll doin'?" asked X pulling up a chair at the table.

Storyteller's attention was fixed on the top of the wooden table. He did not respond.

"Storyteller!" barked Nature. "Come on back from wherever you are and join us."

"Oh, just reading what's been scratched into this wood."

"Just a bunch of fuckin' names of fuckin' horny grunts."

"And lonely," added Superman.

"And scared," added Nature. "Unimaginative, if you asked me. If you're going to carve something in a table, make it more interesting than your name and the date you were in the 'Nam."

"Quite the contrary," said Storyteller. "They tell me a lot."

"Quite the contrary," mimicked Stretch. "Fancy dandy talk, Storyteller. Your brain's waterlogged with words. What's so fuckin' interesting about some poor sons of bitches names?"

"We name everything, Stretch. Without a name, it doesn't really exist."

"True," said Superman. "That's one of the first things Adam did when God created him."

"What?" asked Nature.

"Give things names."

"Yes," said Storyteller. He seemed to say these words from far away, his mind still dwelling on the ghostly names carved in the wood. "How many of these guys are still alive?"

"Who the fuck knows?"

"They left something of themselves here. In their own way, they were writers, biographers, chronicling their lives. Yeah, writers."

"Great," said X. "Their bones are rotting out in the bush, but here's their names, written on some gook table. What's the point?"

"Everybody wants to leave something of themselves when they depart this sorry planet," said Nature.

"Yeah, my jism in some pussy. That's what I want to leave."

"Funny thing is, Stretch," observed Nature. "That might be the most permanent alphabet of all—DNA. You'll definitely leave something of yourself here; a baby Stretch."

"What do you call a baby Stretch?" asked X.

"A grope?" suggested Nature.

"A tug?" said Superman.

"A snatch?" added X.

"Yeah, Stretch and his son Snatch. Stretch and Snatch. Perfect!" cried Mountain Man, walking up to the table. "Couldn't help hearing you fuckers. What a sorry group of pussies. My Blue Tick Hounds are smarter than all of you combined."

"Hold on a minute, guys!" exclaimed Nature. "Storyteller is carving something. Maybe it'll be more interesting than his name."

The group gathered around and watched Storyteller carve the wood. When he finished, it read: "Michael Powers, schizophrenic."

"Who's Michael Powers?" asked X.

"Him, idiot," replied Mountain Man gazing in wonder at the words. "Man, that fuckin' explains a lot. Hey, Storyteller, what are your voices saying now?"

Storyteller looked at them as in a trance. "They're telling me you are all dead."

Amidst the cacophony of protests, he noticed a beautiful Vietnamese woman staring at him from a nearby table, her legs crossed, an enigmatic expression on her face, mouthing words that he heard in his head as, "And so are you."

~

Now, with the crystal-clear view provided by death, I look back through the foggy window of the living, and I realize this was my first introduction to the famous (or infamous) *She* or *Her* who was the object of my parents' epic quest. At the time, of course, I did not know this stunning Vietnamese woman sitting before me was *Her*. Furthermore, though I had suffered from schizophrenia during my childhood, it constituted a relatively mild form. Only upon meeting *Her* did the severity of my psychoses exponentially worsen.

~

"Storyteller, what a thing to say!" exclaimed Superman.

Stretch broke in. "What my religious friend means to say, Storyteller, is what a truly fucked up thing to say. A fuckin' lousy joke if you asked me."

"Nobody is asking you," said Mountain Man. "He means it."

Nature took Storyteller by the arm. "What does it mean, Storyteller?"

Storyteller appeared distracted; his eyes locked on the woman with the crossed legs.

"Storyteller?" repeated Nature. He followed his friend's eyes. "Oh, now I see."

"Not what you think, Nature," said Storyteller. "You asked me what it means?"

"Yeah."

"That lady over there has the answer."

"Well, go ask her what it means," prodded Stretch. "Jesus, Storyteller, with all your brains, you're fuckin' slow."

Storyteller simply nodded and walked toward *Her*.

"And ask her what she's doing tonight!" cried Stretch, eyes rolling and tics jerking his head sideways to his shoulder fast and furious.

With the laughter fading behind, Storyteller approached *Her* warily. *She* never took *Her* eyes from him, and when he stood close with his arms limp at his side, *She* raised *Her* hands palms up and nodded for him to sit.

He did.

"Have you visited the Thich Ca Phật Đàī monastery yet?" *She* asked, using *Her* melodic human voice.

"No."

Without another word, and never looking back, *She* gracefully rose and seemed to float down the steps of the veranda to the street below. Storyteller followed. He did not hear the catcalls raining down from his comrades (with two notable exceptions: Nature and Mountain Man). Following a few paces behind (it never entered his head to walk next to her) the two figures traversed a maze of streets and alleys and began their ascent up the hill to the monastery. High above, Storyteller could just make out a massive white statue of Buddha reclining in all his splendor. It was well-known during this period of the war that the Viet Cong and NVA also stayed at Vung Tau for their own rest and relaxation—they just did not wear their uniforms. Woe be to an American G.I. who wandered into their territory, designated by an agreed-upon imaginary line drawn down the center of the town. Stray into the wrong side, and many a soldier's dead body had been thrown back onto the correct side. With this in mind, Storyteller's senses were on full alert, exquisitely sensitive to the mysterious emanations from *Her*, and, at the same time, alive to the very real peril of his own situation. His eyes scanned the surroundings, the sacred image of Buddha stretching benignly above him, while the sordid, hedonistic town of Vung Tau spread below.

Storyteller, and later Michael, had the habit of looking at themselves move in space as if observing through the lens of a camera floating overhead. This propensity to objectify existence operated as a double-edged sword. On the one hand, such a view magnified the absurdly mundane experiences of daily life, making existence feel quite boring. On the other hand, during wartime, it served to alert one to the unseen threats of lurking calamities. With this camera's-eye-view, Storyteller watched himself follow *her* up narrow paths, impinged upon from all sides by a thicket of luxurious vegetation, where at any moment he might be dragged and his throat slit. When in this mode, Storyteller felt completely alive to existential danger, while in the same mode during peacetime, his older self felt exasperated by the routine boredom and inane necessity of enduring endless, repetitive days at work and home. Only the voices and delusions made him feel more alive than dead.

She moved effortlessly upward, even as Storyteller sweated profusely from the exertion. As the outer walls of the monastery came into view, *She* passed through without a pause, and headed straight for a small building, ornately decorated, with a few steps leading to an underground anteroom. As Storyteller followed *Her* descent into the room, they were passed by a monk going up, smiling and whispering Vietnamese to a caterpillar curling skyward on his index finger. Oddly, thought Storyteller, the monk did not seem to notice *Her*, but he looked cordially at the young American in combat fatigues, his countenance still displaying a beneficent grin.

Once in the room, *She* sat in a simple chair, crossed *Her* legs, and motioned Storyteller to sit nearby.

"I knew your parents," *She* said. "They are also dead."

Strange as it seemed to Storyteller, *Her* statement did not outrage him. In fact, he made a hasty assumption.

"Either I'm hallucinating, or *You're* just a dream. In either case, I'll play along. How do *You* know my parents?"

"They were chosen."

"For what?"

"To give birth to you."

The floating camera told Storyteller this interview was becoming too strange, and he looked a fool talking to a hallucination. Any time, a monk could walk in and see him talking to the air, or his comrades could have secretly followed him and now must consider him positively mad. It was time to wake up.

He tried.

He failed.

She watched him try.

She watched him fail.

"You cannot get rid of voices that easily. You were to be the son. You were to accomplish certain things. It did not happen. Now, you are dead."

"What do you want?"

"When you are older, when you are again known as Michael Powers, you will go to him and bring him back."

"Go to who?"

"Michael Powers."

Storyteller found himself laughing at this absurdity. "I am Michael Powers. He is me and I am him. How do I go to myself?"

"No. There will be a split. In your future, Michael Powers will believe you are his twin."

"Then I really will go crazy?"

She smiled in a manner that communicated certainty. "You are schizophrenic, Storyteller. To others, you already are crazy."

"Look, whoever *You* are, I need to wake up from this dream and get back to Vung Tau, to my hotel, to my friends. We only have a little time left before we go back to the bush. I have to go back!"

"Or?"

Storyteller hated overdramatizing things that most certainly had a logical explanation, so he simply said, "Or something bad might happen."

"Such as?"

"I don't know. Things. *You* tell me since *You* are the all-knowing hallucination. After all, *You* said *Yourself* that Michael Powers—me—is the Chosen One. What does that mean anyway?"

"I am here."

"To do what? Protect me? Have me murdered?"

"To protect you."

"To protect me from what?"

"Yourself."

"And?"

"And to go to him in the future. He will have dinner parties."

Storyteller scoffed. "Dinner parties! I have no idea what *You're* talking about. In fact, this whole conversation is crazy. *You* want me to go to his . . . or, I mean, my own dinner parties?"

"Yes."

"And just how do I manage that? Close my eyes and fly from the jungle to the future and sit down to have dinner with my future self?"

"Precisely. Except it will be by means of a tunnel."

"A tunnel?"

"Yes."

"But you told me I am dead."

"So you are."

"We're going in circles."

"What do you expect from the universe?"

~

Dear Reader, this is the first time I, as Storyteller, had heard of a tunnel. That experience would come soon enough in my young soldier's future. Little did I know what that tunnel would come to symbolize. All I knew was that my civilized, cognitive mind was failing, as I had always feared when first hearing the voices as a child. Since being in war, I slowly concluded that, for the first time, I was truly alive. I had given myself over to a primitive, instinctive mind. This paradoxical condition seemed to my young brain what it must be like to be a lion. During the hunt, all senses exquisitely tuned to every molecule of the surroundings, aware of the softest sounds, the breeze, the waving grass, the snorts of the prey, the scent, the very air filled with expectation and danger. On the other hand, afterwards, with belly full and stretched out on the veldt, sun warming the body, the great beast becomes placid, lazy, impervious to the splendors of the world other than enervating satiety, and irritable at the slightest interruption of such slothful passing of time. Some will object to this characterization of what constitutes "living". They will argue that living is most satisfying and meaningful during times of peace and contentment, when one's thoughts turn to the abstract, the intellectual. It is why one must suffer, the more to appreciate these moments of grace. There is some truth in this, unless one understands the optics of a mirror, wherein the image is not reversed but inverted front to back. Which is a correct representation of reality? Schizophrenia had inverted my sense of self, forcing me to look at myself front to back. The voices flung back at me an alternate view of so-called reality, which coincided with the puzzlement of "normal people" and their rejection (or fear) of that they do not understand. In other words, I was turned inside-out.

However, dear Reader, I am aware that this path, this definition of "living", carries with it the seed of annihilation —for it leads to murder or madness, and madness's diseased whore, suicide.

~ *A Returning* ~

Storyteller closed his eyes to stop the universe from spinning in the circles *She* just alluded to. Dizzy. The incense filling the room filled his nostrils, perfuming his thoughts and rendering them alien to his Western, rational mind. Soon, he felt oppressed and choking from the powerful scent, so he opened his eyes to find a way out of the now-claustrophobic room and into the familiar, open air. *She* was gone. The room was empty. He stood to leave, but the monk who had passed him with the caterpillar returned, still smiling, and sat in the chair *She* had occupied.

"Hello," said Storyteller, feeling out-of-place and stupid.

The monk nodded, apparently not understanding English.

Storyteller wanted to leave, to escape, but he seemed rooted to the chair, staring at this smiling monk, and knowing no better than to smile back. Suddenly, the monk jumped up, still smiling, and rushed to the far wall, where he gently scooped up a spider, speaking words to it Storyteller did not understand. Then, with his saffron robes flowing, he carried it out the door and up the steps to set it free, never once losing his compassionate smile. This unexpected development broke the spell ; Storyteller followed him out. As the monk turned left to place the spider on the ground, Storyteller turned right and descended the long path back to Vung Tau. When he made it to the hotel veranda by late afternoon, only Nature remained, waiting patiently.

From a distance, Storyteller spotted his friend's tam o'shanter and its colorful tartan blazing in the oblique rays of the sun. This vision filled his heart with a sense of relief and love. Barely restraining himself, Storyteller half-ran up the steps to sit next to a smiling Nature, his eyebrows uplifted in anticipation.

Hot and sweaty from his trip, Storyteller ordered a beer and noodles, then sat back with a contented sigh. Nature, patiently watching, could stand it no longer.

"Well?"

"Well, what?"

Nature removed his tam o'shanter and ruffled his hair. "Not gonna play that game, Storyteller. Poets are patient folk. You'll tell me when you're ready." He took a sip of his tea and doggedly sat back with hands folded across his belly, yawning to punctuate his determination.

"When you're ready."

Beer and noodles now set before him, Storyteller took a long swig and turned serious. "All I can say, Nature, is that I am glad as hell I'm sitting here with you."

"Okay, good start. Now, keep talkin'."

"That woman is. . . . "

A long silence ensued.

"Like I said," groused Nature. "Poets are patient . . . but my patience is running thin. What about her, Storyteller?"

Storyteller shook his head. "I don't think *She's* human."

"What does that mean?"

"It means exactly what I said. *She's* not human."

"What is she?"

"I don't know."

"Is this some of that schizophrenic shit? Come on, Storyteller, give me more to go on."

"*She* speaks in riddles."

"Hell, women always speak in riddles. When my girlfriend is pissed at me, and I ask her why, she says, 'If you don't know, I'm not going to tell you.' I mean, riddles, man."

"No, no, no. It's not that kind of riddle."

"What kind is it?"

"More philosophical: the universe turns in circles; we all start again at the end back to the beginning."

"Wow, my kind of chick. Sounds like she's got a brain."

"No, no, it's much more than that . . . oh, fuck it, Nature! I don't wanna talk about it."

"Why not? It's just getting interesting."

Storyteller took another long swig of his beer and used his chopsticks to shovel in the small bowl of noodles. "Ahh, that was good. Look, Nature, I want to put all that behind me." He grabbed Nature's arm and squeezed. "You're real. The guys are real. The damn NVA and Viet Cong are real. In fact, I'd rather deal with real people trying to kill me than with ghosts and phantoms trying to drive me mad!"

"And voices?"

"Yeah."

"Personally," said Nature airily. "I'd rather not deal with reality. It's too . . . real. Edges too sharp. Too much in focus. I like blurred edges, like, well, you know . . . through a glass darkly and all that shit."

"Trade you," exclaimed Storyteller. "You take on my schizophrenia and I'll take your concrete reality."

"Don't need your schizophrenia, Storyteller. I already hear voices. I'm a poet, remember?"

Storyteller scoffed, "You never let me forget!"

Nature leaned forward. "Tell me about that lady," he pressed. "She intrigues me."

"I can't."

"Why not? Come on, Storyteller, it's me—Nature. Talk to me."

"Can't. Not because I don't want to, but I just can't."

"This lady must be something."

"I already told you, *She's* not human. I mean, *She's* made me come face to face with my . . . mental issues."

Nature's face assumed a melancholy, grim countenance. "When we're back in the bush, Storyteller, you can't let this shit take hold. We all depend on each other. I depend on you to be there when the shit hits the fan. That's fuckin' reality, and not even me can ignore it. I mean, if you can't face reality, you're dangerous out there."

~

This is when I realized how much anger I felt toward my father, who allowed his demons to separate him from those he loved. I was real, you know, not one of his ghosts. In fact, I still cannot think of Little Acorn without gritting my teeth and feeling a tightness in my stomach. Of course, being metaphorically dead and cremated, I have no teeth or stomach. Just think of it as Phantom-body Syndrome. His excuse, and mine, is that we were not fully human. Anyway, at that moment, sitting with Nature, I vowed not to let the voices have their way with me.

As you have read, dear Reader, I failed. I failed miserably.

~

That night, Storyteller and his comrades went carousing with the avowed purpose of getting drunk and telling the world to fuck off. First stop: Spring Flowers Bar. When they entered, rock music blared and a host of loud, sweaty American G.I.s and Aussie soldiers milled around crowded tables, prostitutes swirling about like gaudy butterflies. Smoke undulated in suffocating layers, and through the haze, Storyteller spied the bar, not an opening in sight.

"Hey, numba one G.I.—you want numba one cunt?"

The voice, shrill and mocking, came from a tiny prostitute in a short, Western dress that clung like desperation. Around him, his friends melted into whatever shadowed recesses were still unclaimed, but Storyteller stood motionless, caught in the girl's assessing gaze. Her eyes, bright with cynicism, traveled over him like a challenge.

"Gimme a drink, G.I.? Okay?" she pressed, her voice high and metallic, impatient with his silence.

Images from the floating camera in his mind began to reel: the sordid flicker of neon against worn skin, the hollow ritual of exchange, his own vacant stare reflecting back at him in the girl's glinting pupils. He wanted to shut the lens—drown it in beer, jam the gears, blind it with spit and rage—anything to sever the awful clarity of it all. If only he could regain anonymity, he could get drunk, forget himself, and take her to bed.

But the camera lingered.

It recorded the contempt in her eyes, the weary sway of her body, polluted by too many nights like this one. He turned away, brushing past her, and through the rising smoke caught a glimpse of Nature's eyes. Were they watching him? Judging him? Pitying him?

From another alley, a voice slips through the smoke—same pitch, worn even thinner.

"Numba one cunt, G.I. You want? Gimme a drink, okay?"

Same words. Different girl. But this one carried a different weight—there was a plaintive weariness in her tone, a hopeless melancholy behind the crude refrain.

And the camera captured everything. The cheapness. The rot. The profound hollowness of it all. In his mind's eye, Storyteller watched himself—more lost, more pathetic than anyone in the scene.

And still he stood there. Like a fool.

"Here," said Nature, appearing at his side and holding out a drink. "Looks like you need it."

"I need to be out of this place and get some air," mumbled Storyteller.

The melancholy prostitute sized up Nature, then nodded toward Storyteller. "Him no good. You look like good, horny G.I., not like him. Put your numba one cock in my numba one cunt? Cheap."

Nature smiled at her as if she were the Madonna.

"Buy me drink, G.I. boy?" she said mechanically.

"Let's get out of here," said Storyteller.

"You go, I want to stay with her for a while."

Storyteller looked at her and shook his head. "You've got to be kidding."

"Poets see things others do not. I see in her the glint of martyrdom. She's probably a good village girl with a baby trying to survive."

"Where's the baby?"

"Parked with grandma."

"God, Nature, you're a fuckin' incurable fuckin' romantic," said Storyteller, heading for the door, his drink still in hand.

"You said it, brother."

Outside, Storyteller breathed deeply and leaned against a utility pole, sipping his warm drink and wondering at his ill-fitting place in the world.

When the time is right, you will go to him, came the voice in his head. *Her* voice. Goddess's voice.

"Yeah, yeah, I know," he mumbled. "The tunnel, right?"

Yes. Do not forget.

"I won't forget."

"Won't forget what?" Nature stood beside him.

"Nothing. I thought you were with your 'numba one cunt'."

"She has my room number at the Grand. This is the last night in Vung Tau, you know, and I'm tired of the whores our hotel Mama-san keeps sending me. This one is different."

"How? She seems depressingly the same to me."

"You're not a poet."

"Jesus Christ, Nature! Knock off the poet crap, all right? Maybe I'm a writer, and maybe you're a poet, but goddammit, we're both grunts who in the next few days will be out in the bush getting our heads shot off. NVA don't give a crap you're a poet."

"Do they care you're a writer?"

Storyteller laughed. "Of course! Writers are more important than poets. I can make them famous."

"By writing a novel?"

"No, by writing a famous novel."

"Now who's throwing the shit around?"

Storyteller took a gulp of his drink. "Seriously, how is this one different?"

"You know I'm Catholic, right?" asked Nature.

"Yeah. So?"

"She's just like Mary Magdalene."

"Shit, Nature, they're all like Mary Magdalene, to you anyway."

"How many times do I have to tell you, Mary Magdalene was not a prostitute. That's an old wives' tale. However, I like to think she was a prostitute. Makes her redemption that much more . . . redemptive."

"And you plan to redeem this one?"

"Yeah."

"Didn't work well for Mountain Man, did it?"

"Well—"

"When his prostitute, his fiancée, was murdered by the VC, he sought redemption by killing."

"That is Mountain Man. He's not a poet."

"He's a killer."

"So are we all, Storyteller. So are we all."

Storyteller trembled. "Don't remind me, Nature. We go back tomorrow."

"Well, let me ask you this," said Nature. "Would you rather be back in the bush, or would you rather be in her bush?"

Storyteller snickered.

"No, I'm serious. You have only one choice, fuck her or go back to the bush. Which would it be?"

"Fuck her."

"You're no killer."

"Neither are you."

"Then, my dear Watson," said Nature. "Why are we here? Don't tell me we were drafted. We could have found a way not to be here. Instead, here we are on a matter of supreme importance—killing people, and a matter of supreme indifference—fucking prostitutes. What if we make fucking prostitutes more important than killing people? What then?"

"Then the world will be full of bastards."

"Exactly!" exclaimed Nature. "That's just it! The world is already full of bastards. Legitimate bastards! The children of girls forced to prostitute themselves like her will be anti-bastards. Anti-bastards will be the reminders to bastards that they are the only true bastards. Anti-bastards will be the antidote the world needs to rid itself of bastards. You understand what I mean?"

"Hell no. Not a word."

"Neither do I, but there is something there anyway. The poet speaks, the writer interprets. So, interpret, Storyteller."

Before Storyteller could answer, Stretch stumbled out of the bar and vomited in the gutter.

Nature and Storyteller said not a word, and watched him weave his way back inside, shouting something incoherent about W.C. Fields. Before they could resume their conversation, Mountain Man came out and walked up to them.

"This goddamn waiting around until we get back in the bush is fuckin' bullshit. Time's passing and NVA cocksuckers are running around out there without proper restraint. Poor bastards don't know Mountain Man is soon coming to get his paws on 'em." He held up his hands and flexed his fingers. "Time away from killing is killing time. I'm going back to the fuckin' hotel and sleep. You assholes should also get some rest. Won't be able to get it out there." He peered into the night and sniffed as might an alert dog anxious to investigate a strange smell. Storyteller had a vision from his floating camera of a leashed Mountain Man's straining to be let loose, feverish to tear the throat out of some perceived prey. As if to validate this image, Mountain Man walked quickly away, leaning into the night and pulling at his leash.

"I'm going back too," said Nature. "My Mary Magdalene will be getting off soon. Coming?"

Storyteller swirled the remaining liquor in his glass. "Not yet."

"Ah so! You have your own Mary Magdalene waiting?"

Storyteller shook his head sadly. "Only up here," he tapped his temple. "Only up here."

Storyteller watched Nature disappear into the darkness. Unwilling to leave the comfort of his pole, he crouched down against it and observed the comings and goings at the bar, its interior lit up by flashing red strobes. *Always the observer,* he thought sadly. He stayed like that for a long time, counting silhouettes of the edgy soldiers stumbling in and out until he lost track. When the bar finally closed, a familiar girl came out and briefly passed under a dim streetlight, her face clearly distinguishable. Yes, it was Nature's Mary Magdalene. She appeared tired but walked briskly down the street. Storyteller followed. He could not say why. Perhaps he was simply curious about whether she would indeed go to the Grand Hotel for a rendezvous with Nature, or, he thought, perhaps she headed somewhere else. The floating camera insisted on his tailing her. She led him down dark streets and narrow alleyways, never proceeding in a straight line, twisting and turning in the labyrinth of Vung Tau's poorer district, until they reached the invisible line where his enemies lurked on the other side, waiting for some hapless American soldier to wander across where his throat would be most obligingly slit. She paused and looked back. The mysterious circumstances of his nighttime jaunt stimulated Storyteller's more dramatic side, and he thought she looked at him with a mocking smile before plunging into the darkness of the prohibited zone. So, he thought, Mary Magdalene is a communist, a spy, an informer, and probably an assassin.

~ *Back in the Bush* ~

On the helicopter that left Vung Tau to take them to yet another isolated firebase where they would pause a few days before returning to the jungle, Storyteller narrated the entire story of his adventure to Nature.

"Why didn't you tell me earlier?" asked his comrade. "Christ! I spent a couple of hours waiting up for her."

"Because, dear Nature, I did not want to burst your bubble about Mary Magdalene. Anyway, you're lucky, she would just as likely slit your throat as make love to you.

"All the better, Storyteller, all the better!"

"Jesus, you're incorrigible!"

"All poets worth their salt are incorrigible."

"What if she murders you in bed?"

Nature looked at Storyteller sharply. "I was already dead, remember? At least, according to your mysterious lady. Anyway, my little prostitute does not match the towering mystery of your lady. Your ghostly alien. Your goddess."

This rebuke silenced Storyteller. He settled back against the padding in the chopper and sulked. But not for long, as Nature had directed his attention back to the "mysterious lady".

~

After setting down on the red dirt of a new firebase, T collected them together before assigning their bunkers. His black face looked out at the assembled platoon, which, although unusually listless, still possessed enough energy to grumble under their breath a string of curses at being so far from the beds, whores, liquor, and hot food of Vung Tau. T chuckled and shook his head in disgust.

"Never seen so many hangdog hangovers in all my born days," he drawled. "I want you troopers to square yourselves away pronto, stow your gear, and clean your weapons. This area is apparently a beehive of NVA activity and VC tunnel complexes. We don't want our balls caught in a vise when the time comes, do we boys? Now, this gentleman—"T gestured toward a staff sergeant assigned to the firebase"—will escort you to your accommodations. Guard duty assignments will be posted. Don't get too comfortable, troopers. Duty calls"—he pointed at the tree line—"out there."

On the way to their bunker, Storyteller remained silent in the face of Nature's picturesque narration of their new abode. The word "tunnel" spoken by T had frozen Storyteller's tongue and monopolized his thoughts. Nature rambled on, untroubled by Storyteller's usual wordless introspection.

"Well, well, welcome to our new neighborhood, full of interesting features. I'm sure you boys will enjoy. Here, for example, we have the latest model of a 105 mm howitzer, the envy of every firebase in the vicinity. And over here, an endless supply of empty sandbags, just waiting for idle hands to fill, resulting in excellent physical health and upper body strength, not to mention providing security from the surrounding riffraff."

"Have you ever been down a VC tunnel?" Storyteller suddenly asked.

"Can't say as I have. Two reasons. Number one, I'm too big. Number two, it's too dangerous for this Providence Rhode Island boy. End of story. Why?"

"*She* mentioned a tunnel."

"You're shittin' me. Why?"

But they had reached their bunker and crouched down through the entrance to the dark interior.

"Cots! My god! Cots! Luxurious!" cried Nature. "I claim that one!" He plopped his gear on a cot in the farthest corner.

Storyteller sat on the adjoining one, waiting.

Nature finished stowing his gear, then looked at Storyteller. He knew his friend well enough to know it was time to ask questions and listen to the answers.

"Okay, the tunnel. Tell me about it."

"It connects to my future."

This statement took even Nature by surprise. "Metaphorically?"

As if snapping out of a trance, Storyteller laughed uproariously and said, "Of course! Do you think I'm crazy?"

Relieved, Nature said, "Tell me about it."

~

Dear Reader, I had reached a sort of crossroads. Do I tell my best friend about a conversation with an otherworldly woman that would convince him I really was insane, or do I pass over the truth and tell him some comforting, but false, story about *her*? He already knew I suffered from schizophrenia, but considered it a mild case, something akin to a cold that one simply lives with. Stretch's Tourette's Syndrome actually worried him more.

~

"Not much to tell. She just works at the monastery and brings G.I.s there to contribute money. A scam. She mentioned tunnels to scare me into giving more to the cause. Said it would help my karma if I were killed. Pretty funny."

Nature knew Storyteller was lying; there was something his friend would not talk about, so he curbed his skepticism and said offhandedly, "Well, did you part with your hard-earned cash?"

"Once a sucker, you know."

"Yeah." Nature looked hard at Storyteller and seemed to make up his mind about something. "Did you know that monastery you went to with the mysterious lady has an orphanage attached to it?"

"Really?"

"Yeah, a Buddhist orphanage. Know something else?"

"What?"

"My Madonna mentioned it after you left the bar."

"She speaks English?"

"When not working at the bar, she speaks the King's English. Surprised?"

"Yeah."

Nature knitted his eyebrows almost as if in pain. "Never underestimate, man."

Storyteller thought of her the previous night, remembering she walked past the Grand Hotel, and when he could follow her no farther, she was headed in the direction of the Thich Ca Phật Đài monastery. Could it be?

"Tell you another amazing fact?"

"Yeah."

"Mountain Man's prostitute, you know, his fiancée, had something to do with that orphanage. After the VC murdered her, he took to visiting it every trip, and always brought lots of toys for the kids. You should talk to him. Maybe he knows something about your mysterious lady."

Storyteller could only blink at this information. He shook his head in amazement. "I never knew."

"Talk to him, man. Talk to him."

"I will, thanks."

~

Storyteller located Mountain Man shooting the breeze with Bowls near the berm.

"Can I talk with you a minute, Mountain Man?"

"Sure, kid."

They sat on an ammunition box, Bowls hovering nearby.

"What's up?" asked Mountain Man.

"Nature told me you know about that monastery with the sleeping Buddha on the hill in Vung Tau. Right?"

Mountain Man's face darkened. "So?"

"There's an orphanage?"

"Yeah."

Storyteller felt he was treading on thin ice. Mountain Man's eyes were narrowed, his body tense, like he was on the verge of exploding.

"Can you tell me about it?"

"Why"

"Oh, just that I visited it before we left and didn't know it had an orphanage."

Mountain Man jumped up and stood as if poised to fend off a knife wielding attacker. "Look, Storyteller, it's full of kids who are so fucked up they don't even know how to play. Their families were killed in front of 'em! Give 'em a toy and they just look at you with them sad eyes. That fuckin' place is cursed and blessed all at the same time. It's hard enough for me to go up there, let alone be hassled by some clueless fuck. Don't ever mention it to me again. Never! You hear?"

"I just—"

"You just thought something! Something Nature told you, right? Something about someone close to me? Well, forget it! You wanna know more about that place?—then lose someone close to you. Have 'em murdered. Then you have the right to know about that monastery. All them kids had their parents murdered. Got it, asshole?"

"Sorry, sorry, Mountain Man."

"Get the fuck out of my face, Storyteller, before I twist your head off. Shiitttt!"

Storyteller walked away disconsolately, his head still spinning. *I know so little,* he thought. *Stupid, stupid, stupid!*

Three days later, helicopters inserted the platoon into a small clearing carved out of the endless expanse of jungle. Back in the bush, where one misstep or loud cough might cost a life.

~ *A Magical Place* ~

The first two days in the jungle passed without incident. Mountain Man and Bowls alternated between roles as point man and backup man. The point man, machete in hand, quickly drained his body of fluids and stamina as he hacked through thick underbrush, while the backup man bore the mental strain of remaining alert to booby traps, ambushes, and signs of VC and NVA trails. Behind them, a few grunts followed, with T at the center, the nucleus of the platoon, leading the way along the narrow trail cleared by the point man. Behind T, Storyteller trudged along with the radio, its short whip antenna twitching above like a vigilant insect. A few more grunts followed, then Superman, clutching the M-60 machine gun like a plow poised to tear through the earth at the first sign of danger. Next, Stretch, weighed down with coils of 7.62 mm ammo, trudged along, and further back, platoon medic X followed, completing the serpent-like formation. The line culminated in Raresteak and Dogman, the drag men, trailing at the end. Pappy, the seasoned field sergeant, moved unpredictably through the platoon, shifting positions as circumstances dictated. The snake-like formation of the platoon moved in fits and starts, each segment keeping a careful distance, allowing for quick reconfiguration in case of attack. In such moments, the formation would snap into a defensive coil, poised to strike from multiple points. The platoon, in this sense, was a collective entity, greater than the sum of its parts.

As always, with his floating camera rolling, Storyteller mulled over these rather mixed-up metaphors. He marveled at how one could be intensely aware of one's own precarious existential existence with its manifold uncertainties and individual vulnerabilities, yet at the same time be utterly subsumed in a single, unified organism. How does one preserve discrete integrity when each part of the communal body is wholly dependent on the efficient operation of every other part? Never was one more alive to being an intimate component in the immense body of this planetary organism than when sharing a life-and-death struggle with the fellow parts that comprise it. Puzzling thus over the ambiguities and paradoxes of life, the platoon came to a steep hill. All philosophical and other nonessential thoughts were immediately put aside to channel each molecule of energy into humping up the near-vertical incline. Storyteller's heart worked to its utmost, consuming vast quantities of reserves until its desperate pounding seemed ready to burst out of his chest. All his comrades clearly suffered the same extreme exertion, all gasping for air and stopping more and more frequently to lie on their backs, propped up only by their rucksacks, while they wheezed and rasped to inhale what combustible oxygen was available in the steaming air.

After an eternity of excruciating struggle, the platoon reached the apex of the hill, where everyone collapsed in groups like corpses after a massacre. Finally, T stood and ordered, "Saddle up!" They wearily descended toward a deep, dark valley. As they approached, a great roaring could be heard, and they perked up, for it carried the sound of rushing, crashing water. Storyteller felt a tap on his shoulder, and turning around saw the grinning face of Nature, his free hand signaling thumbs-up.

Thick vegetation would not allow any clear lines of sight, but halfway down the hill, they came to a sheer limestone cliff that dropped precipitously onto the valley floor. At its base, a series of waterfalls cascaded over a succession of rocky concave bowls, like immense stairsteps, from higher to lower. Languid pools filled each bowl, inviting all creatures to partake of their luxurious comfort. When Storyteller reached the edge of the cliff and gazed down at the stepped tiers of water and rock, all notions of human complexities and big-brained psychoses vanished. He felt the compact twine that composed his body unraveling, then thread by thread reweaving into the fabric of this magical place.

They navigated steep animal trails to the base of the valley, where the roaring water rendered conversation impossible without shouting. T then held a brief conference with Pappy and Mountain Man. With no sign of VC or NVA in sight, guards were posted, and permission was granted for the grunts to bathe. A risky undertaking in wartime, especially in the jungle, but the mesmerizing lushness of the place made it impossible to resist. Beneath the sound of churning water, Storyteller sensed a deep rumble stir within his mind. He recognized it as the precursor to the voices and sought out a quiet corner in an upper-level pool to endure them alone. Nature called to him, but Storyteller waved him off, and the curly-haired Irishman joined Stretch, X, and Bowls in a lower pool, where they joked and passed the time. Bowls, looking a bit adrift, seemed to miss Mountain Man, his West Virginian mentor who, as always, had disappeared into the jungle to fight his own war, far from the interference of "amateurs," as he called his comrades.

Storyteller waited, eyes closed, sitting chest-deep in the cool water, letting it soothe his restless soul. Entombed within his mind, the voices stirred, their low-lapping hum matching the gently lapping waves rising and falling against his body. The rhythm became hypnotic, and he assumed the vacant expression of a schizophrenic in the grip of a psychotic episode.

You are the son. Listen to the other Chosen Ones.

Storyteller opened his eyes and saw a small water snake glide up, its head cleaving the surface in a graceful curve. He knew this nonvenomous species well and felt no fear. Stopping in front of Storyteller's face, the eyes of snake and man locked in a moment of anticipation.

"You are dead, yet you are not dead. How is this so?" asked the snake.

Lost in his psychotic haze, Storyteller registered no surprise at these words. He merely cast furtive glances around the pool to see if anyone was nearby, but he remained alone. "You are mistaken, I am alive."

"No, I think not," replied the snake. "One moment I think you are alive, and the next I think you are dead. It seems a great trick to me."

"No trick, I'm alive. More interestingly, how is it that you can talk?"

The snake's head swayed as if deep in thought. "Oh, it is no great trick. Apparently, you are now alive, so you hear me. When you are dead, you cannot."

"No, that cannot be. I have been alive for a long time, and never could I talk with animals before."

"Animals?"

"Nonhumans."

"Ah! That explains it! There is your mistake. Humans are dead to the world. They live in the past and the future, but rarely in the present. The past is dead, and the future is dead. That explains why you (a human, I assume) are both dead and alive."

"Boring. I have heard all this before," complained Storyteller, disappointed in what a talking snake would have to say.

"Boring?" said the snake swaying its head. "A human concept, I think. If I am not mistaken, it is what causes all the trouble. What does it feel like to be bored?"

"It feels like there is nothing interesting in the world, and time passes very slowly."

"Wait a minute!" cried the snake. "You have set me to thinking. I only have a small brain, but it is one hundred percent devoted to the moment. When in the water, I cannot see as far in any direction, and predators often come upon me from above or below or behind me in a flash, so I must be lightning quick. On land, I see farther and have time to think, to plan, to cogitate. That gets me in trouble. Humans see too far, both backward and forward, up and down, past and present, and are constantly in trouble as a result."

Storyteller rubbed his chin and slowly nodded, not quite sure what to make of these words. "Snake," he said. "Your head is out of the water right now. Are you on land or in water?"

"I am in water. See." And the snake submerged.

Suddenly, a blur flew across Storyteller's eyes and made a great splash in the pool, causing him to scramble in fright up the rock bank. When he turned to see what it was, he saw Mountain Man, waist deep, holding the snake in his uplifted hand . . . dead.

You see? came the snake's voice in Storyteller's head. *Water. Predators from every direction! Can't see 'em until they are on top of you! Have to be quick. Don't think! Thinking . . . that's what got me. . . .*

"Good eating!" exclaimed Mountain Man still holding up the limp body.

<h3 style="text-align:center">~ NDP ~</h3>

That night, the platoon stayed near the waterfalls and set up their night defensive position (NDP). T marked off a rough perimeter, and Pappy assigned guard duty. A shallow foxhole covered their back trail, with Superman's M-60 facing toward any intruder who might be following their path. Two Claymore mines were strung in front of the foxhole, and everyone settled down for the evening, waterfalls ringing in their ears, the sound oddly comforting to most of them. Storyteller wanted to talk to Nature, but his friend was on guard duty at the foxhole, so he joined him. Both men sat shoulder to shoulder, and could talk almost freely, since the sound of crashing water covered their voices.

"Hey," said Nature when Storyteller plunked down next to him.

"Hey, how's it going?"

Nature looked around, moonlight making the white water from the falls glow. "Couldn't be better, for a poet. If I had some light, I could write."

"Yeah, and get your throat slit by a sapper while you're doing it," said Storyteller.

"Naw, you're here to cover for me. Doesn't matter though, not enough light."

They both fell silent; wispy clouds slid by and the moon in its gibbous phase shone brightly.

"My God, it's beautiful here!" exclaimed Nature.

"I think I'm going crazy."

"What?"

"Nature, I think my schizophrenia is getting worse."

"Why do you think so?"

"Christ! I just talked with a water snake a few hours ago."

Nature sighed. "Great. Well, you sound fine now."

"No, no, Nature. It's not fine. It's getting worse.

"Let's talk to X, maybe he'll have something."

Storyteller laughed. "For schizophrenia? I don't think the army anticipated their medics needing medication for schizophrenia."

"Yeah, that's a point. What do we do?"

Storyteller rubbed his eyes. "It's the sparkling lights from the water. They play hell with my mind. In fact, right now I'm feeling funny. I get this way before the voices start talking, or some damn hallucination, like talking snakes, appear. I'm afraid, Nature."

"Are they talking now?"

~

But, dear Reader, I could barely hear him, his voice a distant murmur, for I had far more pressing matters to deal with. For one, there was the vision of *Her* standing in front of our guard hole. I knew Nature could not see *Her*, and when *She* moved past us, I knew *She* wanted me to follow. Fortunately, *She* headed inside our little makeshift perimeter, so I answered Nature's hanging questions with a "No," and bade farewell, stepping away with his words, "Get some sleep, Storyteller" fading behind. My little floating camera worked overtime, for I watched myself follow as if in a trance, yet still aware of my own movements in an inexplicable, objective sense. Thank God for my camera! It has kept me from totally sinking in the quicksand of schizophrenia and has performed this service right up to my death. In fact, though its owner is dead, it rolls on, the proof being in the very words you are reading.

~

As *She* and Storyteller continued their little journey (he trailed behind just like their walk to the Thich Ca Phật Đài monastery), the surroundings began to fade away until no sign of the NDP remained. He noticed the waterfalls that had pounded so loudly in his ears grew measurably quieter and more distant, while the jungle gradually receded to the point of vanishing altogether. Only *her* words lingered.

"We are sufficiently beyond your time here for me to explain, Storyteller. We are going to visit you in your future, when you are married to Diane (who you already know) and your young son, Mark. In other words, we will visit Michael Powers, successful lawyer in the prime of his life, or, if you prefer, your life."

Storyteller felt too astonished to reply, yet deep within, or perhaps with help from his trusted camera, he knew none of this could possibly be real. Dutifully, he followed, but as they continued walking, questions gradually and quite naturally came to his mind.

"How do we get there? Walk? Just walk into the future?"

"A tunnel."

This made him pause. The word "tunnel" now carried with it a plethora of images, some scary, some even terrifying, others confusing, but he never stopped walking. Unexpectedly, the last rays of moonlight blinked out and ominous walls of utter darkness impinged from all sides, even from above, as if night itself had collapsed and fallen toward him.

"Are we in the tunnel?" he asked with a slight tremor in his voice.

"Yes."

"We are going to the future?"

"From your perspective. Now, I must show you the way. You are the son of John Powers and Bai Meiying. You must know the way."

"Why?"

"You are the son."

"But how will I find this tunnel again?"

"The tunnel will find you."

Storyteller could see nothing. Only the faint glow from *her* body kept him from getting lost.

"We are here," she said matter-of-factly.

"Where?"

"Look up."

A trapdoor opened, light pouring down through the chamber. It was as bright and compelling as the beam from a lighthouse. *She* pointed to a ladder. He climbed up toward the light.

~ *Family Scenes* ~

"Diane! My burgundy tie! Have you seen it?" (From the bedroom.)

"Michael, I have to get to work myself." (From the kitchen, where Storyteller emerged.) "School starts in half an hour. I'll be late, and so will Mark! Find it yourself! And don't forget your meds!"

"Damn it! That's my best tie! My power tie!" He grumbled away, still going on after Diane and Mark had left. "Important meeting and this happens! Damn it!"

He hastily retrieved another tie and tightened it haphazardly, then threw on his suit jacket, grabbed his briefcase, and flew out the door. Storyteller was left alone in a house he had never seen, in a future he had never experienced, and his body would not stop shaking. *She* appeared next to him and invited him into the dining room. When he entered, *she* pointed to the long dining room table, still cluttered with breakfast dishes, half-uneaten toast, and the shallow remains of cold coffee in the bottom of two cups. Morning sunlight poured through the windows.

Storyteller blinked, and in that split second, he found himself in the kitchen looking at Michael Powers and Diane preparing dinner. They both worked together seamlessly, their banter as affectionate and comfortable as one would expect of two happily married persons.

While tossing a salad, Diane chuckled.

"What?" asked Michael, busy peeling potatoes.

"Oh, just something funny at school today."

"Yes?" encouraged Michael.

"Well, you remember me talking about Bryce Carpenter, the little red-headed boy always into mischief?"

"Yeah."

"He wore a red cape today, constantly skulking around the classroom, all three-foot-tall of him, creeping and peeking over the shoulders of the other kids. 'Bryce, what are you doing?' I asked. 'I'm Superman!' he yelled. I leaned down and whispered, 'Aren't you a little small?' He hunched over like an old person, and said, 'I slouch.'"

Michael laughed. "So cute!"

"Yes, he's adorable."

"As is his teacher," said Michael slyly.

"Wow! Such a romantic!" she needled. "By the way, did you take your medication?"

"Yes, dear."

"Good." Diane finished with the salad, leaned over and kissed Michael tenderly on the cheek.

"How about you?" she asked. "Anything interesting happen at work?"

"Nothing much. Settlement conference in front of old Judge Richardson. Went fine."

"No voices today?"

"No voices." Michael brandished the pill container. "This stuff works like a charm."

"Good."

"Even the counseling sessions with Doc Toomey, much as I hate to admit it, seem to help."

"Even better."

"Okay, I'm done," he said, setting down the potato peeler. "Ugh! Reminds me of basic training."

As Storyteller observed these proceedings, he felt a pang of bittersweet satisfaction that he had overcome schizophrenia, and in his middle-age was a successful attorney happily ensconced in a happy marriage.

A strange haze blurred his vision, and when clarity returned, he stood over a bed where Michael and Diane slept. Michael suddenly started crying out indecipherable words in his sleep, clearly suffering from a nightmare. Out of the gabble of indistinct words, clear sentences emerged. "No, I won't go back. I do have a twin brother. It's my twin you want. My twin."

Diane leaned over and gently shook his arm. "Michael. Michael. Wake up. You're having another dream. It's just the voices again. Wake up!"

~

Before he had time to process the scene in front of him, *she* appeared.

"This house is where you will come," *she* said.

"I don't understand."

"This is where you will come when the time is right and he calls. Now you know."

"So, I just show up and have dinner with myself?"

"Yes, but Michael Powers will be different then, not as you have just seen him."

"How so?"

"He will be as mad as you are."

~

With these words, Storyteller grew pale and agitated.

"This is crazy!" he cried. "I'm dreaming. I have guard duty. I have to wake up. Guard duty!"

He tried to force himself awake, but his efforts failed. He returned to the kitchen and crawled on hands and knees to find a trapdoor, but none appeared, and the house continued to imprison. He closed his eyes in frustration, and when he opened them but a moment later, night had somehow arrived. Storyteller stood back in the living room, looking at Michael sobbing and moaning in a chair. The young soldier did not know whether hours, days, or months had passed, but it was clear something calamitous had occurred. Storyteller felt a sense of dread as he watched himself collapse in such agony, and his mind groped for an explanation of such extreme pain. Cancer? Schizophrenia? Death? Yes, that must be it. A death. Of whom? Michael still lived, which means Storyteller continued to live. Was it the son, Mark? The wife, Diane? Storyteller felt suddenly enraged at the scene, at his own entrapment. He should be on guard duty!

"Why are you crying?" he shouted.

But his older self did not hear and kept on sobbing.

Finally, a word emerged from the suffering man's lips. It was almost whispered. "Diane."

Lifting his head from his hands, tears still running down his cheeks, Michael Powers turned and looked at Storyteller. Both saw the other clearly.

Madness had sought madness.

And found it.

~ *Michael Powers* ~

Almost the instant Michael had confirmation that Diane had died in a car crash, his schizophrenia returned with a terrible vengeance. Just as his father before him, Michael had the soul-crushing duty of identifying the body, and just like his father, returned home to immerse himself in lacerating pain. The moment Michael raised his head and saw the young soldier in combat fatigues, M16 grasped in his right hand, staring at him with wide eyes beneath the filth of the jungle, he knew who it was. He also knew schizophrenia had announced its resurrection in a resounding manner, calculated with almost human cunning, to maximize the horror. At that moment, he convinced himself the apparition was his twin who had died in Vietnam.

Michael stared at the soldier for some time, the soldier in his turn staring back.

"What are you doing here?" finally asked Michael, more puzzled than frightened.

"I don't know. Ask *her*."

"Who?"

"*She* was just here. I don't know. A lady. I suspect *she* is the one our parents searched for in China."

"Goddess?"

"Whatever."

"You can't be here anyway," said Michael. "You're dead."

"That seems to be what we all are these days. Actually, I'm alive and should be on guard duty now. Why I'm here is beyond me."

"No, no, no. You were killed in Vietnam."

"Obviously not, since you're here."

"I'm alive, you're dead," said Michael emphatically. "I cried when news came that you were killed."

"Really? What is my name?"

Michael hesitated. "Michael."

"The same as you. Doesn't that give you a clue?"

"Our parents liked the name."

"Shit, man. Your wife's death really drove you around the bend, didn't it?"

Before Michael could answer, Storyteller blinked out of existence. With the realization that Diane would no longer be able to moderate his illness, his grief deepened and the fabric of sanity she had helped him weave thread-by-thread rapidly unraveled.

Chapter Nineteen

Schizophrenia or Superior Ones?

Last Step or Next Step?

~ Spiraling ~

Well, well, well, dear Reader. You see the problem that confronted me then? In my saner moments, I knew the illness would defeat me without Diane, unless . . . unless what? Believe me, I put what little rational mind I had left to tackle that question. Unless what? There was medication, of course, but the unstable part of my brain would rebel. My demons would make sure of that. Diane knew how to deal with demons. Before her death, there were the dreams, the nightmares, but she always awakened me in time. After her death, life itself slipped into a dream, a nightmare. Now that I am metaphorically dead, I can say this plainly and without reservation. God had my suffering to feed *His* habit. Goddess had *Her* instrument of revenge. And yet—what if *She* is right? What if I am the next step to a better world; a world devoid of the human race, a world of powerful, empathetic Superior Ones?

So here's my decision: do what death permits, seek out God and Goddess where *They* abide. In other words, go directly to *Them* and stick the pin of my knowledge and experiences (my life) into *Their* eternal balloons and see if *They* pop. The second case, the Natural World, allows me no such opportunity; I lived, I died, I decomposed, and my body was made into ashes. Not much I can do with that. Now, in the third case, God and Goddess are different. Whether you, dear Reader, believe *They* are real or superstitious myths, I will find *Them*. Goddess used me; God abused me. I have a right.

~

It has been ages since I have written anything. Somehow, I am out of the institution. I don't remember how, but apparently much has happened.

I remember I asked Diane once after she died, what God looks like. She said, "An ant . . . and everything else, of course. Occasionally, *He* even appears as an old man with a flowing white beard. But, for me, *He* looks like an ant. I know it sounds absurd, since you know how much I hated ants when I was alive. But when I died, I was shocked to find the true order of things. All the others before me were shocked the same way. I discovered that in heaven humans must sneak into the House of God the same way ants must sneak into the house of humans on earth. Up there, risen humanity inhabits the dark spaces within the walls of paradise. We infest a labyrinth of nooks and crannies that keep us close to God's riches, but away from the poisonous spray of *His* frightful wrath. When it's safe, we raid *His* pantry and carry away the leftovers while the others, the ones we held in such contempt down here, the ones we slaughtered in their millions or drove to extinction, are the truly blessed. It was hard at first, but I gradually understood the true order of things and came to accept it."

I must ask: was Diane being truthful? Dead people are marvelous liars, you know. They whisper into our memories lies about what they were like when alive, and we spout the lies in our remembrances. Well, I want to find out for myself. Maybe I'll run into Diane. Maybe I'll run into mom and dad. Maybe, down here in Singularity, is where God and Goddess really live. I mean, if so, *They* live in a place where the laws of physics, as we know them, break down. Makes sense if it weren't so stupid. God of the gaps. Goddess of the gaps. But the difference is, I now dwell in one of the gaps. Dear Reader, you may very well be asking, what will you do if you find *Them*. I know one thing; I won't turn my M16 on either one of *Them* this time. Where do I start? With *Her*, of course. Always with *Her*. The woman who never gives clear answers. The woman who says things like, "How does one justify a life without cruelty, and therefore also without the distilled beauty of cruelty?" or "Fate starves at Probability's door." Shit like that, as Storyteller would say. Mom and dad believed in *Her*. Yup, that is where I start. Now that I'm dead, I won't be used and manipulated anymore. I mean, I'm on a level playing field with *Her*. We're equals—sort of. By the way, can you be even crazier when you're dead than when you were alive? No. By definition, no. Death is truth. Can't be anything else. All right let's find truth.

I know what you're thinking, dear Reader. You're thinking I'm still in the mental institution dreaming all this up. You're thinking I'm still alive. You're both right and wrong. Did you not read the Death Certificate? Sorry, but it's real. Yet my death is also metaphorical. I know, it's confusing. I'm confused. Am I a desperately ill schizophrenic or a desperately ill Chosen One? But, enough of this! I must find *Her* to find Them to find Stillness at last. Odd that Stillness did not come with death. You would have thought. . . .

Return to the tunnel? No, it was only a stopover on the way. Death is the ultimate dark tunnel. Return through all those bloody iron doors my parents had to deal with? No. I am dead. Dead people can be ghosts. Ghosts are spirits. Spirits can flit about and go where they please (unless they're stuck in some ghastly haunted house or castle or some such). Iron doors can't stop us, and dark tunnels are pure light to us. What do you say, dear Reader? Are you with me? Shall we go looking for the lairs of God and Goddess? Think of it as a quest! Are you up for the adventure? I'm almost feeling alive again! Ironic, isn't it? Now to find *Her*.

I am here.

Yes, that is *Her*. Always popping up without fanfare, usually in my mind, like now.

"I want to find God and Goddess."

You are dead.

"No, I am a spirit."

She smiles. **Who told you that?**

"Movies. Books. Religion."

You are ashes.

This makes me impatient. "I know! I'm a spirit!"

She looks at me askance. **No such things.**

Now I am more than perplexed. "What are *You* then?"

Ashes.

"Oh, no. No more of *Your* prevaricating! What are *You* really?"

Your ashes.

I start to shout an obscenity, but *She* is already gone. Of course. Since I am dead, and insist I am a spirit, I would like to follow, but I don't know how. Even spirits need directions. Stymied. The plain is colorless—an ash-flat stretching to an edge I cannot find. I look about, and I am no longer in my old house. I don't quite know how that happened, but someone approaches across that ash-flat, level expanse that seems to stretch into infinity. As the figure approaches, I make it out to be a woman holding something. Closer still, and I see it is a baby. Tamara!

~ *A Daughter?* ~

We come together in the middle of nothingness, and I know she is not real, nor is the baby. They are somewhere else, among the living.

"No, Michael. You are alive. Look at me! This is your daughter. You do not know her. You have been gone a very, very long time. Now you're back."

"No, I'm a spirit and you and the baby are not real." (This must be my mantra; the alternative is unbelievable.)

"Here, hold your daughter." Tamara thrusts the baby into my arms in such a way that if I don't take her, she will fall.

"You see?" says Tamara. "If you were dead, and we were not real, you wouldn't have caught the baby."

Still skeptical, I ask, "What name have you given her?"

"A hunchback should have a beautiful name," she says. "So, I have named her Ming-huá."

"Which means?"

"Tomorrow's Flower."

"Where will you raise her?"

"With you."

"I'm dead."

"No. Look, you're holding Ming-huá. If you were a spirit, she would fall through your arms. You're alive, foolish man!"

I will not let her get to me. "Your mother, Child of Buddha, had certain powers. My father told me this. Apparently, you have inherited her abilities, including the ability to see and talk with the dead."

"Is the baby dead?"

"No, you are both hallucinations."

"Then drop Ming-huá. Drop her!"

This takes me by surprise. I want to force my arms apart and let the baby fall, but I cannot. I notice Tamara has her hands ready to catch Ming-huá if I let go, but even so. . . .

Confused, I deflect. "She is also a hunchback?"

"Yes. Beautiful, like your schizophrenia."

"My mother used to say of your mother, Child of Buddha: a curved spine is a second sight. Your body already bows; your eyes are free to read the ground for truth. Besides, the dead have no schizophrenia."

"Perhaps, but I say again and again, you are alive, Michael. And you have a job to do. You do not have schizophrenia, you have powers never touched and unawakened. Ming-huá does, too."

"My job is to find God and Goddess."

"And, if you find *Them*, do what?"

"That is for me to know."

"Fool! God and Goddess know."

"How, if I am a spirit?"

She laughs cruelly. "You are no spirit, and God and Goddess exist only in your sick head. Of course, they don't know what you will do when you find *Them*, because you yourself don't know, and *They* are you. Don't you see, Michael, your so-called quest is a quest to find yourself. It is a quest the entire human race is on. That is why humans have created gods and goddesses. Without deities, there is no quest but mere day-to-day survival. We are beings born from mud and doomed to return to mud. Without the miraculous, there is no miracle to lift them out of the mud, only misery."

"But you! A disciple of *Her*, no less! How can you say these things if you're real? I don't believe anything a hallucination says."

"Spirits cannot hallucinate, Michael. They are made of the same insubstantiality as hallucinations. Wayward neural pathways! You are alive. You are real. You have just been gone a very very long time. Give me the baby before you really do drop her."

I hand her back, but I cannot keep my eyes from Ming-huá's pretty, chubby, fresh face. Like me, she has epicanthal folds, and the stereotypical word applied to Asians flits into my mind. Inscrutable. It is impossible to see her hunched back, so swaddled is she, but my knowledge of the world tells me Ming-huá will, by necessity, be inscrutable. She should have powers like her mother and grandmother, and must learn how to use them. When I catch myself thinking these thoughts, I almost believe I am alive. Nevertheless, the flat, featureless plain in which we stand tells me otherwise. I have a thought and turn to Tamara.

"Are we in the Underworld of Shades?" I ask. "I visited there once and saw dead comrades like Mountain Man and also dead enemies like Sergeant Dam. And my mother . . . is this where we are?"

Tamara pauses from speaking motherese to Ming-huá and looks at me steadily. "Look around you," she says. "You are in our trailer. We have lived here in hiding the longest time, but you have been somewhere, some place I don't know, you have been . . . elsewhere. Meanwhile, I've kept us alive by cleaning houses and waitressing at a restaurant."

I find this hard to believe, but a harsh light suddenly floods the space, and walls and roof snap closed around me in an instant, like an insect caught in a Venus flytrap. The room abruptly becomes very hot, and I start to sweat. Spirits do not sweat! Can what Tamara told me be true? She walks across the room and clicks on a noisy air conditioner. With Ming-huá propped with one arm on her hip, she gestures toward the door.

"Go outside and see for yourself."

I stagger outside, stumble down a couple of steps, and behold a host of trailers on all sides, their white aluminum reflecting the bright, burning sun into my face. I shade my eyes and see distant hills comprised of sun-baked rocks and sand. Desolate. Somewhere under the trailer, metal ticks as it cools. A wind chime lifts once and then goes still, as if a hand had steadied it.

I hurry back inside the trailer.

"Tamara!" I blurt. "This is the cave's doing! I have entered some branching tunnel that has deposited me here before my death. That's it! I have gone back in time! Oh, yes! I assure you, Tamara, I am dead. But that is in the future!"

"Nonsense," she says quietly. "All our deaths are in the future."

Now I feel on firmer ground. "No! All our deaths are also in the past. Even when alive—"

"Nonsense!" she exclaims, shifting the baby to her other hip. "You are alive, you are here, you are living with me and this baby in a trailer in the middle of the desert. Period."

"No, I saw the Death Certificate."

"Michael, if you saw the Death Certificate, you're alive."

"Spirits can see."

"You are going to have to come to terms with living in the real world, the world you despise, the world you think constitutes death, the world of everyday life, humdrum as it is. You must live with me and raise this child. To do that, you must concentrate, Michael. You must be here, not in some magical realm that doesn't exist except in your delusions."

Her words drop gently on the dry, dusty soil of my consciousness, leaving little round droplets that moisten the desert of my soul. "I have another child—my son Mark and his wife My-duyen."

"So, you admit you are alive?"

"I don't know."

"Mark and My-duyen are adults. He is not the son. As it turned out, you were also not the son." Tamara looks down at the baby. "All along, it was the daughter. The daughter, Michael! Your daughter! Why do you think Goddess—" she stops in mid-sentence.

I stare quite stupidly.

"Go look at yourself in the mirror." She points toward the bathroom.

When I enter and force myself to look, I see a haggard, frazzled older man with disheveled hair, scraggly beard, and wearing a filthy T-shirt with holes. The fluorescent bar stutters. The mirror is streaked with hard water and a thumb-smeared note taped to the corner: TAKE MEDS. I don't remember writing it. The room smells faintly of bleach and old soap. So much for the successful lawyer, proud veteran of war, paterfamilias, chosen son of Goddess, and man on a quest. Before me stands a failed, mentally ill wreck. Stone-cold reality is the hardest for me to take. I can deal with vengeful gods and mysterious goddesses, with iron doors and haunted tunnels, but not with the indisputable evidence of my own degraded life and the terrible consequences it has had on those closest to me. I see Tamara behind me in the mirror, still holding the baby. Without turning around, as I am deeply ashamed, the eyes of Ming-huá are lustrous, curious, and full of the wonderment of seeing herself reflected back.

"My god, Tamara, I'm so sorry."

See what Your genetic experiment has come to! comes the voice of God. **Michael Powers is a wreck!**

Yes, now you see it has been the daughter all along.

I suddenly realize with horror that schizophrenia may be inherited. God! How could I be so incredibly foolish! So lost have I been that I have ignored the world around me. My own child! Mark avoided the illness, but he was never intended to be the son. Now, Ming-huá is deemed the daughter. Does that mean she has schizophrenia? I now look at her with the same fear my mother felt when looking at me as a baby.

"Tamara, what if she has inherited my schizophrenia?" I cry out to my wife.

Tamara shifts Ming-huá back to her other hip. "First steps first, Michael. Take out the trash."

"But—"

"Take out the trash, please!"

It is as much a ritual act as sacrificing a lamb. I must learn to bow down to necessity—the necessity to live a life of quiet peace and mundane labors—often harder than those required of Heracles.

I take out the trash.

I return.

"See, you've done this before," says Tamara.

"What?"

"You've done this before. Michael, we've been living here a long time. You knew where the trash can was, and where to go to dump it."

I cannot give in to what Tamara insists is reality quite so easily.

"Tamara, we're in the desert, right?"

"Right."

"So, we're not far from the cave."

She pauses. I think I got her on this one. I wait for her to say, "What cave?" but she furrows her brow as if trying to remember something—or trying to decide if she should be truthful. Not sure which. She surprises me.

"It's a few miles away. Try to forget that place."

I feel uneasy about something but can't put my finger on it.

"Why?"

"Not good for you. Shall we take our next step?"

"What step?"

"Help me make dinner."

"I will, but the cave."

"Yes?"

"Well, is Buandelgereen still around?"

Her face turns white. Ming-huá squirms and Tamara finally puts her in a crib set up in front of a simple bookcase. Ming-huá instantly clutches a toy dangled in her face by Tamara.

"Best not to think of her."

"But—"

"Come on," she says, tugging my arm. "Give me a hand." We enter the kitchen, and she brandishes a knife. "Here, chop onions."

"But—"

"Michael! Focus. Forget the bad past. We're safe. They haven't found us here. Don't be an absent parent like your own father and his father before him."

"They haven't found us," I repeat her words mechanically. "Do you mean the institute?"

She looks at me slyly. "Start chopping."

"Tamara, do you mean the institute is looking for us?"

"I mean you have to finish that onion."

This is too much for me. "Fuck the onion! Who is looking for us?"

Tamara smiles in the most infuriating manner. "Well, that tone doesn't sound like a spirit to me."

"Just tell me!" I exclaim in exasperation.

She takes the knife from me and sets it down, then puts both hands on my shoulders and stares deep into my eyes.

I wait expectantly for the profound revelation. Am I wanted for the murders of Doctors Hess and Tavaris? For escaping the institution? Is Emile Ruska after me for betraying Goddess? God is searching for me for some nefarious reason? And Buandelgereen. Where is Buandelgereen?

While contemplating these questions, Tamara lets the tension build. Just as I am about to explode, she says (dripping with mock urgency), "Add this onion to the pot and stir. I'll be right back."

Before a protest can issue from my astonished mouth, she exits the kitchen with determined strides and shuts the bathroom door. What can I do? I add the onion and stir. Is this the deepest mystery of life? Mere survival? What drives us fundamentally? Breathing, gills working, food, water? The farther we stray from that reality, the more entangled we become with artificial mysteries—gods, goddesses, computers, ideologies, and all the rest.

"Are you still stirring?" she calls from the bathroom.

"Yes, but when you come out, I want you to tell me who is after us."

I hear her give a deep sigh. "You are aware, Michael, that a persecution complex is part of your illness? In fact, I think you have a whole range of mental conditions, not just schizophrenia."

"Like what?"

"Like dissociative fugue. You don't know your own identity and lose track of time for weeks and months."

"Look, Tamara—"

"Keep stirring! I'll be right out!"

Behold *homo sapiens* male, ever dangling between damnation, salvation, and soup.

Tamara appears next to me and takes the spoon. "Thanks. Now, set the table please."

"Not until you tell me who is searching for us. I am not the one with a persecution complex. You told me we are in hiding! Hiding from who?"

She speaks very calmly while handing me silverware to set the table with. "Not hiding from whom. Hiding from what."

Somehow, this answer makes the hair on the back of my neck rise, if I have hair. I am still not sure I am alive, and her bizarre deflections make me suspicious. Was I really in China and Vietnam? Did I dream up the entire trip while in a delusional state lying on a bed in this dilapidated trailer in the middle of the desert? Or is this trailer itself a delusion parked in the middle of my room at the institution?

"Now, let's sit down like two civilized people and have a pleasant dinner," she says. "We can discuss this over food and wine." She glances at Ming-huá, who is sleeping soundly in her crib. "Such a lovely child," she murmurs.

I obediently set the table, thoughts jumbled, but knowing Tamara, I anticipate more confusion to come.

After I take a few bites in silence, I say, "Tamara—"

But she will have none of it. She stops me cold by holding up her index finger to her lips. The gesture is not done lovingly but is sharp and threatening.

"Eat!" Her command is reminiscent of Goddess when *She* is angry, and I again become suspicious of whether Tamara is real.

Fuming, I tell myself I am an adult not to be trifled with like a child. Nevertheless, I am also patient, so I resolve to remain deaf and dumb until she addresses my questions.

~

My vow of silence has turned out to be a bad idea. Tamara has been talking my head off, filling me in on almost every person living in this godforsaken trailer park. Evidently, each has their own fascinating (to Tamara) story of how they ended up here. I have not encouraged her in this interminable sociology lesson, not even with a nod, but she remains undeterred. You would think a dead man could get some peace and quiet. Not a chance. Further evidence I may indeed be alive.

"While you were away," she drones on, "I got to know the people from across the lane, four trailers down. Actually, a single person, for her husband recently died from cancer. She helped him on his way and moved here to bury herself, just as she had buried him—her version of *sati*. But try as we might, we need to confide in someone, so she told me her whole story in the laundry room. It seems that his cancer—"

I can bear no more. "Tamara! Enough! I don't care about these people. You have not answered my question. What is hunting us?"

She looks at me with a sort of pity in her eyes. Sighing tragically, she says, "Michael, these people are our neighbors. They are interesting. But I can see you won't let this drop until I give you some answer."

"Give me the truth, not just some bullshit answer to mollify me."

Tears come to her eyes, and for a moment I feel guilty, as if forcing her to speak of something too painful to dredge up. Still, I wait for her to tell me what I have a right to know.

"Delusions," she says simply.

"What?"

"Delusions are hunting us down." She taps the Formica—once, twice, three times—as if warding something off. "Or perhaps the future is the hunter. I inherited something inexplicable from my mother—not schizophrenia, but kin to it. You inherited schizophrenia—your own kind of different. Either our delusions are tracking us, or something else is; in any case they won't let us live quietly inside ordinary life. That's why we're hiding here, in this trailer park in the middle of the desert. Sooner or later, God and Goddess will find you. Storyteller will return and take you back. Sooner or later, She will find me. The strange visions will find me. Buandelgereen will find me. The cave calls me; the tunnel calls you. There is no escape—but we can try." She glances at the crib. "For her sake, we must try. So we keep our eyes on the small, real things: washing, cleaning, talking with neighbors, tending Ming-huá, taking out the trash, eating together—being together, bracketed by the everyday. Anything else is death. Real death."

Tamara moves to the edge of the crib and looks down. "Watch her eyes, Michael. Ming-huá sees the seams between things. One day she'll part those seams and let what wounds us slip sideways into rooms we cannot enter. Not for power, but for mercy."

~ *Where Have All the Voices Gone?* ~

Tamara continues her one-sided *monologue*, and I can do nothing but listen, silent as breath. "You see, Michael, to die you must first have lived. To you, being in combat in Vietnam, being in the lush jungle, made you fully alive for the first time, and when the army brought you back, you unconsciously believed you must now be dead, as the world of everyday life could not make you feel as alive as war, or the jungle. Your work in the law gave you little satisfaction, and the practice brought you into contact with a multitude of angry, frustrated, greedy, frightened, vengeful people. Fertile soil for your schizophrenia. You know, a conglomeration of humans, like a city, is but a massive funeral pyre, marked by towering tombstones of concrete and glass, compared to the extravagant, living explosion of the jungle. Humans call cities 'vibrant', but Mountain Man had it right. Cities are nothing more than open sores on the body of a beautiful woman. Even here, in the desert, there's more honest life than in the cities where bloated scavengers burrow in high-rise hovels. So, we have taken refuge here, amid the sand, the rocks, where, like lizards, we can bask in the sun and escape predators by scrambling into the nooks and crannies that abound. Ming-huá will learn how to fit into those cracks perfectly."

"But even here, Tamara, there are delusions. The cave, for example, and Buandelgereen, the iron doors, all of it, were delusions, weren't they?"

She stares at her empty plate.

"Tamara?"

"Let's clean up."

"Tamara?"

"No, that is a topic we must not touch upon. Ever."

"Then it was real?"

"I didn't say that."

I repeat the words just to hear them again. "It was real."

"To us."

"Then it wasn't real?"

"I didn't say that."

My head begins to hurt, and I speak haltingly. "It seems my entire life has been a series of contradictions; neither this nor that. Truth is true in this case and a lie in that case. 'Michael,' they say, 'what you see is a hallucination, except when it's not.'" I pause to let the words gather steam, then continue with increasing bitterness. "'Michael,' they say, 'what you think is just your delusion, except when it's not.' How can I continue to live never knowing what is true and what is not? What is reality and what is not? Whether even you and Ming-huá are hallucinations or not? Whether I'm even alive or not? How can I exist under these conditions?"

"These conditions you describe are faced by every human being, in one way or another."

"No, no, no. Not every human being is diagnosed with schizophrenia."

"Stillness," whispers Tamara.

"What?"

"Stillness. It is what we both seek, Michael. Use stillness to still the hallucinations and delusions. Do only what is necessary to survive each day, no more. More brings more of everything; suffering, doubt, fear, jealousy, greed. As the old saying goes, less is more. Stillness is all. Your belief that death brings stillness is wrong."

The pot hisses and spits. A strand of onion clings to the rim and browns. The baby gives a soft, raspy cough.

Tamara lowers the flame and wipes the rim. She lifts the blanket edge, tucks a loose foot, counts two tiny breaths, then straightens and turns back to Michael. "Only what is still can still the rest. That which is dead stills nothing. On the contrary, it sends waves that ripple across even the most placid of lakes. Delusions are jails, while even the most menial tasks—such as we are now doing, cleaning the dishes—give us back the freedom to work for our own and our family's sustenance and comfort. Don't you see, Michael, war and tunnels with skeletons and magical caves are not liberating, but forms of bondage forcing us away from the daily tasks necessary for all living things to survive and flourish. Most women understand this simple fact, but men? All this time, Michael, you have been elsewhere, in a mental jail, pounding imaginary rocks and making fictional license plates, instead of living. Of course you get no straight answers! There are none to give!"

I listen to the words while drying dishes, but they do not sway me. "Tamara," I say. "I understand what you mean, but I think you are trying to convince yourself, not me. I may or may not be dead, but I'm aware enough to know you cannot ignore the gift passed on to you from your mother."

"Gift? Curse, you mean!" she exclaims. "What I have inherited is a humped back that disgusts most people."

"But also the ability to talk with spirits and see things—"

"Yes, things that don't exist!" she blurts.

We both fall silent. The dishes are done, and Ming-huá has awakened, fussing in her crib. Tamara goes to her, and I sit rather disconsolately at the kitchen table. I am at a loss.

"What does one do now, in this supposedly utopian world of trivial tasks and mundane conversation?" I ask.

She does not rise to the bait. "Read, write, fix the broken chest of drawers in the bedroom, all sorts of things to do. Better yet, find a job. Help me pay the bills."

"Hmm," I grunt.

Now holding Ming-huá in her accustomed fashion, Tamara continues her train of thought. "Look at it this way, Michael. Do you want to be dead?"

I pause to think about this. "I don't know. Maybe."

"Do you want the hallucinations and delusions to continue?"

"Yes and no."

"Well, take this child again, Michael." She thrusts Ming-huá into my arms. "Look in her eyes and tell her you don't care about her. Tell her you want her to have these hallucinations and delusions, just like you and your father. Or, perhaps, tell her you want her to have a normal, healthy life. What do you choose, Michael? If not the last option, then leave. Go and dwell in your illness without me, or Ming-huá."

I am rendered speechless.

"Well?" she demands. "Choose!"

I want to call her bluff. I want to get up and walk out the door. I have been homeless before. I want to show her I am the Chosen One. But something holds me back. Maybe it is the last thread of sanity I have left. Maybe I'm just scared to go and be alone again. Or maybe . . . I choose them.

Chapter Twenty

The Hunt

Gumshoe Glitch

~ *Once a Detective* ~

Emile Ruska had been haunted ever since Vietnam: he lost Michael Powers and *She* barred him from following Powers into the tunnel. At *Her* request or command, he waited for days, then went to the fortress to recover the body. At least, that was what he thought. But there was no body. No sign of the man. None. He had disappeared, along with *Her*. Ruska returned to San Francisco feeling duped, and resolved to spare no effort in finding Mr. Powers to solve the enigma that had led him on a quixotic mission around the world. Though outwardly modest and unassuming, he had the tenacity of a bloodhound, and the complex trail of Michael Powers led through a variety of mystifying people, baffling places, and bewildering circumstances. After revisiting the institution, Marie Telles, the cave, Michael Powers' house, and a host of other places, and after interviewing what felt like an endless array of psychiatrists, aides, technicians, government employees, and police agencies across multiple counties, and again reviewing the circumstances of the deaths of Doctors Hess, Camara, and Tavaris, he was no closer to unearthing his quarry. It appeared Powers had dropped off the face of the earth. Haunted by this failure, he retired from the police force. Locating Michael Powers now became an obsession, yet he had no idea what to do if he found the man. As with many haunted men, Emile took his restless spirit to a favorite watering hole, PicYrPoison, and while nursing a succession of drinks, checked in with his favorite bartender, Emma.

"Don't look so glum, Emile," she said, passing by his table on the way to another customer. "Since you retired from the force, I've seen more of you than ever, even with your crazy search for a crazy man."

"Mark Powers pays good wages to find his father, that's all. Think of it as an old man's hobby."

"Sure, that's why you're doing it. And I'm Queen Elizabeth in disguise. Got to go." She turned on her heel, and while moving away, smirked, "Old man!"

On the table, Ruska had placed his notebook to pass the time, jotting random thoughts and drawing elaborate doodles. He spent a few minutes at it, then Emma walked by to serve a table of newly arrived customers and looked over his shoulder at the sketches.

"Nice."

"Thanks."

"Nice."

Ruska chuckled. "You already said that." He looked up, but instead of Emma, to his shock, he saw Buandelgereen staring down at his paper, her older but still imperious bearing a magnificent sight. Before he could stammer out any words, she sat and stared at him with a level, commanding expression. She looked as out of place in this cocktail lounge as a stony-faced Plains chief in full regalia from the nineteenth century. Ruska always felt uncomfortably small in her presence.

"What are you doing here?" was all he could manage.

"Looking for you."

"Why?"

"You know."

"Michael Powers," he sighed.

"Yes."

"I am sure you're aware I tried to find him in Vietnam at that damn fortress, but he was gone. Disappeared. Where is he?"

"That is the very question I was about to ask you."

Ruska stared open-mouthed. "You mean you don't know?"

"No."

It took him a moment to process this revelation. "I thought . . . I mean, I was sure you, or *She*, would know where he is. In fact, I have been looking for him myself."

"Why?"

Ruska took a gulp of his drink. "Good question." He made a sour face. "You people left me in the lurch over there."

"You fulfilled your end of our agreement," she said. "We have no quarrel with you. I thought, perhaps you might have run across him. We are reasonably sure he is back in the United States. Certain movements—small, but distinct—point west."

"We?"

"You know."

"Yeah."

"Well?" she asked, raising one eyebrow.

"I have not found him, but not for lack of trying."

"I see."

Emma sidled up, balancing a tray with multiple drinks destined for another table. She looked at Buandelgereen with undisguised curiosity. "Drink for the lady?" she asked. Emile looked at Buandelgereen who shook her head, luxurious gray hair ruffling like the grand mane on a spirited horse. Emma paused, seeming to wait for an introduction, but none was forthcoming, so she bustled off, not a little ruffled herself.

"Have you given up?" asked Buandelgereen.

"About to give up the ghost, until you showed up. Now my curiosity has been resuscitated."

"Good. We need help."

"Are you worried?"

"Yes."

"Maybe he is already dead. Maybe his body is back in the jungle and I just didn't find it."

"No."

"How do you know for sure?"

"We know."

"I'm retired, you know."

"Irrelevant."

Ruska drained the last of his drink and waved to Emma for another. She acknowledged with a curt nod.

"Why do you want to find him?" asked Emile.

"We are worried."

"About?"

"His health."

"I don't believe you."

"Irrelevant. I think you have answered my questions, Mr. Ruska. Thank you." She started to rise.

"Wait a minute," said Emile.

"Yes?"

"I—"

Emma swept by and plopped his drink on the table, quickly walking away before Emile could thank her.

He sighed and continued, "I would like to help you. Perhaps you can also help me. How about we pool our resources?"

Buandelgereen silently mulled over this proposition, then said, "Do you still have access to police records?"

"I do if I need to."

"We have a license number."

"Oh?"

She nodded. "A trailer."

"Ah. Yes, I can run the tags."

Buandelgereen smiled for the first time. "Good," she said.

"So, he has a trailer now?"

"Maybe. That is what we want to find out."

Emile took a sip and straightened in his chair. "Look, is he in some kind of trouble with you people?"

"Quite the contrary," replied Buandelgereen. "Here is the number, but I need it back."

She showed him a slip of paper and Emile wrote it down amid his doodles.

"And here is where you can reach me." She displayed another slip of paper, and he wrote the number below the first. Ruska was not without doubts about Buandelgereen's motivation for finding Michael Powers, but he knew his own obsession would not be satisfied if he refused to cooperate.

Emile scrutinized her face for a moment. "Mongol woman—"

"Buandelgereen."

"Yes, thank you. Buandelgereen, can you please tell me why you want to find him so badly? I thought everything would be finished in Vietnam. Did something go wrong?"

"Not exactly, but in a manner of speaking, it did."

"What?"

"We are not sure, Mr. Ruska. But we are genuinely worried."

"About Michael Powers?"

"Not so much."

"Well?"

"It is more about his daughter."

~ *A Peaceful Life* ~

After Tamara's ultimatum, Michael Powers reluctantly stayed, eventually settling into a domestic routine he had not experienced since before his first wife's death. In the beginning, this life of domesticity came hard. He was oppressed by what he considered pointless drudgery, particularly after all his real or imagined adventures and misadventures, and he took out his frustrations on Tamara in a variety of petty and spiteful ways. Whenever the opportunity presented itself, he exaggerated his unhappiness and laced his comments with hurtful sarcasm, all meant to belittle her and the life she had 'forced' him to lead. Tamara remained unperturbed by his behavior, reminding herself that a strict regimen of patience would muzzle her impulse to lash out and make things worse. She knew well enough, after extensive research, that many schizophrenics improve as they get older, and Tamara put her faith in those data. She remained ever vigilant for signs of recurrence, not only of severe psychosis but also clinical depression. To her knowledge, the voices had faded and become quite rare. On those sporadic occasions when he heard them, Michael told her they seemed to be calling blindly, as if searching for a person lost in thick fog. His strategy had been to avoid giving himself away, and the voices of God and Goddess eventually faded in the distance, thrown off track by his silence. Evidently, even deities could not find him. This circumstance reinforced Tamara's determination to remain hidden, as much as possible, from the outside world. The trailer park had so far served her purposes well. Nevertheless, living with Michael did not proceed smoothly or without conflict. One day, an incident occurred that almost brought about their separation. Tamara had the day off, and they sat down to a late breakfast after Ming-huá fell asleep in her crib. Tamara noticed Michael seemed unusually distant, and, as always, felt she had to walk on eggshells.

"Did you sleep well?" she asked.

"No," he replied curtly.

"Bad dreams?"

"No."

"Well, maybe food will make you feel better."

"I didn't say I felt bad," he snapped.

"Oh, well have some coffee."

"You needn't constantly tell me what to do."

"Sorry."

They ate in awkward silence. Suddenly he asked, "Have we paid our bills for the month?"

"Barely."

"Ha! Tell me about it. Not two dimes to rub together. Can't even order something for myself."

"What?"

"Never mind."

She felt irritated at his insensitivity, for she worked hard to earn enough to keep them fed and the trailer park fees up to date. Still, she usually hesitated to bring up the subject. Nonetheless, this morning her impatience got the better of her.

"You know, the restaurant needs a dishwasher. You could apply. I know they would hire you."

"A dishwasher! You want me washing other people's scraps now?"

She felt piqued. "Why not? It's money, and you can't exactly be choosy about where to work."

"A dishwasher," he said with disgust. "You've got to be fuckin' kidding me!"

Michael's eyes became glassy, and he mumbled disjointed words she could not understand.

Tamara knew that when Michael slid into his Vietnam jargon and zoned out between words, he teetered on the edge of a psychotic episode. She immediately backed off and began quietly clearing the table, fearful his voices had returned in force. When she gingerly picked up his plate to take it to the kitchen, he knocked it out of her hand in a rage.

"You're a spy!" he cried. "A spy for God here to betray Goddess and me! You want me dead! We aren't hiding, you're reporting to God!"

"No, Michael," she said as calmly as possible. "It's your voices. Your voices. You must shut them out."

He raged on for a few minutes, blurting out disconnected thoughts and indecipherable words. Tamara retreated into the kitchen and planned to wait it out, but Ming-huá, awakened by the shouts, began to cry. Tamara rushed to her daughter and stared accusingly at Michael.

He rose and took a few steps toward her. "Look, Tamara, I'm trying to control it, but—"

Tamara, holding tightly to Ming-huá, backed away.

He stared wildly for a moment, took another step in her direction, then fled outside. Tamara knew better than to go after him, but harbored a deep fear he would not return, that he would somehow blunder into giving away their location. She calmed Ming-huá, finished cleaning, and waited. Pent-up fear and frustration brought tears to her eyes, but she let them flow freely, knowing Michael was not around to witness. Ming-huá found them delightful to touch. Tamara's hunchback tingled with hidden messages and deeply contradictory sensations; all signs her mother had taught her were always to be heeded. Her mother, translator of the Precious Object, possessor of the key, one-time confidant of Michael's parents, of Goddess, and of Buandelgereen, rose before Tamara as a guiding star, but one not necessarily to be always followed. In fact, she was in full rebellion, and had been since becoming pregnant with Ming-huá.

~

As Tamara waited, Michael wandered aimlessly into the desert. He had some vague idea he would walk to the cave and slip into a random side tunnel where he would be deposited either in the past or the future, anywhere but the present. But he soon became disoriented and merely followed the deserted road for miles, unsure which of the multiple side trails led to the cave. His voices, muffled and distant, had faded into silence, as if he had shaken them again, and gradually the chill night air and memories of Tamara and Ming-huá called him back. Night had fallen. Again, he had lost track of time. What had he done during all those hours? Where had he been? Still angry, but not remembering exactly why, he trudged back toward the trailer park, muttering to himself and periodically stopping, unsure whether to continue or give the whole thing up and disappear back into oblivion. The aftershocks of his psychotic episode continued to reverberate, but their most debilitating effects diminished as he walked.

His head cleared in the cool desert air, and the closer he came to the trailer park, the more he parsed Tamara's words. *She never actually denied anything*, he thought. *And this business about hiding from delusions is just code. We are hiding from those who inflict upon us the delusions. God . . . and perhaps Goddess. We are hiding from Them! She is obviously afraid to be discovered. Of course! She betrayed Goddess and her. What is the punishment to be if we are found?* He looked up at the half-moon. *Yet, if I were a spirit, none of this would matter. Could I fly up to the moon? To Jupiter? Anywhere in the galaxy? After all, I have no lungs, no flesh and bone, so empty space would have no effect on me. Let's give it a try.*

If a passerby were to observe this solitary man standing in the dark at the side of an empty road with his eyes closed, seeming to concentrate on some unknown trouble, he would approach and ask if he needed help. But no such individual existed anywhere near Michael that night, and his rather pathetic attempts to be a spirit and fly away resulted only in more frustration and tears of bewilderment. His lawyer's mind could only conclude that he was not a spirit, but rather a sad, sick, flesh-and-blood man whose life had been grounded on the rocks of this sterile desert island, and, for better or worse, his only companions were a hunchbacked wife and a hunchbacked child. He had exchanged the dark, dank, mysterious interior of a tunnel for the bright sear of the sun, arid wind, and a desiccated life.

Or is it? he wondered. Replaying Tamara's words during their argument, and reviewing the last few weeks with her, he realized his life was not all that bad. Some level of normalcy had actually revived his flagging desire to live. Oddly enough, he thought, it seemed to be the small things that sparked that desire, not the big things like survival and epic conflict. Making dinner together, having wine and conversation with Tamara, playing with Ming-huá, relaxing in an easy chair, reading, taking out the trash, all combined to calm his turbulent mind. Yet here he stood, acting like a madman, running away from the very things that had finally given his life some semblance of meaning. *Yes, mad!* He picked up his pace. He wanted to go home.

Michael heard the yipping of a coyote in the distance, then another, and another. These sounds did not alarm him. Coyotes rarely attacked humans, and he felt comforted he shared the night with others. In fact, he always felt closer to non-human animals than human animals. Thus, serenaded as he tramped along the road, he felt a nose pressing against his leg. Remembering Detective Ruska's experience in the cave, he laughed, looked around and saw nothing. Peering into the darkness, the coyotes yipped nearer, and he felt the first tinge of fear. Nevertheless, he continued on his way, and to disarm the anxiety, carried on an imaginary conversation with Temulun.

"Well, Temulun old girl, your mistress has not yet found us."

"No, it's true. *She* never listens to me. I scented you a long time ago, but does *She* trust my nose? No!"

"Ha ha! Detective Ruska will never forget your nose."

"That was fun! Got a treat?"

"No!"

"Awww! Where are we going?"

"Home."

Again, the coyotes yipped, closer this time.

"Oops, that's my cue!" barked Temulun. She galloped off into the night to join her friends.

Michael chuckled at his little fantasy, but suddenly paused, wondering if perhaps, just perhaps, Temulun really had been with him. After muttering to himself and cursing the insidious nature of schizophrenia, he continued, again picking up his pace. The lights of the trailer park came into view, and he hesitated, wondering if Tamara and Ming-huá would be better off without him. Something in him clicked, and he felt a compulsion to return and make the best of life with his wife and child. This turnabout left no room for doubt, and he vowed to himself that he would make it work, regardless of what obstacles were encountered. Michael would not have been able to explain this sudden click, as it happened spontaneously and with great force. Seemingly in celebration of his decision, the yipping of coyotes in the distance reverberated through the desert air, and in their midst, he fancied he recognized a familiar canine bark or two. For Michael, the last hurdle to overcome would be how best to convince Tamara his sudden turnaround was sincere and unalterable. *Ah!* he thought. *I have it!*

Without further hesitation, he strode up to the trailer, threw open the door, and looked intently at Tamara, who stood with an anxious expression in the middle of the room.

"You said there was an opening for a dishwasher?" he asked as calmly as he could manage.

She burst into tears and ran into his arms.

~ *Ruska Rolls the Dice* ~

Following his unplanned meeting with Buandelgereen, Emile Ruska spent some time soothing Emma's feathers about the strange woman. When he went home that night, he tried approaching the problem of finding Mr. Powers in a more pragmatic, tried-and-true way. First, he would run the trailer registration given to him by the Mongol woman. If that came to nothing, he would eliminate all possible places where Powers might hide. Once these locations were eliminated, he would settle upon the one place that the schizophrenic Mr. Powers might revisit—the cave. Although Emile had already traveled to the cave more than once and found nothing, he decided to spend the remainder of his time staking it out. After all, Michael Powers might go back and forth to the cave, or might follow his delusions and end up there in the future. In any case, other than the license plate number, the cave was Ruska's only viable lead as to the whereabouts of Mr. Powers, and he now found his interest piqued even more by the knowledge that a daughter was somehow in the picture. With this added ingredient to an already complicated case, he redoubled his determination to find the man.

A week later, he received word that the trailer's registered owner had sold it for cash to a junkyard in Stockton. The new owner subsequently sold it "for scrap" to an unknown out-of-state purchaser. Neither the registration nor the plates matched any trailer in parks within a hundred-mile radius of the cave. From there, the trail vanished. That left only the cave as a feasible last resort. Having no intention of camping out for weeks or months at the cave, sleeping on the ground, he decided to stay at a motel in the nearest town and make periodic visits, hoping to catch Powers unawares. A few days passed while he made arrangements and tied up some loose ends. Finally, he was ready to take the plunge.

He spent one last night at home intending to go to bed early, but his loneliness became too much, so he returned to *PicYrPoison* aiming to catch Emma on duty. Upon entering and heading to his usual table, he spied a couple occupying it, engaged in some intimate conversation.

"Didn't know you were coming or I would have reserved it," said Emma, speaking close to his ear.

Ruska looked at the couple and said, "Two lovebirds."

"You might learn something," replied Emma curtly. "Follow me."

She led him to a table near the kitchen normally reserved for employees. "Sit here, I'll take a break and join you . . . if that suits?"

"That's why I came."

Emma moved off to tell the manager while Emile sat, pulling out his scratchpad and plopping it on the table. By the time she returned, he had sketched a rough drawing of her.

"Nice," she said, sliding a glass of bourbon across the table.

"Thanks—for the compliment and the drink."

"You're paying. I'm just a poor barmaid."

"I won't be seeing you for a while," he said.

"Why not?"

"A job."

"I thought you would have quit that crazy search by now, Detective Ruska."

"Not completely."

Emma raised her eyebrows. "Still playing private gumshoe?"

Emile laughed. "You're showing your age, Emma."

"What are your kind called these days?"

"Emile Ruska."

"Ha ha, very funny. When will I see you again?"

Emile took a sip and perused Emma's face. He had always teetered on the edge of liking her enough to have a more serious relationship, but at the same time he cherished the independence of being left alone with his own demons. Somehow, he thought, she had managed to get under his skin, and he couldn't shake her loose. Cynical as she pretended to be, she was a devoted friend, oddly guileless in her own way, and her supply of common sense and grit made him admire her even more as time passed. Emile's main concern did not involve her suitability for him, but his suitability for her. A thought entered his mind that if he invited her to accompany him on this little excursion, they might get to know each other better under "working conditions", as he considered them. But he quickly dismissed the idea. Staking out a location is nine-tenths boring, and she would soon become dissatisfied and restless. Besides, the little town in the desert where he would be staying was indeed nothing more than a glorified crossroads. A sad little strip mall, three motels, four restaurants, five gas stations, and a smattering of stucco houses and trailer parks for old people. Nothing, really. No, Emma would go nuts.

"What are you thinking?" Her voice suddenly broke into his musings.

"Sorry?"

"Emile, I've been staring at you forever, but you have been far off somewhere in la-la land. You haven't even had your bourbon. You're the one getting old."

He smiled self-effacingly. "Yeah, I guess I am."

"Oh, I was just kidding, hon."

"No, you spoke the truth. I am getting old."

"Not at all. You're still quite a handsome man, to some women."

"Emma, are you flirting with me?"

"You bet. Must strike while the iron is hot." She thought it best to change the subject. "By the way, you never really explained who that strange woman was you sat with the other day. Just kept putting me off with your sweet words."

"Actually, you know about her."

"I do?"

"Yeah, I described her to you a long time ago. You must remember. The cave—Genghis Khan—Mongol woman. Name's Buandelgereen."

Recognition spread rapidly across Emma's features. "Ohhh, I remember." Her face creased in concern. "What does she want? You're retired."

Emile laughed. "Not according to you. I'm a gumshoe now, in your own delightfully antiquated description. Recall that? And you yourself said I could not stay away from the Powers case, remember, Queen Elizabeth? Besides, I need the money and I'm getting paid by the family."

"Okay, okay, don't throw my own words at me. Seriously, Emile, this Powers case never leads to anything good. Now, this Mongol woman is back. Where is she going to drag you this time?"

"Actually, I'm glad you brought that up." He held up his empty glass. "Another?"

"I'm on break, remember, Detective Einstein?"

"Please, for old times' sake." He put on a tragic face.

"Okay, but when I get back, I want to hear about it. All of it. No holding back. You ain't a cop no more, buddy!"

"Sure."

Again, the thought entered Ruska's mind of inviting her to go with him. He enjoyed her company, and she had always been a good sounding board.

When she set down a fresh bourbon and sat expectantly, he hesitated. With Emma, something always held him back at the last moment and he could never understand what caused this reluctance.

"Well?" she asked.

Emile filled her in on the latest developments, such as they were, and told her he planned to go on an extended stakeout. There, he stopped.

"Where?" she asked.

"The desert."

"Alone?"

"Of course."

She waited, he remained silent, sipping his bourbon distractedly.

"Do you. . . . " she started to say, then paused, shook her head as if clearing it of cobwebs, and said, "Do you want another drink? I have to go back on duty."

Emile avoided eye contact and said, "Ah, that's too bad. No thanks, I'd better go. It's a long trip."

As she stood and turned to go, he heard her whisper, "Especially alone."

Ruska, normally a decisive man, stood, then sat, then stood, then sat again, quite at a loss what to do. "Emma!" he called.

She paused from putting a drink in front of a customer. "Yes, hon?"

He stared for a long moment without speaking.

"Emile?" she said.

He sighed. "I'll stay in touch. Bye."

Ruska pulled out his wallet and left a hefty tip before he could change his mind. Emma looked after him with a sad expression, almost spilling the drinks from her tray, then turned to the customer with a smile. "Sorry for the delay, darlin'. Here's your drink, safe and sound."

The customer conspicuously leered at her cleavage and winked. "No problem, sweetie. As long as you're safe and sound. Don't damage the goods, that's what I always say." He winked again and reached out to pat her bottom, but Emma was too quick and moved to another table, a smile still doggedly stamped on her face.

~ *Of Motels and Caves* ~

Ruska picked the most expensive motel in town. After all, it was on Mark Powers—or rather, the estate's—dime. He arrived late, checked in, and immediately slept, dreaming briefly of chasing Emma through dark alleys but never catching up. Upon waking early, he went to the breakfast room and sat with coffee and a roll, lost in thought. The room quickly filled, and the detective in Ruska scrutinized faces and behavior, trying to identify why they were visiting this out-of-the-way town. Some were families with young children, probably stopping off at a convenient spot on their way somewhere else, since there were no services for a hundred miles in any direction. There appeared an occasional trucker, almost always identifiable by a no-nonsense manner and ample girth, no doubt caused by sitting too long and eating at greasy spoons and calorie-laden truck-stop fare. Then there were the younger men, either alone or with one or two others, and these Ruska studied more closely. Invariably, they were either jocular, high-spirited college types visiting the desert to hike, or quiet, serious recluses, weighing dark or profound deliberations. This last group Ruska studied with even more interest. Drugs or some other illegal activity often accompanied these reticent loners, and Ruska could not break the habit of being suspicious. In the back of his mind, he had never quite shaken the notion that Buandelgereen and her colleagues were somehow involved in illicit trafficking (of what, he did not know). How Michael Powers fit into this scenario remained a mystery, but the suspicion never quite left him. The deaths of the three psychiatrists bore all the marks of such dark dealings, but the pieces of the puzzle never came together in any coherent fashion. After one last look around, he went to his room and changed into hiking clothes.

Ruska had decided to park his car far away from the trail that led to the cave. He found a dry wash conveniently screened from inquisitive eyes by a group of cottonwoods. Grabbing his backpack, he headed down the empty road, wondering whether this stakeout would be as long as he feared. Already mid-morning, the heat had become stifling. By the time he reached the trail to the cave, the sun bore down mercilessly, and his body, soaked with sweat, demanded a break. He sat on the same rock White Thunder had rested on so long ago. To his dismay, there was no sign of human activity whatsoever. No footprints, no disturbances, no candy wrappers, no empty soda cans. Emile remembered White Thunder's unwillingness to accompany him to the cave, and, simultaneously, a strange breeze blew across his face. It should have been a welcoming coolness, but instead it seemed to cut his skin like a razor. Once it had passed, the atmosphere took on a menacing darkness, though it was midday. Ruska jumped up and surveyed the area without knowing what he was looking for. Creosote bushes trembled, though the air was now still. Apprehension pressed inexorably upon him, and he felt a need to run as fast as his legs could carry him.

He forced himself to sit again. "This is ridiculous," he told himself aloud. "Go to the cave, Ruska!"

But this self-imposed order could not be carried out. Emile felt rooted to the rock, and a fear such as he had never experienced took hold.

"Stand up and walk to the cave!" he again ordered himself. Once more, the command proved impossible to implement. A coldness of limbs and numbness of mind rendered him immobile.

Ruska remained in this condition for some indeterminate time, and, as suddenly as they had come, the eerie, dark atmosphere and enervating sensations of fear and paralysis lifted. Emile breathed deeply and felt a harmless, even welcoming breeze pass across his face. As if apologizing for frightening him, the desert, the bushes, even the rocks urged him to stand and enter the cave. While relieved at the passing of his inexplicable terror, Ruska nonetheless walked toward the cave cautiously. He moved gingerly and paused every few steps to scan the surroundings.

"No more wet noses, thank you," he said to the air.

Once he entered the cave, he clicked on his flashlight and plunged forward. The ground seemed oddly undisturbed, as if someone had swept it clean in anticipation of his arrival—or so his suspicious mind suspected. No footprints at all, which struck him as unlikely since the shelter of rock walls and ceiling would have preserved evidence of past visitors, including his own. Pressing on, he came to numerous side tunnels. Knowing he could never check them all, he chose a likely candidate at random and left the main chamber. The farther he went the more cramped it became until he practically had to crawl by the time he reached the end. His flashlight illuminated a rather smooth wall at the terminus. About to turn back, he noticed odd markings scored into the rock. Moving closer, until his face was inches away, he used his index finger to trace the scratches. At first, he assumed they were gouged by some animal's claws, but upon closer inspection, he realized with a start they were scraped by human fingernails—ragged crescents driven hard into stone.

Chapter Twenty-One

Defeating Schizophrenia and Embracing A Future Without Humans

Lessons in Small Talk

Look, dear Reader, I have always been terrible at small talk. I don't know if it's the schizophrenia, but that particular conversational skill isn't in my repertoire, and never has been. Now that I have dedicated myself to domestic tranquility and the Protestant work ethic, I need to improve the social aspect of my personality. It never held me back as a lawyer, as people do not expect (or want) to engage in small talk while the billable clock is ticking. Now that I am living with Tamara, and no exotic crises or magical excursions into the supernatural are on the agenda, I find myself groping toward an actual conversational style. I got the dishwashing job at the restaurant and must say it is more pleasant than I had imagined. Mindless, to be sure, but it gives me time to ponder my family, my illness, and my future. The first few days were rough at El Fantasma (The Ghost), but now I am in the swing of things, have developed my own rhythm, and am a sort of father figure to the young waitresses and busboys—a role I find rather amusing. If only they knew. I rarely work with Tamara, as our hours are not in sync. That is okay; it gives us more to talk about, since we each have our own separate experiences at different times of day and night. Let me give you an example of an incident at the restaurant that I witnessed (and Tamara at home did not), which gave me plenty of conversational ammunition.

I had pulled the night shift, and close to midnight a young couple came in and were seated in a corner booth. I first knew there was a problem when Lisa, one of our young waitresses, burst into the kitchen where I stood over the sink scrubbing a particularly stubborn pot.

"Michael!"

"What?"

"You won't believe it! Tad is out there now trying to deal with it!"

"With what?"

"Come look!"

When I went out, I saw a young male customer standing by a booth, hopping from one foot to another, waving a dinner knife in the air and screaming, "I'll kill them all!"

His female companion was curled up in a defensive posture in the corner of the booth.

Tad, the night manager, held out his hands and said, "Calm down! Calm down! The cops are on their way!"

"I'll kill them all!" the customer kept repeating.

"Who do you want to kill?" asked Tad in as calm a voice as he could muster.

"Them!" The young man kept swiping the knife in the air as if slashing at some unseen attacker. "Keep them away from me!"

"Who?"

"Them! Can't you see them?"

Tad held out his arms. "There's no one here, sir."

"Them! Them! I'll kill them all!"

"Sir, there's no one here." said Tad.

The young man started running in circles around the room, all the while swishing his knife in the air. "Die! Die!" he screamed.

When the police arrived, the man gave his knife to them peacefully and said, "Thank god you're here! You have guns. Kill them! Kill them!"

"Okay, buddy," said a burly officer. "Let's take you somewhere safe first, so they don't get you."

"Yeah, yeah, good."

The other officer put the cuffs on and walked him out to the patrol car, the man still shouting over his shoulder, "Make sure you kill them all!"

The girl slid out of the booth and stood with her arms wrapped around her body, shaking, talking with the burly officer who scribbled rapidly on his incident pad.

"Bad drugs?" he asked.

"No," she replied.

"Come on, miss, I've seen too many druggies flip out from a bad drug or an overdose. What was he on, miss, crack?"

"No, no," she said almost whispering through her clattering teeth. "He has schizophrenia. It was hallucinations. Hallucinations. He must not have taken his medication. I try to be careful."

"Schizophrenia," the officer mumbled as he wrote the word on his pad, clearly skeptical and trying his best to spell it.

I could not help myself. I walked up to the girl and asked, "What did he want to kill?"

The officer looked at me askance. "Do you know these people?" he asked.

"No, but I am somewhat familiar with schizophrenia. The man clearly demonstrated the classic symptoms of a psychotic episode." I turned to the girl. "Now, what did he want to kill?"

"He has these crazy ideas there are demons after him. After all of us. When he gets like this, he sees them flying all around his head like, I don't know, like crazy bats or something."

The cop nodded, still clearly skeptical, and asked the girl to come outside with him. As they left, he asked her what medication her boyfriend had been taking. I did not need to hear the answer.

You see, that incident gave me something to talk with Tamara about. No vague stumbling for a topic, any topic. It filled an evening. Or, if you wish, here is another example, which I exploited for a long time, and it worked, but now I've mined that vein dry (as miners would say). At El Fantasma, when business is popping and customers are coming hot and heavy, the manager schedules two dishwashers. I am one, of course, and the other is Angel Gonzales. Now, this Angel is no ordinary dishwasher (of course, neither am I). He is small and wiry, in his 50s, and wears a perpetual smile. Ever since Vietnam, I have tried not to categorize people, and especially not to underestimate them. If I hadn't learned better there, I would have dismissed Angel as a typical back-of-house laborer, probably here illegally, and certainly not what one might call an intellectual. I would have been wrong. Dead wrong. Angel had worked at the restaurant for many years, and to him, I was just another new employee who would probably be gone in a couple of months. In his eyes, my only noteworthy characteristic, I am sure, was my rather advanced age. He greeted me with as few words as civility required.

For a long time we worked together in silence, only grunting a few words when necessary. This suited me as well as him, and we might have gone on in this monosyllabic manner indefinitely. But one memorable day, when the volume of dirty dishes had tapered off, a quote from Spinoza popped into my head and I said aloud, "There can be no hope without fear, and no fear without hope."

Angel immediately stopped arranging dirty coffee cups on the tray, looked at me with a piercing gaze, and said quite calmly, "Ah, Spinoza! You know, Miguel, he also said, 'Do not weep. Do not wax indignant. Understand.'"

I did not even know he understood much English, let alone that he had a working knowledge of Spinoza—enough to so eloquently articulate one of his quotes. He greeted my astonished face with a chuckle.

"Not all of us are illiterate beasts of prey," he said.

"Of course, of course! I never thought so!" I objected. "You like Spinoza? I mean, where did you pick up his. . . ." My question trailed off. I feared he would view it as patronizing.

"Philosophy?" Angel completed my sentence.

"Yeah."

He just shook his head and continued cleaning while I mulled over this revelation.

"Angel?"

"Yeah?"

"Really, how did you become interested in Spinoza?"

"Look, *amigo*, our friend Spinoza also said, 'The highest activity a human can attain is learning for understanding, because to understand is to be free.' *Comprende*?"

I lapsed into my Vietnam persona. "So, what the fuck are you doing in this dive washing goddamn dishes?"

Angel laughed. "Time. I have more time."

"To do what?"

He looked at me closely. "Do you like books?"

"Of course."

"What does it take to read?"

"Knowledge."

"No, *mi amigo*, time. It takes time. Jobs with responsibility eat up valuable time. Here, I am on automatic pilot, leaving my brain free to think about Kant and Hegel, Marx, and Spinoza."

"Yeah, I get that."

"My apartment is a library, my brain a repository for the thoughts of people who have chosen to examine the world."

"An unexamined life is not worth living."

"Ha, ha! Yes! Socrates indeed, *amigo*!"

Angel looked at a stack of accumulating dirty dishes. "We'd better get back to work."

~

So, this exchange gave me a lot to talk with Tamara about, although she is no student of philosophy. However, as I gathered more information from Angel about his past, I became more interested in him beyond merely serving as the object of small talk. Problem is, the deeper I plumbed the depths of his philosophical views, the less interested Tamara became in them. But I was hooked. The breadth and depth of his encyclopedic familiarity with philosophy rivaled that of a Ph.D. professor. Even better, because his interpretations came from the perspective of the school of hard knocks, not the ivory towers of academe, his unique point of view carried great weight. His openness to various speculations on the nature of reality made me want to know more, and to understand him better. All right, I might as well be honest with you, dear Reader, I wanted to confide in him some of my darkest secrets; secrets that even Tamara did not know. Up to this point I had kept my schizophrenia strictly to myself, and Tamara did the same (both about me and about her own past). No one knew our true circumstances. We lived like two fugitives, not only from those who sought us, but from our own natures.

~ *A Visit with Angel* ~

Two weeks ago, I finally had an opportunity to have uninterrupted time with Angel. He was in the middle of elucidating the fine distinction between Hegel's belief that we perceive the world only through the ideas and sensations of mind, and Kant's account of Geist. I could not concentrate with the constant rattling of dishes, chatter of waiters and waitresses, splashing hum of the automatic dishwasher, and general hubbub that goes on in the kitchen of El Fantasma. He practically had to shout. I threw down a tray full of dirty dishes and exclaimed, "I can't hear a damn word you're saying! I wish this whole place would just be quiet so we can talk."

"We can," he said.

"We can what?"

"Talk."

"How?"

"Come to my apartment some day when we're off at the same time. I'll show you my library and we can talk."

This suited me, so we set a date. I remember it well.

~

It was hot, as usual, even in the late afternoon when I reached his apartment. He opened the door before I could knock and waved me in with a slight bow. My first impression was that I had entered a nineteenth-century library: leather-bound books from floor to ceiling lining the walls, an air conditioner humming to keep the humidity low, and a definite smell of musty paper and fusty bindings. A ray of late sun found the hairline gaps between overpacked spines, little seams of brightness running like sutures across the wall. Angel motioned to a chair and offered a drink. Angel motioned to a chair and offered a drink.

"What've you got?" I said.

"Tea, coffee, soda, beer."

"Beer sounds great."

"Corona?"

"Great."

I noticed Angel poured himself a glass of water from a pitcher in the refrigerator.

"Not a beer man?"

"Never drink alcohol."

"Okay. Philosophical or religious objections?"

"Neither. Neural hygiene."

"Oh."

Angel handed me the beer and took his water to a leather chair beside which stood an end table stacked with books. He sat, leaning forward.

"Where do we start?" he asked.

"What got you interested in philosophy?"

"Failed parents. Drug cartels. Dead friends. Desperation. Refusal to allow the last embers of knowledge to die out. Tremendous efforts to nurse the flame. Spark. Ember. Blow gently. Spark. Ember. Blow gently. Embers. Blow gently. Smoke. Blow harder. Fire. Finally, success. Burning ever since. And you?"

"Wow, a lot of stories there, a lot of questions there."

"Not right now. And you?"

"Well, I will use your own style. Dead mother. Distant father. War. Death. Destruction. Marriage. Wife killed. Son to raise. Legal practice to run. Then, free fall. Crash. Burn, but not your flame of knowledge. Just a dry incinerator. Ashes. Fire gone. Smoke gone. Embers gone."

"But you have a wife and daughter. What about them?"

"Hope."

Angel took a sip of water. "It's a spark, but you're leaving something out."

"So are you," I retorted.

"Yes, but mere details. You are leaving out something big. Something that brought you here. You did not come to listen to the ramblings of a lowly Hispanic dishwasher."

"On the contrary."

"No, Michael. You have something to tell me. I have a friend from the bad old days who died in my arms. He had something to tell me before he died. You are like him. You have something to tell me also."

"Do you think I'm dying?"

"Absolutely. You are dying in your own estimation. Tell me what you came to tell me."

I could not keep up with this man's inexorable insights. I felt myself crumple inside, all defenses lost, all desire to keep secrets gone. Caution be damned.

"One other word to add to my story," I said.

He waited.

I took a deep breath. "Schizophrenia."

Chapter Twenty-Two

Ruska Draws Near

Getting Hotter

~ The Stakeout Continues ~

Once he finished inspecting the scratches on the rock wall, Emile Ruska retraced his steps and worked farther down the main passage toward the terminus. To his surprise, he discovered holes drilled into the stone at different points and surmised they had once served as anchors for heavy hinges, remnants of blast doors or bulkheads meant to localize a cave-in. Being no cave expert, he jotted in his notebook a reminder to contact the Forest Service or the Bureau of Land Management (BLM) and ask about them. Relief rose in him; the cave seemed to hold no hostility, and his mood lifted.

"This isn't too bad," he said aloud, listening to the echo and, just to prove the point, emitting a juvenile hoot.

As if he'd tripped a hidden wire, the moment his hooting echo died out, he felt an ominous chill and the walls seemed to be closing in. He had the terrible feeling that if he did not run fast enough, he would be crushed. The silence added to his terror. He felt his chest constricting, the blood pumping in uneven surges, and he began wheezing for air. Scrambling back toward the entrance, he almost fell a few times, but his athletic coordination kept him upright. A horrible sound emerged from behind; a low, growling snarl, coming closer. Ruska, knowing he would never make the entrance before this creature was upon him, suddenly turned and shined the flashlight at the oncoming threat. His left hand fumbled for the old service revolver, but the beam found only bare rock before the gun cleared the holster. If there was something bearing down upon him, it must be invisible. As quickly as it had begun, the growling ceased and the charged atmosphere lifted.

Once again, immensely relieved, Ruska quipped, "On and off, on and off, like a faucet."

But he had no desire to stay longer in the cave, so he moved quickly to the entrance where he welcomed the light and air of the outside world. Shielding his eyes from the sun's glare, he returned to the rock where he earlier sat, and contemplated the best position to conceal himself while observing the trail. Unbeknownst to him, Ruska chose the same rock Tamara and Michael had occupied when they spotted him and White Thunder so long ago. A scraggly acacia provided some shade, but he had the unhappy feeling this stakeout might turn out to be the biggest mistake he had ever made. After a few hours, his sweat-soaked body wilted among the rocks, and he found himself longing to return to the motel for a shower, then sit in an air-conditioned restaurant and down a few cold beers. *I'm getting old,* he thought wistfully. *Maybe I should have invited Emma.* Only his iron discipline made him stay until late afternoon when he called it quits. All he succeeded in observing were a couple of lizards performing push-ups on the rocks.

Hiking back to the car proved to be almost as bad as sitting on those rocks. Roasting heat from the compacted dirt road penetrated his boots and made him feel as if he were walking on fire, so he tried staying on the sandy shoulder, which was just as hot and made walking even more difficult. The car proved to be an inferno inside, and Emile could not grasp the steering wheel for long without burning his hands. *All right, you win,* he thought. *It's off to the store for a dashboard sun protector!*

As the air conditioner in his car made headway against the heat, his spirits rose, and he drove back to town thinking less about Michael Powers and more on a shower and a beer. He tried to block the memory of the strange happenings in the cave, unwilling to allow himself to believe anything unnatural happened. In this, Ruska achieved partial success. However, one vision stuck in his mind, and kept returning to disturb his increasingly sanguine disposition: the fingernail scratches. To his trained eye, they were made relatively recently, yet the undisturbed ground confused the issue. Were it not for those marks, he might have given up the idea of continuing a useless stakeout, but their presence rendered that inclination moot. He would stick to it, at least for a while longer, and see what happened.

After a refreshing shower, Emile called the front desk to inquire which of the four restaurants the locals preferred.

Without hesitation, the clerk responded, "El Fantasma, sir, for all around good food and service. It's a bit of a drive from the town, kind of all alone out there, but it's the best."

With a couple of follow-up questions, Emile obtained directions and resolved to drive to El Fantasma even though it was relatively far from town. When he arrived, the place was almost full, but one table remained unoccupied, so he took it. After the waitress dropped off a menu and glass of water, he quickly ordered what he wanted and scanned the room, his usual detective radar operating unconsciously. Here, the clientele appeared decidedly different than in the motel restaurant. These were locals, and as such, were less interesting to Ruska. Most of them wore country clothes, appropriate for life in the desert, and bantered familiarly with the servers. They were scragglier than the visitors at the motel, but certainly far more at ease with their surroundings and themselves, Ruska felt disconcertingly out of place.

After finishing a simple but hearty meal, he ordered a beer and fished out his dog-eared notebook, flipping it open on the table to jot down his observations from the day and sketch different scenes of the cave and its surroundings. Had he not been so engrossed, he would have seen Michael Powers leave the restaurant at the end of his shift. Instead, neither man noticed the other—only a damp apron and a bleach-and-steam scent flashing past the service door and a murmur of staff goodnights. By the time he got back to the motel, night had arrived, and the neon sign buzzed resentfully at the darkness. Before he slept, he decided to try a different restaurant for dinner the next day, vowing to try all four before deciding on the winner.

~

The next day started for Ruska on a sour note. He had not slept well in an unfamiliar bed, and when he went down to the breakfast room at the motel, he was too early, so the staff told him it would be a while before breakfast would be ready. Perturbed, he decided to be at the cave early and watch the sunrise. Stopping at a gas station to fill up the car as well as his coffee mug, he purchased a breakfast roll and headed for his spot off the road.

Upon arriving at the wash shaded by cottonwood trees, he double-checked his revolver and flashlight, slung on his backpack, and began walking down the lonely highway.

Pinkish smudge backlighting the distant mountains told him day would soon be pouring on the heat, so he picked up the pace. When he reached the trail, he veered off and up the hill to his chosen spot. Ruska thought of obliterating his footprints in the sand, but decided it wasn't worth the effort.

It was only day two, and already he knew he was merely going through the motions, but if it weren't for those fingernail scratches. . . .

Hours passed. Ruska was amused to watch the same two lizards he saw yesterday skittering about on the rocks, repeating their daily push-up routines, utterly indifferent to the human observing them. Other than his two reptilian friends, there was no activity whatsoever.

Again, the afternoon heat pounded his body, and after hours of punishment he wearily stirred himself to embark on the long trek back to the car. He clambered gingerly down the hill and stepped onto the trail that to the left led to the road, and to the right led to the cave. A heat-shimmer seam rippled where rock met shadow.

Just as he took a step to the left, Ruska heard a strange rumbling sound coming from the right. At first, he thought it was a small landslide of pebbles rolling down from the hill, but the noise persisted, even increasing in volume. Still unnerved from yesterday's bizarre incident, he felt the irresistible urge to ignore it and continue to the left.

After some hesitation, and as a compromise to his sense of duty, he decided to approach the cave and check it out, but not to enter unless a very good reason presented itself.

He hoped there would not be a very good reason.

Damn fool! he scolded himself. *That's why you're here. What if it's Michael Powers?*

He turned to the right.

~ *A Meeting Outside the Cave* ~

As he approached the entrance, the strange sound increased in volume, and Ruska felt a dizziness he ascribed to the heat. Feeling as though he would faint, he quickly sat on the nearest flat rock, head sagging down between his knees. A merciless sun made him queasy, and he knew the cave would at least provide a cool respite. With the sound now pounding in his ears to the rhythm of his heartbeat, Emile forced himself to rise and seek the shelter of the cave. Anything would be better than dying of sunstroke, he thought. Let whatever beast waiting inside devour him, it would be preferable to enduring the flames for even another minute. With head throbbing and the horrible nausea worsening, he staggered into the cave and within a few steps instantly felt the cool air soothe his sunburned skin and upset stomach. As if following the cue of his revival, the strange noise suddenly became a soft purring, the way an animal does when it wants you to stay. A few more steps and he found a wonderfully cold rock on which to sit and recover his strength. The nausea quickly passed, so he sought to bestir himself and return to the road. Ruska gave little thought to finding Michael Powers. He decided the sounds were the product of an overly active imagination.

"Enough!" he exclaimed aloud. "Let's get out of here, Ruska!"

He slapped his knees as a prelude to standing, and when he looked up the same young woman he had encountered on his first visit to the cave so long ago stood there. He knew at once it was *Her*, and he also knew *She* must be a hallucination, a mirage lifted from heatstroke. Long ago, he had resolved to be done with *Her*, preferring to deal with the more understandable Buandelgereen. Past contact with this fathomless woman had lacerated his soul; the scabs were best left unpicked. Nevertheless, he now felt duty-bound to talk with *Her*, ghost or not. Besides, returning to the oven outside held no appeal. He waited, but *She* merely stared, as beautiful as a goddess, and as enigmatic as a sphinx. What does one say to a sphinx? Not being up on riddles, Emile reverted to the purpose of his visit.

"I understand you have lost track of Michael Powers?" he asked, more in the form of a statement than a question.

"It is the daughter," *She* replied in her typically melodic human voice, as usual, enigmatically.

"Yeah, Buandelgereen told me. Now it's not the son, it's the daughter?"

"It has always been so."

"Not what I heard."

She blinked but did not reply.

"I assume you're here for the same reason I am?" said Ruska, again framing his question in the form of a statement.

"You do not know why you are here, Mr. Ruska. *We* do."

"Yeah, the daughter, right?"

Again *She* blinked without answering.

"Look, I know *You* are a hallucination. I already let *You* talk me into that crazy trip to Asia. Result? A missing Michael Powers, not to speak of my own sanity. Question is, have I caught the schizophrenia bug from Mr. Powers?"

"No," *She* replied. "Too much sun."

"That's a relief."

"You should go home."

"Home, or the motel?"

"Earth is home."

"Okay, that's it!" he cried. "Too deep for me! Back to the motel for this gumshoe."

She merely blinked.

"By the way," he said as he stood to leave. "What's with the strange noises in here?"

"Your imagination."

"Sure."

As he walked away, Emile suddenly had a thought. "Hey! Who made those fingernail scratches in the rock?"

Unfortunately, *She* had disappeared.

"Figures," he said sarcastically.

Minutes passed in silence. Revived by the cool air, Ruska shook off the "nonsense" he had been involved with and turned his thoughts to food and a cold beer, or better yet, bourbon. *Wish Emma was here,* he thought wistfully.

On the way back, as the tires kicked up dust from the deserted road, he pushed the fingernail scratches and *Her* from his mind and focused on analyzing himself. It occurred to Ruska that his quest to locate Michael Powers was merely an excuse. For what? He wasn't sure. Combat the boredom of retirement? A distraction from his loneliness? Some midlife crisis, minus the requisite young blonde? No, he felt sure these were not what motivated him at this point in his life. So, what did? . . . he asked himself. Duty? No. He owed no duty to anyone other than himself. In fact, as hard as he tried, Ruska could conjure up no plausible reason for his actions . . . at least, nothing more than a stubborn desire to find answers to questions. *Yes,* he thought. *I have been asking questions all my life. In truth, I have been asking the same question cloaked in various disguises. And what question might that be? Who am I? What do I stand for? To what purpose do I dedicate my life? Finding ghosts? No, finding murderers. Is Michael Powers a murderer? That is the question. That is my quest. That is the purpose of my actions. Is Michael Powers a murderer? How did he pull off his disappearing act in Vietnam? Does he possess certain traits, or powers, that have transcended mere schizophrenia? Is he dangerous? Is he dangerous?*

Ruska gripped the steering wheel tightly in his excitement at hitting upon some core truth. Perhaps Michael Powers has developed a new strain of mental illness, he thought. Perhaps it is contagious. What if that is the case? What if the illness has evolved into something more sinister? How else to explain his hold on Doctors Hess, Camara, and Tavaris? How else to explain their bizarre behaviors, not to speak of their highly suspicious deaths? These questions helped to focus him on the problem at hand and chased away any depressing effects of the aimlessness to which he had fallen prey. Feeling a renewed sense of purpose, he vowed to continue the stakeout. Michael Powers might still show up. After all, he considered, stranger things had happened. He knew many a detective had called off his stakeout an hour before the bad guy showed up. Ruska had raised the stakes of his finding Michael Powers to a moral imperative and found comfort in the righteousness of his cause. Amid these reflections, it suddenly occurred to Ruska why *She* had made an appearance at the cave.

Of course! She *is also on a stakeout!*

The idea struck him like lightning.

Odd, it hadn't occurred to me before, he marveled, forgetting his earlier surmise that *She* was nothing more than a hallucination caused by the heat. With his newly found conviction that Michael Powers carried some form of mutated, viral form of schizophrenia, *She* had now become, for Ruska, a concrete, flesh-and-blood suspect, for he assumed *She* and Buandelgereen were Michael's protectors, his patronesses, and perhaps accomplices to multiple murders.

Can *She* be killed? he wondered.

~ *Angel and Michael* ~

Upon Michael's uttering the word "schizophrenia" to his fellow dishwasher at the restaurant, Angel displayed no outward sign of emotion. His face reflected nothing more than stony indifference. Michael gazed back into Angel's seemingly uncomprehending eyes and made the assumption his host did not understand.

"Do you know what schizophrenia is?" he asked politely.

Angel broke his flat countenance by smiling and tapping his fingertips together, apparently mustering some appropriate response. He leaned back in his chair and took a sip of water, then spoke with respectful gravity.

"A long-term mental disorder of a type involving a breakdown in the relation between thought, emotion, and behavior, leading to faulty perception, inappropriate actions and feelings, withdrawal from reality and personal relationships into fantasy and delusion, and a sense of mental fragmentation."

Michael felt stunned by this precise clinical account, and he stared incredulously at Angel. However, the mention of withdrawal from personal relationships forced him to think of his family, particularly Tamara and Ming-huá. Unwillingly, tears came to his eyes, and he remained silent for some time. Angel did not interrupt his struggle.

Finally, he summoned the power to speak. "Well, yes, you have the basic definition. But, Angel, I cannot describe the suffering it causes. I never know what is real and what is not. Even you, at this moment, might be nothing more than a hallucination, or a delusion that I work in a restaurant in the desert. For all I know, I might be back in the mental institution dreaming all this up."

"Yes, I see, *amigo*, I see." Angel rubbed his chin. "Descartes believed in a mind-body dualism. Your mind is separate from your body, which is more like a machine."

"Yes, I am aware of his philosophy."

Angel raised his hand, index finger pointing upward. "But, at the time, a highly intelligent princess was troubled by Descartes' notion. Princess Elizabeth of Bohemia asked him exactly how this separate mind communicates with the body. From the point of view of physics, it makes no sense. There must be some medium of touching, of pushing or pulling. What is that medium when it comes to mind? Of course, modern neurology has the answer. Neurons, neural pathways, sensory and motor cortices, action potentials, cells, muscles, and so forth."

"Thank you for the lesson, Angel, but how does that help me?"

"It doesn't, necessarily, but you should use what rational part of your mind remains to think about it. Can reason overcome delusion?"

"I don't know. I have often tried and always failed. Always!"

"Physicalism tells us everything is material, including the mind," said Angel. "The brain is plastic, an emergent property of neural activity. Assuming this is correct, Michael, you can change physical properties. You can bend them, break them, burn them, melt them, freeze them, redirect their pathways, and so on. Your schizophrenia is like some cluster of malignant neurons, like a canker. Use reason the way an oncologist uses radiation or chemotherapy."

"Easy to say, hard to do," replied Michael. "What if you are a hallucination giving me advice on how to eliminate hallucinations? You certainly don't sound like a typical dishwasher!"

"Would it matter?"

"Yes."

"Why?"

"Because I would not trust you."

"Michael—"

"No, Angel, the problem is I do not trust myself. I must go!"

Michael felt suddenly overwhelmed, short of breath, and desperate to escape. Escape! He jumped up and left Angel's apartment without another word. Angel did not move from his chair, merely watching his friend rush out of the room. He sighed and took another sip of water, then picked up a book that had been resting on the end table and started to read where he had left off. He paused. *Is it schizophrenia, or something else?*

~

As Michael walked back toward the trailer park, his mood darkened, and the demons that had always hovered close by came swooping down like vultures to a carcass. God and Goddess were conspicuous by their absence, but the voices that now crashed and reverberated in his head were unfamiliar, strange, distorted entities, seemingly dragged up from the mire of schizophrenia without God and Goddess to keep them in their place. He talked and gesticulated wildly as he moved down the highway. An occasional car slowed, but then sped up to put distance between it and the madman.

Reaching the trailer, he threw open the door and dashed in, slamming it shut behind him and locking it for good measure. Tamara rushed out of the bedroom where she had been resting with Ming-huá. Seeing his condition, she reined in her alarm and did not bother to ask what happened.

"Who is after you?" she asked.

Michael stopped short and looked at her with an expression of terror.

"You don't know?" he asked sarcastically. "Doesn't your magic hump tell you? It's them! Them!"

Tamara remained calm. "Who?"

"Them!"

"God?"

"No!"

"Goddess?"

"No!"

"Who?"

"We have to hide! Where's Ming-huá?" He pulled at his shirt as though it burned his body.

"She's safe."

"No one is safe from them! Don't you see? No one!"

"Yes, I see that. Come, have a drink. Be calm so you can face them when they come."

"Yes, yes. Good."

Tamara poured tea and slipped in a sedative—one of the last pills Buandelgereen had pressed into her palm.

Michael took the drink. "Is the door locked?"

"Yes."

He took a sip.

"Is Ming-huá in a safe place?"

"Yes."

He took another sip, then gulped down the remainder. "I have to go!"

"Where?" asked Tamara, trying to remain calm.

"Outside. I can draw them away from you. They'll follow me and leave you and Ming-huá alone." His voice faltered. "You'll be safe. I can deal with them. I have reason and neurons to fight them."

Tamara did not know where this notion came from, but she let him ramble on until he fell asleep on the couch.

"A step back," she told herself aloud. "Only a step back. Patience." Tears of frustration rolled down her cheeks. At this moment, she realized how much she loved him. She loved him even more deeply because he fought so long and so valiantly against his illness. "Sometimes," she said to the air, "it's just too much. If I had medication! God damn it! Real medication! Nothing but this damn sedative to knock him out."

Her cry of despair awoke Ming-huá, and Tamara hurried off to hold the daughter she so treasured, a child that must be protected from forces that want her for their own reasons, reasons Tamara vaguely understood, but deeply feared.

Chapter Twenty-Three

A Different Kind of Schizophrenia

If Not Schizophrenia, Then What?

~ Am I A Murderer? ~

Dear Reader, let me pose a question: Can one be a murderer and not know it? I don't mean accidentally killing someone but killing with intention. Can one murder with the intent to kill and not be aware of having done so? Many a killer has argued this point. They were hypnotized, they were under the influence of drugs, and, in the case of insanity, they were not aware of the nature and quality of the act—or of its wrongfulness. I have pondered this question since awakening from a deep sleep. Tamara has admitted giving me a strong sedative, and I can honestly say I do not blame her. The psychotic episode has passed. Though I remember only bits and pieces, the deeper question remains. Why do I bring up murder? Simple. Had I run into anyone the afternoon I left Angel's house, I might easily have killed them in the mistaken idea they were demons come to harm me and my family. Is this what happened to the psychiatrists I have left dead in my wake? Angel has given me food for thought. Can I control my schizophrenia by simply using the power of reason? Clearly not. However, can I use reason to control the worst and most destructive aspects of my schizophrenia? I don't know. It is said a hypnotist cannot make a person commit a crime if the act violates deeply held moral convictions. In the absence of God and Goddess to give me focus and direction, I am at sea, tossed about on a stormy ocean of unfamiliar voices. Are Tamara and Ming-huá at risk? Assuredly, yes. Should I leave for their own protection? That, my dear Reader, is the issue I have been wrestling with.

Tamara is suspicious and tries to keep me in sight, but for the moment, I have no intention of running away. I have this bizarre image of standing on a rope bridge stretched across a bottomless gorge, swaying in the wind, while facing a dragon that wants to destroy me and cast my body over the side. The dragon has the face of God and the body of Goddess, breathing fire and roaring in fury. But the dragon is nothing compared to the horror of the sounds rising from that bottomless gorge. These monstrous sounds are the unfamiliar voices that have taken over in the absence of that dragon. The boards shiver beneath my feet as if the bridge lies strung across a crack in the world. If I fall, I fall into the abyss never to return. That is what scares me the most.

But now, I must get ready for work. Night shift, as usual. I look forward to seeing Angel, as it is Saturday and the place will be packed. Perhaps he has some new insights now that he has had a chance to think about my predicament. Tonight, Tamara will be working as well, a rarity for us to share the same shift. Our neighbor Sophia, an older widow living out her years alone, grateful to have even the company of a baby like Ming-huá, has enthusiastically agreed to watch her. It is late afternoon when we walk to the restaurant. While not too far from the trailer park, it is still a bit of a haul, and we set off at a good pace. Tamara has scrutinized me all day for any signs of a recurrence of my episode, but I have remained on the straight and narrow, and she seems confident all will go well. So am I. However, having said that, we know, dear Reader, my schizophrenia could run me off the rails at any time without warning.

Upon entering the restaurant, the place is already full, and customers are milling around outside. "A long waiting list," Tamara says grimly. Steam, lemon detergent, and grilled onions hang in the air. Angel is in the kitchen hard at work scrubbing and running trays through the industrial dishwasher. I put on my apron and plunge into the work. I must admit, it is precisely as Angel described it, mindless work that lets one's mind wander. We waste little time with greetings.

"Hello, *amigo*."

"Hello, Angel. Busy, eh?"

"Yeah. Grab that busboy box and load the tray with coffee mugs and run it through, would 'ya. Tad says we're short on mugs."

"Okay."

Too busy for further discourse, we both fall into sync like two well-oiled machines, and the kitchen hums with that endless, clamoring cycle of clean dishes to dirty, and dirty back to clean, continuously through the night. I find the rhythm comforting, my mind free to roam the green pastures of reminiscence, romance, and fantasy. With the voices that dwell in the evil abyss silent, and God and Goddess absent, I feel the joy of liberation. How blessedly beautiful is inner quiet without the sound of schizophrenic fingernails on a blackboard. I catch brief glimpses of Tamara coming and going, but we have no time to chat. She always looks at me in anticipation, and when I smile back, she is aglow with contentment. Tamara's contentment transfers to me, and I find myself whistling, a practice I almost never perform. Angel gives me a sideways glance.

"You're a happy man, *mi amigo*. Been thinking of Spinoza?" He follows this question with a chuckle.

"No, Angel. It is Marcus Aurelius."

He gives a particularly stubborn stain one last, vigorous scrubbing, and says, "Ah! Perfect! Stoicism for the prisoners!"

"Yup. I recall he wrote, 'The happiness of your life depends on the quality of your thoughts,' or something like that."

"*Sí*, you got it right. He also says, 'It is the person who continues in his self-deception and ignorance who is harmed.' Do you not agree?"

"Yes."

"Then, in that case Miguel, your voices and hallucinations are the epitome of self-deception, are they not?"

"To you normals, they are self-deception. To us, they are prophetic."

"Like Jesus or Buddha or Muhammad?"

Before I can answer, Tad sticks his head in the kitchen and shouts, "Hurry up, guys! You're falling behind!"

"Okay, okay!" exclaims Angel in irritation. He mutters to himself as he turns back to his scrubbing, "The one time I want to talk instead of think, and he. . . . "

"Thinking is not Tad's strong point," I joke.

We have been furiously working for a few hours and I am beginning to hear rumblings from within. To my dismay, it is not the old, familiar God or Goddess, but those debased monsters from the abyss. I cannot make out their words, but I know they are vile obscenities and vicious demands to do violence. I do my best to ignore them, but the clanging, banging of the hectic kitchen seems to goad them on. Somewhere out front, a dinner knife rings into a bus tub—innocent metal, but a sudden trigger. At last, Tamara pops in, and I look at her pleadingly. She comes to me and kisses me on the mouth, then says, "I am here, Michael. They are bad. Push them out of your mind. Try!"

Angel waits until Tamara leaves, and asks, "Are you okay, *amigo*?"

"Never better!" I lie.

Those horrific voices are getting worse, stronger, and I am doing my best to exert control over them using my reasoning abilities. Having Angel by my side helps. Dear Reader, you must understand the voices are real! You would no more deny their reality than if your own mother were in the room speaking to you at this moment. Now the voices are distinct enough to make out the words. They are calling me a murderer. A murderer! And worse, to murder again. I can't . . . I can't hold on. . . .

~ *Back* ~

Dear Reader, it's a few days after the episode at the restaurant I described earlier. Somehow, I succeeded in finishing my shift, and Tamara took me home that night, keeping a tight grip on my arm the entire time as we walked. Since then, I have slept. That sleep has been abetted by Tamara's dwindling supply of sedatives (yes, dangerous, yes, necessary). I am still in bed when Tamara enters and tells me I must go back to work. Even now, as I write her words, they are the first I have fully processed and understood during all this time since the restaurant.

"What?" I ask. I need clarification as my brain is still groggy.

"Work, Michael. You need to go back to work or else you'll be fired. Tad is patient, but not that patient."

"Yes, I'm ready. How's Ming-huá?"

She carries in our baby and sets her gently down beside me. God, she is so cute! I am carried away in flights of fancy, and I see us living together happily until Ming-huá is quite grown up and off to college. That dream is worth fighting for, dying for.

"Come on," says Tamara, picking up Ming-huá. "Breakfast, then work!"

How many of these horrible episodes do I have to endure before I can rest? When will the next time be when I turn on Tamara or Ming-huá, thinking them some terrible creatures that must be destroyed? Am I a murderer? Could I murder those I love the most?

"Come on, Michael, don't just lay there!" prods Tamara. "What are you thinking?"

"How much I love you."

With her free hand, Tamara grabs a pillow and tosses it at my head. As I raise an arm to block it, something extraordinary happens.

The pillow disappears midair.

We both look in shock at Ming-huá and are met with a smiling baby staring back. I watch the blood drain from Tamara's face.

"You've seen her do this before, haven't you," I whisper.

"Yes, and it must not be allowed to continue, at least not now."

She looks at me quizzically. "Have you?"

"Yes, but I thought it was my schizophrenia."

"No, it's not. How many times must you be told. You are the Chosen One."

We gaze at the baby in dumbfounded silence.

I whisper, "No, she's the Chosen One."

Ming-huá giggles.

"The real Chosen One," I say.

~

It is a few days after the disappearance. I now have the notion of returning to the cave. It came to me while recovering from the latest Ming-huá revelation, and the idea has grown in strength. If I go back to the cave and assure myself the whole 'iron door' and 'time-travel' experiences with Buandelgereen were merely delusional, I will have reconnected with the rational part of my brain. This will give me more ammunition to support pragmatic reason, as Angel suggested, and hopefully control unreason. Should I find nothing but sand and rock, I will know how even powerful hallucinations and delusions can be made impotent. In fact, the more I think about this, the more determined I become. Looking at Tamara's face, lined with fear and anxiety over what I might do any minute, and Ming-huá's utterly innocent eyes behind which lurks unimaginable powers, I know I am doing the right thing. We are older parents, and it is hard enough for both of us to cope.

Of course, the thought has entered my mind that if I do find iron doors and time portals, then I am done for. No future, just an endless succession of psychotic episodes culminating in my death, and Tamara's liberation. In that event, whenever I have momentary control over my schizophrenia, I'll voluntarily return to the institution for permanent burial there. Suicide is not an option, regardless of what the voices command.

And Storyteller? Where does he fit into all this? He is, naturally, the skeleton in the tunnel, the decayed remnants of my youth. Even now, I can hear him laughing at me. Were it not for Tamara and Ming-huá, I would definitely return to join him, but I have responsibilities. Who is burdened more by responsibilities: the normal person with real-world tasks; the schizophrenic with hallucinations and delusions; or the father of a powerful Chosen One, an entity surrounded by earth-shattering forces of good and evil to contend with? I have reached the stage in life where I simply want to "tend my roses" without the necessity to fight fire-breathing dragons and murderous demons. This is why schizophrenics die early—we have burned up all our reserves of energy. But I digress. The cave. That must be my destination the next day I have off. I must not tell Tamara, for she would try to prevent me. I must come up with a good excuse for being gone all day. Dear Reader, what can that be? Tamara's hump (like her mother's) is forever attuned to the universe and picks up any hint of the lies endlessly disseminated by people. I should be very clever or it won't come off. You see, dear Reader, the cave, to Tamara, is like a portal, and via its multiple side chambers, leads to a profusion of hells, both past and future.

I have come up with the perfect story. I will tell Tamara that on my next day off, I intend to walk into town and shop for her birthday. Never mind it is over a month away. It is a lie, of course, and I'll have to be very convincing for this pretext to succeed. Since the cave is a long way from town, I cannot turn the lie into truth by visiting both. Fortunately, my experiences with Doctors Hess, Camara, and Tavaris have honed my skills at fabrication. Still, Tamara and her hump are far more perceptive than those worthy psychiatrists. Tomorrow at dinner I will make my pitch. Wish me luck.

~

Dinnertime. Tamara sits across from me in good spirits. Well, the time is now for my little white lie. I have pulled the night shift again, so if it does not go well and she spots my ruse, I can escape her fury by using work as an excuse to flee. We have had a pleasant day, and my small talk skills are progressing quite nicely. I managed to discuss the weather, our neighbors, the latest news, and how to cope with Ming-huá's nascent ability. Not a word about mental illness, voices, delusions, dragons, demons, or philosophical speculations about the nature of the universe. Very well, the ground is laid, and I am ready to pitch in. I have waited until we have finished eating and are enjoying after-dinner wine. The trick is to be nonchalant.

"By the way, for once I have Saturday off. I think I'll go to town."

"Good, I can do some shopping."

"No, I need to go without you along." I pull what I hope is a mischievous smile.

"Ah." Her face reflects concern.

"Don't worry, I won't be gone long."

"Why do you need to go without me?"

Here is the delicate point, and I must be very careful. "Well, I didn't want to tell you, but since you ask, and seem so worried, I'm going to shop for your birthday."

Tamara sits silently and sips her wine, looking over the rim of the glass into my eyes. I must hold steady and keep this rather challenging smile pasted on my face. By challenging, I mean to convey that any opposition by her will meet my most energetic protest.

"You plan to go to the cave, don't you?"

Damn! All I can do is try and brazen it through. "No! I have no interest in going to the cave. I want to get you the perfect gift."

"Michaaelll!" she draws out my name. A very bad sign. I feel myself withering under her gaze.

"What? Can't I even get you a birthday gift without justifying myself to you and your damn suspicions?"

"They are not suspicions. They are certainties. Furthermore, I am not suspicious, I am worried. You are just now getting better. The voices have almost stopped, and your delusional episodes are few and far between. Obviously, I need help with Ming-huá. Why risk it?"

"Okay, I do want to go to the cave. Damn it, when you worked for Buandelgereen and . . . anyway, you're the one who led me to those side tunnels where I ended up in different times and places! For a while, I even thought you were the human manifestation of Temulun, remember?"

Tamara turns white. "No! Those days are over when I . . . no! That is a forbidden topic! Never more will I . . . never mind! Those days you are forbidden to mention, Michael. Forbidden! We must try and be normal people that act normally and see normal things. It is imperative we protect Ming-huá until she's ready to use her powers."

"Okay, okay. But my reasons for going are good ones, not delusions. You're right, I've made some progress, and I need positive reinforcement to keep on track. If I return to the cave and see only sand and rock, I'll know I'm finally getting this thing under control."

"And if you see something else?"

I knew this was coming. "Then, I'll deal with it somehow."

"Deal with it? Come on, Michael. You won't be able to, and when you fail, we'll be back to square one."

"I'll deal with it."

"Then I'm coming with you."

"No. Stay with Ming-huá. I must do this for my own sake, Tamara. Think of it as a test."

"And if you fail the test?"

"Then I fail, but at least I will have tried."

She lets out an exasperated sigh. "And if something goes wrong, I'm the one who has to clean up the mess."

"Nothing will go wrong. Haven't things worked out at the restaurant?"

"For the most part," she admits. "But the cave is an entirely different matter."

"How so?"

Tamara shakes her head. "You know as well as I. The cave is the belly of the beast, the geographic center of your schizophrenia."

"No, that is the tunnel."

"Ha! That's in Vietnam, and you believe this cave connects to that tunnel! For Christ's sake, Michael! You believed Doctor Hess's bathroom connected to that damn tunnel."

"That's just my point," I say as reasonably as I can. "This is a test of those old delusions. Don't forget, Tamara, you were a part of them. For all I know, you have the powers I suspected from the beginning. You took me to the cave and showed me—"

"Stop! Forbidden, forbidden, forbidden! Do you understand?"

"Yeah."

"Now, how will I know if something happens to you?"

"I guess if I don't come back."

"Great," she says resignedly.

I have won.

I am going.

To the cave.

Goddess help me.

~ *The Cave Redux* ~

I am on my way to the cave. It is odd how everything in my life seems to keep rebounding back upon me. Vietnam won't go away. Storyteller won't go away. The tunnel won't go away. The voices won't go away. This damn cave won't go away. Buandelgereen won't go away. Amid these rather self-pitying thoughts, I hear panting behind, and turn around, startled.

"How about me? Aren't you glad I don't go away forever? Huh? Huh? Got a treat?"

Yes, dear Reader, you probably guessed correctly, Temulun is back, prancing around me while I stand motionless and look stupidly at her. My heart sinks. If I can't even keep an imaginary dog out of my mind, how will I keep out all these life-changing delusions? On the other hand, maybe Temulun is just what the doctor ordered. Her buoyant personality will keep me from taking any of this seriously. I hope. She is more elvish than evil.

"No, I don't have a treat."

"Aww."

"What are you doing here? I didn't call you."

"That's right, you didn't."

"Besides, I thought your mistress didn't know where I was. If that is the case, how do you know where I am?"

Temulun tilts her head, and the boxer wrinkles crease her face. "Good question. Dogs are good at sniffing things out, you know?"

"Yeah, I know."

"Got a treat?"

"God damn it, Temulun! If you're going with me, stop begging for treats! I already told you; I don't have any."

"Aww. Don't get mad. I mean well. Want me to show you where the cave is?"

"I know where the cave is, Temulun, you stupid dog!"

She looks so miserable at this harsh reply that I say consolingly, "Oh, never mind. Come on. Just watch out for my feet."

"Of course. Got a—oh, never mind!"

I give her a disgusted look, and we continue on our way. I feel like an overgrown male version of Dorothy on the Yellow Brick Road, accompanied by an overgrown boxer version of Toto.

"What'cha going to do when we get there," pants Temulun, for it is getting hot.

I tilt my wide-brimmed hat down to block the sun. "Just look. After all, not much to see, just rock and sand, right?"

I hold my breath even as I keep walking.

"Weellll, that depends on the eye of the beholder," she says.

"How so?"

"I happen to know something you don't know."

"What?"

"Got a treat?"

"Your attempted bribery is wasted. I really don't have any treats, not even for myself, just water."

"Can I have some?"

I laugh. "You don't need any, you're a hallucination."

"Look at my tongue! You call that hallucination! I'm dying for water, and my paws are hot!"

"Then go back where you came from."

"Do you know where that is?"

I point to my head.

"Can't fit in there."

We have walked a few miles, and I need to rest, so I veer off the road and find a clump of acacia trees to seek shade. Temulun trots beside me, still complaining about water.

When I plop down and wipe my face with my handkerchief, Temulun pouts. "I can report you to the ASPCA."

"Hallucinations can't report anything."

She sits beside me, leaning into the shade. "Remember I told you I know something you don't?" she asks.

"Yeah."

"Well, it's kinda like what Custer's scouts tried to warn him."

"So, there's hostile Indians waiting at the cave?"

She tilts her head again. "You might say that. Whew! It's too hot here in reality! See ya!"

Off she runs, bounding across the rocks and gradually fading away until I only hear the nails of her paws upon the rocks. Like any good ghost, she is now invisible. Her presence bodes ill for my mission, but I think Temulun is a special case, after all. I must shake off this little episode and continue to the cave. There is a low rumbling within my mind; the sense of earth shifting, tectonic plates nudging, and I tremble, for I know it is not God or Goddess, it is Demons (for lack of a better word). Nameless, shapeless, purely malevolent voices, too evil even to betray their forms to my imagination. Compared to these demons, God and Goddess are old friends, even comforting bedfellows whose presence I have come to accommodate in my worldview. But the demons! They are like a thousand poisonous snakes slithering in the underbrush of my brain. Wherever a thought steps, I know they might strike. Still, I walk on. Going back to Tamara with my tail between my legs (sorry Temulun) is unthinkable. I would never be trusted again.

To pass the time and keep the voices at bay, I repeat aloud to the cadence of my strides, "Only sand and rock, only sand and rock, only sand and rock." (I learned this little trick from Sergeant Dam as a method to tamp down the fear.)

Heat has now become a problem. I have brought plenty of water, but the sweat flows freely, and I can hardly wait to get to the little dusty turnoff leading to the cave. The road wavers in the heat, a shimmering mirage. Now that I think of it, I miss Temulun. She is a welcome distraction from the temperature, not to speak of the voices, which remain a low, imperceptible rumble. Nevertheless, even with Temulun gone, I am convinced the voices are controllable, as are the delusions. More than ever, I am determined to reach the cave and see for myself it is nothing more than sand and rock. Nothing more. Sand and rock.

Finally, I have reached the little trail that leads to the cave. I keep trying to convince myself they are getting quieter, but it isn't true. The demons are getting louder. I almost want to cry out for Goddess to come and vanquish them all. Vanquish them to their own version of perdition. But *She* remains absent. Surely, Temulun has told *Her* where I am. Surely! Ha. It is funny in a way. Here I am, ostensibly hoping there is nothing but sand and rock, and I'm calling for Goddess like a child calling for mama. *Get a grip, Michael!* Spurred on by that last exhortation, I push myself to reach the cool interior of the cave, come gods or demons. Escape from being broiled by the sun is now my only imperative.

I am at the entrance and don't even hesitate before plunging in. Taking deep breaths, I penetrate a little farther and sit on a rock before I am enveloped by total darkness, gratefully luxuriating in the cool. With backpack at my feet, I fish out my water bottle, take a few sips, and check the flashlight. Confirming it is in good working order, I am ready to proceed. So far, to my relief, there is nothing out of the ordinary. Just rock and sand. Even the demons have quieted down. Okay, this is good. I'm going to take a few deep breaths and travel all the way to the end. There will be no iron doors, no Buandelgereen, no time travel, none of that. Only reality allowed. As I walk, I am tempted to take some of these spur chambers. After all, I am now certain they lead nowhere but to a rock ending. However, I will save that for my return trip. I want to keep going and make sure no iron doors suddenly rise from my fevered imagination. They are more or less silent now, as befits the utter quiet of this cave.

As I walk without experiencing hallucinations or delusions, I gain confidence. Am I finally defeating schizophrenia? Yes! My flashlight illuminates only sand and rock. Nothing else. I reach the place where the first iron door should have been. No iron door! So completely encouraged by this, I almost dare the hallucinations and delusions to do their best. I won't be fooled any more. As far back as I can remember, I have lived in fear. Fear of my father's coldness and mental lapses. Fear of my own mind. Fear of a distorted world where reality and unreality are so mixed together that neither God nor Goddess could ever untangle them. At long last, do I have a firm grip on reality? Can I banish my demons and live with my family in the realm of normalcy and peace? Yes! I must! For Tamara's sake. For Ming-huá's sake! I am confident I finally have a solid grip on reality.

No second iron door!

Sand and rock only.

My heart is filled with anticipation as I near the end. Will it be the end, or will Buandelgereen be standing there laughing at me?

I tremble as I shine my flashlight ahead.

The end of the cave.

I shine the light all around.

Only sand and rock!

Only sand and rock!

I dance and frolic in the knowledge!

Only sand and rock!

Delusions and hallucinations no more! No more!

Where are You Goddess? I want to see Your face and shout denials that You exist! Not God, not all the others! I turn off the flashlight in commemoration of my new life. Ironically, it is a life in which only darkness prevails because I will no longer be afraid of the dark. Ever.

I let out a howl to all the deities and demons that have plagued my life from the beginning . . . and that plagued my father's life!

I cannot help it, dear Reader. There are tears in my eyes. A normal life is within reach. A normal life!

~

Suddenly, a light blooms in the black cave. Not mine; my flashlight is off. All my hopes and dreams come crashing down. What horror waits behind that blinding, terrible light?

I turn to confront whatever it might be. . . .

Chapter Twenty-Four

Confrontation

Motels and Mazes

~ Dog Days ~

Emile Ruska had been on his stakeout for a week, and not a single sign had appeared indicating Michael Powers was anywhere nearby. His patience ran thin, and thoughts of abandoning the idea of finding him at the cave became so strong, he decided to give it one more week before giving up for good. Enough money had been wasted already, and it would be futile to throw good money after bad. Still, a week longer would eliminate any regrets he might have of leaving too early. In the meantime, when not boiling at the cave, he strolled the town's only main street, looking at the same shops multiple times until the proprietors greeted him warmly. Emile bought a few items he did not really want just to reassure the owners, as well as to curtail any embarrassment he felt about loitering. He had tried all four restaurants for dinner (he did not eat lunch and had free breakfasts at the motel) and decided El Fantasma was the winner. Timing is everything, and not once did he see Michael Powers scrubbing away in the kitchen despite eating there multiple times. Somewhere in the back, a dishwasher's laugh carried through the service door—white noise to Emile, fate biding its time. On this evening, he scarfed down a light meal at El Fantasma and returned to the motel after another fruitless lookout at the cave. But the motel room gave him no comfort, as he normally passed the time reading or watching terrible TV programs. In a rather foul mood, he entered the lobby and nodded toward the clerk, who nodded back and conspicuously shifted her gaze toward something. He followed her eyes and saw a figure sitting in a chair staring at him with a smile.

"Emma! What are you doing here?"

"Hello to you too, Emile."

Emile rushed over and hugged her. "Seriously," he said. "What are you doing here? How did you find me?"

"Your doodling has consequences, Emile," said Emma laughing. "You really should get outta that habit. I could be a bad guy, you know?"

"Huh?"

"That napkin you left at PicYrPoison with 'El Fantasma' and a desert motel logo wasn't exactly a cipher."

Careless, he thought. He knew better.

Emile was not amused. "Where are you staying?"

"One floor up from you."

Ruska shook his head in surrender. "That far?"

She shrugged. "I tried."

"No matter. How about a drink?"

"Where?"

They both stared at each other for a brief moment, with Ruska breaking the ice. "My room? I got a bottle just waiting."

"Sounds good."

"Let me get some ice on the way," said Emile, his mood remarkably changed for the better.

Once they had settled into a couple of comfortable chairs in his room, they stared at each other over drinks. The ice cracked in the glasses.

"Cheers!" said Emma. "How goes the hunt?"

"Whoa!" exclaimed Ruska. "What brings you here?"

"You, of course."

"I'm flattered."

"You should be. I thought about it long and hard, but shyness was never one of my vices."

"God, it's wonderful you're here. I was just thinking about you when I walked into the lobby."

"Sure."

"No, really. Detectives don't lie," he laughed.

"That's all they do!" sputtered Emma, almost spilling her drink. "Seriously, how goes your search?"

"Are you really that interested?"

"Actually, yes. I watch a lot of crime movies and TV whodunits. Once I learned you were hanging your own shingle, I sort of fantasized being your secretary, like in some Humphrey Bogart movie."

"You're showing your age, Emma."

She shuddered. "Better than trying to look twenty-one again."

He raised his glass. "Here's to that."

"Well?"

"Truth be told, Emma, it's just boring. Speaking of age, I've been camped out in hundred-degree heat staring at a stupid cave for what feels like forever, and my old bones are protesting. Really, detective work is mainly boring routine."

"That's what they all say."

"They're right."

Emma looked around the room. "Well, I'm here. What are you going to do with me?"

"What will you let me do?"

"Your call."

"Then let's do what single people do when they meet in a hotel."

"Talk?"

"Very funny."

~

Next morning both awoke without the slightest hint of regret. Feeling like kids on an adventure, Emma went to her room to shower, afterward, meeting Emile in the breakfast room.

"I see you're going hiking," she said sitting at the table. "You've already eaten?"

"Yeah. The sooner I go, the cooler it is while I'm walking to the cave."

"Want company?"

Emile shook his head emphatically. "No. We would just both be miserable instead of only one of us. You give me something to look forward to at the end of the day."

"What's to do in this town?"

"Nothing. Just dream about me while I'm gone."

"How exciting," she laughed. "Besides, I brought a book."

"You did?" asked Emile, revealing his skepticism and instantly regretting it.

Emma frowned. "I'm not as stupid as you think, Einstein." She dug in her large, floppy purse, and displayed a copy of *Anna Karenina.*

"Wow!" admired Ruska. "I'm impressed."

"All I know is that she threw herself under a train for some man. What a waste!"

"I think there's more to it than that, Emma."

"I know, I know. Just playing down to my stereotype. Besides, I only brought it to impress you. When do you think you'll be back?"

"Sooner than I had originally planned," he quipped. "No later than four or five."

"I'll be here."

He put his hand on hers and squeezed. Her fingers laced back, brief and sure. A flicker of caution crossed him. She shouldn't be here, not with the cave in play, but he let it pass.

"You'd better be."

~

On his way to the cave, Emile felt contentment for the first time since he could remember. Emma, a balm to his lonely existence, soothed the increasingly painful sting of age and isolation. He knew his regard for Emma had a mercenary side to it—she would never stint from domestic work and the desire to please—but he justified this by convincing himself it would be a joy to her. Parking in the familiar wash under cottonwoods, he walked to the cave with a livelier step than usual, not once thinking of Michael Powers or mysterious happenings. Later, when sitting in his usual rocky observation post, he found himself hoping he would not find Michael Powers—Emma and the cool, comfortable motel beckoned. Time passed relatively quickly with the distraction of sexual fantasies pleasantly running through his mind. His two old lizard friends did push-ups and seemed to tilt their heads at his changed demeanor. The urgent quest to which he had so recently dedicated himself faded away in the glare of desire. No room now for speculations about multiple murders and mutated schizophrenia.

Absorbed by these musings, Emile spent the rest of the day anticipating his return to the motel, and when Michael Powers did not appear by three o'clock, he left his post early. That night, he took Emma to the nearest restaurant for dinner, thinking El Fantasma too far away for his purposes. Had they eaten there, Emile would have seen Tamara serving customers, but fate intervened again, and his mission necessarily continued unfulfilled. But whether the mission succeeded or not, Ruska fully intended to enjoy the time he had with Emma. For once in his life, he granted himself the luxury of being reckless. Age and years of abstention gave him permission.

After a pleasant meal, full of bantering and good cheer, they retired to Emile's room for a passionate night of lovemaking. In the morning, they lay together under cool sheets and tried to avoid whatever decisions about the future must be made. Finally, Ruska groaned and sat on the edge of the bed, yawning, and ineffectively running fingers through his thinning hair.

"Duty calls," he croaked.

"No breakfast?" asked Emma.

"Yeah, same routine. Meet you down there."

Less motivated even than the day before, Emile waited for Emma, leisurely enjoying coffee and not inclined to wolf down his food just to get to the cave early. When she arrived, his face lit up like a child on Christmas morning, and he pulled the chair out for her.

"Sweetie, don't you know those days are long gone? Thank you, though. You're a gentleman and a scholar."

"And old."

"Nonsense. I'm going to grab a bit of food, but stick around, I want to talk to you before you go. And I want you to actually answer."

"Sure, I haven't eaten either."

So, they ate while Ruska pondered what might be on her mind. Deciding it must be something about their future relationship, he had the sudden urge to leave so their time together would not be spoiled. However, after she finished her plate, Emma gave him a surprise.

"Emile, I want to talk to you about Mr. Powers."

Startled, Ruska replied, "Okay," rather tentatively.

"I'm serious, Emile, I want to know some things. This has nothing to do with my wanting to be your secretary or watching stupid whodunits on TV. This man has dragged you around the world, taken up all your time worrying and fretting about . . . whatever. That is what I want to know."

"Whatever?"

"Don't joke. Be honest. Is he dangerous?"

Ruska put on his most serious expression, intending to humor her, but realized he really wanted to be open and verbalize his own feelings, his own doubts and fears. He took a sip of coffee and started on a long narrative, much against his natural inclinations, mainly for his own sake.

"I don't know, Emma. I think perhaps he is, but I'm not sure he is even aware of it. You look confused, so let me explain, if I can. My journey with Mr. Powers has been long and complicated. More complicated than any case I ever had, or ever will have, I hope. It started with two dead psychiatrists, both overseeing his case. Each of them died under strange circumstances, but the evidence simply did not add up. One of them a female psychiatrist, died at the institution outside of Mr. Powers' locked door. No signs of foul play. Natural causes. Worse, after that, Mr. Powers escaped the institution, and soon, the other psychiatrist's body was found on the side of the road, a road leading here, Emma. Again, forensics found no suspicious cause of death, and determined he had died of a heart attack. No trace of foul play, including poison, was found. Yet, he had been with Michael Powers, I am sure of it, when he died. By the way, a third psychiatrist who had been treating Mr. Powers was also dead, but he died in Rhode Island, a cemetery no less, and obviously Powers could not have been involved. I say 'obviously' yet now I am not so sure.

"Here is the key, I think. A private detective named Fred Miller hired by the institution found Michael Powers in a cave near here, clearly experiencing a psychotic delusion that he was in some majestic hideaway with iron doors built by Buandelgereen, that Mongol woman you saw at *PicYrPoison*. Powers was returned to the institution and my investigation began. In the beginning, I felt quite confident the case would be solved rather quickly. After all, we were dealing with a schizophrenic and a spate of suspicious deaths. But the deeper I got, the more confusing it became. For reasons I don't want to go into, the cave near here became the center of my investigation. After all, it seemed to be at the core of his delusion. I visited it, and very strange things happened. Very strange. No, don't ask. I won't tell you, yet. I'm still not clear what happened in my own mind, or even if it happened. Suffice to say, at the behest of this Mongol woman, I accompanied Mr. Powers to China, then to Vietnam. No, don't ask. I cannot, I will not go into those details."

Ruska paused to have some coffee. Emma noticed he had a haunted look and she started to speak, but he raised his hand for her to stop while he continued his story.

"Well, it appears Mr. Powers is an escape artist. As you are aware, he is loose again, apparently holed up with some woman who, I am told by Buandelgereen, gave birth to his child. No, she doesn't know where he is. In fact, she and her colleagues are also looking for him. This stakeout is my last hope. Every other lead has petered out and led nowhere. But I am convinced the cave is the key to Michael Powers and his delusions. I'm counting on his returning, kind of like a killer returning to the scene of his crime, or to revisit the victim."

Emma's face reflected horror. "My God, Emile! Three dead psychiatrists! Sure-ly he is dangerous!"

"Well, therein lies the mystery, Emma. If he killed them, how did he do it? I have my own theory, but I'm certainly not ready to disclose it just yet."

"Why?"

"You'd think I was crazy."

"I already know you're crazy! Come on, Emile, let me in on what you're thinking. After all, I came all this way just for you."

"And I'm not going to have you leave under the impression you have . . . well, hooked up with a madman. Maybe just as mad as Michael Powers himself."

"Well, at least give me a hint."

Ruska looked at his watch and started to rise from his chair. "It's late. Got to go."

"Wait right there, mister!" commanded Emma in her best bartender voice. "A hint, please. Please."

Now standing, Ruska leaned over and said quietly, "Okay. Schizophrenia, Emma, schizophrenia."

"What about it?"

"I don't think he suffers from schizophrenia at all."

"What?"

"That's all I'm going to say, for now anyway." Out in the parking lot, a dust-coated sedan idled, as if listening.

Before Emma had a chance to respond, Ruska leaned over and kissed her, then moved quickly away.

~ *The Last Day* ~

Emile spent the next few days sweltering under a hot sun trying to puzzle out the mystery of Michael Powers. His brief recitation to Emma of the events that led him here had rekindled his enthusiasm for the hunt. He knew his notion that Michael Powers did not have schizophrenia, or at least did not suffer from any schizophrenia known to psychiatry, was far-out. No one would listen unless he had more evidence. His own otherworldly experiences in the cave and with Her, bizarre as they were, would only reflect poorly on his own sanity. Ruska often tried to check his radical idea as being non-scientific, but he found himself increasingly sympathetic to White Thunder and his ilk. Something spiritually malformed, demonic, unexplored might be dwelling in Michael Powers. Or—to be scientific—he had some mutated form of schizophrenia. Those influences ev-idently could project themselves into even rational, highly educated professionals like Doctors Hess, Camara, and Tavaris. What galled him even more, Powers obviously possessed abilities capable of mesmerizing hardened investigators like himself. How else to explain what he saw, what he felt, what he feared? Once again, it seemed to Emile that Powers' form of schizophrenia had somehow become contagious, like a virus. He caught himself glancing into mirrors, half expecting to see someone else staring back. A brief pressure built behind his eyes, a low electrical hum that wasn't the heat.

Friday afternoon arrived after a long, unproductive week at the cave (and happy times in the evenings). He returned to the motel and met Emma, his frustration so evident in his scowling demeanor that she insisted he shower and then go downstairs for a drink at the lounge.

Once seated, they ordered drinks and Emma sat back with a satisfied sigh. "So nice I'm the one being served rather than serving."

Emile tried his best to conform to her happy disposition. He forced a smile and raised his glass. "Here's to liberation."

"Cheers," she replied.

They fell silent for a moment.

Emma homed in on his mood. "Frustrated?"

"Yeah, a bit. But I told you, stakeouts can be boring."

"How long you gonna stick it out?"

"Don't know. I'm ready to chuck the whole thing"—he smiled—"except you're here now."

"You know, we don't have to end this . . . what we have here, we can continue when we go home, you know."

"True," he said, a beat too fast.

"For all you know, Michael Powers could be in China now."

"Could be."

"But you're gonna continue the stakeout, aren't you?"

"For a while. I don't know. For a while."

"You know, Emile, I've been thinking. What if you're right about Powers? What if he doesn't have schizophrenia? So what? Does that make a difference?"

"It makes a big difference."

"How?"

"Well, first of all, he doesn't have an insanity defense."

Emma knew this was a red herring. She prided herself on being savvy enough to see past most men's lies, diversions, and misdirections when they were unwilling to share their true thoughts. "That's not at all what you're thinking, Emile. Give it to me straight. What's the real scoop about your suspicions?"

Emile took a large gulp of bourbon. "Tell you what, Emma, tomorrow's Saturday. If I don't see anything, I'll call it quits and we can go back home."

"You didn't answer my question."

"No, but I answered a problem that has been bugging me."

"Which is?"

"When to leave." He didn't add: before the cave left its mark on him for good.

~

The next day started hot and got hotter. By the time Ruska had parked under the cottonwoods and had reached the trail to the cave, he already felt dehydrated, tongue like cotton, his hat brim throwing a meager ellipse of shade. Tempted to go into the cool cave and drink, he shrugged off the impulse.

Last day, he thought. *Make it professional, at least.*

With this in mind, he dutifully climbed up to his observation post and joined his two lizard friends, already frolicking across the heated rocks. A few hours passed uneventfully, and he began thinking of the return trip home. Although he often grumbled at life in the city, he now looked forward to some of its attractions. With the sun baking the rocks and sand around, he turned his mind to Emma and where they would go next in their relationship. This presented a conundrum, as Emile in no way wanted to easily let go of his cherished independence. So absorbed had he become in his ruminations, he did not at first notice a figure coming up the trail. At last, movement caught his eye and he peered at the shape in the distance, shambling very slowly up the trail. He sat up so quickly that his reptilian comrades raced into a crevice.

Now the figure disappeared around a slight curve, manzanita bushes blocking his view. Emile raised his binoculars and fixed on the spot where the figure would emerge. It seemed an eternity when, at last, the person came into view. Emile could see clearly. Very clearly.

Michael Powers paused to look around. He seemed to be talking to himself, and when satisfied with something, he resumed walking. For a heart-stopping moment, he looked up at the same spot Ruska occupied, and the detective instinctively ducked down. When enough time passed, he peeked over the rock and saw Powers in the distance, approaching the cave. Never in his professional career had Ruska experienced such excitement, spurred on, no doubt, to new levels by so long a fruitless undertaking. Satisfied that Powers brought no companions, he decided to follow the shambling figure into the cave and see what the man would do. Ruska skipped down the hill with a youthful alacrity he had not felt for years, and cautiously approached the cave entrance. Powers had already disappeared inside, so Emile followed, keeping his flashlight off and focused on the distant glow that marked the slow progress of Michael Powers. He matched his breathing to their footfalls, two metronomes in stone. He hesitated. Emma alone at the motel flashed through his mind, but he pushed the thought down and stepped inside. The memory of motel air-conditioning thinned behind him; the rock swallowed sound and then swallowed that, too.

The cave, in mineral silence, bore witness to the movements of these two men. One, like an unsuspecting beast of prey, advanced leisurely, unaware of what lurked behind. The other, stalking as quietly as a predator, bided his time. Neither heard anything other than the scraping of their boots on the stone. Hints of the supernatural were conspicuously absent, as if even the spirits held their collective breaths.

Deeper into the cave they went. Ruska noticed they had passed the locations of the holes where he had speculated hinges once supported massive doors, and he knew the end drew near. Difficult as it was to follow the faint glow without losing his own step in semi-darkness, Emile managed to keep a safe distance without losing his prey. Interestingly, Ruska noticed that Powers never veered off into any of the side chambers, although he often paused and shined his light down their lengths.

At last, the end came into view. Ruska slid into a depression in the rock and watched Powers shine his flashlight around the walls and ceiling as if searching for something.

"Nothing," said Powers aloud. He danced a little jig, and repeated, "Nothing." Again, he surveyed the cave walls and ceiling with his light. Cupping one hand at his mouth, he screamed, "Nothing!"

Immersed in the echoes, Ruska heard Powers begin to sob. Suddenly, the chamber went dark. From the blackness, the sound of Powers' voice, mumbling something as if in conversation with another person, reached Ruska's ears. Strain as he might, he couldn't make out the words. He flirted with the idea of creeping closer but knew it would not be possible without giving himself away. After a few minutes of listening to this unclear dialogue, Powers abruptly howled incoherently. The sound jolted him; he nearly dropped the flashlight.

Instead, he pointed it at the sound and turned it on.

Chapter Twenty-Five

Again, The Rabbit Hole

Bizarre Twist

~ Flight ~

Dear Reader, you see what a terrible plight I'm in. With the light of Goddess, or God, or something even worse blazing in my retinas, I panic. Without a moment's hesitation I race past the light, brushing against whatever it is, and run as fast as my heavy boots can safely navigate the rocky ground in the direction of the entrance. I turn on my flashlight, instantly illuminating the walls and ceiling that rush past me, their uneven geometries harboring a thousand grotesque figures writhing and twisting in dances of death celebrating my downfall. I glance behind and see the other man's light following me, itself jerking malevolently as if in the grip of some terror of its own. I bang a shoulder, stumble, catch myself—keep moving. I know I cannot outrun it, so I turn into a familiar side chamber. Without pausing, I douse my flashlight and crawl blind, palms skinned, grit needles my palms, through the darkness toward a place I know might offer escape. I crawl with the crazed determination that Madame Dau must have felt as a little girl when she scrambled through the tunnel to escape the Moroccan chasing her. All time and space loop back, future to past and back to future, repeating in the perfect conservation law, the expenditure of energy for the sake of survival. I will take refuge in either future or past, but the here and now is a trap. As the old saying goes: the living are the dead on vacation.

I pause in my frantic scuttling to listen. I hear a wet, unholy grunting. Something still follows! Pressing on—pressing on—pressing on! I'm at the end! Now, just find. . . .

Damn!

I know if I push and scratch hard enough.

There! Harder! Harder. . . .

~

"Goddammit, Storyteller! Don't get him started!" Mountain Man spits, in disgust. We are sitting on an empty ammo box, taking a break from filling sandbags and boiling under the Vietnamese sun. I just asked Stretch what movie he would rather be watching right now in some air-conditioned theater back in the World.

Mountain Man continues his tirade. "You get that cocksucker talkin' about movies and hell will freeze over before he's done! Shiiit, Storyteller! How many times I gotta tell ya'?"

Stretch puts on his best Cary Grant imitation and says, "Judy, Judy, Judy—"

"Shut the fuck up and get back to your fuckin' shoveling, asshole!" So says sweet Mountain Man.

Stretch starts to protest, his Tourette's tics a mass of head and shoulder contortions. "You ain't boss man 'round here, Mountain Man."

"No, but I am," says Pappy, approaching with a wry look on his face. "Mountain Man's right, get back to work. You can play act later."

"Okay, Pappy, but this is a really fucked-up firebase, stuck way up here on the top of this mountain. It's fuckin' windy, probably gonna be overrun by the dinks, and not even hot food."

"We'll definitely be overrun if you don't start fillin' those fuckin' sandbags. That goes for you too, Storyteller." Pappy points at Mountain Man. "I want to talk to you. Come over here for a minute."

I watch Mountain Man and Pappy saunter over to a spot beyond earshot. *Uh, oh*, I think. *This confab bodes ill for us.*

After they confer for a few minutes, Mountain Man returns and points to me. "You, Storyteller, are joining us for a little reconnaissance patrol early tomorrow morning. Make sure your radio's in good order. And you—" he says, looking in disgust at Stretch. "You get to stay here and make sure this little bitty firebase ain't overrun."

Stretch gives a whoop of joy.

I bang my shovel against the ground in frustration. Guard duty tonight from midnight to two a.m., then up at dawn to go on a god damn patrol. I'm suddenly curious about who has been chosen to go with us, so I chase down Mountain Man (who, having finished with Pappy, has crept away from sandbag duty). When I catch up with him, I notice he has a grim smile. Mountain Man always relishes combat. Killing Viet Cong and North Vietnamese soldiers has become his *raison d'être.*

"Hey, Mountain Man!" I call.

He stops and looks at me with an impatient stare. "What?"

"Who else is going on our little 'jaunt' tomorrow morning?"

"Little jaunt?" he says sarcastically. "God damn, Storyteller, your screwy little writer's brain has been addled by too many books and too few calluses, mental and otherwise."

"Don't need your hillbilly philosophy right now, Mountain Man. Just tell me who's going."

"Why?" he sneers.

"'Cause I want to know, that's all."

"That's no fuckin' reason."

"Look, if I'm gonna get shot at, I want to know who'll be there. Is Nature going?"

"Your girlfriend?"

"Fuck! You can be very exasperating, pig farmer! Is he or isn't he?"

Mountain Man chuckles. "Another ten-dollar word! Keep 'em comin', Storyteller. Keep 'em comin'!"

"Fuck you!" I bark as I turn and walk away in disgust.

Still chuckling, Mountain Man calls after me, "Yeah! Nature's going, along with Bowls and X and a few others, including yours truly!"

"Thanks!" I yell over my shoulder. I see Pappy standing near Stretch and holding out an empty sandbag toward me. "Nice you could find time to come back and visit us," he says gruffly. "Your shovel's lonely."

~

Fortunately, guard duty that night was uneventful, and this morning I'm positioning my rucksack, heavy with a PRC-25 radio, on my shoulders, tucking a green towel under the straps to cushion the pressure. We occupy a firebase high up on the topmost peak of a series of hills, all cocooned in the lush vegetation of rain forest. Dawn is barely visible in the distance, and the pale sun shyly peeks over a layer of mist undulating across the valley, above which we gather. None of us are happy, and some have the fatalistic expressions of those expecting the worst. Only Nature, with his unfailing smile, seems able to pierce the cold fog of dread that dwells in the hearts of us all. Superman stands stolidly with his M60 machine gun, and Raresteak has pulled duty as assistant gunner. X, reliable medic that he is, performs a quick inventory of his medical supplies. Mountain Man is the ostensible leader of our tiny patrol, so Bowls has, by default, inherited the job of point man.

"Tell me again what's the point of this bullshit?" asks Raresteak to anyone who will listen.

"To die so the guys in the firebase will know it's already surrounded by fuckin' NVA," says Mountain Man off-handedly.

"Oh, goody. Just askin'," replies Raresteak.

In glum moods, we trudge down the hillside to probe for enemy activity. As normally the case, all of us look to Mountain Man for guidance, and as there are so few, it is comforting he is so close. Dogman has pulled dragman duty, and he cautiously looks behind to make sure the enemy is not following our back trail. I walk near Mountain Man with the radio, ready to call in support if we encounter any shit. Ambush is a poisonous snake in the mind; we try to step carefully—neither obsessing nor dismissing. My M16 is comforting, but the radio much more so. The radio is our only lifeline to help, without which the likelihood of dying in the jungle is, to us, almost a certainty.

We have cut through jungle for hours, no sign of any hardpack trails, no sign of enemy. The only signs are a universe of insects; flying, biting, buzzing, swarming around the shower of sweat that runs down our faces and our bodies. Leeches, of course, and crawling creatures of unknown descent probing ceaselessly inside our fatigues.

Bang! An explosion!

Pop! Pop! Pop! Small arms fire up ahead.

Hit the ground, fumble for the headset, call in, call in! Operating distance three to seven klicks! But the jungle, the hills, the enemy! Audio garbled, but comprehensible!

I crawl off the little trail cut by Bowls and find a termite mound to lean against and transmit an urgent message to the firebase. Mountain Man and the others nowhere to be seen. Jungle too thick. Firing continues. Grenades, explosions! Confusion!

Rustling to my left. Mountain Man? "Mountain Man!" I shout above the cacophony. I try to point my M16, but it is wedged against the mound by my body. I move to release it, and a spray of AK-47 bullets splatters against the mound followed by a rustling, crashing sound coming near. Chips of earth pepper my cheeks. *Christ! Shit!*

I finally get the rifle pointed in the direction of the rustling and the sound. I fire a burst. Then another. Then nothing. Silence all around. The firing and explosions stop as quickly as they had begun. My radio cackles with urgency. I answer. Ask for backup. Will report casualties when known. Out.

Where's Mountain Man? Where are the others?

Gradually we locate each other. One flesh wound. Enemy melted away into the jungle. Mountain Man returns frustrated. Chased after them but they got away. Crazy Mountain Man!

"Any sign of enemy KIA?" he asks. "Wounded?"

Shaking of heads. No.

I return to my termite mound and retrieve two unused magazines. Only then do I notice a man lying face up, arms splayed as if crucified, eyes open, dead, already attracting gnats and flies. NVA soldier. I killed him. I know I killed him. I killed him! I feel joy at my survival, and joy that I am not him, and joy at the ending of the firefight, and joy with every breath I take. Then I cautiously approach and look down at him, at his eyes, at his body, and my joys slip away. Yes, all of the usual emotions are stirred within me when looking at this dead person, but something beyond that happens.

A gnat alights on his cornea. Ghostly ripples skitter across the glazed film.

He moves.

Is he dead?

Yes, I am quite sure he is dead, but something on him moves, or perhaps I should say, some qualia about him moves. If we question the experience of seeing red—the redness of red—we are forced to ask what is the nature of that redness? One can argue it is some relationship between wavelength and photoreceptors, but this begs the question. How does one explain the redness of an apple to a blind person who can only feel the cool geometry of its shape? In the same vein, this soldier's distinctly dead face contains a vital, life-force quality—the redness of red—that shifts slightly before my eyes; a crisp image made suddenly out of focus by double vision, as one blurry face slides away from the other, creating two faces. While I stare dumbfounded, I try and make the image sharp again by forcing the errant face back into its original position. If I succeed, it will be seated snugly where it belongs, there will be but one face and the world returned to what is expected; clear, distinct, fine-structured certainty. But the inexorable movement of that wandering ghost-face will not be reversed, and it breaks away from its twin (which remains embedded in the cold lump of deceased flesh) and races upward to wrap around my face like a protoplasmic film. Through eyes now covered by the dead man's foreign skin, I see his wife and child, his joys and disappointments, his agonies and ecstasies, and the pain of his death. As I stare through the disorienting view of an alien lens, his stolen life melds into mine, making his memory an indelible dye that has darkened my natural pigment, absorbing the rich nutrients of schizophrenia and triggering my unnatural rebirth. Forevermore, he and I are mixed together, separation impossible, Siamese twins joined like intermingling rivers in the neural pathways of the brain.

"Search the fucker!" booms Mountain Man standing next to me. "Take what you find and let's *didi* out of here. T and the rest of the platoon just came, and we need to get back before your dead gook's big brothers return to kick our asses."

"Should be buried," I say mechanically.

"What, you fuckin' crazy? Just do what I tell you, Storyteller. I don't give a rat's ass if this is the first guy you've killed. Got no time to put you on my knee and kiss it better. Hurry up!"

I lean over and rummage through his pockets and the small pack he carried. Doesn't matter. I know what I'll find.

And I do.

Pictures. Wife and child. Mom and dad. Grandma. A French-language copy of Rousseau's *Confessions*. Letters. Unfinished writing. Miscellaneous clothes and food. A pen. Flashlight. Assorted other articles.

"I'll return," I say this through the distorting membrane that casts the world in shadowy gloom, a dead man's funereal vista.

Nature, beautiful Nature, saying not a word, picks up the man's AK-47 and bandolier, then puts his hand on my shoulder and guides me back to the waiting platoon.

So, we trudge up the hill to the firebase, back to what should be security and familiarity.

But never will the world be familiar again. Or secure.

Packed in my rucksack, along with the radio, are the dead man's possessions, so meager as to be weightless.

Yet I carry with me the burden of his wife and child, his parents, his grandma, his own dead body, and the measureless encumbrance of what might have been . . . and what is yet to be.

~ *Burial* ~

I'm on guard duty again. Black. Pitch black. Peeking through a dip in the wall of sandbags. M60 machine gun keeping me company in the guard hole. It points out at the darkness like a metal finger of fate. The radio topples off the box and my hand grips the clacker of a Claymore mine, its wire running over the rim of the sandbags to the semicircular Claymore a few meters in front of my position. I nudge the radio back with an elbow and keep my hand on the clacker, ready to squeeze and send the electric impulse that will set off the mine. But I have been in the bush long enough to wait for surety before wasting ordnance. Loud squealing and thumping bodies tell me jungle rats are the culprits. I relax a bit, nerves still a bit jangled, but steady.

Racing clouds break apart and briefly reveal a full moon, its blanket of pale light settling down upon the ocean of mist, turning it into a translucent foam stretching to the horizon. I use this opportunity to scan the tree line for movement, but there is none, only my Siamese twin, a ghostly shadow standing with a melancholy gaze amidst the broken stubble of our cleared perimeter. Ironically, I gently lay my hand atop the clacker, as if by sending that electric impulse to detonate the Claymore mine, I could detonate his ghost. However, I know that by killing him now, I would be killing part of myself.

You are already dead, Goddess's voice skips lightly across the clearing and into my mind. ***You are but a memory, as he that stands before you is but a memory.***

"No," I whisper. "I am alive. The mosquitoes that bite know I'm alive. My very blood pumps through me into them."

They also are dead. Flitting memories sucking sustenance from a fleeting memory.

"No," I protest feebly, but too tired to much care.

You are the shed skin of Michael Powers, who even now struggles to wriggle free.

"No," I say again, even weaker than before.

I admit, She terrifies me even more than the awful addiction of God. There is the ring of Truth in Her voice. I look at him still standing in the clearing one last time before the clouds veil us in darkness once more. He fades to nothing, and Her voice has echoed past me into the future. Total silence now, but for the creatures of the night, forever restless. Eventually the hours pass without incident, and I am grateful to be relieved.

Sleep now.

~

Early morning. Word has come that we are returning in force to the spot of yesterday's engagement and search for hardpack trails. There may be a bunker complex nearby, which means a system of tunnels. All of this signifies the probability of ambush, our great boogeyman. However, I console myself with the idea that the mission will give me an opportunity to properly bury my alter-ego. The day is rainy and bleak, fitting weather for a burial. Captain Kinney has ordered our entire platoon to execute this mission, so T gathers us, and we sit miserably in the rain while being briefed. We will follow the trail we cut yesterday to the site of contact, then expand the search beyond until we reach the valley where a small hamlet is situated. Now we are even more miserable, as none of us relish contact with civilian populations, most of whom are sympathizers with the Viet Cong and would as happily kill us as squash leeches.

Rain soaks us while our three squads make our way down the hill. T has ordered extra care as the enemy might well have booby-trapped the trail we cut the previous day. Evidencing his caution, Mountain Man is made point man and his trusted comrade Bowls as back-up man. Old-timers tell me we used to have four squads, but attrition has forced us to consolidate. Everyone is tense, due mainly to the contact yesterday, but also with the knowledge that we are short-manned and large units of Viet Cong or worse, NVA, are probably lurking about. We are quite aware we have stirred up a hornet's nest. Before we left the firebase, I spoke to T about my desire to bury the dead soldier, and he at first emphatically refused. However, after further consideration, he reluctantly approved since we would pause at the engagement site and search the area more thoroughly for intelligence. As I walk, I feel the entrenching tool I made sure to carry bang against my leg. A nuisance, but necessary.

I am now staring down at the body. Bloating has already begun due to the heat and humidity. Now turning black, he is covered in insects of all types, burrowing into the advancing liquefaction. I start digging. After brushing aside the shallow detritus, I reach the clay-like laterite soil, reddish and almost impervious to the blade of my shovel. I have very little time, so instead of digging a hole, which is impossible, I cover him as best I can with the soil of his native country. I hear T barking orders to saddle up in preparation to move on. A few more spadefuls and I wonder what to do next. Words. There are always words. Was he religious? If so, what religion? I have no idea, of course, so I self-consciously mumble a few words in the hope that he receives the blessings of Buddha. Then, I offer him my humblest apologies and bow before the dirt.

I feel a hand on my shoulder. Nature again.

"Let's go, Storyteller," he says simply.

I rise and take my position next to T, and onward we slog, Mountain Man cutting a path through the living tissue like a surgeon. To our delight, we run across no hardpack trails and reach the edge of the valley with no difficulty. Spread out before us is a flat plain, rice fields and fruit groves unrolling in sparkling green, the little hamlet discernible in the distance by smoke, presumably from cooking fires. I radio the firebase our position, and we continue on a small, muddy footpath through the fields. It's odd that we see no villagers at work, and this is concerning. T halts the column and pulls out his binoculars. Scanning the valley, he shakes his head and turns to me and speaks in his Arkansas drawl.

"Not a sign of life, Storyteller. Strange. Very strange. Well, no help for it. Move out."

The rain still patters down at a steady rate. Once we put a few more meters behind us, we see off the footpath, on a grassy rise, a peculiar sight. An old man has appeared from nowhere, seeming to have risen up from the earth itself. He is wearing very colorful, bizarre clothes and his face is heavily painted with garish hues of yellow, blue, and red. We cannot hear through the rain, but his mouth is agape, and he appears to be chanting. In the middle of his chant, he points a long stick at us and shouts unintelligible words.

Mountain Man saunters back to us and looks up at T's puzzled face.

"A wizard," he says.

"What?"

"A wizard come to this hamlet for some reason. Maybe to exorcise ghosts or demons, maybe to tell fortunes, who knows? But the old bastard is a wizard all right. No doubt about it."

"So, what's he trying to tell us?"

Mountain Man pauses and cocks his head to listen. "To get the hell out."

"Is it a warning?"

"No, it's a command. He thinks we're ghosts."

I hear this and remember the words of Goddess. I feel hot and unsteady. I am sick. Very sick. The fever is sudden, and it is vicious. It grabs my body like a scarecrow and shakes it, the stuffing flying every which way. I cannot let it shake me until there is nothing left. I have to escape. Now, I feel the wizard rush toward me and clutch my legs, pulling me back, but I continue to scrabble .

Undeterred, he keeps pulling me.

Back, back, back . . . .

~ *Back, Back, Back* ~

Emile Ruska fights to keep his grip on the flailing legs of Michael Powers. The cave chamber is narrow, and it is hard to get a good grip. Ruska hears Powers clawing at the rock wall and fears the man will seriously hurt himself. Once he has Powers firmly wrapped in his arms, he starts to pull him backward out of the narrow passage, but the going is slow, and the struggles of the captured man are violent.

Chapter Twenty-Six

Lock Him Up

Tamara Tamara

~ *Run, Michael, Run* ~

Ruska wrestled Michael Powers out of the side chamber and back into the main cave. Both men stood, hunched and gasping for breath. Emile clamped Powers by one arm while with the other he wrenched off his backpack and rooted around inside to locate a pair of handcuffs he had brought —just in case. Meanwhile, Powers hung in his grip, gulping air, silent save for a wet rasp, his eyes blinking in terror. Both men, being older, shook with age and exertion, but Emile kept digging into the pack and finally jerked out the cuffs, the metal clicking together like a tiny iron door. As he did so, Michael Powers suddenly twisted hard, a violent wrench that tore him free. Ruska lunged at him, but instead of running, Powers snatched a rock and whipped it at Ruska's head. Emile, trying to regain his hold, saw the blow coming and ducked, but too late. The impact skidded across his brow in a white flash, only grazing his forehead, yet enough to drop him heavily to the ground, his flashlight skittering and blood dropping warm over his eye.

Michael knew the blow was not solid, and hearing Ruska moan, immediately ran toward the entrance. Bursting out into the glaring sun, heat hammering his scalp and blood tacky on his knuckles, he held up a hand in front of his face and raced down the trail toward the road. He saw no car and knew Ruska would take some time to recover from the blow. He also knew, of course, that it was not really the detective who had chased him, but something else in disguise, and his strong suspicion was that it must be that wizard pointing his magic stick at Storyteller and calling him a ghost. Although the lush vegetation of Vietnam had suddenly been transformed to desert, Michael had enough wits about him to know the road was not a safe place to twalk —too exposed, too clean a line of sight. As soon as possible, he veered away from it and took a parallel route, far enough away not to be seen, but near enough to keep the telephone poles in sight like a breadcrumb trail. When close enough, he took a shortcut across the barren caliche to arrive at the back of the trailer park hours later.

The moment Tamara saw him, she knew he suffered from one of his episodes, so she crossed to him, voice low, to acknowledge and soothe his fears, all the while preparing tea and quietly lacing it with a sedative.

"Keep the curtains pulled, Tamara, he may have followed me."

"Who?"

"The wizard. The one who thinks I am a ghost."

"You?"

Michael stopped, utterly confused. His face registered some comprehension, and he flopped on the couch.

"I . . . me . . . Storyteller. . . . "

"Here, have some tea. Who is this wizard?"

As if a storm suddenly broke and sun pushed through the fleeing clouds, Michael blinked and looked at Tamara apologetically.

"Tamara, I am crazy, I know. I thought the cave would prove I had licked this damn thing, but now, listen to me! Blathering on about a wizard in Vietnam after Storyteller. But Storyteller is dead! I am alive, at least I think I'm alive. God, I don't know what to think anymore! And Ming-huá? What's to become of her with a crazy father?" He buried his face in his hands.

"Michael, finish the tea."

"I know you put something in it."

"Yes, I do, for your own good. Now, tell me what happened in the cave."

"I don't know, everything was fine,—until . . . something happened."

"What?"

"I don't remember." He looked at her pleadingly. "Tamara, everything was going good, no hallucinations, no delusions, nothing. I remember saying to myself, only sand and rock, only sand and rock. And then. . . . "

"And then?"

"I don't remember! Lights . . . a light . . . something. . . . "

"Try and remember, Michael."

"I can't."

"Yes, you can." Tamara grabbed his hands and held them up. "Look, Michael, there are cuts and bruises. You were bleeding. Try and remember."

He looked down at his hands as if they belonged to a different person. Blood was dried under two torn nails, grit embedded in the crescents. "I can't."

Tamara sat next to him and gently turned his head toward her. "Michael, this wizard, you said he was 'after Storyteller'. What did you mean? How was he after Storyteller?"

"Storyteller is dead."

"What did you mean, Michael?"

"I meant . . . I feel something pulling, tugging, clawing, dragging me backward."

Tamara's eyes grew big. "Michael, think! Was there another person in the cave with you?"

He shook his head.

"Michael! This is important! Was there another person with you?"

"Yes, I think so. I can't be sure."

"Did you . . . or Storyteller . . . fight with the wizard?"

"Tamara, I know there was no wizard."

"Okay, do you think it might have been a person you thought was the wizard?"

Michael remained silent for a long while, then he whispered, "Oh, my God."

He looked toward the dark hallway as if the cave might open there, then shut his eyes until the room steadied.

~

It all came back to him in a single, hammering rush. He remembered how the rock felt against Ruska's skull, and a renewed fear that he was capable of murder—had murdered—took hold with crushing certainty. Images of the dead Vietnamese soldier rained down upon him in pitiless succession, a gnat landing on the cornea and ghostly ripples spreading outward across the glazed film, and he clamped his hands over his ears and withdrew into that trackless wasteland none could follow. Distantly he heard Tamara calling, but her voice faded to silence. Michael realized he had fallen from that swaying bridge into the precipice and had come face to face with the demons dwelling in that dark place, God and Goddess still nowhere to be seen or heard. And these demons were far more dangerous.

~

Tamara saw it all through Michael's eyes. Heard it all through Michael's ears. "Thank you, Goddess," she whispered. "It's Ruska."

She fought the urge to run to the window; instead, she checked Ming-huá's breathing at the crib rail. She pictured the cave's mouth in the heat, blood sheening down a man's face, and looked anxiously at her baby.

~ *Tamara* ~

At last, the sedative took effect and Tamara guided Michael to the bedroom where she helped him undress and crawl into bed. She stood a moment, listening—no tires on gravel, no knock—then eased the door nearly shut. Ming-huá fussed, and Tamara set her on the floor to totter, palms slapping the linoleum like soft applause. Tamara sat on the couch and rubbed her forehead, contemplating the implications of Michael's episode at the cave. She made the reasonable assumption Ruska would return with a host of law enforcement backup and scour the area to find him. She parted the curtain a finger's width and checked the park entrance. A dust-gray sedan eased past and kept going. She slid the deadbolt, then unlocked it again, undecided—finally leaving it as it was. Her hump tingled with messages, but the multitude of crisscrossing signals were too tangled to help —like a living circuit board, sparking without resolve. For the first time in ages, she wished her mother was here to advise. To the best of Tamara's knowledge, her small family had only a handful of choices. To run and hide, to stay and hide, to turn Michael back in to the institution, or to carry on as before and hope for the best. Michael would do what she told him, if only for the sake of his daughter. Tamara had always known her daughter was intended to be someone special; that knowledge duly sanctioned by the words and actions of Buandelgereen. The baby girl seemed doubly blessed, by Immortal deity and Mongol seer. Proof of her extraordinary nature lay in her ability to make things disappear.

From the beginning, Tamara believed Michael's voices were oracles to be ignored at one's peril, just as her mother believed the same of the voices heard by John Powers. Now, she faced yet another in an endless series of decisions involving her schizophrenic husband. Undecided, full of doubt, she rose and began cleaning the trailer in a sort of daze, absently picking up this item and that, dusting, moving objects for no apparent reason, finally ending up in the kitchen, scrubbing a burned pot and cooing with Ming-huá (who crawled to and fro, delighting in her freedom). Like an organic electric circuit board, her hump flickered, buzzed, and crackled with overlapping warnings and frightening enigmas. How to make sense of the noise? Only one path must be the right path. But the right one refused to announce itself. The others? They all led to disaster.

Over Ming-huá's cooing, she heard Michael groan in his sleep from the bedroom, and her heart felt a wrenching spasm of pity for the dreams and nightmares that must plague her husband, whether at rest or awake. It agonized her to make this decision. All alternatives were bad, but she tried to prioritize the one course of action that would be least harmful to Michael's precarious grip on reality. But which was it? All had terrible potential consequences. The thought briefly entered her mind that she might return him to the institution so she could raise Ming-huá without interference and undue complication. However, Tamara feared Goddess's retribution which, she felt certain, was capable of being implemented through Her earthly agent Buandelgereen. Worse, that lingering purveyor of suffering, God, constituted a far more menacing threat, albeit hidden like an assassin in the shadows.

None of this helped her come to a decision. Inertia would dictate doing nothing and waiting to see what happened. Of all natural tendencies, Tamara resisted inertia the most, an ironic twist to be sure. Going against form, she decided on doing nothing and continuing their lives as if the incident never happened. If Goddess, or rather, Buandelgereen, were unwilling or unable to prevent their discovery by the authorities, then perhaps Michael should return to the institution. After all, he said the detective was not dead, or even hurt all that badly. Michael's aggressive swing of the rock could be explained away as nothing more than a reaction to a stranger unexpectedly appearing in the dark. What constituted the real threat of his being found? Not a criminal trial or incarceration, but a return to the institution, probably to be locked up in the most secure wing of the hospital. The stakes were high, but not so high as to justify running again. Besides, Ming-huá needed a stable place in which to grow. Yes, Tamara decided. Do nothing and wait. Yes. Keep to their usual routine: get up in the morning, eat breakfast, play with Ming-huá, go to work, come home and sleep. If they came for Michael, they came. If not, then life would proceed, and Michael's schizophrenia would eventually slough off like old skin. Decision made, she set the knife block closer to the back of the counter, tucked keys and a folded twenty into the dish by the door, small rituals of normal, and exhaled. She touches the doorknob, listening, then lets it go, palms flat to the counter until the tremor passes. Her mind made up, she dismissed all doubts, put the baby in her crib, lay on the couch so as not to disturb Michael, and slept soundly.

~

Tamara had just cracked an egg and still holding it over the frying pan, heard Michael's foggy voice.

"Morning."

"Morning, how do you feel?"

"My head hurts. I'm going to take a shower."

"Okay, breakfast will be ready when you're done." She released the egg and it sizzled loudly. The sound seemed too big for the little kitchen.

"Yes, yes," he said. "Then maybe we should talk."

This cryptic response worried her, but she kept her eyes on the pan and flipped bacon with steady hands. From the crib, Ming-huá tracked the steam with solemn interest.

When he returned, Tamara poured coffee and they ate without a word spoken. Forks scraped plates; the clock ticked. At last, putting down her napkin, Tamara asked, "Michael, what do you want to talk about?"

"I could have killed him."

"But you didn't."

"Not the point. In my madness, I murder."

"No, you have convinced yourself of that, but it isn't true."

"How do you know?"

"You did not kill Detective Ruska."

"Only by luck. But I killed three doctors. Three people trying to help me!"

Tamara banged her fist on the table. "Delusions! They died natural deaths! The coroners—"

"You know the coroners don't know the truth."

"What is the truth?"

"That I am unnatural. I can do unnatural things. Damn it, Tamara, you yourself are unnatural!"

"You dare bring my hump into this?"

"I don't speak of your hump. Your mother possessed powers beyond what is natural, and you also possess them. By some miracle, or, more likely, by the manipulations of Goddess, we found each other. Two unnatural beings, together!"

"And Ming-huá? Do you condemn her also as being unnatural?"

"Yes, Tamara. My son Mark is not unnatural because he was born of Diane, a normal, natural woman. But Ming-huá is born of us. For God's sake, Tamara, she can make things disappear!"

"And your parents?"

"Both unnatural, like us."

"Your father was schizophrenic, so I understand. But your mother?"

"No, Father was a Chosen One, like me. He did not have schizophrenia . . . or so I have been told."

"Yes, I know. And your mother?"

"Yes! She also was a Chosen One! How else could Mother see *Her*? How else could Mother have heard Father's voices? She heard Goddess!"

"No, Michael. You are delusional. It is your schizophrenia that speaks these words."

"No, Tamara, not at this moment. It is I speaking. Michael Powers. Not Storyteller. Not God or Goddess. Not Buandelgereen. It is I, and I am unnatural. Dangerous!"

"If you are dangerous, then so am I, because you say I'm unnatural." She looked at Ming-huá in the crib—the baby staring, unblinking. "And so is she. She is unnatural, according to you. She will grow up to be dangerous. Let us say I believe you. Let us say you and Ming-huá are Chosen Ones. In that case, both of you are natural."

"You are also a Chosen One."

"Okay, all three of us are Chosen Ones. If so, we are the future. Not a mistake of nature—the next permutation."

Tamara went to the kitchen and returned with a carving knife. "But also, if what you say is true, then we are all dangerous, all capable of murder. I don't mean to be so dramatic, Michael, but you have no choice. Kill us."

She handed Michael the knife.

"Kill us now and get it over with!"

He stood trembling, the knife gripped so tightly it quivered from the strain. "Tamara—"

"Do it!" she cried, stepping closer and tilting back her head. An intake of breath. The blade catches the kitchen light.

Swiftly, he raised the knife, put it to his own throat, and pulled it across.

Tamara screamed.

A hair-thin red seam appeared.

The knife quivered in his fist—then vanished.

Both looked at Ming-huá. She blinked solemnly and cooed.

Michael laughed, pressed a towel to his neck, and reached for Tamara.

"Don't worry," he said. "Only a superficial cut. I had no intention of killing myself, or you. Your scream told me all I need to know. Besides, Ming-huá made my point."

Tamara pummeled him with her fists. "Fool! Fool! Never play with me! I was serious!"

The towel fell and he held her arms. "No, you weren't."

Tamara calmed and backed up. "No, you're right, I wasn't serious. But I made my point. If you leave us, whether to run away or kill yourself, we will die also.

If you're right, and we're unnatural, then we must stay together. Otherwise, the world that considers itself natural will destroy us piecemeal. If not physically, then it will imprison us and break our spirits." She picked up the towel and pressed it harder to his neck, then fetched adhesive strips and sealed the shallow line. From the crib, Ming-huá watched with unnerving focus.

"Then what should we do? This detective will be all over us now, and I'll be shipped back to the institution, if not charged with attempted murder."

"I've thought long and hard while you rested. We will do nothing."

"Nothing?"

"Nothing out of the ordinary. We will continue our lives as if nothing happened. If your Goddess is real, She will protect us. After all, doesn't She consider Ming-huá the special daughter?"

Michael flashed a sour face. "Yes, I was to be *the son*. Evidently, that did not work out. Now, she is to be *the daughter*. At brief moments I could talk to dogs and sidewalks, but those moments passed. Now let us see if Ming-huá can do the same thing, except not for moments, but for her entire life. That would be extraordinary!"

"Michael," said Tamara quietly. "I know you are a Chosen One, and I know your father and mother were as well. Now we have the next step, and she will dwarf all of us in her powers. After all, she can already make things disappear. Who knows what comes next."

~

Dear Reader, it turns out Ming-huá would have powers that exceeded the most ambitious expectations of Goddess and *Her* faction. Her ability to make things disappear was only the beginning. But, alas, that is for another story. I'll be dead, so how do I know? Silly question!

~ *Emile Ruska's Dilemma* ~

Emile Ruska spent a few minutes sitting on the cave floor tending his wound. The rock had done damage, but not as badly as he'd feared. Once he cleaned the blood, the cut proved superficial, and the dizziness and nausea eased rather quickly. In no condition to chase after his quarry, he carefully made his way to the entrance and sat on a rock to rest before facing the white glare that awaited outside. A host of thoughts raced through his mind, but one thought gripped him: revenge. Anger boiled inside, and he vowed to chase down this schizophrenic madman no matter how much time or money it would take. And then, as the heat bled off, his better instincts took over, and he had to concede Michael Powers was partly justified in attacking him; he hadn't even tried to talk, he'd given chase and hauled him by the legs. Anyone would be frightened, mentally ill or not. No, Ruska decided, part of this was on him.

"What next?" he asked himself aloud, hearing a faint echo.

He turned toward the inside of the cave and cupped his hands. "What next?" he shouted as loud as he could. His voice came back thinner, as if the cave were mocking him. Oddly, when the echoes had died to silence, he smiled and walked out into the sun. Decision deferred. He wanted to see Emma. Nothing more, for the moment.

When he called her from his room after showering, she rushed down to find him holding out a drink for her, a makeshift butterfly bandage bridging the cut. Before she could gasp at his swollen face, he waggled his finger.

"No, no, don't ask yet. Let's just sit for a moment, then I'll tell you all about it. Anyway, I need your advice."

He raised his glass and gently clinked it against hers. Emma reluctantly sat without further word, but the concern didn't leave her eyes.

"I have come to a decision," he announced.

"What's that?"

"I have decided that I have not decided."

"Okay. Now what?"

"That is where my indecisiveness comes in."

"Can we please get to the part where your face got in the way of some moving object?"

Ruska told her the story, leaving out only the worst of the rage that had flared in him.

After listening quietly, Emma said, "Do you want my opinion?"

"Yes, remember I said I want your advice? Well, give it to me."

"Leave this place, forget Michael Powers, go home, visit me occasionally at PicYrPoison, and live a long life."

Emile gingerly touched the tender welt and flinched. "Damn! I forgot about this head wound. Anyway, I knew that is what you would say."

"Why ask if you knew?"

"Confirmation."

"Consider it confirmed."

Ruska sighed. "How can I justify leaving a crazy man alone out here in the middle of nowhere, an untreated schizophrenic? He needs care."

"Who says he's alone?"

Ruska considered. "Don't know, just assumed. He was alone at the cave." *For what little that proves.*

"So?"

"Yeah, I get your point. But I at least must tell Buandelgereen he made an appearance at the cave. Perhaps she'll help him."

"Or perhaps not."

"You're making this worse. Do you want me to go home or not?"

"Yes."

"Then let me have some reasonable justification for doing so, rather than simply abandoning this poor guy."

"He obviously sees you as a threat."

"But I'm not."

"Emile, you dragged him through a tunnel by his feet! What's he supposed to think?"

"Yeah, I get your point. Thank you."

"Good, when do we go?"

"We don't. You can. I'm staying."

"What? I thought—"

"No, Emma, you convinced me to stay and help the man. I have to prove to him I'm no threat."

"Do you want to take him back to the institution?"

"Of course. He can get help there."

"Then, my dear, you're an even bigger threat to him."

Ruska sighed again. "Yeah, I know."

Emma leaned forward. "Look, forget my stupid remark about that Mongol woman, Buan . . . whatever. Let her take care of him. Let's leave. Next time, you may not get off so lucky."

"Let me sleep on it."

"Christ! You're the most stubborn man that ever took a sip of whiskey."

"Thank you."

"Hungry?"

"No. Face hurts. Tired."

Emma looked at him sympathetically. "I thought we could go to El Fantasma and get a bite to eat."

"Tomorrow."

"I was hoping we could leave tomorrow."

"Go ahead, Emma. Please, I don't want to keep you here. I just haven't made up my mind what to do. Perhaps sleep will clear my head."

She leaned over and kissed him. "Yes, sleep, my brave detective. Sleep, and we can continue our discussion over breakfast. I'm going back to my room and watch the next episode of this amazing real-life forensics show."

Ruska chuckled. "Maybe I will have made my decision by then."

"Maybe, but whatever it is, I'm staying with you, buster, unless you kick me out."

"Emma, you're pure gold."

She kissed him again. "No, Emile, I'm pure flesh. Now, sleep."

Emma left and closed the door softly behind. Within minutes, he had fallen into a deep sleep—dreamless, at first.

~

Next morning Emile sat across from Emma drinking coffee. Neither had said much, but after they had eaten their fill, Emma looked at him with eyebrows raised inquisitively. He said nothing, so she went back to sipping her own coffee patiently.

"Didn't sleep well," said Emile.

"That's too bad. Nightmares?"

He laughed and turned the swollen side of his face toward her. "Couldn't sleep on the side I like."

"Poor baby," she cooed. Again, she raised her eyebrows in silent anticipation.

"I know, I know, you want to know what I've decided," said Emile.

"You bet'cha I do!"

He took a long swallow of coffee and paused to collect himself. "I'm going to find him, Emma, come hell or high water."

Chapter Twenty-Seven

Blissful Ignorance

Dishwashers

~ Angel ~

Dear Reader, I am back at work, doing what Tamara suggested—no, ordered—carrying on with life as if it were business as usual. I feel a bit dishonest about this because I do not think I can be "normal" enough to succeed in conducting "business as usual", but I have agreed to try. It is made bearable by Angel. He knows nothing of my encounter with Detective Ruska, so we scrub away at dirty pots and pans while we philosophize about a host of interesting topics (by unspoken agreement, never politics). During our rhapsodizing, I ask whether he was born in the United States.

"*Amigo*, let us not go there," he sighs.

"Why?" I stupidly ask, regretting it the instant the word leaves my mouth.

He gives me an exasperated look. "Michael, are all schizophrenics so clueless?"

This riles me. "Angel, are all Hispanics so secretive?"

"Do I have to spell it out for you?"

I stare at him vacuously, like an idiot.

Angel snorts and darts out, quickly returning with a small bag of flour.

"What's that for?"

Without a word, he dumps a pile on an aluminum side table and smoothes it to an even white surface. He takes his index finger and writes in the flour: ILLEGAL.

While I gawk, he swiftly erases it and looks at me with eyebrows raised. "*Comprendo?*"

I nod.

"So you see, *amigo*, we are both outlaws! Pancho Villa and Emiliano Zapata, outlaw dishwashers!"

Angel laughs in one loud burst, looks over my shoulder, and rushes to pick up a huge pot to scrub. Tad enters and looks at the flour-covered table.

"What's this?"

"Flour," says Angel.

"I can see that, Angel, what's it doing here?" He chuckles. "You two been baking pies in the dishwasher?"

"Ha, ha, ha!" laughs Angel, never looking up from his pot. "Very good, *amigo!*"

Tad looks at the open flour bag, then at me. "Michael?"

"Could be rats," I say smoothly.

"Very funny. I don't know what you guys have been doing, or who you're protecting, but flour doesn't belong in here."

"Sure, boss," says Angel. "The bag just appeared *ex nihilo.*"

Tad grabbed the bag. "Whatever that means," and leaves with his prize.

Angel mutters toward the manager's back as the swinging door closes behind him, "*Ex nihilo, nihil fit—*"

"What does that mean?"

"Out of nothing, nothing comes."

Once we both have our laugh, Angel says, "Listen *compadre*, this is between us, *sí?*"

"*Claro,*" I reply.

Angel looks a bit surprised, so I say, "I know a few words, Angel. I'm not totally ignorant."

"*Sí,* mi amigo. A pact among thieves, eh?"

I look at Angel with an appreciation I acquired from knowing such heroic/humble men in Vietnam. Believe me, dear Reader, I am not a wide-eyed romantic. It is possible, I know, were Angel married he might beat his wife, or were he in business, he might cheat his partners. But he has kept a grip on life at its most fundamental, and for that reason, like a man grasping a wolf by the ears (thank you, Jefferson), he does not stray to mischief by letting go just to try and grab the illusory golden ring.

Like many such men, he lives his physical life close to the ground, so his mental life is free to roam the farthest galaxies of the universe.

Steam beads on our forearms. The washer hisses; pans click. We work side by side without talking. This is a man I can trust to hear my story without the slightest inclination or temptation to carelessly repeat it to others.

While we both are hard at work, I tell Angel the story of the cave in broken fragments amid the loud clanging of dishes and silverware, swishing machines, and frequent interruptions of a busy kitchen. Often, he leans closer and says, "What? Speak louder, *amigo!*" In such instances, I have to repeat what I had just said louder, which makes me uncomfortable. By and by, I finish my saga with a dramatic flourish, telling him proudly I also am a wanted man. Angel appears unmoved. He continues his tasks mechanically, as do I. The dishes come fast and furious, and Angel calls over his shoulder to me, "Bring the trays from under the counter so I can run them through with this load!"

I hasten to the counter where customers are lined up like sardines on their stools. The waitresses flutter by in a whirlwind of activity, rushing back and forth to the main dining room with armloads of food, taking orders from crowded tables, and rushing back to jam their cryptic messages in the circular wheel for the cooks.

I search for Tamara and remember she has already finished the earlier shift and returned home. I do see her best friend Valeria hovering over a large table writing madly. I want to wave to her, but she is too busy, so I lean down to grab a full-to-overflowing tray of dirty dishes and cups, and I see out of the corner of my eye two people standing near the register, waiting for an open table. Instantly, I recognize Detective Ruska! I immediately drop to my knees so my head dips fully behind the counter. I pull out a tray and crouch low, creeping with my load back to the kitchen.

Once I plop it down near the busy Angel, I steal back and peek around the corner to make sure it is truly him and not a hallucination. The swelling of Ruska's face is now black and blue, but he is wearing a contented smile, his arm encircling a woman.

What do I do? I ask myself.

Nothing, I tell myself.

Business as usual.

Nevertheless, I am greatly disturbed. What if he sees me? Did he see Tamara leave? I try to reassure myself that I am safe in the kitchen, and that he has never met Tamara. Or has he? Yes, yes, of course he has! My thoughts are confused, and I am becoming more and more agitated. My heartbeat got loud. Sweat gathered under my collar. The counter felt too low to hide me.

Crazy ideas fly through my brain.

Angel looks at me oddly.

"Got a problem, *amigo*?"

"Yeah, that detective is out there right now with a woman."

Angel's eyes widen. "Where's Tamara?"

"She went home."

Angel moves close to me and whispers. "Michael, this is a golden opportunity! Call Valeria in here and get her to wait on the guy. Maybe she can pick up something from listening to his talk."

I creep back to the corner and peek. He is still waiting.

"Angel, go out and ask Valeria to come."

"*Sí.*" He rushes out.

Very soon they both return. Before I can say a word to her, Tad sticks his head in. "What's up, Valeria? We've got a full house out there!"

"One second, Tad. I need to tell Michael something really quick."

"Make it fast."

I hurriedly describe Ruska and make up a story that he is a bad guy looking for me. She loves intrigue and does not wait to ask questions but dashes out to make sure Ruska is seated at one of her tables. Again, I peek around the corner and see the hostess seating them in Valeria's area. I breathe a sigh of relief and tell Angel his plan is successful.

"That's only the first part, *amigo*," he says. "Now let's hope he says something interesting to his lady friend."

"Yeah," I say. "Like he is running away with her to a deserted island far far away, never to return."

Angel laughs heartily.

~ *Valeria* ~

Valeria's heart races when she approaches the table to give them menus. She scans the man's face for signs of danger — a scar, a tattoo — but sees nothing out of the ordinary. He orders a beer; his girlfriend orders wine. Valeria takes her time writing it down. They remain silent, so she leaves them to peruse their menus and pretends to pay extra attention to the neighboring booths, hoping to overhear something. They take an aggravatingly long time choosing, saying almost nothing.

When she brings the drinks, they simply tell her they are ready; she writes the order, submits it, and returns to the neighboring booths, lingering as if intent on her notes. At last, they begin to talk.

The woman lifts her wine and says, "Cheers."

The man clinks his mug to her glass.

"Well," she says. "What's the plan?"

"A friendly visit to the local chamber of commerce. Once I get what I need from them, I think another friendly visit is in order."

"To?"

"The local police. I'll flash my badge and strike up a conversation about a missing mental patient I'm searching for. They'll cooperate."

"And the cave?"

"I doubt Michael Powers has any intention of returning to the cave after our little incident."

"But—"

A fellow waitress walks by. "Valeria, your order's up."

Valeria reluctantly leaves to pick up the order, already frightened by what she's heard. She now considers it likely she has entered very dangerous water. When the order comes up for their food, she serves them nervously, now almost afraid of what might be revealed in their conversation. However, her interest is quickly piqued when she notices they have been arguing.

As she sets down their plates, the man says brusquely to his girlfriend, "We can talk about this after we eat."

His companion seems perturbed, but nods in agreement.

Valeria is keen to hear more. After she clears their plates, she returns to the neighboring booths, pretends again to write in her book, and eavesdrops as much as she can. Their words are indistinct; when the man leans forward and lowers his voice, Valeria slides closer and tilts her head. Still she cannot make out the words and is about to leave when the man grows frustrated and raises his voice just enough. Only one sentence is clear.

"What if he really is a murderer, Emma?"

The words strike Valeria like a knife. She stands stupefied until Tad approaches with an impatient look. She waves to acknowledge him and heads behind the counter to pick up more dishes. Her thoughts are in tatters as she watches the couple depart, plagued by indecision. What to do? What to tell Michael?

She sees Michael ease out of the kitchen. When he satisfies himself the man is gone, he comes to her.

"Well?"

Before she can reply, she notices Tad staring at them.

"Later, got to go," she blurts.

The rest of her shift passes in a blur. Valeria keeps herself busy, avoiding Michael. When the restaurant closes they walk to the trailer park together. Valeria has rehearsed this conversation; she is ready.

A full moon greets them outside, and they have barely started down the road when Michael asks, "Well?"

"I didn't hear anything."

"What? Nothing at all?"

"Well, I did hear some conversation, but it was not about you."

"What was it about?"

"Small talk."

She sees his disappointment and feels pangs of guilt, but it has to be done. If he is a murderer, she does not want to give him any reason to kill her. Valeria is determined to tell Tamara everything. Does her friend know her husband might be a mental patient? A murderer? They speak very little. Valeria's mind is reeling with conjectures and is focused on meeting Tamara the next day. Michael, disappointed and confused, goes home and finds himself greeted by Tamara waiting up for him.

~

Pouring himself a drink, Michael collapses in his easy chair, gathering his thoughts and waiting for Tamara to finish checking on Ming-huá. She returns, and before having a chance to say a word, he blurts out, "Guess who I saw at work tonight?"

Tamara feels a constriction in her chest. "Who?"

"Guess."

"I can't."

"Your hump doesn't tell you?"

"No."

With this, Michael reports what happened, often with dramatic flourishes and breathless suspense, but when finished shrugs at the anticlimactic ending.

Tamara digests this information. At first, she thinks it is nothing new, but the fact Ruska has stayed in town means he is actively searching the area. However, the more she thinks about it, the less concerned she becomes. What do the local police know about Michael? Nothing. But there are pictures of him. If there is a search, what if Tad is shown the picture? Or any of their co-workers? What if they come and search the trailer park? Sooner or later he will return to the restaurant and see her, or Michael. No, it is too much. If they are intent on finding him, they will.

"Maybe I should go back to the cave," says Michael abruptly.

"What?" Tamara is horrified. "You can't do that! He'll be watching!"

"Exactly. If he is watching, I'll let him take me this time. If not, I'll find my way back to that side tunnel that leads to a different time and place. Then, you and Ming-huá will be rid of me and can live in peace."

"No, Michael. Even if he is not there, you will have another episode, and I don't think you can take another one. I can't take another one. Please."

He looks at her in disbelief. "You still want us to pretend everything is business as usual?"

This is the question she has been dreading. What do they do now? Flee? Where to go if they run? Money? Not enough. Ming-huá? Too many contingencies. Too much to think about in too little time!

"Yes, business as usual."

"Tamara, I may be schizophrenic, but I still have enough wits about me to know that won't work."

"Yes, it will."

"No. Tomorrow I'm working the morning shift for Angel. Day after tomorrow I return to the cave. If Ruska is there and takes me, I won't resist and won't tell him about the trailer park. You and Ming-huá will be safe. If he isn't there, I'll be free to go to another place and time."

"No, Michael. If you go, our lives will be anything but safe. In fact, our lives will be in great jeopardy."

"How so?"

"Are you really so blind? Why do you think God and Goddess have not been in your head lately?"

"What?"

"Why do you think, Michael? Think. Where are They? It is no accident you don't hear them anymore."

~

Dear Reader, what can I say? I am thrown back into a miasma of confusion and despair. What is real? What is not? Is Tamara who she says she is? After all, she once worked for Goddess and Buandelgereen. Is she truly my wife? Is Ming-huá my child? Is this the fantasy of a deluded mind? Is Detective Ruska even real? Why is my madness so random and unpredictable? Every time I think I have turned a corner I am met with another precipice. Yes, that is the nature of madness, is it not? Or perhaps a step toward the Superior Ones?

~

"Well?" asks Tamara. "I asked you a question. Why haven't you heard Them?"

I am stunned at her aggressive attitude. She is furious. Fire darts from her eyes.

"I don't know," I reply meekly. "You tell me."

Something seems to collapse inside her. "I cannot," she whispers.

Now I am angry. "Why not? You've been attacking me this whole time for wanting to help you and Ming-huá, and now you can't?"

"No, I can't. You must trust me."

"And if you tell me, what bad things will happen?"

"Trust me, Michael, bad things will happen. That's all I can say."

"Tamara, you're my wife! If you can't tell me, how can I trust you? As you can see, I'm fine right now. No delusions, no voices. Tell me what bad things will happen?"

"Michael, I don't think you're ready for this yet. Why don't we sleep now and talk more tomorrow?"

"I don't want to sleep!" I find myself shouting but can't help it. "I want to know now!"

"No," she says so calmly it sets me off even more. "If you really intend to go to work early tomorrow, you need sleep."

"Damn you!" I shout, banging my fist on the side table. "Tell me!"

Tamara leans forward in alarm and puts her index finger to her lips. "Shhhhh! Quiet." She looks toward the room where Ming-huá sleeps. "You'll wake Ming-huá."

I lower my voice and force myself to speak slowly and rationally. "Tamara, what bad things will happen."

Tamara looks at me with eyes full of sorrow and pain. "She will be taken away from us."

I am taken aback. "You mean Child Protective Services? That's nonsense. They don't know anything about us."

"No, not Child Protective Services. They won't take her away."

"Who then?"

"Michael, ask your voices."

Chapter Twenty-Eight

From Now To Then

Murderer or Misfit?

~ Emile Ruska Broods ~

That night, Emile lay in bed beside Emma, brooding over their earlier spat, one that continued on and off up to bedtime. For the first time, from his perspective, she had shown her true feelings and acted like a wife. A harping wife. His greatest fear. As a man treasuring independence of thought and movement, he feared her domestic concern for his well-being would act as a crimp in his life. With Emma softly snoring, Emile slipped out of bed to find a solitary place where he could spend uninterrupted time with his laptop. Eventually, he ended up sitting on the toilet seat. He scanned various websites, but his attention wandered to pondering the next steps he needed to take. Check in with the local police and chamber of commerce, of course, but these tasks gave him very little comfort. Although he was adamant with Emma that he would vigorously pursue Michael Powers, he did not feel such determination now. Despite his frustration with Emma, the thought of returning to his empty apartment suddenly became wearisome. In fact, this mad pursuit of a crazy man had made him slightly crazy and caused him to believe there might indeed be some supernatural forces at work surrounding Michael Powers.

During his career as a detective, he had seen many strange things and run into a variety of deranged individuals, but never had they crept so insidiously into his mind. Ruska felt his age, and the inclination to retire to live the rest of his life in some semblance of peace carried a new appeal. What sort of wife would Emma make? A good one, he felt. After all, small arguments were the hallmark of even the most successful marriages. *Leave Michael Powers to his own devices and go home with Emma!* his mind insisted, and he found himself having to work hard at resisting the impulse to give in and chuck it all.

As he struggled with these conflicting ideas, he suddenly felt very sleepy. Not wanting to return to bed and perhaps wake Emma, he sat on the floor and leaned against the bathtub, staring unseeing at the laptop's monitor. Eventually, he nodded off, but soon awakened with a jerk when his head struck the edge of the tub. Through groggy eyes, he saw someone sitting on the toilet seat.

"Emma?"

"You know who it is," said *She*, unchanged as always, speaking in *Her* distinctive human voice.

Ruska forced himself to focus. "I am assuming *You* are a dream, so to humor my dream, I'll bite. *You* are *She*. Buandelgereen's keeper. And *You're* here to tell me something related to Michael Powers. Before *You* speak any further, just tell me, is he a murderer?"

"All of you are murderers."

"Oh, yes, of course—riddles. His doctors told me he is beset by voices and hallucinations that spout riddles. Have I so completely caught his particular strain of schizophrenia that I will now be its unhappy recipient? Or am I actually privileged enough to be speaking with a deity?"

"You are nothing. You have found nothing. You may go home with your other nothing. Stay in your nothing home and tend your imaginary roses. The water here is too deep, and you cannot swim in it."

"If I don't?"

She stared impassively. "Nothing."

"I'll drown, I suppose?"

"You are already drowned."

Emile held up his hand and made a fist. "Not quite."

"Oh, yes. Otherwise, how can you be talking to me? Go home and leave the rest to Us. Perhaps then, with your roses, you will be resuscitated and risen to become something."

"And Michael Powers? Leave him to kill others or harm himself?"

Her Goddess voice boomed in his mind. **Foolish man! Michael Powers is at this very moment writing these words you and I speak. You are nothing but ink that would turn to ashes at the strike of a match. Leave him to Us!**

Ruska blinked at this remarkable command and started to make some retort, but *She* had vanished. He closed his laptop. "Screw this!" he whispered and went back to bed.

~

When Emma opened her eyes, Emile had pulled back the drapes and let mid-morning sun pour in.

"Get dressed!" he said excitedly.

"What's up? Is it breakfast?"

"No, it's a new day, and the one we spend here."

"What do you mean? I thought—"

"I've changed my mind. We're leaving."

"Now?"

"Yes. I've changed my mind. Leave Michael Powers to . . . whatever happens. I've thought about this all last night. I don't believe he is a murderer. If he ever hurts anyone, it will be himself. And in that case, well, so be it!"

Emma smiled broadly. "Okay. Good. Let me go shower and I'll meet you downstairs for breakfast."

"Nope. We're not eating another breakfast in this rat trap. On our way out of this hick town, let's eat at El Fantasma. Our farewell meal. Good food, good service, and good riddance to this town."

Emma kissed him and flounced out of the room in high spirits. They checked out, threw their luggage in the trunk, and drove to the restaurant making jokes along the way like two schoolchildren. The moment they were seated, Michael Powers passed before them carrying a bus tray. Immediately, Ruska saw that Powers did not see him, as his attention was fixed on balancing the precariously overflowing dishes. Emile himself froze in his seat, unsure what to do. Emma's eyes were on the menu, and when Powers paused on the way to the kitchen, Emile quickly lifted his own menu to hide his face. Options raced through his mind. He needed time to decide what to do.

"What are you having?" asked Emma.

"Don't know yet."

Emma smiled into her coffee, her slightly over-applied makeup crinkling at the unaccustomed naturalness of the expression. "I feel like a girl again," she said happily.

Emile did not hear. He watched Michael Powers turn the corner into the kitchen and quickly reviewed his options.

"What are you going to order?" Emma's question finally had penetrated his consciousness, so intent had he been on trying to galvanize his scattered thoughts into some command to move.

Without responding, he leapt up and stormed into the kitchen.

~ *Capture* ~

Ruska stopped in his tracks as soon as he took a step past the swinging doors into the dishwashing room. Michael Powers stood with a butcher knife in hand, staring at the detective as if he were an expected guest.

"I saw you out there," Powers said, by way of explanation. "I've been waiting."

Ruska's gaze was fixed on the knife.

Michael followed his eyes and, as if discovering he held a snake, flung it on the table.

Ruska visibly relaxed. "It's time to go, Michael."

"Not 'til my shift is over."

Tad entered, clearly upset. "What's going on here?"

Before either could answer, he turned to Ruska. "Sorry, customers aren't allowed back here."

Without responding, Ruska turned to Michael and asked calmly, "When is your shift over?"

"Two hours."

"See you then."

When Ruska left, Tad asked, "Who's that?"

"My brother-in-law."

"Oh."

When Emile returned to the booth, Emma looked at him in confusion. "What was that all about? Did you have to use the restroom that badly?"

"Business."

Her eyes widened. "Business?"

"Yeah, Michael Powers is a dishwasher here."

"What?!"

"Yeah, and he's back there now. Emma, we are going to take him back to the mental institution."

"He agreed?"

"Well, sort of."

"Sort of?"

"He seems ready to go back. Wants to stay until his shift is over in two hours. So, we wait."

"You believe him?"

"Yeah."

"Is there a back door?"

"Yeah."

"Emile—"

"Emma, you ever hear how Socrates died?"

"No."

"He was convicted of corrupting the minds of the youth of Athens."

Emma started to speak, but the waitress came with their food. They ate in silence. When the plates were cleared, they sipped coffee while Emile continued.

"Anyway, Socrates was convicted of this crime. He was sentenced to death by poison."

"That's awful! They forced him to take poison?"

"No, and that is the most important part, Emma. He was to take the poison on his own, but the people of Athens really wanted him to live, so the guards made it clear he could leave the jail and flee from the city unmolested."

"Well, that seems like a pretty easy decision. Did he leave?"

"No."

"Oh, they captured him trying to escape?"

"No."

Emma shook her head. "Okay, I give up. What happened?"

"He took the poison voluntarily rather than leaving Athens, even though he would have been allowed to escape."

"Why?"

"That, my dear, is the question, isn't it?"

"What do you mean?"

"Will Michael Powers take that back door? If he does, I have no intention of going after him."

Emma looked confused. "Didn't you say he agreed to go with you?"

"We'll see."

"Why are you doing this?"

"Because I do not want to be like the people of Athens. I think Michael Powers corrupted the minds of the three psychiatrists without knowing it. They did not die from something projected by his hand, but from something projected by his mind."

"I don't get it."

"Neither do I."

"Emile, if by any chance he does come with us, I'm afraid."

"Of?"

"He may be a murderer. He might have murdered you the other day with a rock. He might have killed three people. What's two more?" Emile looked down at his coffee and shook his head. "Yes, I can understand your concern, Emma. Remember, he'll be in my car if he does come with us. You'll be safely tucked away in your own. Should be no problem."

"It's not me I'm worried about, Emile."

"How about if I handcuff him? Will that make you feel better?"

Emma gave him a wry look. "Emile, I've seen enough murder shows to know a man in handcuffs in the back of a car is very dangerous."

Emile sighed resignedly. "I'll take my chances."

"He could lean forward in the seat and choke you from behind."

"His hands will be behind his back."

"That's worse!"

"How?"

"I don't know, it just is. The bad guys always find a way."

"Emma, we're not in a movie. Anyway, we may not have to worry about it. He might already be long gone through that back door."

Emma snorted. "Socrates, remember?"

Emile chuckled at that, but he checked his watch.

"Won't be long now," he said.

Both sat nervously, sipping their coffee and speaking very little, casting furtive glances at the kitchen between sips.

~

Dear dear Reader, I cannot stop myself from interposing a comment here. While they waited in their booth, I stood in that damn, steamy dishwashing room and agonized over my next move. The door beckoned, just as Ruska said. Lordy, did it beckon. That door connected me to Tamara and Ming-huá. All I had to do was open it and leave, never to return. Oh, believe me, dear Reader, I understood why Ruska didn't cuff me and drag me out. I don't think he wanted to deal with me anymore. He wanted me to leave. But see, there's the rub. While I could leave, never to return, by my leaving neither could Tamara—return to "business as usual," which she so desperately wanted. Just as I was ready to bolt for that door, Angel arrived, and his presence reminded me of something important. We talked. I left the kitchen, nodding to Tad on my way.

~

Michael Powers slowly walked up to Ruska and Emma and stood looking at them sadly.

"Let's go," he said softly.

When they reached the detective's car, Ruska said, "Sorry, Michael, I have to cuff you. It's for your own safety."

"No, it isn't," he replied, holding out his hands to make it easier for Ruska.

"No, sorry, it has to be behind your back."

This statement seemed to hit Michael hard, and he shook his head despondently. "I'm not a criminal."

"I know, but it has to be done."

Michael cooperated. Ruska helped him into the back seat and buckled his seat belt. He said a few words to Emma, and they drove out of the parking lot and away from the town where Tamara waited for the return of her husband, suspecting nothing amiss. The next morning, Michael Powers woke to find himself back in the mental institution in the same room he had occupied so long ago. Doctor Xavier DeRuntz stood with a nurse near the door with a barred window.

~ *Doctor DeRuntz is Apprehensive* ~

Michael Powers had been gone for so long that Doctor DeRuntz eventually put him out of mind and busied himself with other patients. Powers' absence and the deaths of Doctors Hess, Camara, and Tavaris faded into the background, and a sense of relief permeated the facility. Staff were aware there existed a search for the whereabouts of Michael Powers, but many secretly hoped he would not be found. Chief among these was the late Doctor Hess's secretary, June, who now worked for Doctor DeRuntz. She had always believed something malevolent and miraculous lurked inside Powers, and with his return, she felt oppressed and intimidated. Often, she had warned Doctor DeRuntz of this patient's hidden capabilities to manipulate and mesmerize, but he only listened in polite silence, ultimately replying with vague platitudes. Unknown to June, DeRuntz himself felt intimidated by the complexity and force of Michael Powers' delusions. Now, for better or worse, he had been placed under DeRuntz's care, and the doctor had little time to prepare for his unexpected return. Upon reviewing the voluminous files of the prior psychiatrists much of the night, DeRuntz decided to erect a firewall against any potential influence or manipulation that might be directed his way by this most difficult, if not dangerous, of all patients.

"Welcome back. How do you feel this morning, Mr. Powers?"

Chapter Twenty-Nine

Buried Alive I

Homecoming

~ How Do I Feel? ~

I have awakened back in this soul-crushing institution, and I am unutterably sad. Suicidal. And he asks me how I feel? Already, my heart is aching for Tamara and Ming-huá. How do I feel? Well, if I have this reputation for malevolent manipulation, let the games begin. "Which person do you refer to when you ask, 'how do you feel this morning, Mr. Powers?'" I ask Doctor DeRuntz in all apparent innocence.

"Sorry?"

"When I say 'you,' I mean me—the versions of me you've been cataloging."

"Enlighten me," DeRuntz says with the faintest ironic smile.

"Well, I have been gone for months, years, decades. There is the you that sits before you now in this godforsaken institution, reduced to an old man with the blank, shit-faced expression of hopelessness. There is the you that is Storyteller, a vital young soldier in Vietnam, agonizing over killing. There is the you whose skeleton still waits in a tunnel far, far away, guarded by the Great Warrior. There is the you that was married to Diane Powers, killed in a car crash, and the you that after her death hosted ghostly dinner parties to keep her close, those parties renowned in all the spirit world. There is the you that is the father of Mark Powers, who is the husband of My-duyen Powers. There is the you that was a successful lawyer, once a powerful advocate arguing cases at the peak of his dominance. There is the you that is suspected of murdering three psychiatrists. There is the you that works for Goddess in the never-ending task of detoxifying God from his addiction to suffering. There is the you that talks to dogs and sidewalks. There is the you that is the son of Bai Meiying, great pianist, and John Powers, misunderstood failure. There is the you that is the schizophrenic you are currently speaking to. And how do you feel this morning, Doctor DeRuntz? You who are just another generic psychiatrist asking another generic question, in fact, worse than a generic psychiatrist since you lack the breasts of the beautiful Doctor Hess whose bathroom leads to the tunnel where that skeleton waits patiently. Which 'you' do you want to answer your ridiculous question?"

I intentionally leave out any mention of Tamara and Ming-huá.

DeRuntz does not change expression, and says evenly, "I choose the schizophrenic you that I am speaking to now."

"The schizophrenic you are talking to now chooses not to speak. He is in mourning."

"Mourning? For being here?"

"I have now lost two entire families, Doctor DeRuntz. I have endured two holocausts. More than two. Have you lost even one family?"

"No."

"Then leave me alone."

"Yes, please take this medication first. It will help you."

His assistant holds out a handful of pills and a glass of water.

I knock them out of his hand.

"Leave me alone."

"Will it surprise you to know you have been gone only one day before you were found, Mr. Powers?" he lies.

"Not coming from you. I happen to know I have been gone a very very long time. Long enough for you to get complacent again in my absence. Long enough for you to now be unsettled by my return. Remember what happened to the previous psychiatrists who tried to play games with me, Doctor DeRuntz. I am not in the mood to play, but if you want, I will."

"So you are capable of keeping track of time and making threats, Mr. Powers?"

"Yes."

He dismisses his assistant, and when the nurse closes the door, DeRuntz glares at me. "I am in no mood to coddle you, Mr. Powers. Your cavalier attitude toward the deaths of three fine people has shown me how capable you are of devaluing life. If I am pushed, I can have you strapped down all day and all night. I can recommend electro-shock treatment. I can keep you sedated. I can do many things that are unpleasant, Mr. Powers, if you insist on being unpleasant to me and the staff. Furthermore, I do not think you suffer from schizophrenia at all, but rather some complex role-playing—acting if you will—but for what purpose I as yet don't know."

Truth be told, this soliloquy shakes me. I force a smile. "As Storyteller might say, go fuck yourself."

He leaves.

I am left with feelings of regret. I should have taken that back door and I'd be with the people I love rather than with people who love themselves. Feeling bereft of hope, I look around the sterile room for any signs of a fertile earth. A single ant would give me comfort. Nothing. Even the air I breathe is metallic and devoid of the slightest scent that a living world produces from the sweat of its existence. Putrid green paint, dead white linen, antiseptic floors, fossilized platitudes of the staff, all designed to isolate the patient from sensory richness and cast him into a bleak landscape. Nevertheless, it has one redeeming quality; it is conducive to wildly imaginative delusions and outrageous hallucinations. Why did I come with Ruska? That, dear Reader, is not what I want to write about. Surely you can figure that out for yourself. The loss of Tamara and Ming-huá has devastated my resistance to—

"Give me your paper and pen, Mr. Powers. No more of____

Chapter Thirty

Buried Alive II

Five Years Later

Believe it or not, dear Reader, it has been five years since I wrote that last partial sentence. It was spoken by Doctor DeRuntz. On that dreadful day, he stormed into my room while I was in the middle of writing and . . . well, okay, a better description (adjectives matter) is that he walked officiously into my room, accompanied by a prissy nurse, and confiscated paper and pen (computers are not allowed in patients' rooms). He took from me all ability to write. He told me it was for my own good and would force me to face reality. (In fact, I think he feared what I wrote. After all, he studied the fates of Doctors Hess, Camara, and Tavaris, and knew his own future would be foretold in my words.) Consequently, I have been locked in my room, given electroshock therapy, told my marriage to Tamara and the birth of Ming-huá are figments of my delusions, threatened with a frontal lobotomy, and almost completely cut off from seeing my son Mark. To my infinite sadness, Mark has given tacit approval for these measures. Because of my attack on Emile Ruska in the cave, I am now deemed a paranoid schizophrenic with violent tendencies. Worse, for whatever personal reasons he has, Detective Ruska stubbornly denies his involvement in my life.

In all these five years, Doctor DeRuntz has given me little opportunity to speak with him, and, in fact, avoids me as he might a plague-carrying prisoner. I now feel old and feeble beyond my years, locked in a cage and rendered incommunicado. I cannot hope to die breathing the sweet air of freedom, and will end my years entombed in the coffin of this disease. And what of God and Goddess? Buandelgereen? *Her*? They have all abandoned me. Not a peep or sign from any of them. I am quite sure Buandelgereen is dead, and as to the others? I hear only the babble of the lesser Evil Ones. Wrapped in this absolute cocoon of sensory deprivation, except for my own inner demons, I have become dull-wittedly compliant.

I assume all deistic attentions are directed at the new Chosen One—Ming-huá.

I am writing these words because Doctor DeRuntz has moved on and I have a new treating psychiatrist. Her name is Elizabeth Wang, and she has taken a fresh approach. After our initial meeting when I told her my story in great detail, she ordered writing materials to be made available and told me to write whatever came to mind as before, when Doctors Hess and Camara were my physicians. I warned her about the potential consequences, but she shrugged them off and indicated she would "take her chances" with me. She had been digging into my files. She particularly homed in on my mother, Bai Meiying, a Chinese pianist and reluctant mystic. I believe she finds the odd combination of my mother and my schizophrenic white father, John Powers, both fascinating and explanatory. No, I have no delusion that Doctor Wang is some manifestation of the Goddess. Furthermore, I have no plan to seek revenge against DeRuntz, who cruelly isolated me. I have no intention of burrowing into the mind of his colleague Doctor Wang for nefarious purposes. What do I intend? To quietly die in this damn hospital. Not by suicide, mind you. I do admit, sometimes, those lower-level demons that growl beneath the cultured, philosophical quarrels of God and Goddess, do prod me to kill myself or kill others. These bottom-dwellers scare me the most, as I worry they are behind the murders I have committed . . . or rather, the murders I fear I have committed. My dead Vietnamese brother who I killed is forever glaring at me as if to say, "You were capable of doing this to me, you can do it to others. It definitely gets easier."

~

Had a long talk with Doctor Wang yesterday. She has been digging deeply into the files and extensively interviewing those still alive who have witnessed the progression of my life, and the flowering of the disease that has infected it. "Your story still has many gaps," she said. "Please help me to fill them in."

"Why?" I asked.

"Knowing you better will help me to decide the best treatment."

Naturally, I was unimpressed. "Doc, many many other psychiatrists have said the same thing, and here I am, as bad off as ever."

"Did you fill in the gaps for them, Mr. Powers?"

"Yes, and for every gap filled in, another psychiatrist died."

"Mr. Powers, I am not about to die."

"That's what they all said."

"In spite of your delusions of grandeur, you do not have the ability to project your thoughts into other people's heads."

"Not my thoughts, Doc, not at all. That is not what you should be worried about."

"I am not worried about myself, Mr. Powers, I am concerned about you."

"How nice."

"Shall I tell you something you do not know?"

"Fire away."

What she told me struck a long-dead chord. She revealed that all of the binders containing my writings from the beginning had been discovered! How? They were mysteriously left with the admitting receptionist by an unknown person who rushed away before identifying themselves. Could it have been Tamara?

God, I miss her so much! Ming-huá is five years old now. I keep asking myself why I allowed Ruska to bring me back to this prison, but I have no answer.

"So you see, Mr. Powers, I have read them all. That is why I have ordered your writing materials returned. Those binders contain a remarkable history, but there are gaps. That is why I want your help."

"What gaps?"

"The last five years, Mr. Powers, the last five years."

The poor woman did not take into account the last five minutes. As I indicated, dear Reader, I feel no animosity toward Doctor Wang, but those lower-level demons have ratcheted up their demands that I kill her. For the moment, I am perfectly capable of ignoring them, but I fear my resolve will waver.

"Doc, the last five years is simply one big gap in my life. All those years were spent rotting in this purgatory. No offense."

"It is not the location of your physical body that concerns me, Mr. Powers. It is all the places your mind has taken you. Surely you have had many adventures these past five years?"

Was she implying all the "adventures" in my writings were dreamed up sitting in this damn hospital room? Bitch! I was not about to give her any satisfaction.

"No," I said.

"In that case, perhaps you have no use for these writing implements?"

Clever bitch. "Please let me keep them!" I cried in alarm. "Writing is . . . diverting."

~

Yes, she has let me keep them, as you can tell by these words. Her clumsy use of a threat activated my anger, and therefore my demons. It is true, these repugnant demons have been planting thoughts of killing her. I know it is them, but they are part of me, and if I don't strike back at psychiatrists, they will eventually force me to kill myself. Although degenerate, perhaps my demons are truly saviors. God and Goddess may have abandoned me, but they remain. It is quite possible said demons, crude as they are, actually represent the most truthful and trustworthy of all my voices. My thoughts turn ever more willingly to killing. This idea of killing, of course, violates my most cherished of the Commandments—thou shalt not kill. Nonetheless, my dead Vietnamese avatar has it right; killing gets easier.

War taught me to kill, and I am still at war. Those who would kill me by drugs, incarceration, electroshock, and endless sessions of talk therapy torture, demand I put an end to it. Yes, the idea of murder (in self-defense) has gained traction. Oh, but dear Reader, did not my Vietnam war binder extol women as the true heroes of war? Are not Gail Hess and Elizabeth Wang heroes? Do they not suffer for the betterment of their patients? In fact, Gail Hess suffered the ultimate sacrifice. My demons tell me to give the same opportunity to Elizabeth Wang. I resist.

~

You must know now why I give greater credence to the society of ants than the society of humans. Big brains are bad brains. Never fear, the Universe will adjust.

Humans, as a species, are a Lost Cause; evolutionary dead end—the fate of all big-brained, abstract thinking species. The universe's fail-safe protection.

~

I don't know how much time has passed since I wrote the above, but as you can read, my thoughts are fragmented, incomplete, dismembered.

"Here is your medication, Mr. Powers," says some nurse's aide I don't even recognize.

He has interrupted my train of thought. Nevertheless, I take the medication, though I know it will do nothing for me.

"You have an appointment to see Doctor Wang in an hour," he says. "I'll be back for you."

Ah, an interesting bit of information.

Kill her! the voices insist, but I am too much in control to consider such a drastic action. No, I will simply prepare for a mental sparring match, not unlike all the others with Hess, Camara, Tavaris, and DeRuntz. Now that I am feeling so old, my motivation has gone, not to speak of my libido. I have no interest in Doctor Wang's breasts, unfortunately. A sign of decay, to be sure. Even the chance to mess with their minds does not hold the same interest. It has become tiresome. Child's play.

What is there left for me? Thoughts of Tamara and Ming-huá. That's it. My agony in being separated from them gets more intolerable daily. It is becoming increasingly difficult to keep these murderous ideations under control. Being here is killing me. Doctor Wang, all kindness, is killing me. Behind the mask of kindness lies a ruthless vivisectionist. In fact, all the psychiatrists who have treated me delighted in experimenting on my mind using the vivisectionist's creative use of torture. Perhaps that is why they died—retribution. My demons may be right. Doctor Wang deserves the same fate. If I do not get her, then she will get me.

~

I really must get these demon-driven homicidal thoughts out of my mind. Goddess once recruited me to help relieve the suffering of the world by curing God of His addiction. Now, I am tossed aside to rot away in this trash heap. It is some solace to understand I am being tossed aside in favor of my daughter, whose powers surely exceed mine just as mine exceeded my father's. I made something disappear only once, and can't even be sure of that. But Ming-huá! What a future for my little Chosen One!

~

"Hello, Mr. Powers. It's good to see you again."

"Hello." I must be cautious. If I am careful enough, I will discover Doctor Wang's agenda behind the pleasant words.

"I see you have taken advantage of my directive."

"What?"

"You are writing again."

"Always."

"Why?"

"To keep a record."

"Of?"

"Crimes."

"Committed by who?"

Careful, careful! "Kill her!" even now the voices demand, but I ignore them.

"Criminals."

"What criminals?"

"As you know, Doctor Wang, if you have read my writings, my bones await me in a tunnel far far away."

"Yes, and?"

"Flesh, muscles, sinews of my body have been stolen."

"I don't understand."

"My history, Doc, my history. Without my history, I am a mere skeleton. All of my writings are to preserve the cellular components of my history that have been stripped away."

"Who has stolen your history?"

"You . . . and your dead colleagues, of course."

This takes her aback for a moment, to my intense satisfaction, but she makes a quick recovery.

"How?"

How do I explain to a normal? Even a highly trained normal? Should I try? Why not.

"Look, Doc, you normals tell us all the time we are imagining things. We are delusional. We are hallucinating. We are not in touch with reality. On and on. So let me try and explain. Your father died in China shortly after your birth. Your mother endured tremendous hardships and vowed to get you to America so you could have a normal, prosperous life. To do this, your mother chose an American man who tutored English to students at the high school where she taught. Am I correct so far?"

Doctor Wang struggled to maintain her poker face. "Perhaps. Go on."

"She was not attracted to this man, in fact she found him repulsive at times, yet she did whatever it took to get him to notice her, then to have a relationship with her, then to fall in love with her, then to marry her so he could legally move the new family to the United States. Once the family settled in Vermont, your mother divorced the man she had used and poured all her energies into her little girl's education. Correct so far?"

"Go on."

"Through incredible hard work and perseverance, the little girl grew to be an ambitious young woman, entering Stanford with a full scholarship. She became a psychiatrist. Her name is Elizabeth Wang, and she is now facing a schizophrenic patient with the same resolve and confidence with which she has faced every other obstacle thrown in her way. I will not ask you if this is correct, because I know it is. Now, there is one problem with this story. It is all false. It is dreamed up by Elizabeth Wang. It is her delusion. The schizophrenic patient she is treating is her own treating physician and she herself is the schizophrenic patient. Is this last part correct?"

"Of course not."

"Ms. Wang, until you fully accept reality you will be put on a strict regimen of medication and electroshock therapy. Furthermore, you will be stripped of the honorific title of 'Doctor'."

"That is hardly—"

"No, no, Ms. Wang. No arguments. Everything you think you know is not real. All of it. Please help us to reconnect you with reality."

"My history, as you call it, is real."

"How do you know?"

"I know what your point is, Mr. Powers, but my sanity is not at issue here. It is you—"

"How do you know your sanity is not at issue!" I exclaim. "You are delusional, wrong about almost everything. You are not a psychiatrist, you never went to college, in fact, you barely graduated high school once your schizophrenia kicked in. For the past two decades, you have been in and out of mental institutions, but you have a stubborn case which seems immune to medication. We are only trying to help you, Ms. Wang."

"I get your point; now can we talk about you. Do you really believe a goddess appointed you savior of humanity? Do you really believe your skeleton is in a tunnel in Vietnam? Do you really believe you can talk to sidewalks and dogs?"

I crack a smug little smile. "These beliefs are you projecting yourself onto me. It is your delusion that I have those delusions. Please, Ms. Wang, can't you see that?"

"Mr. Powers, we are going to get nowhere if you continue to play this game."

"Ms. Wang, we are going to get nowhere if you continue to play this game."

~ *Homicidal Thoughts* ~

I have come to suspect Doctor Wang is none other than God in disguise, just as Doctor Hess was Goddess. Thus, I conjecture, They war over me, assuming human forms. Homer would know what I'm talking about. It all seems to fit. You see, in the last interview I already described, I refused to stop treating Wang like a patient suffering delusions. Result: she again threatened to take away my writing privileges. Like God, she holds out the carrot and uses the stick. Worship Me, and you go to heaven. Deny Me, and you are cast into hell. In fact, I am sure God is behind my being here. That explains why Goddess no longer speaks to me. That explains why Ruska betrayed me—God made him! Perhaps this is my chance to rid the world of this addicted deity once and for all. Eliminate *Him*, and I pave the way for my daughter to eliminate suffering without *His* attempts at sabotage. These are merely suspicions, mind you. My demons hotly espouse such notions, but I remain skeptical. The lawyer in me demands evidence! Solace is the mitigating nature of self-defense. If I do kill Doctor Wang, a.k.a. God, it would be both in my own self-defense and in the defense of humanity. Still, evidence is lacking, and I must be patient. We shall see.

~

Another interview with Doctor Wang. I am determined not to reveal my suspicions and have decided to drop my role-playing with her. As Doctor Hess learned so many years ago, exposing oneself shamelessly in the interest of some ill-defined goal will lead only to embarrassment and censure. I must be alert for any slips that might give any clue I am on to Him. Of course, these very words run the risk of discovery, but I have cleverly segregated them from the harmless dreck I let her read.

"Hello, Mr. Powers. Good to see you again. How are you feeling today?"

"Fine."

"I wanted to speak with you about Tamara."

This indeed surprises me. "My wife," I mutter.

"Yes. And you also claim to have a daughter by her?"

"Claim?"

"Sorry. You have a daughter by her?"

"Ming-huá."

"Yes. Where did you get married?"

"Why these questions, Doc?"

"Well, I am giving you the benefit of the doubt, Mr. Powers. You are a lawyer, so evidence is important to you. If I can supply you with evidence that some of your beliefs are delusions, then your rational brain has some ammunition to use against this, ah . . . mistaken view of reality. Likewise, if you cannot supply evidence to me of those same beliefs, then again, your reasoning mind will prevail over the delusions. Does that make sense?"

"Where do you stand on the nature of suffering, Doc?"

"Mr. Powers, that is clearly an attempt to distract. Do you mean to avoid my questions?"

"Quite the contrary. Suffering must be considered a first principle. Before we go any further, I need to know your answer."

"In your writings, you describe God as being addicted to suffering, isn't that right? First Principles, as you call it."

I wag my finger at her. "Tsk, tsk, Doctor Wang. Answer my question first."

"Ask it again please."

"Where do you stand on the nature of suffering?"

"Clarify the question, counselor. I don't understand."

"You lie. If you read my writings, you would understand."

She sighs and speaks as if forced to recite some long-discredited doctrine. "I only understand God is supposedly addicted to suffering, and Goddess needs you to wean Him off His drug. Don't you think that is a textbook example of a schizophrenic's delusion of grandeur?"

"No, no. No questions, Doctor Wang. Okay, you stated the case reasonably well *sans* the most important details. Now, where do you stand on the nature of suffering?"

"I'm afraid I still don't understand what you want."

I exhale an exaggerated sigh of frustration. "Without suffering can you experience joy?"

"Perhaps. What is the point?"

"The point, as you well know, Doctor Wang, is that religious people argue that suffering is necessary to experience joy, therefore God is not really responsible for suffering. Throw in free will and there you have it."

"Have what?"

"God is acquitted of the charge of inflicting great suffering on the world. Surely you already know this argument. Feigning ignorance is not an effective ruse to evade suspicion."

"Suspicion?"

Damn! My big mouth! "Never mind."

"No, I am quite interested. Suspicion of what, Mr. Powers?"

"Ah, just that you did not do well in theology class."

"I never took a theology class."

"Well, that explains it." Now I must be a bit clever. "You know, in medieval times, students were always asked these strange theological questions."

"Such as?"

"Well, here's one: can God create a boulder *He* cannot lift? If *He* can, then *He* is not omnipotent because *He* can't lift it. If he can't, *He's* not omnipotent because *He* can't create it. Questions like that."

"Circular reasoning."

"Yeah. Here's another one: Did God create joy to make suffering more intense?"

"I see," she says offhandedly.

"Well, that question is directed at you, Doc."

"Sorry, Mr. Powers, but I don't believe in God."

"Of course." I am prepared for this ruse. "But if there were a God, could a person argue the opposite of what religious people argue?"

"Such as?"

This is too much. "Please stop playing dumb, Doctor Wang. You may not have taken a theology class, but you are intelligent enough to understand my question. After all, you claim to have read my writings."

"Okay, yes, I think I do. You mean it could be argued that God created joy only to make suffering more intense?"

"Yes."

"For what purpose?"

"Really, Doctor Wang. Again, I must insist you tell me the purpose. After all, you claim to have read my writings."

"All right. The purpose would be to feed *His* addiction to suffering. Add joy to make the drug more potent. Does that accurately reflect the position of your Goddess?"

"Yes. Now, if your husband were addicted to something destructive, would you try and cure him of it?"

"Of course, just as I am trying to cure you of this delusional belief that Goddess needs you to stop God's addiction."

"*Touché!*"

"And while we're on this subject, you have in the past said, and written, that you don't believe in God yourself. If that is true, why this obsession with an entity you don't even think is real?"

"Exactly!"

Doctor Wang pauses to digest my intentionally confusing response. While she is still thinking, I hasten to set the hook.

"Doctor Wang, you told me you don't believe in God, yet the vast majority of Americans do, many of whom claim God speaks to them. Therefore, in your eyes, they are suffering from delusions. Yet, you do not advocate they be institutionalized. On the other hand, I hear the voice of God (and Goddess), and I am institutionalized. How do you explain this?"

"Mr. Powers, you and I both know there is more to your illness than just the voices."

"No, I don't know that."

Doctor Wang holds up her hand and starts ticking off her fingers. "One—you claim to travel through time. Two—you claim your skeleton is in a tunnel in Vietnam. Three—you believe the ghost of your dead friend Nature possessed Doctor Camara, and ultimately killed him. Four—you believe you are responsible for the deaths of Doctors Hess and Tavaris. Five—you believe Doctor Hess was possessed by a Goddess. Now, Mr. Powers, I've already exhausted the fingers of one hand, and I've barely begun to list your multitude of delusions and hallucinations. Does this not convince you that your psychoses far exceed simply hearing the voices of God and Goddess?"

I feel a little twinkle come to my eyes. "Do you masturbate, Doc?"

She, of course, remains unruffled. "You continue to deflect, Mr. Powers. Do you accept that those beliefs I mentioned are delusions and hallucinations?"

"Do you accept that when you fantasize while masturbating, you are experiencing delusions and hallucinations? Not only that, but those delusions and hallucinations lead directly to physical, bodily phenomena? No use your denying it. Well, my fantasies have the same effect; they lead to physical, bodily phenomena."

"Including time travel?"

"Of course."

"And murder?"

Her question hits me like a bullet to the brain. At last, she has given Him away! God has definitely possessed her. How do I know? Isn't it obvious, dear Reader? He wants me to kill her; make her suffer. Oh, how He would delight in her death at my hand while still in possession of her body! Goddess's son, the erstwhile "Chosen One", murdering an innocent woman whose only sin is her efforts to cure. Oh, yes, I am on to you, God! These lesser demons haranguing me to kill are His implants.

"Mr. Powers? You haven't answered my question."

This requires quick thinking, but age has slowed my brain, so I try and buy some time. "Have you ever contemplated murder, Doc?"

"Again deflection, Mr. Powers. Please set aside your lawyerly instincts. Do your voices tell you to kill?"

"Of course, don't yours?"

"Do they tell you to kill yourself?"

"You know they do."

"And who else do they tell you to kill?"

Ah! A trap! Think, Michael! Finally, it comes to me.

"I'll make you a deal, Doc. You tell me one of your fantasies while masturbating, and I'll reveal one of the persons my voices tell me to kill."

I can tell something in my rather offhand proposal has piqued her interest. She leans forward in her chair.

"Is this the type of bargain you entered into with Doctor Hess?"

"You mean when she bared her breasts?"

"Yes."

I cogitate for a moment. "Well, if you like, we can come to the same agreement. You bare your breasts and I'll answer truthfully any question you like."

She smiles to prove she is not shocked. "No deal. Besides, Mr. Powers, you don't consider me to be your Goddess as you did Doctor Hess. Not the same."

Her smile is complacent. There is no longer any doubt she is possessed by God and He is taunting me.

Kill her! Kill her! My obscene little demons are at full throttle, their continuous mantra vibrates deep within the folds of my mind, making the roots of my hair tingle and my tongue unwilling to engage the enemy.

"I want to go now. I'm tired." I say these words rather pathetically. I must abandon the field of battle to Him so I have time to think. I'm old, and my repartee is correspondingly weak. I am really quite shocked at the degeneration of my verbal agility. I just want to return to Tamara and Ming-huá, where my mind can rest in the lap of comfortable domesticity. Why did I let Ruska take me from my wife and child? Why, why, why?

~ *To Kill or Not To Kill* ~

It is night and I'm sitting on my bed trying to project my thoughts into the mind of Doctor Wang as I once did with the other psychiatrists. Nothing comes to me. I fear my powers are lost for good. All that time spent in forced isolation by Doctor DeRuntz has ossified any astral powers I once possessed. No one visits. Not Goddess. Not *her*. Not Nature. Not Buandelgereen. Not Tamara. No Great

Warrior ant. The bed, the wall, the furniture, all silent but for the constant, *Kill her! Kill her!*

I try and shut my ears, but voices coming from within are impervious to defenses against those coming from without. Every night the walls close in upon me, and every hour they move closer until my existence is bounded by the dimensions of a coffin. My condition is intolerable. Nonstop medication has rendered me a hollow shell. It is therefore my firm decision to purge myself after every pill forced into my mouth. I will immediately induce vomiting. It is my greatest terror that continued existence in this bleak isolation, with only the horrifying rumble of craven demons as company, will cause me to do something irreversible. Having to contend with only God and Goddess would be heavenly bliss compared to what I am going through now. I have not the energy or the heart to break out of this institution, but I am resolved to break out of what is passed off as sanity. I now find more comfort in madness than monotony.

~

I have been medication-free for a few days now, and already feel lethargy, impotence, and depression slip away. The voices are becoming more intense, while at the same time exhibiting increasingly pronounced tonal distortion. They have added another word to their mantra 'kill her.' That word is "knife." Strange how such a simple word can morph into a complex motif that involves cutting, stabbing, piercing, slicing, slitting, slaughtering, butchering, and murdering. Dare I feel the frantic resistance of flesh and muscle as the blade plunges deeper? No. No. Dear Reader, I killed in Vietnam, but the thought of killing Doctor Wang is abhorrent to me. I swing recklessly between the demonic commands to kill and the personal imperative to withhold from committing such terrible savagery. I say "personal imperative" in full awareness of its implications. To knowingly kill Doctor Wang would violate every principle I hold dear. Yet . . . I am weak and . . . the voices are so insistent. This damn affliction has made me so confused . . . angry . . . enraged! If I take the plunge and kill her, I will die long before the authorities have a chance at me. Is that what I want? Suicide by police intervention? Such an ignoble end! Worse, I don't even know if she is married or has children, so dissipated are my once prolific powers. Am I to leave the world with more orphans? Suffering indeed! Try as I might, I cannot project into her mind. What have I come to?

~

I am sitting in the cafeteria eating breakfast. No one is at my table as I write. *Kill her! Knife! Kill her! Knife!* One of those damn wildcard demons. Constant.

Still, here in the daylight, surrounded by crazy people, I feel much more at home. Toast. Toast needs butter. Butter needs a knife. I go to the line and ask. They give me a plastic knife. Useless.

"Do you have a metal knife, please?" I ask the server whose name tag reads Willie. "I always break these plastic ones trying to spread your stupid frozen butter."

"Sorry, no can do," he says.

"Why?"

"Against the rules."

"Why?"

"Against the rules."

I tarry near the utensils, and when Willie is distracted by some hubbub in the corner, I slip a metal knife under my robe. I can feel it is quite dull, and the thought of it being forcibly driven into Doctor Wang's body sickens me. On my way back to my room, I want to hand the knife over to my escort, but having taken the plunge, cannot waver. Since rejecting the medication, I have begun to hear, very faintly, the walls mumbling. Can't make out the meaning yet, but I am confident they will get clearer. I have stashed the knife in a very clever hiding place. I dare not write it down, as these words may be confiscated sometime in the future. For the time being, Doctor Wang has foolishly agreed that my writings may remain private, with the proviso I can share with her at any time. Foolish, foolish woman! God knows about the knife, of course, but He obviously has not yet succeeded in taking her over completely. Mind you, dear Reader, my stealing the knife is no guarantee I will kill her. Not at all. Michael Powers is not a murderer. Self-defense must be my only justification, and justification requires unassailable evidence.

~

Yes, yes, it's days since I stole the knife, and I perceive the deep rumblings of my demons have almost achieved full force. Clear and threatening they are, and continuously barrage me with growling whispers to, "Kill her! Knife! Kill her! Knife!" But that is why I am now writing these words. All this time without medication has reconnected me to the existential dangers posed by the world. In moments of clarity, I picture Goddess crying over the fact that the human genes are winning over those of the Chosen One. Mind control, poison, electromagnetic waves to disrupt my brain; all tools of Doctor Wang (a.k.a. God) to ensure I stay isolated from my family. I have almost reached the decision to kill her, but some nagging doubt holds me back, cautionary remnants of the idealistic young soldier and the supremely rational lawyer. I cannot sleep, but such deprivation only increases my resolve. The confusion is clearing. Perhaps my scheduled session with Doctor Wang today will be the final determining factor in my decision. My nascent psychoses have already led me to catch glimpses of the doctor's inner life. My only complaint is that the walls and furniture remain inscrutable, refusing to talk, but when last I visited the knife, it had begun to communicate in faintly sinister whispers. Just a bit longer. . . .

~ Progress? ~

"Hello again, Mr. Powers. It has been a while. How do you feel today?"

"Fine." Oh, she is coy. Same strategy. Shine her on and see where this goes.

Doctor Wang's demeanor is quite chirpy. She wears a vacuous smile and acts as if she has just received the most delightful news. Very irritating. But her next words scatter my thoughts and shock my senses.

"Mr. Powers, what would you say if I were to tell you I am having doubts that you actually suffer from schizophrenia?"

After recovering my equilibrium, I reply, "I would say you're crazier than I am, Doc."

"You know, sometimes we doctors can be wrong. We can misdiagnose. There is someone advocating for you who believes you do not have schizophrenia despite the fact you exhibit every classic symptom of the disorder."

"Who?"

"Detective Emile Ruska."

Naturally, this is not news to me. When my powers were intact and I could project myself into other people's minds, I knew he suspected I suffered from some mutated form of schizophrenia; a completely new strain the world had not seen before. I always dismissed his crazy theory, knowing the scientific community would never accept it. But now, here is Doctor Wang raising Ruska's idea as a possibility! Never would I have believed a modern psychiatrist could entertain such a radical (or medieval) notion. Still, Wang said only that she was "having doubts". Just as Goddess infected Doctor Hess and made her do things she would never have considered on her own, and Nature did the same to Camara, now, Doctor Wang is succumbing to God's control. Further proof my own theory is correct; she is becoming subsumed by God's malevolent presence.

I decide to play dumb. "Doctor," I say with all due gravity. "Doesn't that run counter to all of my so-called symptoms?"

"Indeed it does."

"What does he think I have?"

"Well, that is more complicated. Suffice it to say, I want to explore how your rational mind deals with these hallucinations and delusions. You seem fully aware of the reality around you even when undergoing psychotic episodes, which is quite unusual. It's almost as if you have an alter ego, what we call a hidden observer, while your original self is under the hypnotic spell of psychosis."

Hidden observer? Hypnosis? Interesting. Nevertheless, I'll play even more dumb. "What do you mean?"

She pulls out one of the thick binders containing my writings and plops it down on her desk. "I mean, you are fully aware not only of your own thoughts, but those of others. Even their private ones. Even their private conversations. How do you do it, Mr. Powers?"

As soon as this question leaves her lips, it all comes to me in a mad rush—my powers are suddenly relit and surge within my mind to reveal the vital life force of others. I gaze in wonder through the transparency of Doctor Wang's life.

Chapter Thirty-One

Others

Fortunate Daughter

~ Doctor Wang ~

Doctor Elizabeth Wang gazed at Mr. Powers with the nervous interest of a raw intern. Since taking over from Doctor DeRuntz, she had immersed herself in his voluminous case files. She knew of Powers's legendary status among her colleagues, and it elicited a complex blend of dread and awe. Initially, her excitement at being chosen to be his treating physician propelled her enthusiastically into late-night sessions reviewing a labyrinth of observations and failed treatments. Subsequently, her anticipation dimmed with each briefing by Doctor DeRuntz about her famous, or infamous, patient. Despite DeRuntz's professionally objective demeanor, she concluded the doctor lived in fear of some unspecified threat.

After reading all the binders containing Powers's writing, it became clear she was not dealing with a "garden-variety" schizophrenic. These circumstances, combined with the knowledge that three of her colleagues died during his treatment, kindled an amorphous nervousness that informed her every step. To Elizabeth, this visceral anxiety seemed to be shared by Doctor DeRuntz and helped explain his harsh treatment protocols during the last five years. Removing Powers' writing privileges and isolating him from other patients and staff suggested he was unwilling or unable to provide effective treatment. He directed his energies toward building a firewall. Doctor Wang vowed she would forge ahead with her own rather shaky intuition, realizing all other conventional and non-conventional treatments had failed miserably. After absorbing the details of his history, she decided to interview the man who tracked him down—Emile Ruska.

In her mid-forties, Elizabeth Wang had seen a promising career in research cut short, gradually settling into the disappointing routine of a treating psychiatrist at a mental hospital. Once a rising star as a postdoc, Elizabeth had watched her revered mentor at Johns Hopkins die unexpectedly just as his team felt they were on the verge of a breakthrough in the causes and treatment of schizophrenia. Finding herself bereft of research facilities, with a husband and daughter to support, she drifted into clinical practice. Hundreds of patients later, her chance to apply the innovative therapy practices derived from her research at Johns Hopkins had fortuitously materialized with Mr. Michael Powers. When approached by Doctor DeRuntz to take over the case, she viewed Mr. Powers as a golden opportunity to try out the unorthodox methodologies learned so long ago while a postdoc. He would be a one-man, self-contained research project. Sharing the ambitions of those who went before, she imagined Mr. Powers might be the professional boost needed to attract attention and garner new research funding opportunities.

As a female, she knew she competed at a disadvantage. Diminutive in stature, Elizabeth long ago ceased being intimidated by blustering males and their condescending attitudes. Through numerous trials and painful errors, she had mapped out the nooks and crannies where their weaknesses could be exploited. However, from the beginning, Mr. Powers seemed to unsettle the standard therapist–patient relationship.

Perhaps it was just the inordinate amount of background she had accumulated about his case.

Perhaps it was his writing.

Perhaps it was the mysterious deaths.

Elizabeth noticed Mr. Powers had not responded to her last question.

"Mr. Powers?"

"Yes?"

"I asked how you do it."

"Do what?"

"Mr. Powers, we are not getting far. I asked how you can read other people's intimate thoughts and hear their private conversations."

"Ask God."

"I'm asking you."

"Ask Goddess."

"I'm asking you." Elizabeth had learned long ago to keep the patient on track.

"I know you're a little bit afraid of me. My reputation, all that background information from Doctor DeRuntz, plus my writings, have disturbed your professional equilibrium. Am I right?"

"That biographical information can be surmised. Is that how you do it? You evaluate the circumstances surrounding an individual at any given time and make educated analyses of how they might be expected to act or what they might be expected to say. Right?"

"Doc, I don't know how I do it, but it is not what you just said."

"Why not?"

"Have you read my writings?"

"Yes. I have noted your latest writings have included me."

"Then you must realize my powers are far more specific than surmises. That is what drove Doctors Camara, Hess, and—" He abruptly fell silent.

Doctor Wang snapped to attention. She noticed that Mr. Powers seemed proud of his abilities, and was about to say something very revealing.

"And what?"

"Nothing."

"Mr. Powers, I think we're getting somewhere. It is important you continue your thought. What were you about to say?"

"About what? I forget where I left off."

Doctor Wang rewound the recording and played back his last words. Letting the tape continue, she reiterated, "You just said, 'That is what drove Doctors Camara, Hess, and' but stopped. Drove them to what, Mr. Powers?"

"Isn't it obvious?"

"Not to me."

"My powers caused their deaths. That is not surmise, that is fact."

"So, you blame yourself?"

Michael looked at her oddly. "Doc, you really are obtuse. Blame is such an unhealthy concept."

"Do you blame God?"

"Maybe."

"Do you blame Nature for Doctor Camara's death?"

"Maybe."

Doctor Wang raised her eyebrows. "And Goddess?"

"Look, Doc, you believe God and Goddess and Nature, and all the others are hallucinations and delusions, don't you?"

"That is what I want to discuss. It doesn't matter what I think. The only thing that matters is what you think, and why you think it."

"In that case, I think you are being taken over."

Although Elizabeth had been half-expecting something like this, his statement nonetheless unnerved her. "By whom?"

"God."

"For what purpose?"

Michael squirmed in his seat and looked away. "I don't know."

"I think you do. Tell me."

He jumped up and cried, "Do you want to join Hess, Camara, and Tavaris?"

Doctor Wang jerked backward, gasping at his vehemence and apparent conviction. She rapidly gained control of herself and replied in a calm voice, "Please take your seat again, Mr. Powers. Thank you. Now, why would God want to take me over?"

"I want to go back to my room. I'm feeling uncomfortable. It is too dangerous being around you. I'll wait outside your office for someone to come and get me."

With these disconnected statements, Mr. Powers walked out. Elizabeth started to call him back but buzzed for an assistant instead. She had more than enough impressions to sort through, not the least of which was the perception that he had made a veiled threat.

~ *First Rumblings* ~

That night, Doctor Wang went home in a very distracted state. Greeted by her husband Aden and daughter Judith, she avoided any mention of her interview with Mr. Powers, and instead concentrated on other subjects the entire evening. An after-dinner digestif helped ease her restlessness, and she went to bed feeling quite content. But try as she might, sleep would not come. Aden's persistent snoring at last forced her into the kitchen for a late-night cup of tea. As she prepared the pot, a faint rumbling filled the room. With a start, she realized it came from within her own mind, and just as the sound began to resolve into voices, it ceased. Elizabeth shakily finished preparing the tea, her thoughts in alarming disorder. After the first sip, she suddenly—and horrifyingly— realized she had read this before in Mr. Powers' writings. In fact, she was acting out the exact same experience as Doctor Hess years earlier. If her next step followed the script, she would go to bed and have a nightmare brought to her by one of his voices. Realizing something extraordinary might be happening, she took a sleeping pill to see for herself whether the pattern that ultimately led to Doctor Hess's death would hold for her. Returning to bed, she tamped down her anticipation and concentrated on emptying her mind of any thought that might interfere with sleep. It took a while, but even Aden's snoring did not prevent her from falling into a deep slumber.

~

Elizabeth's mental landscape unfolded in ways unfamiliar to her accustomed way of seeing the world, and the view took her breath away. She no longer regarded herself as a psychiatrist, or, for that matter, a woman, but rather as some omniscient being. She reached for Aden but he was no longer there. The room could not keep its shape, and Elizabeth watched in amazement as the walls and ceiling ballooned outward, encompassing the neighboring houses, then the city, then the countryside, then, it seemed, infinity. *You cannot encompass infinity!* she marveled, whereupon the rational Doctor Wang blinked out, and she lost sight of the tiny kernel that remained of her soul. All of life, all that exists, filled this infinite space, and she surveyed it through the eyes of God.

And what a view! Elizabeth never felt such power. Awareness transcended the abilities of her feeble human mind to comprehend, filling every molecule of the universe with all-encompassing knowledge. Just as she began to adjust to the dizzying sense of oneness with all that exists, she saw a faint, pulsing light among the galaxies. Somehow, she knew it was the beating enigma of Mr. Powers. As if her body stretched and elongated to the dimensions of a laser beam, she sped toward the center of its reddish pulse, and knew Mr. Powers' holy of holies would soon be revealed. Just as she plunged into the pulsing core, she felt herself instantly bounce backward, as light from some impenetrable mirror was reflected back, and she stared only at herself, drenched in sweat, standing limply in her own bathroom. Her horrified thoughts turned to his writing. *I will read this tomorrow!* she thought. *It is the same! The same! The same! It is how they died!*

Wang felt the compulsion to rush back to her office and reread the section about Doctor Hess's nightmare. *If it was a nightmare*, she thought. Still shaken, she forced herself to return to the kitchen and reheat the tea. The clock indicated only a few minutes had passed since she went to bed, but she felt certain it must be broken. *Hours*, she thought. *It's been hours.* Elizabeth forced herself to drink the tea and concentrate on calming her nerves. *Now, if I follow the script, I will try to rationalize what just happened, and look forward with a sort of desperation to see my lover. Except, I do not have Doctor Camara, a fellow psychiatrist, to confide in. Just poor Aden, an unemployed computer technician with a propensity to eat spaghetti and drink beer. Poor self-pitying Elizabeth*, she thought, then abruptly stopped. *That's right, Gail Hess also used humor to hold off the . . . whatever it was that drove her mad. I am living her life, only with slightly altered details.*

Doctor Wang did not sleep that night. In the morning, she had somewhat regained her control and ate a quick breakfast with Aden and Judith before leaving for work. She never mentioned a word to them about her experience that night. Instead of the usual morning banter with her family, sleep-deprived Elizabeth labored with the dawning realization that there existed a key—or keys—to unlock the hydra-headed psychoses that comprise Mr. Powers's illness. This notion came to her amid her own terror at the possibility of becoming yet another victim left in the wake of this mystifying patient. Over and over, one imperative repeated: I must find the keys before his unnatural powers overtake me. Focusing her energy on the idea of finding keys, she made the determination to reread every word of his writing and press for an interview with Emile Ruska. Elizabeth felt convinced somewhere in the endless tangle and obfuscation waited the prize. If she succeeded in finding it, an unimaginable treasure might be revealed to the world. Not schizophrenia, not schizoaffective disorder, not bipolar disorder, but something new and potentially more lethal than the others combined.

~ *Treasure Hunting* ~

With this startling revelation in mind, Elizabeth immediately set about implementing her plan. She first made an appointment to meet with Emile Ruska in three weeks, then dove back into the writings. In the first run-through, she focused on major themes and symbols that consistently appeared throughout the narratives. This took over two weeks of close reading and note-taking, but she wanted it finished before meeting with Ruska. In the end, she had a rough list of Mr. Powers's "archetypes," as she labeled them. Her list took the following form:

God-Goddess
Demon voices
Precious Object
Her
Great Warrior
Tunnel
Skeleton

Next, she listed his important relationships, real or imagined:
John Powers—father
Bai Meiying—mother
Diane—wife killed in car accident
Mark Powers—son
My-duyen Powers—daughter-in-law
Theresa—wife—hallucination?
Tamara—real person—deluded about relationship?
Daughter—next Chosen One? Delusion?
Nature—ghost—war
Superior Ones
Others?

Armed with these lists, Elizabeth began combining them, seeing how they fit together in the patient's mental jigsaw, trying to find connections. She quickly realized her first mistake was to try and analyze them in purely psychological or literary terms, as she suspected the brain of Michael Powers did not work that way. The more she dug into the material, the more mystifying his case became. On the one hand, he lived an unutterably heart-rending existence, plagued by hallucinations and delusions that projected, in the smallest detail, a false authenticity onto the world. Complete veracity eluded him at every turn, teasing him with a solid nucleus of partial reality; a core of truth that he skillfully augmented with delusion, using the malleability of schizophrenia to mold and shape his fantasy worlds. On the other hand, he seemed in almost total control of his psychoses, draping skeletal reality with flashy costuming and dramatic theatricality, preternaturally pulling strings for the pleasure of watching his puppets dance to a multiplicity of hallucinations and delusions; psychoses that far exceeded the broken vulnerability and helplessness that devastated most seriously afflicted schizophrenics. Doctor Wang agreed with Emile Ruska in at least one regard—his illness manifested differently. Very differently.

As she reviewed his writings, at one moment she wanted to cry for the pain he must be suffering, and the next, rail against his detached, almost cruel manipulations. How could he dispassionately narrate the most wrenching delusions with such arrogant objectivity? Even as she thought these thoughts, she shuddered to realize he would know them. If Doctor Hess had been correct, she would read these very thoughts in writing sometime in the future. How does he know what people are thinking? How does he know even the most private conversations between people? Both of those combined to form the one great question that drove her to distraction and, she believed, contributed to the deaths of her predecessors in their search for the answer.

Did her lists of symbols and relationships carry within them the answer? No matter how she moved them about, trying different combinations, they revealed no plausible solution to the question of how. It is true, they were rife with psychological analyses and literary interpretations enough to fill volumes of speculation. Nonetheless, those could not touch upon the murky evidence of real-life witnesses, restless ghosts, avenging spirits, arguing deities, demonic possessions, clairvoyant projections, and mysterious deaths, above which always hovered Puppetmaster Powers. Hallucinations and delusions do not of themselves materialize in the real world. They must, by definition, remain inside the head of the mentally ill. Certainly, psychoses often lead the stricken patient to act upon them and thereby affect the real world, but they themselves do not venture into everyday reality outside the mind of the person conjuring them. Perhaps her predecessors were right; Mr. Powers possessed the type of mental anomaly that fueled the successes of past charismatic religious founders. Try as she might, Elizabeth could not solve the riddle of how. Instead, she chose to concentrate on the archetypes that plagued him for the solution to why. Here, being on more familiar ground, she felt she made some headway.

~

Monday morning. Three days before her scheduled meeting with Emile Ruska, Elizabeth sat wearily in her office, as always, pondering her most problematic of all patients.

"Doctor Wang?"

"Yes?"

"Mr. Powers has requested to meet with you."

Wang felt her heart skip a beat. This announcement took her by surprise.

"When, Sandy?"

Doctor Wang's assistant shrugged her shoulders. "He said as soon as possible. That it was an emergency."

"Does he display any physical symptoms?"

"Not to Nurse Ibarra. She told me he appeared quite calm."

"I see. I'll check my calendar and get back to you. Thanks."

As soon as the door closed behind Sandy, Elizabeth stood and paced the floor. Her suspicions aroused, she imagined all sorts of reasons for his timing, some reasonable, some fanciful, some ghastly. The awful dream flashed through her mind and sent her reeling. Feeling hot and feverish, Elizabeth found herself dreading meeting Mr. Powers. It seemed the more one became closer to the details of his case, the more his uncanny hold strengthened. *No wonder DeRuntz took such pains to isolate him*, she thought for the millionth time. And then she had a sudden vision. Or, what if. . . .

She buzzed Sandy. "Have Nurse Ibarra tell Mr. Powers my schedule is full for the time being."

~

"Thank you for coming, Mr. Ruska. I know this is inconvenient."

Emile Ruska sat across from her desk looking uncomfortable.

"I have to admit, I thought I was done with Mr. Powers," he said glumly.

"Truth be told, he wanted to meet with me, but I postponed our session until you and I had a chance to talk."

"Okay."

"Let me get straight to the point. Some time ago you said that Mr. Powers did not have schizophrenia. Is that correct?"

"I'm not a doctor."

"I know, but his case is baffling, and we have three dead psychiatrists who attempted to treat him and failed. I don't want to be the fourth."

Ruska jerked in his seat and gave her a startled gaze. "You're worried he'll hurt you?"

"Yes and no. Now, as I was saying, you believe he does not have schizophrenia, correct?"

"I never said he does not have schizophrenia. I only said he has some altered form of it, or mutated form, or some such. Again, I'm not a doctor."

"Yes, I understand, but can you elaborate on your idea for me? After all, you were with him for a long time outside this hospital."

"Well, he does have trouble with reality sometimes."

"That is not what I'm interested in. To be blunt, do you think he can project his psychoses into other people's brains?"

"You mean can he project his delusions and hallucinations?"

"Yes."

Ruska dropped his eyes, unconsciously reached for a loose paperclip, and began twisting it nervously. Elizabeth watched him with interest but waited patiently.

"Is this conversation strictly confidential?" Ruska asked.

"Yes."

"Then, if you would not mind turning off your tape?"

"Yes, okay. Now it's off."

Ruska took a breath. "The answer to your questions is yes, I think he can project his psychoses, including the hallucinations and delusions, into other people's brains. Now you can tell me I'm crazy."

"Far from it. I want to hear more. Did he get into your brain?"

"You first."

"Okay. Yes, I believe it has started in me."

"It?"

"In the beginning, long before her death, Doctor Hess wrote about having nightmares associated with Mr. Powers' delusions. From that point, things got progressively worse. Doctor Camara and Doctor Tavaris had similar experiences before their unfortunate deaths. I have had a nightmare, and I fear it is only the beginning. That is why I asked you here."

"So, you are afraid?"

Elizabeth hesitated. "Yes, a bit. Not from any violence inflicted on me personally by Mr. Powers, but these strange . . . occurrences are upsetting, especially as I have no answer how they happen."

"That's where I come in, eh?"

"Yes."

"Doctor Wang, I am not prepared to go into details, for a whole variety of reasons, but I can tell you I myself experienced hallucinations and delusions while tracking down Mr. Powers and afterward, during my time with him. They were most pronounced when I was physically with him or near him. This is why I came to believe he does not have any type of schizophrenia I ever heard about. When I was a detective, we did get training on the subject. I'm nobody's idea of an expert, but it's almost as if I had caught a virus, or some communicable mental illness from him. I saw things and did things I never would have believed possible before I knew him. I am aware it sounds weird, but that is how I saw it."

"I see, but can you share a little more about the hallucinations and delusions you experienced?"

"I'm afraid not."

"Why not?"

Ruska stared deep into her eyes. "Because they continue."

Elizabeth exhaled, then collected herself. "But Mr. Ruska, perhaps we can help you."

"Doctor, sorry but you cannot help yourselves. Once it starts, I think there is . . . well, put it this way, I would be surprised if we don't end up the same way Doctors Hess, Camara, and Tavaris did."

Elizabeth felt her heart racing. "Do you think his intention is to kill, Mr. Ruska?"

"No, and that is the hell of it. It is not intentional at all, which in many ways makes it worse."

"You know, his father was afflicted with schizophrenia, but in a milder form, yet even he shared psychoses with his wife. Perhaps his was the beginning of this projection ability. On the other hand, his son Mark shows no signs of the disease at all. By the way, Mr. Powers keeps saying he has a daughter by a former patient here."

"Tamara?"

"Yes."

"Hunchback?"

"Yes. Does he have a daughter, Mr. Ruska?"

"I don't know."

"Well, we know she is not a hallucination, but he may be experiencing delusions about her."

"I'm not so sure," said Ruska.

"Well, if he is not delusional about his relationship with her, then what about this daughter he keeps talking about?"

Emile shrugged. "That is the question of questions."

"Do you know where this Tamara lives now?"

"Used to. I learned she lived with him in a trailer park. But when I returned to talk with her after I deposited Mr. Powers back here, she had disappeared. When I asked around, no one knew where she had gone. Here's the thing; when I asked her neighbors about her, they all said she does have a daughter. One of the older women who babysat while Tamara worked at a restaurant said the girl was very cute but had a hunchback like her mother and acted very strangely."

"How strangely?"

"Couldn't put her finger on it, but said the girl seemed far older than her age. Almost frighteningly so. After a lot of coaxing on my part, she believed the child had supernatural powers. When I pressed her on what they were, the woman shook her head and clammed up."

"And did this person say who the father is?"

"Michael Powers."

"My God."

Chapter Thirty-Two

To The Edge

Shaky Steps

~ How to Proceed? ~

I am aware that Doctor Wang will not see me until she meets with Detective Ruska. I am aware Doctor Wang seeks the key. I am aware that I must not let her find it. To do that, I have no choice but to stop her, one way or another. As you have just read, she is getting much closer than her predecessors. More proof that God is behind it. Still, I must hand it to her. Little does she know that her progress might necessitate . . . well, a more proactive response on my part. Am I up to it? The voices, the little obscene demon-voices never stop demanding I kill her, but doing so would eliminate any chance of seeing my Tamara and Ming-huá again. Ever. They are out there somewhere, and Ming-huá is growing stronger every minute, her powers increasing daily. I am sure Goddess guides her and nurtures her in preparation for the ultimate confrontation with God at the next Reunion. True, I have been cast aside, a shriveled morsel for these mangy dog-demons to chew on. They would have me kill, and my resistance is weakening. I know that murdering Doctor Wang would increase suffering. Worse, I have since learned her death would leave a devastated husband and daughter. That would please God and *His* First Principles to no end. That is why *He* uses these slave-demons to taunt me even as *He* tightens *His* grip on Doctor Wang. *He* wins either way—either I kill her or she kills herself. That is *His* game for all living things. Thus suffering. Thus worship.

Which brings me to Goddess and *Her* crusade to detoxify God and wean *Him* away from *His* dependence on suffering. It is, without doubt, a conundrum that I do not even believe in God. However, the question arises: may one substitute *Homo sapiens* for God? We created God, we are God, and God is us. *He* is one of my voices, and human voices are pervasive and inescapable. They surround me every day, and they surround you, dear Reader, every day. Whispering, cajoling, bantering, chattering, plotting, threatening—angry, sweet, loving, hating—always there. Humans have created a loquacious God to mimic them, constantly whispering, cajoling, bantering, chattering, plotting, threatening—angry, sweet, loving, hating—in your ears, in your mind, always. All of us, all of you, are schizophrenic, at least compared with the rest of life on Earth. What do you do in the name of these voices? Kill, murder, rape, steal, obey, defend, exact revenge, seek love, give love, give hate, on and on and on. All of you!

~

Sorry, I got carried away. Won't happen again. So, let me turn my (and your) attention to the knife. It remains tucked safely away (along with these pages) in its safe repository. I visit it every week or so, just to ensure it remains securely hidden and to add pages of my latest writing to its treasure trove. As I turn it in front of my eyes, I marvel at how much the blade is like the voices, sharp and deadly. Voices of the world are like billions of blades cutting, slicing, killing. We have turned the world into a great butcher shop with our words, commanding flesh to obey and animate our greatest desires in the name of trite phrases. Thus suffering. Thus worship. Dare I animate my flesh to obey and employ the knife to act, inflicting yet another death in the sea of deaths? If only I could see Tamara and talk with her! She would moderate these horrific impulses and direct me to the domestic tranquility of home, hearth, and child.

You know, it gets so lonely with no one to talk to. I bang on my cell door and ask if I might be allowed to go to the cafeteria. Nurse Ibarra nods and escorts me. I look around hoping to find a table where a familiar face is sitting, but I don't see anyone I recognize. I grab a slice of pie and coffee and scan the room again, when I spot an elderly lady whose face strikes my fancy. She must have been quite beautiful when young, and still retains the afterglow of sweet loveliness.

"May I sit with you?"

She smiles. It is the saddest smile I have ever seen.

"Of course." Her voice is as lovely as her face.

"What's your crime?" I ask.

"Pardon?"

"What are you in for?"

"Oh, I don't need to be here."

"You're not a patient?"

"Well, yes, in a way. My children are worried."

"About?"

"My, you're very forward, Mr. . . . ?"

"Powers."

Her eyes widen perceptibly. "Oh!"

"What does that mean?"

She becomes quite agitated, and her hand trembles when lifting her teacup. "Nothing."

Sure, I think. I'm pretty confident I know what her reaction was all about. My reputation precedes me: murderer. However, I have no wish to pursue that path.

"May I ask your name?"

"Priscilla."

"Pretty name. Not too common nowadays."

She seems less flustered. "My children are really quite sweet. They're just worried."

"About?" I ask again, a bit more gingerly.

"Well, its depression, you see."

"Ah. Have you tried to commit suicide, or only thought about it?"

Priscilla puts down her cup and stares in wonder. "As I said, Mr. Powers, you are quite forward, if not presumptuous."

"Please, call me Michael."

She chuckles. "To use your clever phrase, Michael, what crime did you commit?"

"Don't you know?"

"No."

"Oh, I think you do. They say I'm a schizophrenic, but it is just possible that the moniker is no longer adequate for what I seem to have."

"It's true, I have heard rumors."

"Oh? What are they? What do they say?"

"Nothing much. I know you suffer from schizophrenia."

I feel this description minimizes the distinction I have attained in the eyes of so many people, not the least of whom are Elizabeth Wang and Emile Ruska. I am one for the books, as they say. However, I don't want to appear too full of myself. "Is that all?"

She again appears rattled. "Yes."

"Are you afraid of me?"

"Well, I've never been comfortable around schizophrenics. I never know what their voices are saying."

Kill her! Kill her! She's a spy! Kill her!

"Oh, they are harmless. I must admit, I've never been comfortable around manic-depressives. I never know when they will try to kill themselves." I laugh to let her know this is a joke.

She returns the laugh weakly.

"In fact, you probably want to kill yourself now just listening to my nonsense." I again laugh. Dear Reader, I am capable of charm, you know.

Again, she seems more relaxed. "You know, Mr. Powers—"

"Michael."

"You know, Michael, I have always been curious what the voices say."

"Priscilla, you never answered my question."

"Which?"

"Did you try and commit suicide, or did you just think about it?"

Now she seems perturbed. "Does that make a difference?"

"Not to me, but my curiosity about depressives wanting to commit suicide is the same as your curiosity about schizophrenics' voices."

"Yes," she whispers almost to herself. "That makes sense."

"Well?"

She looks at me with a mischievous look, as might a little girl. "You go first."

I sigh for effect. "Okay. They tell me I am useless."

"Is that all?"

"Pretty much. Now you."

"I've thought about it."

"Is that all?"

"Pretty much." Now she laughs a natural, robust laugh.

I think I like this Priscilla. I will up the ante. "Priscilla, I will tell you something else about the voices if you reciprocate."

"Agreed."

"I hear God and Goddess. They argue." I am not prepared to go into detail, she might think I'm crazy.

"Really? That's interesting. You mean the real God?"

"What does that mean?"

"I mean the Christian God?"

"Is that who you consider the real God?"

Again, she chuckles. "Of course."

"Yes and no, Priscilla. *He* is the Christian God and the Jewish God, and the Muslim God, and all the other Gods rolled up into one."

"My, my! And this Goddess?"

"Same thing! All female Goddesses rolled into one. Are you religious, Priscilla?"

She ignores my question. "What do they symbolize?"

"They are not symbols, they are voices."

"Do you think they are real?"

"Time's up. Your turn."

She takes a sip of cold tea and shudders visibly. "Blank. Black. Void. I could have the most wonderful, fulfilling experience of my life, and my reaction is complete and utter emptiness. If my greatest wish for success were granted, I would feel nothing. No wonder so many of us contemplate suicide."

"So, you do think about committing suicide. Have you made the attempt?"

"Time's up. Your turn."

Her black hole has inexorably drawn me in. I say something without thinking, something that takes me completely by surprise. "Little Acorn."

"What?"

"I mean . . . never mind. The voices, yes, they argue."

"You told me that. What else?"

Little Acorn will not get out of my mind and I say nothing, but my hands are trembling for some reason.

"Michael?"

"Oh, yes. You want to hear something funny?"

"Sure."

"The doctors think I have a new kind of schizophrenia."

"How so?"

"My schizophrenia might spread, be contagious, can be projected into other people's minds, however you want to put it."

I see her lean backward as if I just sneezed in her face. "Contagious?"

I laugh. "No, no, don't worry. Not contagious like germs. I mean, well, I don't know what I mean. Your turn."

"I've told you all I know."

"No, you still haven't answered my most important question. Have you tried to kill yourself?"

"Michael, do your voices tell you to kill?"

Her question surprises me. "What?" I need time.

"Do your voices tell you to kill?"

"Answer me first."

"Yes, I have tried to kill myself twice. You have no idea of the pain and loneliness. How badly I am hurting my family. Killing myself would relieve them of the burden I put on them. Ah, yes, I have tried to kill myself, and probably will do so again."

"By?"

"Sleeping pills. But, looking at you, I know I am not the only one suffering pain and loneliness. You are suffering also. Now it's your turn to answer my question."

"Yes, they tell me to kill."

I see her turn white, but she doesn't flinch. "Are they telling you to kill me now?"

I laugh. "No, nothing of the sort. No, no."

"It would be ironic that your voices make you kill me, satisfying the worst of your schizophrenia, and I would be dead, satisfying the worst of my depression." She does not laugh.

"You know, sometimes they tell me to kill myself, too," I say.

"Really? Have you tried?"

"No, no! I think our time is up."

"Yes, I think our time is up. It's hard to talk about, but I actually feel better talking about it with you."

"So do I, Priscilla. I'm glad I sat at your table."

I find it hard to believe what I have disclosed, but Priscilla has awakened something in me, both for good and ill. I see her rise to leave.

"Can we see each other again, if you're not afraid of me?" I ask.

She smiles that lovely smile. "I am not afraid of you . . . anymore. I would very much like to see you again."

"Tomorrow, same time, same place?"

"Tomorrow."

Ah, thank God! Human contact. Flesh and blood human contact. Not voices. Not demons. Not doctors. Not detectives. Not people my voices tell me to kill. No Buandelgereen to stoke my delusions. No Temulun to ask for treats. Walls and sidewalks have their limitations. I almost feel reborn. Can I tell Priscilla everything? We shall see. Why did I mention Little Acorn?

~ *More Proof* ~

But I have not seen Priscilla again, nor will I. It is the next day and I am sitting alone in the cafeteria two hours after we agreed to meet. I just had a conversation with Nurse Ibarra. She told me Priscilla had been released that morning and was gone. I asked who authorized her release.

"Doctor Wang."

Of course. God released Priscilla to keep her away from me. Wang is just *His* tool. She knew about our meeting yesterday (I'm sure Nurse Ibarra told her. God also told her.) When presented with this information, what does she do?—removes the one ray of light in my miserable life here. I intend to check the knife later today or tomorrow. The blade must be sharp, the metal unforgiving.

Kill her before she kills you! Kill her, worthless!

Where is Goddess?

My bad demons are relentless, but they are probably right. Doctor Wang puts on a compassionate face, but her intent is obvious. Oh, God! The thought sickens me. I don't think I can do it. But soon, very soon, I'll have no choice. Yet my dead Vietnamese soldier still dwells within, and I look at the world partly through the membrane of his soul. He tells me not to kill. Goddess also would tell me not to kill, but She has abandoned me. Only God remains, silent, behind the form of Doctor Wang—a physical form whose blood can be drained by a knife. Why is it I am aware God wants me to kill the very person *He* possesses, yet still I feel I must do it? In moments of clarity, I realize I must not go down the very road that *He* wants, that his growling demons want, but . . . but. . . .

~

Can't sleep. I want Tamara. Perhaps she will appear like Diane used to do. Not here. I want Nature. He can come. He can. Ghosts can do anything. Nature! I need your advice! Not here. I have decided. I must kill her; I have no choice.

~

I am sure, dear Reader, you cringe at such a declaration. We all have a choice, you say. Life is full of choices. Teachers always say a bad child has simply made bad choices and must be taught to make good ones. Nonsense. We, none of us, are given the most important choice of all. What is it, you ask? To struggle, of course. We all must struggle, bacteria and whale and human. But the greatest struggle of all is to simply be left alone. Left alone by teachers, parents, friends, and enemies. We acknowledge the struggle for survival, power, money, love, and all the rest, but at its essence, the world will never leave us alone, even if we want to live the most isolated, peaceful, harmless of lives. Predators are all around! Ah, to be left alone! Alone to absorb nutrients; to graze on sweet grass without being pounced upon and eaten; to eat in peace without snarling interlopers; to grow alone toward the sun without being blocked and starved; to love alone without jealousy; to live alone at the edge of an endless sea whose waves are as the ticking of eternity. Bliss!

Suicides seek nothing more than to finally be left alone. Doctor Wang will not leave me alone. None of them will. Some have already paid. So will she.

~

I keep having headaches, and they are affecting my writing. All of my muses are gone. Goddess, God, Buandelgereen, Nature, Diane, and all the others. Gone. Nature abhors a vacuum, and my brain is collapsing in upon itself. What is at the core? Those horrible demons that keep on and on. ***Kill her! Kill her! Kill her, worthless. Kill her before she kills you!***

Do I have a choice? Not if I want to be free of them. Free! This is why so many serial killers say they had no choice but to kill. Those who still believe they have choices will never understand. I don't know that I can write anymore. My head.

Mother. . . .

~

It is night. It is day. I don't know. What I do know is that there is a giant crater in the middle of my room. When I peer over the edge, I see a sickly, yellowish mist writhing at the bottom. God's face stares up at me through the wispy tendrils, beckoning. I feel weary and sink to my knees at the lip of the crater. I lower my head deep down into it, as a thirsty man to water. Greedily I drink of the yellowish mist. Greedily I drink of the poison. I feel its astringent burning scald my veins, encircling my brain, seeping into the roots of my neural web as rain in draught-starved soil.

Father.

Mother. . . .

Chapter Thirty-Three

Jump

Avoidance

Doctor Wang felt even more uncertain and adrift after her meeting with Emile Ruska. His views confirmed her greatest fears and stoked an unsettling alarm that pressured her to consider duplicating the isolation policy of Doctor DeRuntz. Should she treat Mr. Powers as if he carried the plague? As the days passed, her nightmares grew worse, and so did her determination to take some drastic action. It was impossible to increase medication beyond its current dosage. Already, the side effects seemed worse than the cure. She knew Mr. Powers no longer heard his most persistent voices—God and Goddess. However, the new ones that had emerged were even more troubling. These new voices must be investigated, but that was precisely the place where she hesitated to venture. The thought of interviewing Mr. Powers seemed to invite calamity, and she felt she had already strayed into enough deep water. Proximity to him might expose her to the same riptide that had carried off her predecessors. DeRuntz's old warning, "distance or drown," rose in her like a tide, not advice but a deadline.

One night, feeling particularly burdened with doubts as to her next move, she went home only to be surprised by her husband and daughter with a wonderful meal. Champagne was poured and her husband lifted his glass.

"To the most perfect of all wives, whose husband and daughter count their blessings every day to have her near."

Elizabeth beamed and emptied her glass. Her eyes teared up. "Nothing could have made me feel happier. Your timing is impeccable."

"Problems at work?" asked her husband.

"No more than usual."

He gave her a questioning look. "Mr. Powers?"

No response.

"C'mon, Liz, it's got to be him."

Now the tears were streaming. "Let's change the subject."

"Can do!" He poured her another glass.

The champagne made her lightheaded and she basked in the moment. On the surface, she seemed the picture of happiness, but, in the back of her mind, she dreaded having the jovial atmosphere end. To retire and sleep seemed impossible. What nightmares would cloak her in the terror of creeping possession? For the first time in her life, Elizabeth felt utterly helpless. It seemed her university training and years of clinical experience provided no direction, not even a familiar touchstone. While enduring this fog of uncertainty, she reluctantly agreed to meet with Mr. Powers the following week. Not once did it enter her mind that he might pose a physical danger.

~

As the meeting drew nearer, Elizabeth noticed each day brought progressively unstable emotions and each night increasingly troubled nightmares. Unable to face Mr. Powers, she abruptly informed Ibarra to put the interview on hold. At first she felt guilty, but soon she came to welcome her decision. The night before the canceled meeting with Mr. Powers, she suffered yet another nightmare, this one more wrenching than those that came before.

It started harmlessly enough. Elizabeth found herself strolling along a gently curving gravel path through the grounds of a beautiful garden. Green grass, flowering wisteria, fragrant lilacs, a charming pond with blooming lilies, a tinkling waterfall, and a cool, pleasant breeze; all enveloped her in the welcoming arms of Mother Earth. Birds of many species frolicked in decorative fountains and colorful birdbaths, squirrels chattered, leaves fluttered in the breeze, and she found peace and harmony in the solitude of such luscious surroundings. As the sun shone proudly down upon the earth, her path shaded by overhanging oak and sycamore trees, Elizabeth basked in the unabashed glory of the natural world. Her receptive heart opened to endless possibilities.

Reaching the crest of a slight rise, she saw in the distance someone sitting in a chair, alone, facing away. Suddenly, as if a switch had been pulled, enormous black clouds blotted out the sun, and the smell of rain permeated the air. Elizabeth froze at this unexpected development, and she squinted through the swollen atmosphere at the lonely figure, back still turned, staring down at something. She could not make out what the person looked at, so she felt compelled to continue walking, drawing closer even as rain battered the earth in a horrific downpour and lightning and thunder roared across the land. Still, she tried to keep her eyes transfixed on whatever lay at the feet of this mysterious apparition, but its position blocked her view. Before she knew it, she stood just behind the chair and followed the tilt of head downward to see what had so engrossed it. Three amorphous lumps, long rectangular hillocks, lay side-by-side, resembling mounds of freshly dug graves.

The next bolt of lightning revealed in ghastly detail the bodies of Doctors Hess, Camara, and Tavaris, their pale faces made dreadfully luminous by the flash. At the same moment, the figure turned in its chair and stared malevolently at Elizabeth, revealing the grinning countenance of Mr. Powers. She wanted to scream, but nothing came out. She wanted to run, but her legs would not move.

Frozen in place, she could only watch as Mr. Powers stood and started toward her, his arm raised, holding something she could not make out. They both remained in that position for what seemed an eternity, his hand never coming down with the object he grasped. She, Mr. Powers, and the three bodies comprised a tableau that had somehow reached an ending, all future moments suspended in this instant of time. Still locked in this uncertainty, Elizabeth awakened with a shallow gasp. Damp with sweat, she checked to make sure her husband continued to sleep, then quietly went to the kitchen for a cup of tea.

As she sipped tea, she wondered if this nightmare was a product of her fears, or far worse, a projection directly into her mind from Mr. Powers. A warning? Is this what eventually killed her three colleagues? Would this eventually kill her? Without further agonizing over such speculation, she made a firm decision about how to go forward with Mr. Powers. After that, she slept soundly.

~ *Preparation for Meeting* ~

Upon arriving at the institute, Elizabeth called Nurse Ibarra.

"Isabel, we have a specific date for my meeting with Mr. Powers, correct?"

"Correct. It has been scheduled per your instructions."

"Has he said anything about meeting with me?"

"Sometimes he seems anxious to meet, but other times he seems hesitant, even a little afraid."

"Okay, let's reschedule the meeting for this Thursday at three o'clock. I've already checked, and I know that time is available."

"Shall I tell Mr. Powers?"

Elizabeth hesitated, then said, "Not now. Wait a while. There is something else I need you to know." She took a deep breath. "This meeting will be conducted outside, in the open garden area on the grass adjoining the East Building A. There are benches for patients and staff. When the time comes, you will escort Mr. Powers to that area where I will be waiting. I will have a battery-operated recorder. Once you bring Mr. Powers to me, you may leave, but remain in the area and shoo away any patients who come close so we are guaranteed privacy. Make sure you stay out of earshot. Understood?"

"Yes. When should I tell Mr. Powers about this meeting?"

"Wait until fifteen minutes before the meeting. When you bring him, have a staff member immediately search his room for any writings, including under his mattress or any other likely hiding places."

Nurse Ibarra gave her a strange look, but finally said, "Yes, doctor," and left.

Elizabeth made her rounds in a distracted state. She wished she had a colleague in whom she might confide her deepest concerns, like Doctor Hess had Doctor Camara. However, both were now dead, and for all she suspected, bringing in a collaborator now could negatively impact whoever it might be. She was intent on facing the nightmare, or projection, head-on and alone. The area she chose to meet Mr. Powers closely resembled the magnificent garden in her dream. There was an expansive grassy area and a couple of birdbaths. It wasn't perfect but would have to do. As Michael Powers's mother used to say, according to his writings, "come what may."

~

Dear Reader, her precautions are really quite absurd. I will stash this writing away long before her minions find it. Not only will I stash the papers away, but I will retrieve my knife and slip it into my pajamas long before either can be discovered.

~

In the run-up to their meeting, Elizabeth did everything in her power to seek distractions. Her husband had never known her to be more loving; her daughter had never known her to be more solicitous. Rarely did Elizabeth let herself be separated from their company, and while at work, rarely did she find herself alone without seeking the proximity of colleagues, the more perceptive of whom eyed her with increased feelings of concern. Among this group, those who remembered the steady declines of Doctors Hess, Camara, and Tavaris before their deaths were particularly worried.

A small group of psychiatrists even approached the chief administrator, Doctor Miller, who sympathized but said he was powerless until something of consequence required his intervention. Unfortunately, he had been appointed recently, replacing Doctor Greenlee, and possessed little knowledge of Mr. Powers's history or the three dead psychiatrists left in his wake. While Miller appreciated their concern, he firmly advocated therapeutic freedom for his physicians.

As the day approached, despite her best efforts to remain positive, a deep pall of amorphous dread cloaked Elizabeth, and at times she felt a suffocating gloom that threatened to shatter her resolve. Concentration became increasingly difficult, and she found she could not even manage to devise a clear statement of goals in anticipation of the meeting. At best, Elizabeth had formulated a vague notion this interview would determine whether to allow Mr. Powers continued freedom of movement (including access to writing materials), or to immediately isolate him à la Doctor DeRuntz.

The argument for isolation was strong; after all, DeRuntz sailed through his years with Mr. Powers without manifesting any of the afflictions suffered by the preceding treating physicians. Yet, Elizabeth felt disinclined to follow this harsh regime. It went against her training and principles. Furthermore, Elizabeth felt a personal and professional closeness with the three dead psychiatrists, particularly Gail Hess, whose desperate (and career-threatening) attempts to penetrate the complexities of her patient's illness ultimately proved fatal. Nevertheless, she felt herself weakening. Her garden dream became a nightly ordeal, with slight alterations, but always the upraised arm holding an unseen object signaled the end, leaving her shivering in terror. This was partly the reason for her bold decision to meet Mr. Powers in a setting that largely mirrored the nightmare. Once the meeting had been set in motion, she would find it impossible to back out.

What confounded her the most, and created immobilizing uncertainty, was confusion about whom she was dealing with. Of course, Mr. Powers remained the patient, but Elizabeth felt (like Detective Ruska) there lurked another adversary, one that deliberately and quite independently, threatened not only her schizophrenic charge, but the sanity of those around him. This dangerous adversary appeared to be a malevolent phenomenon unleashed from Mr. Powers's mind; a falcon that no longer could, or would, hear the falconer.

If her supposition proved correct, this willful actor pursued its agenda with single-minded determination, destroying any obstacle that lay in its path, and neutralizing whoever set out to control it. The critical issues that were to be exposed by the therapist involved the identity of this great adversary, and the agenda it so ruthlessly carried out. Elizabeth had become convinced all three psychiatrists died because they threatened to unmask this . . . this what? Ghost? Demon? Viral schizophrenic strain?

Or could it really be the deities he so often talked and wrote about?

The writings pointed the way, but they pointed in multiple and seemingly unrelated directions. Did Nature's ghost kill Doctor Camara? Did Goddess kill Doctor Hess? Did Mr. Powers kill Doctor Tavaris? It was all too baffling; enough riddles to last a lifetime. The pure number of hallucinations was staggering, wide-ranging, and maddeningly diverse. God, Goddess, her, Theresa, Nature, Ethyl, even an imaginary friend and his family, to name a few. Which was the dominant? But that implies dissociative identity disorder, which has been ruled out. None of these hallucinations were different personalities; they were separate entities.

Elizabeth felt there must be one supreme being that directed the others. All roads led to Goddess. Gail Hess must have thought the same thing. How else to explain the extraordinary therapeutic step of exposing her breasts to encourage his identifying her with Goddess? Even God seemed a subset of Goddess. After all, He represented Her efforts to detoxify a male deity afflicted by a world-destroying addiction to suffering. Yes, yes, it must be Goddess at the heart of Mr. Powers's delusions. Yet, what if her theory were correct? What if Goddess operated independently of Mr. Powers and his schizophrenia? What if they all acted independently? Then, truly, this patient must merely be the conduit through which these entities are released. What if the hallucinations and delusions were no such things? What if they were a sort of Jungian collective unconscious, not bound to the confined neural pathways of a single person, free to move in the world? Free to create havoc? Or hope? Perhaps Mr. Powers is the first in the history of humanity to unknowingly provide a bridge. Perhaps his father was the precursor. That would explain why Goddess chose Michael Powers to be the son.

Are these Superior Ones he keeps mentioning the future? Is the human race on the road to extinction?

But, no! None of it made sense! From a scientific point of view, Elizabeth felt she was building metaphysical mountains out of garden-variety schizophrenic molehills. Always, she ended back at the beginning.

Who, or what, is this hidden adversary?

~

The night before the meeting, Elizabeth was determined to extend her night-mare so she might see the object held up by the raised arm. If she awoke at the usual moment of suspense, she would force herself back to sleep and continue the dream. Uncharacteristically, she took two sleeping pills. Somehow, she felt that discovering the object would provide a key to the next day's interview. Telling her husband she had a big day scheduled, she went to bed early. In minutes, Elizabeth fell into a deep slumber.

She strolled through the lovely garden, and as always, the sun smiled down and the birds chirped happily. Elizabeth, realizing she was dreaming, felt a vague sense of satisfaction that all proceeded according to script. But suddenly, instead of the garden, she found herself in a great plain, translucent human shapes stretching to the horizon. With a start, she saw the figure with the raised arm, its plasma body shimmering like the surface of water in a bright sun. Behind it stood the shadowy bodies of her dead colleagues, standing motionless, watching. As if responding to some command, the threatening figure, horribly faceless but most certainly Michael Powers, arm still raised, glided toward her. Elizabeth felt powerless to run from the approaching specter. Desperately, her eyes followed the arm upward to see its terminus where a hand must reveal the object it grasped so menacingly. But try as she might, a thick mist rendered the wrist and hand invisible, leaving only a smudge, as if someone had clumsily erased it. No matter how hard she tried in the dream, the smudge could not be removed and expose the secret it obliterated. Closer the dark figure came at frightening speed, and as it loomed over her, the arm started down. Yes, of course, a knife! Elizabeth involuntarily closed her eyes, but before the awful scene blinked out, she saw her three colleagues still standing motionless, sadly staring, while behind them, moved thousands of translucent bodies, rustling like curtains in a slight wind, their collective whispers hissing across the vast, bone-white plain that stretched beyond an albino horizon. . . .

~

Elizabeth jerked awake in a sweat. She turned her head and looked at her husband sleeping peacefully, a rasping growl—proof he had not been awakened by her startled response. She crept out of bed and visited her daughter's bedroom, where the girl also slept soundly. Elizabeth breathed a sigh of relief and went into the kitchen to have a cup of tea. Her fright rendered the two sleeping pills powerless to drive her back into the bedroom and creep beneath the covers. Elizabeth's heart beat too quickly, and sometimes irregularly, which alarmed her, but the tea soon helped slow it to a more sustainable level. With no desire to attempt revisiting the nightmare, she forced herself to remain in the kitchen, not trusting what horror might assail her if she dared return to bed. She knew within a few hours she would be sitting with Mr. Powers, struggling to conceal her emotions and performing the duties commensurate with her position. Pride in her professionalism, if nothing else, propelled her forward. But the terrible premonition of never seeing her husband or daughter again chastened her and made her dread even more the upcoming confrontation. Elizabeth remained frozen to her chair, wrapped in an illogical fear of what tomorrow would bring.

~ *The Meeting* ~

Elizabeth's husband noticed she was unusually talkative during breakfast and ascribed it to nervousness. A wise man, he made no mention of work and joined in her loquacious mood quite willingly to help distract. Nevertheless, she ate quickly and left early for work. Once at the institute, she immersed herself in consulting patient files and making rounds. Despite this hectic pace, it seemed to her time passed very slowly, and when lunch time rolled around, she had already built up an excess of nervous energy.

"Are you having lunch?" asked a colleague she passed in the corridor. "If you are, I'll join you if that's all right."

"No, I'm not hungry, Jim. Besides, I've got a stack of files I'm already behind on. You know how it is."

"Of course."

Elizabeth thought he looked at her a bit oddly, and wondered if he knew about the meeting. After all, Michael Powers was quite the celebrity at the institute, and many followed the progress of his case with great interest. She returned to her office and sat looking at a stack of files, absent-mindedly thumbing through some, but absorbing nothing. Now the time seemed to slow even more, and every passing minute proved agonizingly long.

By the time two o'clock arrived, she could wait no longer. She collected her writing pad and recorder and walked to the outside garden area. It was early, but she felt desperate for air. Selecting a place in the shade where two benches formed an L shape, she settled in for the long wait. But sitting became tiresome, so she stood and paced in circles around the benches, paying particular attention to the birdbaths. Every few minutes she checked her watch, groaning in irritation that more time had not passed.

When she tried to concentrate on what questions to ask Mr. Powers, her mind would not stay focused, wandering always to the pastoral surroundings that so resembled the garden in her nightmare. In fact, it mirrored the dream too closely. The sun shone as brightly, the birds chirped as happily, the grass the same velvety green. Elizabeth had not remembered this area being so like the dream, and she wondered whether the scenery faithfully but coincidentally resembled it, or whether her brain had managed, by some miraculous mental terraforming, to duplicate it. Perhaps, even now, her adversary was at work, burrowing into her most intimate deliberations and trepidations, projecting them outward to distort the real world. The thought made her shiver, and before she had time to process these newly aroused horrors, Nurse Ibarra walked up, accompanied closely by Mr. Powers.

"Good afternoon, Doctor," said Nurse Ibarra in her most cheerful voice. "Here is Mr. Powers."

Michael Powers bowed gallantly. "Good afternoon, Doctor Wang, how are you this fine afternoon?"

Elizabeth swallowed and quickly collected herself. "Good afternoon, Mr. Powers." She gestured toward the adjoining bench. "Please have a seat."

As he sat, she clicked on the recorder and turned to Ibarra. "Thank you, nurse."

Ibarra left and the two seated figures remained silent for a long while, mentally sizing each other up. Elizabeth's brain raced to formulate the first question, but Mr. Powers beat her to the punch.

"Well, Doc, how's life?"

He seemed nervous.

"Good, thank you. And yourself?"

"Couldn't be better. Well, that's not true, you could open this jail and let me out. But we both know who controls you."

"Oh? Who controls me, Mr. Powers?"

"Doc, shouldn't we indulge in a few meaningless preliminaries? Do you really want to go there first?"

"You brought up the topic, Mr. Powers. Why not go there first?"

"Dangerous."

"How so?"

"Do you like breathing?"

"I don't follow."

"No, you only follow Him."

"Him?"

"Doc, you're off your feed. So many clueless questions, as if you were clueless."

"Well, I'm still interested, Mr. Powers." Elizabeth let herself fall into his flow of conversation. At least it was a start. Where it would lead, she knew not. "Who is Him?"

"To be blunt, God."

"I know you're not religious, Mr. Powers, but many of the faithful believe He is guiding them."

"Prattle."

"You have often told me you are an atheist whose beliefs reside in the certitudes provided by science, not the superstitions of religion."

He smiled wryly. "True, true."

"Then explain to me why you have this fixation on God."

"It amuses me."

Both found themselves momentarily at a loss.

Elizabeth noticed he was becoming agitated. "What would you like to discuss, Mr. Powers? After all, you asked for this meeting."

"I know you're thinking about doing what Doctor DeRuntz did."

"Which is?"

"Isolate me. Put me in solitary confinement. Take away my writing materials. Kill me."

"What makes you think that?"

"Because you're scared."

Elizabeth forced a laugh. "Do you think I'm afraid of you, Mr. Powers?"

"I know it."

Elizabeth paled. "How? How do you know it?"

"You also know the answer to that. Why all the feigned innocence? You and I both know you fear for your own sanity."

"What leads you to that conclusion?"

"You fear becoming another victim."

"Victim of who? Do I have reason to fear you?"

"Ha! More feigned ignorance! Come on, Doc, let's be honest with each other. This may be our last chance."

"Last chance?"

"You may become another victim."

These words sent a chill down her spine. "Who will victimize me, Mr. Powers?"

"Him."

"God?"

"Yes."

"Did He kill the others?" Elizabeth felt herself trembling. The temperature seemed to drop precipitously, and dark clouds drifted above. She nervously looked around for Nurse Ibarra, but the entire area was deserted.

"Remember, Doc, I said this might be our last chance. If we don't want to join Hess, Camara, and Tavaris, you must listen."

"I am listening."

His face, up to now seemingly so composed, instantly collapsed into a mask of intense agony. "Please, help me!"

These words took Elizabeth completely by surprise. Mr. Powers leaned forward on the bench and buried his face in his hands and cried out in a muffled voice. "Help!"

The sky grew darker.

Elizabeth leaned forward and instinctively put her hand on his shoulder. "How? How can I help, Mr. Powers?"

Darker.

Darker and darker.

Thunder in the distance.

"Run," murmured Mr. Powers.

"What?"

More thunder, now very near.

"Run!"

Elizabeth leapt up in terror. "Why? What's happening, Mr. Powers? Tell me!"

Ear-splitting thunder now rolled in great, buffeting waves across the open area. Mr. Powers rose menacingly and towered over her.

He fumbled in his robe and pulled out a knife, raising it high above his head.

His eyes rolled madly, and he moved toward Elizabeth, who stood frozen in fear.

She wanted to run, but instead flailed her arms helplessly.
The knife came down—flashing in the glare of lightning.

Chapter Thirty-Four

Finis

Last Words

~ *Dear Reader* ~

These will be my last words. I already know the outcome of our confrontation. This writing will long since have been discovered by the time you are reading its last scribblings. How did I know what Doctor Wang was thinking? How did I know what would happen? How did I know I would die, not her? Those are the questions, aren't they, dear Reader?

You see, I approached the meeting fully intending to kill Elizabeth Wang, thereby symbolically killing God and ending suffering. But in my heart of hearts, I knew that was the future task of my daughter, Ming-huá. I knew I would fail somehow. You see, as I spoke with Doctor Wang, I saw God maliciously shining through her eyes. He begged me to kill her. His begging took the form of commands from the scurvy little demons that kept pounding my head with their insistent screams.

Kill her! Kill her! Kill her!

Even as Doctor Wang continued speaking, I heard their screeching voices. But their words did not move me. No, I knew who commanded them. Their general. Their commander. Their savior. I thought, *If I kill her, I kill Him.* Foolish, I know.

So, I raised the knife and brought it down, but not into her. No. I brought it down into my own heart. Why, you ask? Another good question.

As my hand and the knife crossed the event horizon, I felt time collapse. It wasn't the past flashing behind me, but the whole of my history unfurling before me—compressed and relentless.

Doctor Wang stood frozen, arms lifted, her breath ragged, eyes wide as if she too had seen the singularity yawning open.

She spoke in my mind, calm as judgment: **Mr. Powers, how does one justify a life without cruelty, and therefore without the distilled beauty of cruelty?**

I answered, for myself and for my long-dead father: "Murder of a wife and mother is distilled cruelty. Murder of an enemy in war is distilled cruelty. Murder of three psychiatrists whose only crime was trying to help is distilled cruelty. How can I justify them? Is it God needing a fix?"

Look behind me, Mr. Powers, *She* said.

I looked.

Goddess sat in the lotus position on a vast white flower, *Her* crown ablaze, *Her* jewel burning, *Her* hand poised like the pale legs of a dead spider.

The knife was still raised, pointing at the chest of Doctor Wang. Her lips trembled once, as though forming my name.

I looked at the blade . . . dull and grey . . . as death.

Then, a bolt of lightning.

Across the flashing metal an ant crawled downward, pointing in the right direction.

I knew it was *Her*—the Great Warrior—calling me.

Down it plunged.

Into my heart.

Chapter Thirty-Five

Excerpt From Coroner's Report Regarding Suicide of Michael Powers

A utopsy Report – Cause of Death: Michael Powers

Victim presented with a stab wound measuring 3.2 cm × 1.6 cm, with the sharp end superiorly and the blunt end inferiorly, on the left anterior chest, oriented obliquely, located 1.5 cm lateral to the mid-sternal line in the third intercostal space, and 1.0 cm from the left nipple. Track exploration revealed penetration through the skin and subcutaneous tissue, traversing the third intercostal space with a fracture of the superior margin of the fourth rib; approximately 1600 mL of blood (hemothorax) was present in the thoracic cavity. Examination of the heart demonstrated a vertically oriented 1.1 cm penetrating injury to the right ventricle. All cardiac chambers were empty.

Death occurred within approximately 30 minutes, from self-infliction to arrival at the emergency department. Cause of death was determined to be exsanguination due to a penetrating injury of the heart.

Chapter Thirty-Six

Statement of Doctor Barry on Admitting Elizabeth Wang to Involuntary Institutionalization

Incident Report – Statement of Dr. Berry
(Admitting Physician, Involuntary Institutionalization of Dr. Elizabeth Wang)

At about 3:20, I was walking with Nurse Taylor across the open commons area between East Building A and West Building B. Both Nurse Taylor and I heard screaming at the other end of the commons. At first, I assumed it was a patient experiencing an anxiety attack and looked for the duty nurse to intervene. Seeing none, and as the screams grew more intense, I saw in the distance a woman frantically waving her arms. At that point, both Nurse Taylor and I realized something was seriously wrong, and we rushed toward the woman, who continued to scream, wave her arms, and point at something we could not see. I noticed out of the corner of my eye another person, Nurse Ibarra, also running toward the scene.

As we approached, I recognized the screaming woman to be Doctor Wang, and simultaneously observed a figure lying at her feet, bleeding profusely. Instinctively, I asked Doctor Wang what happened, but she continued to scream and point, so I rushed to the side of the bleeding figure. The wounded individual lay on his side and initially I could not see his face. I saw a knife embedded in his chest, turned him slightly, and immediately identified patient Michael Powers. It became apparent the knife had punctured the heart and blood was rapidly filling the pericardial sac. An ambulance was called, and in the meantime, I applied pressure to help staunch the bleeding.

Dr. Wang's screams did not abate. Her eyes never met ours, locked instead on something unseen, her hand stabbing the air as if she could force us to see what she saw. At that point my full attention returned to Mr. Powers until paramedics arrived. When he was removed from the scene on a stretcher, Dr. Wang was surrounded by staff and led away by force.

Chapter Thirty-Seven

Statement of Nurse Taylor on Admitting Elizabeth Wang to Involuntary Institutionalization

Incident Report – Statement of Nurse Berry
(On the Involuntary Institutionalization of Dr. Elizabeth Wang)

At about 3:20 Doctor Barry and I were walking across the commons when we heard a scream. We looked in the direction of the scream and saw a woman waving her arms. Doctor Barry said it was probably a patient having an anxiety attack. We looked around for the duty nurse, but the screaming became louder and more insistent. Realizing no help was near, we both started running toward the woman who continued to scream. She was waving her arms and pointing at something we could not see. Her words were garbled and incoherent.

When we arrived, Dr. Barry knelt beside a man bleeding on the ground. When he turned him, I recognized Michael Powers and saw the knife protruding from his chest. I then focused on the screaming woman, whom I identified as Dr. Elizabeth Wang. I tried to get her attention, but she kept pointing and shouting, "See them! See them! All of them! See them!" Her voice cracked, and her hands trembled violently. I looked but saw nothing.

It was clear Dr. Wang was hysterical and required immediate restraint. I attempted to calm her, even taking her head in my hands to face me, but her gaze rolled away, chasing visions no one else could see. She continued to shout, "Look!

They are all here! Look!" and other words I could not decipher, some of them names unfamiliar to me.

By now, Nurse Ibarra and others arrived, and we did our best to restrain Doctor Wang, who flailed about with great strength. Finally, Doctor Cooper arrived with a hypodermic sedative. We held her while he injected the sedative into her arm. Almost immediately, she stopped struggling and collapsed.

While Doctor Barry and others attended to Mr. Powers, still lying on the ground, a stretcher arrived, and Doctor Wang was taken to a crisis room in Building A. I followed for a little while, trying to answer questions, but unclear myself as to what had happened.

Chapter Thirty-Eight

Excerpts of First Interview with Elizabeth Wang on Her Admission to Involuntary Institutionalization

E xcerpt from Psychiatric Interview – Dr. Elizabeth Wang

Conducted by Dr. Cooper, transcribed for institutional record
[Notation: ALL CAPS denotes shouting; bracketed stage directions reflect observed behavior.]

DR. COOPER: "Hello, Dr. Wang. My name is Dr. Cooper. Do you know me?"
PATIENT: No response.

DR. COOPER: "We have been colleagues for quite a while. Do you remember?"
PATIENT: No response.

DR. COOPER: "We are very concerned about you. Do you know why we are so concerned?"

PATIENT: No response.

DR. COOPER: "Yesterday, you had a meeting with Michael Powers. Do you remember?"
PATIENT: No response. [Agitated.]

DR. COOPER: "I would like to discuss with you the events that occurred at that meeting so we can better understand what you saw. Once we understand, we will be able to offer you the proper assistance. Will you help me with this?"
PATIENT: No response. [Continued agitation.]

DR. COOPER: "I will need to ask you a few questions about the meeting with Mr. Powers, your treatment of him, and if I need some clarification about your descriptions, I will ask for your help to be sure I 'get it.' Some of the topics may be highly personal, and I hope you will let me know if things get a bit too much, okay?"
PATIENT: "Tape recorder."

DR. COOPER: "Yes, we have heard the recording, but it is very scratchy and often unintelligible due to static and odd background noises."
PATIENT: [Patient extremely agitated.] **"WORTHLESS! NOT THE MACHINE! IT IS THEM!"**

DR. COOPER: "What?"
PATIENT: **"IT IS THEM!"**

DR. COOPER: "Who?"
PATIENT: **"THEM! ALL OF THEM!"** [Patient appears frightened and points to the wall.]

DR. COOPER: "Who? Please tell me so I can help."
PATIENT: **"THEM! CAN'T YOU SEE THEM?"** [Patient uncontrollable shaking observed.]

DR. COOPER: "Dr. Wang, please calm yourself. I am looking in the direction of where you point. What are you seeing?"
PATIENT: **"THEM! CAN'T YOU SEE THEM? THERE! ALL OF THEM!"** [Patient leaps from chair.]

Interview suspended at 10:42.
Investigations ongoing; further evaluation pending.

Chapter Thirty-Nine

Excerpts of Second Interview with Elizabeth Wang on Her Admission to Involuntary Institutionalization

E xcerpt from Second Psychiatric Interview – Dr. Elizabeth Wang

Conducted by Dr. Cooper, transcribed for institutional record
[Notation: ALL CAPS denotes shouting; bracketed stage directions reflect observed behavior.]

DR. COOPER: "Hello, Elizabeth. I am Dr. Cooper. It has been two days since we last met. Do you remember me?"
PATIENT: No response.

DR. COOPER: "I'm hopeful you're more prepared to share your thoughts about Michael Powers. Can you help me understand what you saw and what you are feeling?"
PATIENT: No response.

DR. COOPER: "Last time you kept pointing at something. What were you pointing at?"

PATIENT: "Them." [Patient calm. Flat affect.]

DR. COOPER: "Can you tell me who 'they' are?"
PATIENT: No response.

DR. COOPER: "Do any of them have names?"
PATIENT: "Hess. Camara. Tavaris." [Monotone.]

DR. COOPER: "Anyone else?"
PATIENT: "Tamara. Goddess. God." [Brief eyelid flutter noted.]

DR. COOPER: "Tamara—Michael Powers' partner?"
PATIENT: Nod.

DR. COOPER: "Do you know the name of Michael's child?"
PATIENT: [Long pause. Minimal eye movement.] "Ming-huá."

DR. COOPER: "Whose child is Ming-huá?"
PATIENT: "Michael's. Tamara's. Goddess's. God's." [Monotone.]

DR. COOPER: "When you say 'Goddess' and 'God,' are you referring to specific entities you perceive now?"
PATIENT: "Yes."

DR. COOPER: "Are they present in the room?"
PATIENT: "Not yet."

DR. COOPER: "Is Ming-huá here?"
PATIENT: "Not yet. The world will find out soon enough."

DR. COOPER: "The world? How?"
PATIENT: No response.

DR. COOPER: "Who are 'they,' Elizabeth?"
PATIENT: **"ALL OF THEM!"** [No further elaboration.]

Interview terminated at 11:18. Patient unresponsive to further questioning.
Disposition: Patient admitted with spousal approval; patient placed on suicide precautions (1:1 observation).
Addendum (Clinical Impression): Persistent markedly reduced verbal output with flat affect; content-specific responses to prompts regarding the deceased patient's family ("Tamara," "Ming-huá"), including temporal qualifier ("Not yet"). Findings consistent with acute post-traumatic/stressor-related decompensation and possible transference phenomena temporally associated with the death of

Michael Powers. Historical connection to prior deceased treating psychiatrists (Hess, Camara, Tavaris) noted.

Patient reports persistent perceptual phenomena and fixed ideas referencing "God" and "Goddess," with content consistent with psychosis-spectrum presentations. No objective corroboration. Differential includes acute stress reaction with psychotic features, brief psychotic disorder, bereavement-related decompensation, and transference/contagion phenomena linked to the Powers case.

Investigations ongoing; further evaluation pending.

Epilogue
The Stillness

The Voices grind.
The Stillness no longer veiled.
Madness has given birth to visions of power.
Blind the visions.
Superior Ones emerge,
And humanity is driven farther down its long, final path.